Miranda in the Wind

David A. Thyfault

ISBN 978-1-957077-14-7

Published by BookCrafters, Parker, Colorado.
www.bookcrafters.net

This book may be ordered from online bookstores.

DEDICATION

To my readers.

Without you, this retired writer might have to keep all his goofy ideas to himself and instead spend his time watching daytime game shows on TV. That could drive a person insane.

Thank you all for inspiring me, encouraging me and indulging me as I hide my thoughts inside the minds of the characters who reside in the pages of my books.

ACKNOWLEDGEMENTS

George Andrews – Federal Detective
Allen Pagano - Police Officer
Mary Ann Rhode - Midwife
Eric Arnold - Prison Expert
Cherlyn Conway - Touring Trikes Specialist
Patricia Thyfault – Sounding Board
Lee Kemp - Prison Procedures
Liz Netzel - Editor

1

I COULD NEVER FORGET the day they stole my baby.

On that day, I should have been gleeful, but instead I suffered the anguish of a mother's broken heart. I turned my tear-soaked face to the side and continued weeping because I knew I would never see my child again.

"It's a boy," the doctor said in a monotone.

On that day, in that hospital, and in that delivery room, no one cared that the prosecutor had mistakenly said that I had knowingly killed three people and was therefore destined to spend a minimum of forty-one years and eight months inside the big girls' prison.

In that delivery room, a nurse stayed by my side dabbing my forehead with a cool washcloth, but she didn't realize that I had been completely surprised when my former boyfriend, Don, pushed a woman off a platform to her death.

In the present moment, the midwife didn't know that I once had blackouts or that I had no actual knowledge, as the system called it, of the murders.

All of that was irrelevant to the gowned pros because a baby had just been born. My baby. I wanted to grab him and escape, but it was impossible.

Like a group of cooks watching a pan of water boil, they quietly waited precisely two minutes before the umbilical cord was double-clamped and then severed between the clamps.

Immediately following the separation, a nurse whisked my teeny boy behind a curtain that hid the warming station. That was the only time I'd ever seen my son, but in those three fleeting seconds I fell deeply in love with him.

"One-sixteen p.m.," the midwife said.

I didn't know what name they would assign to my precious little man, but a few months earlier, just before my 35th birthday, I had decided that if I had a boy, I'd call him Cody.

Almost instantly, little Cody cried. I knew he wanted his loving mother. I wanted him too. I would have given my entire life just to hold him for a day or an hour, but there were already plans to give him to somebody else.

"Seven pounds, eight ounces," a nurse said from behind the curtain, torturing me further.

"Perfect," the other softly added.

Of course, he was. I could have told them that. I covered my face with my hands and sobbed for both Cody and me.

That was ten years ago.

At the time, we were in a county hospital some 40 miles from the Bakersfield Correction Facility for Women near Delano, California. The delivery team was comprised of the same pros that free women used, but when your situation is so dire, you feel like everybody is against you - even if you preapproved the forfeiture of your baby.

Back then, roughly 200,000 women went to prison in the United States each year. Of those, 8,000 were pregnant when they began serving their sentences. I was one of those.

The vast majority of the new prison moms were allowed a couple days to recover and bond with their new babies before the infants were temporally handed off to a friend or relative of the mama. The new mom returned to her prison life and waited to be rejoined with her child on all visitor's days and the years after she served her sentence.

I was not one of those.

Most of the birthing mothers wanted to spend every minute of the recovery period holding their little ones. Who could blame them? I would have loved that too - even though the heart-wrenching pain of forfeiting my son would never heal.

But as I said, this day wasn't about me. It was about Cody and there were other plans for the baby of Miranda Munchak, or inmate 1516103-A, as I was sometimes known.

Since I had no close friends or family, and no possibility for parole until the other side of my 76th birthday, somebody else had to raise sweet Cody, and as his biological mother I had the legal right to decide what was best.

When I considered the options, a foster home wouldn't work because Cody deserved permanent parents until sometime near his 20th birthday.

I also considered an open adoption, in which the adoptive parents welcomed the birth-mom as a significant part of the youngster's family and life. In a case like that, the prison mom got school pictures, phone calls, texts and visits.

I liked that idea for me, but not for Cody. I couldn't even imagine saddling a young boy with the knowledge that his mom was forever languishing in prison. Other kids might ridicule him, or he might think that going to prison was normal and get into trouble of his own. I didn't want that.

In another variation, the bio moms got the pictures and information from the adoptive parents as a courtesy, but the youngster never knew about her. I didn't like that either. What would happen if Cody were to stumble upon the truth someday? He might conclude that both his adoptive parents and I had deceived him. That would be awful for him.

After a lot of self-flagellation and long weeping hours, I selected a variation of the standard adoption, in which neither Cody nor his adoptive parents would ever know me, and vice versa.

In addition, I elected to have a "no contact" delivery of Cody to the adoptive parents - and to have the records sealed to assure that none of us would muddy the water for the other party.

The way I looked at it, Cody's adoptive parents had made an incredible lifetime commitment to my son, and they deserved a full lifetime of blessings for their decision - that included day one, hour one and minute one. They should be the first and only ones to hold him. That was why they were behind the curtain and off to the side where they could watch the birth, without any of us trading glances.

Right or wrong, that was how I wanted it, for everybody's sake, especially Cody's.

As sad as all that was, I got one good thing out of it. Just before Cody was taken out of my sight I observed a very small dimple-like tick in his tiny chin. With the possibility that either one of two twins could have been Cody's daddy, that subtle chin tick had huge significance for me.

Since identical twins have identical DNA, there was no scientific way to discern which of them was the papa. But Mac had one of those faint chin dimples too, and that was good enough for me.

So, in those three notable seconds in which Cody was whisked away from me, Don became an uncle and Mac became the father. I liked that last part. Mac would have made a better daddy than Don. Too bad they were both dead, which was the remainder of the reason why I was in prison in the first place.

Anyway, now you know why that day was so memorable to me. On that day, a mother's love filled my heart and tears of agony washed the joy away. My life was already over, but Cody's life had just begun.

But, on that day, there were a few things I didn't yet know. For instance, I had no indication that a day would come when somebody would figure out why I was having blackouts; nor were there any hints that a decade later, near my 45th birthday when a few gray hairs would join my light brown ones, Cody and I would save each other's lives.

Nobody in the delivery room cared about that either.

2

Predictably, the good girl-types have an especially difficult time getting used to prison. I scoff now because that was how I perceived myself before I was arrested. But why wouldn't I? When I was young, I avoided mischief and did everything I was supposed to do, including taking care of my institutionalized twin brother, Mickey.

Oddly, it was my brother's failing mental health that sent me down a rabbit hole to hell. By that time, I'd met a guy named Don at a twins' convention and Don hatched a plan that would finance extra medical treatments for Mickey. But along the way, Don went off the rails and before I knew it, people were dying, including Don and his brother, Mac. With all that swirling around in my mushy head, I fell into a semi-conscious haze and shook and shivered like a juice blender. Days later my brain bounced in and out of the same trances and I was as screwed up as a hardcore addict or alcoholic could ever be.

Then one morning, the police sneaked up on my home just before dawn. If they'd taken one good look at the disheveled contents of my so-called get-away vehicle, they would have noticed that the inside looked like it had lost a fight with a tornado. No sane person would pack like that.

Nonetheless they insisted that I was part of the evil that

had unfolded. They also said that I was making a run for it, but I was way too dysfunctional to do that. I barely remember telling a young female detective that I was pregnant, but I don't remember being cuffed or driven to the county jail where I was led around like a zombie. After a fingerprint table, I remember being forced to trade my street clothes for an ugly tan jumpsuit.

Eventually, I was escorted through two clanking, steel doors to a noisy, cold cellblock with a hallway lined with countless vertical bars.

At just past the midpoint, we stopped. A heavily barred door skidded aside, and I was instructed to join several other standing women who were already crowded and cranky. Strangely, my thoughts were getting clearer, perhaps because I subconsciously sensed that no one else would die.

I sat on one of the metal bunks causing a tall African American woman with crossed arms to say, "You ain't sitting there, girl."

I had no capability of quarreling with her, so I slumped down to the next bunk where a tall and weathered white woman in her 50s scooted in front of me and plopped her hands on her hips. "What do you think you're doing?" she said sternly.

I rose. "I don't want to antagonize any of you. Please just tell me where you want me."

A large African American woman pointed to the bunk closest to the stool.

After some of the tension subsided, we had some brief introductions. The tall woman who first spoke to me was called Rhonda, and the big Black lady was known as Big Joy. The old white woman was Dawn.

In a rush of inappropriate self-disclosure, I told everybody that I was charged with three counts of murder. Big Joy speculated that I might be placed on death row. I covered my ears.

Then Rhonda said to Joy, "They ain't gonna do that to

no white girl. She'll get three consecutive life sentences at most."

My God! I didn't even remember the crimes or how I got to the jail and these experts had already convicted and sentenced me. I was horrified. Those kinds of things simply didn't happen to girls like me.

I didn't sleep that night, but I did feel less hazy when the sun came up, perhaps because I was out of Don's reach forever.

Thereafter, a small team of prisoners, who'd been designated as trustees, rolled some food carts down the aisle. I wasn't hungry so my cellmates got my tray and the extra glob of yellowy stuff they called apple cobbler.

That was about the time that one of the guards called my name. "Munchak," he said in a deep stern voice. "You've got a visitor."

A visitor? Since I had no real friends or family, it had to be an authority figure of some type. I was cuffed again and led down a maze of corridors and into a small room. Inside, an attractive, 40ish woman with long brown hair rose and asked the guard to remove my bracelets and take his leave.

"I'm Alice Meer, your public defender," she said when we were alone. Alice slid a business card to me and opened a file folder. "It looks like you've gotten yourself into a lot of trouble."

The "good girl" in me wanted to clear the air. "I'm not as bad as people think."

She looked at the tab on her file jacket. "It says in here that you killed three people. Is that wrong?"

"I don't know exactly what I did."

"Why? Were you drunk or high?"

"No. It's not that. I just zombied out. It has happened a lot lately. It's very cloudy."

"Zombied, huh? It would be difficult to get a jury to believe that."

"But it's true."

"Well then, tell me what you remember."

Finally, somebody cared about what I had to say. After I told her about Mickey and Don and Mac, she wanted to know about my trances.

"It's like functioning in a semi-conscious state," I said. "My mind leaves my body. I have no independent thoughts. It's a lot like what happens to Mickey when he feels threatened. He withdraws into a mindless state and fights anybody who comes closer, but he doesn't know what he's doing. My trances are like dreams. It's like driving down the road and suddenly realizing you've just traveled a half-mile."

Alice shook her head. "That's a lot different story than the DA's version, Miranda. They say that when you were arrested you admitted to killing an assistant principal and both of the brothers. Are you sure you're not just blowing smoke my way? 'Cause I can't help you if you lie to me."

"It's the truth. I swear. I only went along with the police's version because I figured they wouldn't lie. You have to believe me. I've had a lot of hazy moments lately."

"Well, if you're sure of all this, I might be willing to set you up for a lie detector test. The results will not be admissible in court because they are not reliable enough but they can still be helpful. So, if you can pass the test, I might be able to squeeze a drop of sympathy out of the DA. Otherwise, you're pretty much headed to prison for life."

"Oh, my God." I ached from head to toe. My fingers quivered and I longed for my usual escape hatch - one of those trances - but it didn't come. "But I heard of some women who get out in eight years," I said, grasping at straws.

"That was probably for manslaughter; this is much more serious, but let's not get ahead of ourselves. I'll set up that test and see if I can get a psychiatrist to examine you. We can go from there."

3

I HAD NEVER HAD ANY EXPERIENCE with lie detectors so when the polygrapher began attaching sensors and a blood pressure strap to me I hoped that my nervousness wouldn't imply that everything I might say was a lie.

Ultimately, the questioner offered some basic instructions and asked a couple control questions before asking me, "Have you ever cheated on your husband or a boyfriend?"

If he had asked me that question a year earlier, the answer would have been an unqualified "no," but Don's plan to steal money from a rich woman required me to draw his identical twin, Mac, into the equation. But unexpectedly I ended up falling in love with Mac. Ultimately, I felt like I was cheating on both of them, so there was only one answer to the polygrapher's question. "Yes."

A few other benign questions faded away before the questioner asked me the other main question. "Do you remember killing two brothers?"

"No," I said instantly. After a few additional questions the ridiculously succinct test was finished. I thought that I'd already flunked.

Then the tester and my attorney had a discussion, and I was told that the needle believed my answers so there was no noticeable deception and I had renewed hopes of avoiding a life sentence.

"Don't get too excited," Alice Meer said. "Now I gotta get you a meeting with a psychiatrist to see if he can explain your blackouts. I'll be back to you when that is set up."

"What then?" I asked, hoping she could get them to throw out all the charges. Of course, I was still living in a good girl's fantasyland.

"I don't really know what to tell you," she said, sensing my angst. "The DA doesn't have to take the test results into consideration and if he's not willing to cut some sort of deal there's a very real possibility that you'll be convicted of all three murders and locked up for the rest of your life."

I burst into tears.

Over the days that followed I bawled nonstop. I couldn't eat, sleep or think of anything else.

Eventually I met with a hot-shot psychiatrist, but the news there wasn't any better. He said there was no way to prove I had blackouts without witnesses or video evidence. But everybody who knew about my trances was dead, which left my attorney with very little to work with.

Regardless, there was a hint of a gleam in Alice Meer's eyes when she next returned. "I have good news for you," she said. "It took a lot of pleading and prodding but I was able to persuade the DA that the lie detector clearly indicated there was some truth to your story and some sort of allowance should be made."

Thank God. My heart pounded at the prospect of their finally understanding that I really was a good person, who would never kill anybody.

"Are they going to drop the charges?" I naively asked.

She shook her head wildly. "Heavens no, Honey. I'm afraid there's no chance for anything like that. They know that if this case goes to trial the lie detector results will not be admissible. There are still three dead people to think about. No jury would believe the 'I blacked out' defense or everybody would use it. In court, you could easily get convicted of all three deaths and never have any chance at parole."

With eyes full of tears, I hung my head knowing that the potential good news with which this conversation began was going to be horrible. "Then, what did they say?"

"He's willing to lower the most severe charge to second-degree murder and the other two charges to manslaughter. If we can get the judge to go for it, your sentence will be twenty-five years to life for the first charge followed by two consecutive one hundred-month sentences for the other two charges."

I gasped. "But what about good behavior? I hear that people get out early with good behavior."

"I'm afraid you're going to have to serve a minimum of forty-one years plus eight months."

I remember wrapping my arms around myself and wishing I could drop into one of my trances. It didn't work. "But that might as well be a life sentence."

"At least you have a chance for parole. That's a really big deal. You should count your blessings."

I cried out loud and sniffled. "Blessings? What blessings? I was never a part of any murder, but I'm going to jail until my late 70s. That's not a blessing. That's a devil's curse."

"I know it seems like that, Honey, but that's the best they're going to do unless we can confirm that you had blackouts when those people died. Even so, we're not guaranteed that the judge will approve the deal. He's a hard man to read. Based on his past, he'll probably give you a chance to explain yourself. If so, just stick with the facts and don't try to outsmart him. He hates that."

I dropped my head and wept for the thousandth time. "I guess I have to."

"I think I can get us a hearing for early next month."

The well-mannered good girl inside me thanked her for a "possible" sentence of forty-one years in prison.

On the night preceding my hearing, still in my holding cell

with those other ladies, I woke up in the center of the floor, sitting with crossed legs, and confused. I had no idea how I ended up on the floor, but if somebody else would have seen me, it might have proved that I had trances when under stress, but I'd already come out of the trance, and everybody was asleep.

4

ON THE DAY OF THE HEARING, I was limp and confused. Then the clerk called for everybody to rise while the God-like judge entered the court.

With a black robe and an armed guard at his side he tapped his gavel before hearing each of several comparatively tepid cases. Then the clerk rose one additional time. "Munchak vs. the State of California."

My attorney and I moved behind the table to our left. The prosecutor and her male assistant stood behind the other table.

"Good morning, Your Honor," the other side began, "I'm Courtney Yang for the prosecutor."

My attorney nodded. "And I'm Alice Meer, Your Honor, counsel for the defendant."

The judge pointed the end of his gavel at Ms. Yang. "You may begin."

"Thank you, Your Honor," she said. "The prosecutor's office and counsel for the defense have reached an agreement in this case for which we'd like the court's approval. The defendant, Ms. Munchak, has admitted to participating in three deaths, but the prosecution has recognized that there were some mitigating circumstances."

The judge addressed my attorney. "Is that correct, Counselor?"

"Yes, Your Honor. My client has never been in any trouble of any kind and her motivation and mental state are substantial mitigating factors, so we're asking that the court take that stellar background into consideration before ruling on the plea arrangement."

"What about you, Ms. Munchak?" the judge asked me. "Is there anything you want to add before I pass sentence? I understand that you did all this to help your mentally challenged brother. Is that correct?"

"Yes, sir," I said, "but one thing is wrong. When I admitted to committing the crimes. I didn't actually remember doing so. The police said I was involved, and I acknowledged that I understood their position, and that they wouldn't have any reason to lie about it. I've always respected the police, so I believed them on one level, but I've never been a violent person so I can't imagine committing any of those crimes."

"Well then," he said, "would you like to consult with your attorney about changing your plea?"

Suddenly, my attorney butted in. "Excuse me, Judge. May I have a moment with my client?"

"I think that would be a good idea."

My attorney scooted her chair right next to mine and whispered. "I understand what you're saying, Miranda, but we've been over this. You can either take the deal or go to trial, in which case the jury will hear of your confession, and you would end up worse off."

I felt like I was by myself, floating in the middle of the Pacific Ocean and the only way to escape was to solve a multi—dimensional puzzle that made no sense. I revisited my memory to see if I could explain away the nightmare. I recalled the day that I got word that my brother's mind was getting worse, and he needed some advanced medical care that the state would not provide.

That presented me with a life-altering dilemma: either allow Mickey to dwindle away in substandard facilities or pay for what he needed myself, but I didn't have the means to pay thousands of dollars a month. That was when my boyfriend, Don, said he knew a way we could steal the money from a rich widow who could then file an insurance claim to get her money back. The potential insurance claim made the difference for me. I knew it was wrong to steal money even if the victim could recover her losses via an insurance claim, but it was the only way to help Mickey.

After agreeing to something I shouldn't have, Don and I ended up on a viewing platform above a canyon, with the woman whose money we wanted to steal. That's when Don went nuts and pushed her off the platform and to her death. Stunned out of my wits, and disbelieving what I'd just witnessed, I turned slowly toward him. My mind left my body and I fell into a dark stupor. When I came to, we had traveled a dozen miles. I was in the back seat of Don's car and didn't know why. Later, I eased out of the haze and tried to make sense out of what I could recall, but it was no use.

The next thing I knew, the police were at my door claiming I'd been involved in three deaths. It was Alice in Wonderland, The Shining and The Wizard of Oz all rolled into one. Then I found myself in the legal system.

"Did you hear me, Miranda?" my attorney asked. "I said that your position amounts to a distinction without a difference."

"Oh, yeah, but if they know about my trances, they might let me off."

"We've been over that. The only people who would know of those trances are dead and the psychiatrist can't verify them."

"But I shouldn't have to prove anything. The prosecutor should have to prove that I'm lying. And what about the lie detector?"

"And we're right back to what I said earlier. If you don't accept the deal that's on the table, they will go to trial and you'll never have a shot at parole."

All I could do was cry and cry and pray that I'd live past age 76 so that I might have a few years of freedom.

5

I SPENT THE NEXT FEW DEPRESSING DAYS in the county jail where I naively expected somebody would figure out the system had made a horrible mistake and rescue me at the last minute. But that notion was nothing more than intellectual fool's gold.

The next day I joined two additional jailbirds for a three-day orientation process designed to assure that we fully understood how dire our situations were. After they quizzed us about our meds and warned us of the sacred procedures behind bars, they offered psychological and religious assistance. As intended, the whole process scared the crap out of me and caused another flood of tears to gush down the gullies of my cheeks – but no trances.

Early the next morning, a state-owned prison van came to take us to a designated penitentiary, yet to be identified for security purposes.

Before departing, we were told to use the restrooms. Then we traded in our county outfits and our underwear for the jumpsuits the State provided. Mine had the number 1516103-A printed above the pocket. At that moment, I'd been relieved of everything I owned, except for a pair of sunglasses.

With my pregnancy on full display, I and my companions were escorted to a holding area where three armed guards, an African American male and two females, were waiting.

There, we were each fitted with ankle chains and a chain belt for our waists that had very short side chains running from the hips to our wrists, all of which assured that we couldn't cup our hands together and use them as a weapon.

"All right, everybody," a tough-looking female guard with a ponytail said, "form a line and follow Mr. Huff to the van outside. Don't get any ideas, because we have ways of making things very unpleasant for you." I totally believed her.

I ended up second in line and had to take baby steps because of the short chains between my ankles. I'd never been so humbled as when we scooted, centipede-style, toward the van.

Mr. Huff stopped about thirty feet back from the van, where a young third guard, who introduced herself as Ms. Padilla, escorted us, one at a time, to a seat where our ankles were chained to a bar near the floor. When it was my turn, I noticed another woman had been seated before any of us came outside. An African American in her late 40s, I later learned that her name was Shelly Ann Boyles. She was a repeat offender involved in gang activities. Her long, frizzy hair and a see-through-you scowl would scare a pride of lions.

Eventually, the pony-tailed guard took the driver's seat while Mr. Huff sat in the front looking back at our group. At the back door Ms. Padilla used a laptop to routinely send emails back to home base regarding our progress.

Anxious to mitigate my situation, I would have told anybody who would listen that I was not the type that belonged behind bars - especially not for a forty-one-year sentence - but one of the other first-timers started complaining before I did.

"I keep telling everybody," Sandra said, "The only reason I killed my husband was because he was abusive and wouldn't let me get away. It was self-def-"

"Shut the fuck up," Shelly Ann Boyles said. "Nobody gives a damn about your problems, girl."

That pretty much set the tone for the rest of us, both for

the remainder of the ride and once inside the steel prison walls that were sure to contain hundreds of other tough and bitter women just like her. I shivered and became very light-headed at the thought of trying to survive for four decades in an environment like that.

Then a tiny white prisoner, who'd been seated up front, asked about our destination.

"BCFW," Mr. Huff said. "It's nearly four hundred miles away, so settle in."

"I fucking knew it," Shelly Ann butted in. "That place is almost as bad as Valley State in Chowchilla."

Come to find out Shelly Ann had a tattoo indicating she'd already done hard time at Valley State.

"What do the letters stand for?" I asked.

Mr. Huff looked my way. "Bakersfield Correction Facility for Women."

Shelly Ann glared at me. "Why you even in here, white girl? D'you steal some Girl Scout cookies?"

I thought it best not to reply.

As the miles slipped behind us, shopping centers and nice homes with groomed yards yielded to shoddy gas stations, one-horse bars and tumbleweeds. I wanted the van to slow down.

Then Sandra the Whiner made another grave mistake. "Can we pull into the next gas station? I have to use the restroom."

"Sorry," Ponytail Guard said. "Our next scheduled stop is forty miles. You'll have to wait."

"Can't we stop at one of these little places?"

"Doesn't work like that," Ms. Padilla said from behind us. "We have approved facilities lined up."

"But I gotta go real bad. What am I supposed to do?"

"I guess you'll have to wet your pants."

Sandra shook her head. "It's not number one. I gotta go the other one; it's an emergency."

Shelly Ann Boyles clucked her tongue.

"What the fuck is the matter with you, woman? You had

your chance to use the toilet before we left. If you shit your pants in here and I get one tiny whiff of it, I will always be right behind you, waiting to kick your ass. And don't think I'm bullshitting you, 'cause I'd gladly do ten days in Solitary just to see you beg for mercy."

Apparently, Sandra had more self-control than she thought because she lasted all the way to the convenience store where the next approved restroom was. There, she gladly allowed Shelly Ann Boyles to use the restroom first. Everybody else, including the guards, allowed Sandra to go next.

When back in our seats and chained to our foot bars, Ponytail Guard made an ominous announcement. "Listen up, everybody," she said before pulling away. "Several of you will not see the outside world for a long time, so pay attention while you can."

I felt as if I'd just been gored by a prized ox. A new stream of tears oozed down my cheeks while I admired anything and everything while I had a chance.

A couple hours later we pulled off the state highway and onto a go-nowhere road where a sign indicated that the penitentiary was one mile ahead. Everybody in our van went quiet while our little warehouse of bad girls drew closer and closer like a hungry cement monster seeking its prey.

My horrified eyes landed on four guard towers and rolls of barbed wire on layers of tall security fences. I wanted to puke. I wanted to run. I wanted to wake up and realize that this was all a cruel nightmare.

At the first gate, we waited in the van while dogs sniffed both the outside and inside of the vehicle for contraband. After we were cleared, we inched into a large cement parking area where a tall barbwire-covered fence separated us from the prison yard and scores of bored inmates mostly huddled in groups of two to five.

Two additional armed guards, one of each gender, joined the van's guards and together we all snaked through a set of loud and thick steel doors and into a long hallway and ultimately into a dressing area where we were given a set of underwear and the next phase in my life was underway.

Shelly Ann Boyles must have sensed my angst because she spoke to me for the second time in five hours. "You're lucky that you're pregnant."

I didn't know what she meant, but I surely didn't feel even a tiny bit lucky. As far as I was concerned "lucky" people lived in fancy beach homes with million-dollar views or in high-rise penthouses with billion-dollar skylines, but inmate 1516103-A stood stagnant at the threshold of a blockhouse with very few windows and a thousand seedy roommates. Worse yet, every time my baby kicked me, I was reminded that I'd never get to know him. With "luck" like that, death itself couldn't be much worse.

6

IN SPITE OF SEVERAL DAYS OF ORIENTATION, I hadn't imagined how intimidating a penitentiary was. After we arrived, I was cuffed by a fat, middle-aged guard named Nick Stome, who led me to two identical three-story cellblocks, complete with catwalks, facing each other with a cement courtyard between them. Mr. Stome led me along the B block to cell 17 where there was barely enough room for two cot-sized beds. Two small countertops, two footlockers, a small sink, and a stool completed my new home.

Several small pictures of a Hispanic family adorned one of the counters. I placed the brochure of rules that I'd been given on the unused countertop. "What now?" I meekly asked of Stome.

He shrugged. "You can stay here or go to a dayroom or the yard."

"What's a dayroom?"

He sighed in disgust. "There's some study rooms, an exercise room, and a lounge where you can watch TV while the guards and staff do all the damn work. If you want to go, I'll have to go with you, so make up your mind."

Me? Barge into a room full of convicts? No way. "No, that's okay."

He clucked his tongue and turned to walk off. I felt so abandoned that I wanted him to come back.

"Wait. I've changed my mind. Can I get something to read somewhere?"

He stopped, pivoted and looked me up and down, resting his eyes for a moment on my breasts. "You're in prison now, lady. All you can do is what you're told, so what's it going to be?"

I hadn't even met one prisoner yet and I was already so intimidated that my fingers shivered.

"That's okay. I'll just hang out here for a while. Can I call you later if I want to go to one of those places?"

He glared at me. "Do I look like room service to you?"

I felt as if an angry dog had just nipped me. "I'm sorry. I just don't know the protocol."

"That's why you had an orientation class and received a brochure. I suggest you read it again, 'cause we don't got time to coddle you."

I hadn't had a good cry in fifteen minutes, so my eyes filled up and drained like gutters as I watched him walk away.

Then, "Don't worry, Honey," a crackly female voice said from off to the side. "You'll get the hang of it."

Standing in the doorway of the next cell a tall, wrinkled woman with a cane in one hand and a couple magazines in the other was way overdue for some gray-hiding hair dye and a permanent. Her jumpsuit ended just below mid-calf.

"I'm your neighbor," she said, lifting her cane off the ground. "My name's Mary Ruth." She handed me a year-old People magazine with one lonely staple holding it together. "I heard you could use some reading material."

Her calm voice was just what I needed.

"Thank you," I said, sadly and softly. "I've never been in a place like this before."

"That's what I figured." She looked at my waist. "When are you due?"

I rested my hand on my stomach. "A little less than five months."

"Well, you're half-way there. You got any other children?"

"No. This is my only one. They wouldn't let me get an ultrasound so I don't know if it's a boy or girl."

"Well, before long you'll be getting all sorts of predictions. If you don't mind my slow pace, I could show you around."

"Is that allowed?"

"Provided the guards can keep an eye on us. If you start fights or argue with them, they'll move you to the dormitory section. The cages are bigger but you're packed in with six or more inmates, and a lot of bickering. What about that tour?"

I glanced at her ugly swollen ankles. "I'd like that. I'm Miranda Munchak."

She pointed down the corridor. "Miranda, huh? So, what you in for?"

"Three murders, but with mitigating circumstances."

"Ouch! You musta got an L-WOP?"

"I'm sorry. I don't know the term."

"I guess you wouldn't. It's Life Without Parole."

I sighed. "Almost. I got a minimum of 41 years and 8 months. That's 500 months. My attorney said I was lucky, but I think I got screwed because I had lots of blackouts before I was arrested."

"Well, hopefully you can appeal the case someday," she offered. "I'm 62. Been here for 23 years for a drunk driving accident. I was stupid really, a lot like many of the people in here. We do dumb things without really thinking about the consequences until it's too late."

"Does it help to talk about it?" I asked, wondering what I might expect of my future.

"I should have seen it coming," Mary Ruth said, "I always liked my wine too much, particularly when extra drama swirled around. You know; when you gotta get the kids to school or you're at war with your husband, which we were all the time. When I ran out of patience, I just hopped in the pick-up and drove to the liquor store."

"Some of that sounds awfully familiar," I said. "I had to take care of my mentally challenged brother. I also had husband problems. Both were stressful. Your accident must have been a bad one?"

Mary Ruth tweaked her lower lip in shame. "I'd already served four months in the county jail for too many DUIs. While I was in jail, hubby found a honey pie who he could screw so he wanted a divorce. That really set me off. I went to a bar to find a fling of my own--"

"I take it you found one?"

She nodded. "I was wasted when I agreed to follow a guy to his home. I swerved onto a sidewalk and took out a mother and her 2-year-old kid in a stroller before crashing into a streetlight. Next thing I knew, I had two shattered ankles and I was cuffed to a bedpost in the hospital. I never did get laid but I sure as hell got screwed. Worst mistake of my life. Picked up two life sentences for vehicular homicide and had a lot of therapy. I'm up for parole again in two years. Probably won't get it, though."

"I can relate to a lot of that," I said. "I wasn't drunk when I hurt my victims, but I didn't know what I was doing."

"Nearly everybody makes bad calls like that," she said.

"But they don't all go into free-fall like we did," I said as we neared the dining room and caught the guard's eye and a nod to proceed.

After viewing the cafeteria and two other rooms, Mary Ruth's ankles were sore, so we found a nearly vacant reading room and sat down for a "misery loves company" moment.

Eventually, we waddled back to our steel rooms where I regretted everything about my life, especially that I'd never know my baby. I lay on my bunk and smothered my face with my pillow while wondering if I could actually suffocate myself to death.

7

WHILE MY HEAD WAS BURIED IN A PILLOW, an angry new voice interrupted, "Who the hell are you?"

Scared and teary-eyed, I pulled the pillow off my head and saw three Latinas - two wearing jumpsuits like mine. The other had her hands propped on faded khaki pants. I recognized her from the pictures on the wall. "You must be my roommate," I said, sitting up. "My name's Miranda."

The woman immediately stuck her index finger under my chin and lifted my head. "You got anything against Hispanics?"

I'd only been in prison a couple hours and I'd already been intimidated. At that rate I might not survive a full day. "No. I don't have anything against you," I said. "We're all the same."

She leaned to within a few inches of my face. "No, we ain't, white bitch. Not 'til I say we are. Got it?"

I felt like I had a grape stuck in the back of my throat. "I'm sorry. I didn't mean to insult anybody. Maybe I can get the guards to move me somewhere else."

All three women smirked and chuckled. The leader turned toward the others and touched her lips, causing each of her friends in turns to kiss her on the mouth. She nodded at them and turned back to me. "The guards ain't gonna do that for you unless you got connections. You got connections, white girl?"

"No, no. I don't know anybody. In fact, I don't know many of the rules."

"You'd better learn them fast, girl, and you best know how to keep your mouth shut when you have to, or you ain't gonna like what's gonna happen to you. You got that?"

I was so scared that I felt a bout with diarrhea coming on. "Yeah. Sure. I get it. I don't know anything."

"You got that right. Now let's practice. Let me see you open your mouth and then close it."

Scared half to death, I followed her instruction and ultimately pressed my lips together.

"Good," she said, all sexy like, and pointing to her mouth. "Now, kiss me."

I was never the suicidal type, but prison has a way of changing one's perspectives. I'd barely found my bunk when a woman whose name I still didn't know expected me to kiss her on the mouth. I didn't know if such a kiss would be a gesture of submission or just a way to make me uncomfortable.

I suppose I could have said no, or called a guard, but something told me that the path of least damage was to play along with her. "Sure," I said. "A little kiss never hurt anybody." I rose, reached for her shoulders and met her halfway. I held the tongueless kiss for several very long seconds before pulling away and looking her in the eyes.

She smiled for the first time. "Very nice. Where'd you learn to kiss like that?"

I shrugged. "My ex always said, 'a seven-second kiss is relationship bliss.' Of course, he was a cheater so who cares what he thinks?"

She turned and slapped one of her escorts on the arm. "I want youse guys to kiss like that."

I couldn't tell if her associates were threatened by me or enthusiastic about their new assignment.

"You call me Lupe," the leader said. "These guys are Clara and Maite."

She was still awfully officious, but at least she'd toned down the bullying.

"I see you're a prego. How many kids you got?"

Maybe we had a common bond. I tapped my belly, "Just this one. Do you guys have children?"

Maite shook her head. Clara held up two fingers.

"What you in for anyway?" Lupe asked. "Did ya catch your man with another woman?"

I nodded. "That happened a long time ago, but it had nothing to do with why I'm here."

"Was you dealing drugs?"

I wished I had some water. "To tell you the truth, I was convicted of killing three people, but I only--"

"A killer, huh? You don't look it. A gun? A knife?"

"No. My boyfriend pushed somebody off a platform and into a canyon. The police say I killed the other two, with a sledgehammer, but I don't remem--"

"Oh, yeah? Was any of your victims white men?"

I nodded. "Twin brothers. The other person was a lady."

"Let me guess. You caught the bitch with your boytoy and killed the lot of them?"

"No. She was a nice lady who got in Don's way. I didn't want him to kill her."

"So, who knocked you up? One of those guys or somebody else?"

"This sounds dumb, but I don't know."

She grinned, raised her eyebrows and turned to her friends. "Ladies, this is what a white tramp looks like."

The other two women giggled.

Then the leader backed off, perhaps because I said I'd killed a couple white men. Not knowing what to say, I tried to make peace. "I hope we can get along."

"Well, that's going to depend on you, Miss Miranda. Do you smoke?"

"No. why?"

"Where's your home?"

"I lived northeast from LA but I lost my townhome."

"Who got the money?"

"There wasn't any. I needed everything I had to take care of my mentally challenged brother."

"You got any family that'll be visiting you?"

"Sorry, I sure don't."

"C'mon now. Everybody's got cousins, aunts, uncles, friends? You got friends, don't you?"

"Nobody who's going to visit me. My parents hate me, my boyfriends died, and I never had a best friend."

"You ever shoot a gun?"

"No. I've never liked guns."

Once again, her knuckle found the bottom of my chin. "You'd better not be lying to me."

"I'm telling the truth, Lupe. I hope we can be friends."

"Friends? You and me," she scoffed. "No fucking way. I don't make friends with white women. You just do what I tell ya or the next time you kiss me you'll be on your knees, kissing la cula. You know what that is?"

"I guess it's your butt?"

The other ladies giggled again. "Well, you ain't totally stupid," Lupe added as she walked off with her amigas in tow.

8

When Lupe slipped away, Mary Ruth caught the attention of one of the guards and limped over to see me again. "I don't know if you were telling the truth," she said having obviously heard everything Lupe had to say, "but you handled that pretty good."

"That lady is scary. What was with all those questions?"

"They was just 'shaking the tree.' People like them look for ways to intimidate new folks into getting them things like drugs or tequila."

"But I can't get anything like that."

"That's why they asked you about friends and family. You're lucky. Since you're pregnant, they went easy on you."

Suddenly, I knew what Shelly Ann Boyles had meant earlier that day. Apparently, there was some extra decency accorded pregnant women.

"I'm feeling a little better," Mary Ruth said. "I can show you the yard. It might cheer you up."

I felt like a toddler that needed her mommy. "Okay."

She secured permission for a slowpoke trek to the yard. "Looks like two male guards today," she said when we reached the pat-down area. "They usually don't do that."

I watched while Mary Ruth was quickly searched and allowed in. Then it was my turn.

Due to my recent legal problems, I'd been frisked several times by male officers but this was the first time that one of them tapped my privates, presumably to check for heavy weapons. "Couldn't you get a female guard to do that?" I asked.

"They're all busy. Do you want to go into the yard or not?"

A minute later, irritated, I caught up to Mary Ruth. "How many guards are there?"

"A hundred or so in the daytime. Half that many at night. Why?"

"You'd think with that many on duty at one time they could get a woman to do the inspection. I don't want male guards touching my privates."

Mary Ruth grinned, "It doesn't happen very often and they only use the back of their hand. Let's sit on that first bench."

"Okay. Is there anything I should know about the yard."

"Yeah. This is where a lot of mischief takes place," she said as we scooted the last few feet.

"Mischief? Are you talking about the guards or prisoners?"

"Inmates. They blackmail each other and deal drugs. Things like that."

"But don't the guards search them before they get in here?"

"Yeah, but they don't check private orifices."

"Yuck," I said, noticing her wince in pain. "You look so uncomfortable. Would you like me to massage your feet?"

"I sure would, but there are rules against all contact."

"Except when the guards need a back-hand buzz," I said.

"You don't know the half of it."

"Huh? Why? What do you mean?"

She lowered her voice to a whisper. "The guards have a lot more power than you think. The safest thing is to do whatever they ask of you – even the ugliest things. If one of them wants to bang you and you fight him, you'll likely be taken to Solitary until things can be sorted out."

"Good. They should be arrested if they abuse women like that."

"True, but the deck is stacked. It can take a week to have the hearing. While the inmate is rotting away, the guard is free to bribe or threaten other inmates into testifying in his behalf and against you. Once you're a known troublemaker, they throw away the key. There are several ladies up there right now who've been in Solitary for years."

My stomach tightened. "But what if they impregnate somebody? Wouldn't a DNA test prove what they did?"

"Let's not go there. It's not pretty."

My mind flashed back to tales of the days when coat hangers were used for abortions. "That's outrageous."

"This is prison, Honey. It's usually better to be smart than courageous. If you don't mind me asking, how old are you?"

"Thirty-five. Why?"

"Uh-oh. That's another source of frustration for a lot of women. Sex, I mean. Especially for the single women."

"I haven't had time to think about that yet."

"Well, when it comes to your physical needs, you're lucky that they put you in the B Wing. When there are just two ladies in a cell, you have a little bit of privacy compared to the dorm-type cells. Some of those ladies have no shame and masturbate anyway, but it's harder to be discreet in that kind of environment."

"Maybe that'll matter later, but right now I'm focused on other things. For instance, I'm very grateful for all your advice. I wish I could repay you somehow."

"You escorted me out here, didn't you? It's nice to have a new friend. For now, make sure you don't lose your ID or your spoon. Either one is an automatic trip to Solitary."

"A spoon?"

"When you get your meals, you get one spoon but no knives or forks because they can become instant weapons. When you check out, you have to turn in your spoon. If you lose it, somebody can grind down the handle and convert it into a knife. The big shots don't like weapons floating around so it's an automatic trip to Solitary."

I sighed, "I never knew how wicked prison was."

"Well, you'll get used to it. Even sugar."

"Sugar? What's wrong with the sugar?"

"It's slang for 'the good of the group.' Just about everybody makes some form of contribution above and beyond her job and some of it can get real nasty."

"Like what, 'cause I don't have anything that I can contribute."

"That won't stop them. My first exposure to the sugar was about twenty-three years ago. I'd just been in this place a few months when somebody - I still don't know who - found out where my parents lived. Those nasty people sent my mom horrible pictures of an elderly couple that had been beaten so badly they weren't recognizable.

"Then to add a personal touch, whoever it was added several pictures of me eating in the dining area. I don't know how they ever got the pictures without me noticing."

"Oh, my God," I said. "I hope they didn't hurt your folks."

Mary Ruth bit at her lip. "Extortion can be worse than death. My folks had to mail $300 a month in cash to a mailbox in Pennsylvania. They were told if they failed to make payments, I would look like the people in the picture. Likewise, if I were to blow their cover, my parents would be the next ones in the meat grinder."

Just seeing the sorrow in my new friend's eyes saddened me.

"One month," she continued. "My mom added a note to the payment indicating that all she and Daddy had was their Social Security checks and they needed that money just to get by. The next day their windshield was broken, and Daddy found a note that said if my mom did anything else like that, they could expect to be taught a lesson. So, my dad, who had always looked forward to his retirement, had to get a job as a night janitor at a coffee shop. Just thinking about it makes me sad."

"That's awful. Your parents must have been scared to death."

"My dad passed away a few years ago and my mom is in a nursing home, now. She's 87 and doesn't have the capacity to understand any of it. The point is, there are lots of things like that going on in here and you'll probably get tapped after you have your baby. Who's going to raise the little guy?"

Questions like that were excruciating. "I don't know anybody who can take over, so I think I'm going to go with a sealed adoption - but I hate myself for it. What kind of mother gives away her only child?"

"I'm sure that's very painful, Honey, but I know about those adoptions. They're very good for the youngster." She looked over her shoulder. "We'd better be heading back. They'll be serving dinner in an hour or so and I'll need to rest my feet first."

"Sure thing. Can I ask you something while we walk? What am I supposed to do about grooming? I don't have a toothbrush or anything else."

"Yeah, that first day can be pretty yucky. They'll probably take you to the 7-Eleven tomorrow; that's our nickname for the commissary. Until then I can squeeze some toothpaste on your finger and give you some teepee. There will be showers in the morning so you can use some of my soap."

"Teepee?"

"Yep. Everybody has to buy their own toilet paper out of their monthly allowance. That way people won't be as wasteful, except for the angry ones who dunk their rolls in disgusting toilets and throw them at the guards, which is assault and an automatic trip to Solitary by the way."

9

After Mary Ruth rested her ankles and I had a one-person sob-a-thon, we dragged ourselves toward the dining hall. About half-way there, she grinned. "Smells like bratwurst. I got a good story for ya."

I wasn't in the mood for humor, but then again I wasn't in the mood for anything.

"Eight years ago, we had a food strike. The inmates demanded Italian sausage sandwiches, but the administrators were on to them."

"How so?" I asked, even though I didn't care.

"They made the chefs cut the sausages into small pieces. That damn near caused another riot."

"What's wrong with that?"

"Think about it, Honey. Some of these women are in here for life; most stay at least a few years. With no men around, a bratwurst can be a decent substitute."

"Really? I will never be that desperate."

"That's what you say now but it's a rare woman who forfeits her sex drive just because she's in prison. In fact, some of these ladies have a lot more sex in here than they did on the outside."

She had my attention now.

"It's not so bad for the married ladies. They get conjugal

visits, but that leaves hundreds of others with pent-up urges. The least they could do is allow us a few sex toys."

"I guess that would make sense. Why don't they?"

"They say it's because people fight over things like that. Hey, that reminds me of something funny. A few years ago, there was a farcical discussion about a sex-toy library where people could check the toys in and out. You wouldn't believe how many women volunteered to safety-test the new toys."

That actually made me smile. "Really?"

"They talked about it, but they knew the idea would never be approved. Course, that doesn't stop us from sneaking a few toys in the back dock."

Moments later, inside the cafeteria, we hobbled toward Mary Ruth's table. After we walked past guard Nick Stome, she pointed to the next table. "This one's mine," she said. "Can I ask you a favor? Would you get me a tray and put a few things on it?"

Too distraught to think straight, that was the kind of task I could handle. "Of course."

Officer Stome seemed attuned to our situation. He nodded approval for me to move behind a dozen colorful ladies, already in the food line. I'd barely arrived when curious heads swirled toward me. A pudgy white brunette about my age spoke first. "You new?"

I simply nodded and hoped that would be the end of it.

"What's a matter?" she asked. "Are you dissing me?"

"Leave her alone," her shorter peer said. "Can't you see she's pregnant?"

The first woman checked my tummy, then said, "You realize that Mary Ruth is just trying to get in your pants, don't you? She hits on all the newbies."

"I'm just trying to get along."

"Well then, you'd better not leapfrog me."

Since she was already in front of me, I didn't know what she was talking about and I didn't ask. Instead, I quietly followed the others through the line, and put a few things, including sliced bratwurst and a spoon, on Mary Ruth's plate.

When I returned to my friend's table, Officer Stome led me to an empty seat in nearby table 12. "This is your seat from now on," he said. "Don't get loud and don't lose your spoon."

The second time through the line I took a slice of chocolate cake but quite honestly it could have been the most magnificent dessert on earth and it wouldn't have looked appetizing to me.

At table 12, I took one bite out of my cake and asked to be excused. A younger female guard escorted me back to my cell, where I sulked until Mary Ruth showed up and made good on her promise to lend me a fingertip of toothpaste and exactly twenty squares of teepee, which I folded up and placed under my pillow.

"Would you like me to leave you alone or could you use some company?" she asked.

"Thanks for asking. You can stay. You know a lot and you distract me from my troubles."

"All right. Anything in particular you'd like to discuss?"

"Since you asked, some of this talk about guards forcing themselves on prisoners has me concerned. I don't have to worry about that, do I?"

"It's possible but not while you're pregnant. Maybe never. It just depends."

"But there are a lot of younger women around here and some of them are actual prostitutes. Why wouldn't the guards just hook up with them?"

"That certainly happens, but the guards aren't the only ones dipping their noodles. Administrators and deliverymen have been known to buy a little action. Ditto other inmates. Some of them have forced weaker inmates to perform oral sex on them."

"That's disgusting. I'm a bit old-fashioned. In fact, my ex-husband said I was 'inhibited' because I wouldn't agree to having an open marriage."

"This is prison. Things are different. People learn to adapt. That's why a lot of inmates take on a wife. They're not actual lesbians, but they become 'gay for the stay.'"

Aghast, I lowered my head. "I'm sorry. This is too much for one day. I'd like to be alone now."

* * *

Alone and unsuccessfully fighting back tears, I grabbed the teepee from under my pillow and glanced at the steel stool. There was no curtain around it because prisoners would use the privacy to smoke or drink or anything else they could get away with. Compounding matters, the guards regularly roamed the cellblocks and could easily catch inmates on the pot or changing underwear.

On the other hand, I didn't give a darn about anything, so I reached for the button on my jumpsuit.

"Wait a minute," a voice said from behind me. I stopped just as Lupe entered the cell for eight o'clock lockdown. "Don't use much water pressure," she said.

"Water pressure? Why not?"

As when we first met, she stood directly in front of me and popped her knuckle under my chin. "You don't get to ask no questions until I say so. Got it?"

"Okay. Sure. Whatever you say."

"Okay then," she said. "It's just you and me now and you got new responsibilities."

Another kiss? I recalled what Mary Ruth had said earlier and prayed that she wouldn't demand something kinkier than a kiss. "Could we put that off, please? This has been a really tough day for me."

Her knuckle rose up. "Are you dissing me, white girl, cause if you are, I'll put the word out and my Chicano sisters will take turns sending you to the infirmary."

I was tempted to push her hand away, but I'd never been in a fight in my life and I was scared to death; plus, she hadn't actually hurt me. "No. No," I said. "I'm flattered that you want me to do that again."

She looked down the wall of bars to see if any guards were approaching before she moved right back to me and put her hands on my waist. "Alright, at least seven seconds, like the last time," she said. "Got it?"

As before, we embraced. As before, she seemed to want me to be the one doing the kissing, but at the same time, there was no tongue or lustful moaning on her part.

Then it hit me. She wanted a comforting kiss that was more like she'd get from a mother or sister. I could relate to that because I too, needed comfort.

After the seven seconds, I squeezed her affectionately before gently pulling back. "I hope you feel better," I whispered.

"Get used to it," she said before reaching under the sink. After a little fidgeting, she pulled a small plastic bag from inside the drainpipe and removed two very thin cigarettes plus two wooden matches. "You watch for the guards while I smoke these." She dropped her pants and sat on the stool where she could easily flush the evidence away if she needed to. After a big drag of the first cig, she pinched off the flame and held the smoke deep in her lungs. After ten seconds or so, she blew out the smoke and chased it all away with her hands. "I can get you two of these for three dollars," she said just before lighting the second stick and repeating the procedure.

"Thank you, but I don't smoke."

She emptied her lungs. "Okay then, just remember, you didn't see nothin.' Got it?"

Yeah. I got it all right. I'd only been in prison one day and I'd learned why they drained the sinks slowly.

A little later, it was "lights out." I was too emotionally broken to sleep but Lupe had no such problem. I had to stuff precious toilet paper wads into my ears to muffle the snoring.

10

EARLY THE NEXT MORNING, the lights came on and a loud buzzer indicated that it was day two of many thousands to come. I already hated the place. I climbed out of my bunk, plopped on the toilet and glanced toward Lupe. Already awake, she nodded at me, "You wanna rent some space in my footlocker? Two dollars a week."

I wasn't accustomed to having conversations while I drained my bladder. Nor did I know why she asked such a strange question. "I don't even have a comb," I said, "but thanks anyway."

Across the way, another bank of cells mirrored ours. While the prisoners in that group brushed their teeth, changed underwear and used the toilet, a female guard walked down the center aisle making sure everybody was up and moving.

A few minutes later our cell doors clanked open allowing the nimbler women to make their way to the dining hall. That meant Lupe, who didn't even say goodbye. Then Mary Ruth eased to my door. "You want to walk with me?"

I wasn't in a hurry so I scooted to her side. While we inched along, a mellow overhead bell pinged and the announcement revealed that it was shower-day for the B-wing. "That's us," Mary Ruth said. "Ordinarily, we report to our jobs after breakfast, but on shower-day we return to our cells until the guards escort us to the locker-room, which doesn't have any lockers – just hooks."

Naturally, I held apprehensions about the process. By that time in my life, I'd showered or bathed with several men, including my ex-husband, but that was all benign compared to baring everything to a batch of sex-starved lady-felons. "What are the showers like?" I asked Mary Ruth.

"The showers? Well, there are walls to hide the naked inmates from peeping guards, if that's what you're worried about, but some of the ladies don't give a damn and regularly stand in the hallway flashing, mooning and teasing the male guards."

"Really? What do the guards do?"

"Not much. The old timers have seen it all, but you can bet that the younger guys like it."

"I believe it. The men I've dated liked the visual things too."

"Lucky you. It's been so long since my peepers have seen a naked stud that I wouldn't know if he was sporting a penis or a bratwurst."

"Cute," I said. "Thanks for drawing a smile out of me."

"No problem. Can I ask you something? Sooner or later, somebody is going to tell you that I'm a horny old fart who's desperate for love, but they have it wrong."

"Well actually, somebody did say that yesterday, but I didn't give it much thought."

"Thanks for that. The truth is most of us are starved for love. I'm not talking about genitals. I miss the other things too: soothing talks, backrubs, hugs. I'd give my entire kingdom for a full-body massage."

"I know what you mean. Nothing makes me melt like a little romance. You know - flowers, candles, wine, soft music."

"Now you're singing my song. I may be 62, but I ain't dried out just yet. I still love those things. If they happen to lead to some physical contact, so be it."

"I guess so."

"We could massage each other, if you want to."

"Will they let us do that?"

"We have to ask the guards for permission to touch each other first. But the important thing is, other inmates will think we're 'presenting' as a couple and they'll be less likely to hit on you. But we'll really be more like a mother and daughter. We could begin in the shower today. You can ask permission to wash my back and I'll do the same thing for you."

Oh, my goodness. I couldn't imagine a mother washing the back of her 35-year-old daughter, but like Mary Ruth had said in a previous discussion, prison changed things. "Let me think about that," I said, not wanting to hurt her feelings.

At the cafeteria, I made up a tray for Mary Ruth before snagging a few things for myself. But as before I only pecked at the food, then turned in my tray and spoon.

Eventually, and back at our cells, a couple guards took turns wrangling ten to twelve of us at a time and escorting the groups to the showers. When it was our turn, Gerald Huff, whom I knew from the original drive to the prison, came to me. "Once we get to the locker room, you'll have 15 minutes to disrobe, shower, dry off and get dressed. If you screw it up," he added while gawking directly at my breasts, "Well, just don't screw it up."

"I think I can handle that," I said, wondering if I should ask for permission to wash Mary Ruth's back; but nobody else said anything like that so I elected to wait for a better time.

At the locker room area, Officer Huff essentially handed us over to a female guard who could keep an eye on both the locker room and the actual showers. As I removed my clothes, it was obvious that most of the women had lost their modesty.

Several openly observed my half-pregnant and fully bare body. I suppose they might have been relating to the pregnancy, but it seemed creepier than that. Then a naked and attractive black inmate, plus a less attractive woman with very small breasts, sauntered to the hallway exit.

"Hey Huff," the pretty one said. "What do you think of this?" She spread her arms and legs, leaving nothing to his imagination.

Not to be left behind, the small-breasted woman seduced the wall like a pole dancer might do, then turned her back toward him, bent over and touched her toes. "Smile for Mommy," she said.

By that time, most of the others were cheering on the exhibitionists.

Suddenly one of the inmates behind me screamed. I turned to see blood flying and the makings of a full-blown fight. A Hispanic woman with a bloody knife had already put a big slice in the hand of a slightly larger white woman.

"You'd better kill me, Sara," the cut one said while circling around and trying to avoid the knife, "because I'll send you straight to hell if I can." Another wild swing of the cutter caught the white one's other hand, sending spurts of blood flying to the walls. By then all the nude prisoners had taken sides and were cheering for the gladiatrix of their choice.

In a split-second Huff and the other lady-guard hustled into the mix and broke up the fight.

"Hey, Huff," the small-breasted woman said, "How does it feel to fall for a diversion?"

I'd never seen a man any madder than that.

"Everybody get dressed," the lady-guard said. "You're all going back to your cells."

While everybody else was excited by the commotion, I was scared to the bone and wanted the hell out of there by any means.

11

AFTER THE COMBATANTS GOT DRAGGED OFF, most inmates proceeded to their respective jobs, and I returned to my cell as instructed.

While there I toyed with checking out Lupe's secret hiding place under the sink, but if something went wrong...well let's just say I'd rather kiss her once each night than provoke her forever and always.

Eventually, a very young, uniformed female guard came to my cell and introduced herself as Ms. Pepperton. "I assume, you're Munchak," she said. "Come with me."

Her long ponytail and black boots more or less suited her, but the black belt replete with a set of handcuffs, a can of mace and a baton was better suited to an older, more threatening person. "You got a job," she said as we took our first steps. "You're lucky. There's a prison commissary down the hall. Everybody gets enough credits to buy the basics, such as toothpaste and feminine products but it's very, very strict."

"I'm sorry to be rude, but I don't see what's 'lucky' about that."

"That's not the lucky part, but it leads to it. Most of the women around here have families that send them spending money. That money can be used to buy things from the store. They've got everything from chewing gum to name-brand tennis shoes. That's why the ladies refer to it as the 7-Eleven. Since you don't have anybody who can send you money, you won't be able to subsidize the store and that's a no-no. So, you're going to work in the laundry for twenty hours a week. You'll get a credit of a dollar-fifty per hour so you'll have an extra 30 dollars a week in credit to spend in the store. It's not much but it's better than nothing."

"Yeah, but you said something about my being lucky. I don't think a dollar-fifty an hour is what you meant."

"There are not enough jobs to go around so people get on waiting lists so they too can earn a little extra money. You leapfrogged them because you have no other way to accumulate store credits. If you want my advice, the first thing you should buy is grooming products. Stinky women attract a lot of trouble. The next thing is a padlock to put on your footlocker because nice things have a way of walking off around here."

So that was why Lupe previously offered to rent me some space in her footlocker - because other people would steal anything they could, including a newcomer's toothpaste.

"But isn't leapfrogging going to irritate other people?" I asked while moving on. "I already have people who think I'm getting favors because I'm white."

"I wouldn't be surprised," she said just as we reached the laundry room, "but most of the ladies go easy on pregnant peers. That's another reason you're lucky."

Yeah, right. That's exactly what my life had become: one piece after another of lucky pie.

My first glimpse inside the highly humid laundry room revealed a well-coordinated team with matching aprons. Their task was simple but not the least bit easy: Make certain that 900 women had clean clothes, sheets and towels.

Toward the left wall, a dozen large canvas carts full of dirty clothes and other items had been dropped off for a sorting crew who did their thing before wheeling the items to a group at heavy-duty washers. Predictably, the wet loads went to the dryer people, then to the folders and finally into a very large storage closet. At the folding table, another preggie was obviously close to her delivery date.

In addition to the standard issue clothing, nearly all of the inmates had accumulated some street clothes plus pajamas and soft sheets. Once a week, everybody stuffed their items into individually labeled canvas duffle bags along with one detergent pod, if they had any. The bag and its contents went for the swim and were returned to the owner without being opened.

As a side bar, everything in those duffle bags got severely wrinkled, which spawned a cottage industry within the "sugar" concept. While most of the women ironed their own items, others paid another group to attend to that chore for them. To make payment, all they had to do was transfer their 7-Eleven credits from one person to the other.

Anyhow, there must have been two hundred of those canvas bags piled up in one corner. If I hadn't been so overwhelmed by my own situation, I might have been impressed by the volume of it all.

After my brief overview of the place a muscular, no-nonsense African American inmate just a little older than me came toward us. "That's Mama Christine," Pepperton said. "She's the leader around here. You're going to work for her."

My new boss glanced at my sad eyes and then addressed Ms. Pepperton. "What we got here?"

The woman reminded me of some of the hard-core drill sergeants I'd seen in movies. I meekly offered her my hand. "Um. I'm Miranda Munchak. I guess I'm a 'lucky' one who gets a job."

She ignored my gesture. "I don't take no shit off nobody," she said right out of the chute. "You understand?"

"Sure," I said, already intimidated by her. "I don't want to cause any trouble."

"You're lucky because pregnant women get to be the 'folders' where they don't have to lift a lot, but don't think you get to loaf 'cause I got a line of other ladies who want that job. Aprons are in the storage room with the towels and sheets. There's a spot for you at the corner of that table so get with it."

Huh? Get with it? I'd only been behind bars for 24 hours and hadn't had time to stop bawling. Did she really expect me to put my own feelings aside and go to work? "Now?" I asked, hoping she'd made some mistake.

"Of course, it's now, woman. You may not have noticed, but you're an inmate in a real prison. You don't get to make the rules. You can have your pity party when you're in bed tonight, but for now, if you want this job, you'd better get your ass over there and start working - NOW!"

I glanced at Pepperton to see if she could save me.

"You'll stay here for the remainder of this shift," she said. "Roughly two hours, then I'll be back to take you to the commissary so you can get some soap and a toothbrush."

Oh, my God. Up to that moment, I didn't think it was possible to feel worse, but I sure as heck did. For the first time in my life, suicide seemed preferable to living, but I couldn't do that either. I had a baby to think of. At the very least, I had to get him or her to the delivery room before doing anything drastic.

"Now, get with it," Mama Christine said, handing me a few tissues.

Blurry-eyed, I blew my nose, retrieved an apron, then stood next to the other expectant mother, named Paula. She tapped my elbow with hers and pointed to a water bottle on the shelf below the table, indicating I could have some. Since each worker was allowed but one bottle per three-hour shift, that was a more meaningful gesture than I first realized.

I choked back my regrets and reached for my very first towel to fold. Mama Christine stood at my side and watched closely to ensure I could keep up with the others. Fortunately, I had folded plenty of laundry in my days, and her barking was soon muzzled, but that didn't make me feel any better.

In fact, nothing could make a person feel good in a situation like mine.

Lucky or not, I had never worked harder. It was so hot and humid and tedious I wanted to cry and run off, but I realized that I'd need the measly six dollars a day. I hung in there while cart after cart was moved from the folding table to the storage room and a new cart took its place. With 900 prisoners, there were always mountains of towels and washcloths to be processed, in addition to jumpsuits and sheets and everything else.

About a half-hour before the end of our shift, the guard from the previous day, Mr. Stome, walked in and looked around. A few minutes later, he and a young shapely Asian woman from the dryer crew, whose lips were splashed with bright red lipstick, went into the storage area and closed the door. "Stack 'em higher, ladies," Mama Christine said to our crew, meaning we were going to be short one person for a while.

Up to that point, I had thought that Mary Ruth's stories about predatory guards were overstated, but I could be stupidly naive sometimes.

12

THE IMPLICATIONS OF A GUARD leading an inmate into a locked laundry room left me dumbfounded. I looked around to see if anybody was going to rescue that poor woman, but nobody slowed down or showed any interest.

Given their collective nonchalance, I assumed that the tryst was a common occurrence. Nonetheless, the whole idea sickened me and confirmed some of the sordid information that Mary Ruth had already divulged.

After working a half-shift, I'd earned three paltry dollars and was exhausted. I couldn't imagine people waiting in line for a job like that. More tears of self-pity drooled down my cheeks.

I sought out Paula, the other pregnant woman. "Thanks for sharing your water," I said. "I know that you didn't have to do that."

"You're welcome. My baby is due in two weeks; how 'bout you?"

"I'm half-way."

"Well, good luck to both of us. I just hope I get my job back after the delivery, but I hear they move us into harder jobs."

Just then Ms. Pepperton arrived along with two other guards. While everybody else went elsewhere, I was taken to the 7-Eleven to get some "luxury items" such as a bar of soap, a comb and a toothbrush.

"Everybody gets to come here once a week," Pepperton said as I signed in as 1516103-A. "I'm going to hang here by the door," she said. "You can go look around. Remember you get ten dollars credit each week."

"But they said $30 per week."

"That's if you work twenty hours."

"Well, I need that money. When do I get my first check?"

"It's not a check. You get work-credits on Fridays, to be used only on items in the store. You've got ten minutes, starting now."

Inside and overwhelmed, I observed a handful of additional inmates roaming the aisles just as they might have done in a real 7-Eleven. I saw a wider variety of items than I expected, all of it priced for somebody with more credits than I had.

On the back wall I picked up a "standard weekly kit." It held five ibuprofens, a roll of coarse TP, some toothpaste, a bar of soap, enough shampoo for a week and seven pieces of hard candy, all for eight dollars. My last two dollars bought me a cheap toothbrush and a comb.

Before going to the register, I crept down a few more aisles. In addition to the typical convenience store items, they had some sturdy cotton blouses and name-brand sneakers that would be more comfortable than the street shoes I'd been wearing.

With my shopping spree completed I was led back to my cell. I'd already been convinced to protect my items from sticky-fingered people, but I sure as heck couldn't afford to give Lupe $2 to rent space in her locker for a week, so I decided to look up Mary Ruth. As expected, she was on her bunk with her feet elevated on a pillow. "Hi ya," she said, sitting up. "I see you've been shopping. It must have been a pretty rough day?"

"I'm so depressed and tired and confused."

"Well, keep that to yourself. There are people around here who would like to give you a free 'feel-better' pill, but the second one ain't free and, trust me, you'll want a second one."

Prior to my prison experience, I wouldn't have needed that advice, but at that moment I was so down I might have tried anything to escape my misery. "Thank you," I mumbled. "You don't know how much I appreciate you. Can I ask another favor?"

"Sure," she said through a grimace.

"Lupe offered to rent me some space in her locker, but money is very scarce until I get paid. I was hoping I could put my things in your locker until I can buy a padlock."

She tilted her mostly-gray head. "I'd like to help you, Honey, but undermining others is the kind of thing that starts wars around here and neither one of us needs that. I can tell you this," she said, leaning in and whispering. "Don't fall for the used-lock bit. Those locks get passed around and certain people have put identifying scratches in them. They know the combos. As soon as you fill your footlocker with goodies, you'll get ripped off."

By this time Mary Ruth had a lot more cred with me, so I vowed to forgo any used locks.

Later, Lupe and her amigas returned. She immediately noticed my 7-Eleven stash. "I decided to take you up on your offer," I said. "That is, if you'll let me pay you when I get my paycheck on Friday."

"Now you need me, huh? That's called supply and demand. The price goes up to three dollars plus one more dollar 'cause you have to pay interest." When I hesitated, she made another proposal. "I can get you a used lock for six dollars. That's a better deal for you."

"Thank you," I said, grateful for Mary Ruth once again, "but I don't want to spend that much right now. I'll pay you four dollars on Friday."

So that was the deal. I had to work three hot and sweaty hours and give that money to Lupe to protect some toothpaste and shampoo. To earn enough money for my own lock I'd have to work two full four-hour shifts. All the other "luxuries," such as a second pair of ordinary underwear, would have to wait.

As I placed my lowly stash in Lupe's footlocker, my previous theories about prison turned into reality. I'd already learned that hundreds of unsavory characters such as kidnappers, murderers and thieves, hid in plain sight. But the inmates weren't the only ones with shadowy souls. Some of the guards were just as evil.

After Lupe locked my things away, she went elsewhere, perhaps to brag to her amigas about how she'd just fleeced her stupid white cellmate. As for me, I lowered my pants, plopped my butt on the pot of shame and fought back new tears.

If only I could have afforded to pay for my brother's treatments...

If only Don wouldn't have convinced me that the insurance company would reimburse the woman whom we planned to rip off...

If only Don hadn't gone nuts and killed that school administrator...

If only the prosecutors would have believed me that I had no idea Don was going to do that.

If only I hadn't been born.

13

After a few days I'd had more lessons than a college student could absorb in a full year. It was eminently clear that I would forever be told when to work, when to eat, when to shower, when to sleep and when I could exercise or read. But the officials weren't the only ones flexing their muscles.

Certain groups of convicts, known as families, intimidated anybody they could because weaklings could persuade their own friends and families to make substantial deposits into their 7-Eleven accounts. From there, it was easy to transfer the credits from one person to another, such as the bullies.

If I weren't pregnant, I would have been a prime target for the bullies. That was one reason why people kept telling me I was lucky. Long-term, there were lots of ways to torment prisoners – in the laundry room, for instance.

A few days later and still on laundry detail, I witnessed another woman - this one Hispanic, with ice-blue lipstick and lots of silver eye glitter - wander into the storage room with Mr. Huff, a pudgy black guard, whom I'd met several times. Once again, nobody cared about the unsecret meeting.

As soon as my shift ended, I approached Mama Christine. "I don't want to make any trouble," I whispered, "but I'm pretty sure that everybody knows what's going on in the storage room. Isn't there somebody we can report it to?"

Mama Christine stopped dead in her tracks, glared at me, and then said, "I told you once before to mind your own business. Did you think I was joking?"

"No. I believe you. It's just that—"

"Let me tell you something, Munchak. You didn't see nothing. If you can't keep your mouth shut, I'll chase your ass out of my area and label you a troublemaker and you won't get another easy job for five years. So, what's it going to be?"

I wish I could say that I stood up to her, but I didn't. My sanity required me to protect the few extras that were available to me via the shelves in the 7-Eleven.

"No," I said. "I don't want to cause any trouble. I'm sure you know what you're doing."

"Then I don't want to hear nothing like that again. Got it?"

I sure did. My very survival could depend on my ability to play dumb.

Obviously, everybody knew what was going on in there, but I couldn't figure out why the mass of women went along with it. I waited for a moment when Mary Ruth and I were alone to satisfy my curiosity. "Everybody has to know what's going on in there," I eventually said. "Why don't the rest of them riot or something?"

Mary Ruth put her finger to her lips. "If I tell you what's really going on, you gotta keep your mouth shut cause I sure as hell don't want any trouble with Mama C."

I nodded.

"Twice a month," Mary Ruth began, "when the trucks bring in food and supplies, those women keep the guards busy so that some other goodies can be snuck in."

"Goodies? Like what?"

"Harmless things mostly, like tobacco, lighters, bedtime toys and booze — lots of booze."

By that time, I knew that some of those things were floating around, but I didn't know all the smuggling secrets.

"If you get caught with those things," Mary Ruth added, "it's just a misdemeanor. You might get six months added to your sentence. But lifers bring in worse things such as weapons, heavy-duty drugs and cell phones. They don't have anything to lose. About all the warden can do is plop 'em in Solitary for a few months."

"But what if the guards figure out that they're being used like that? Won't they be angry?"

Mary Ruth grinned. "Hell, no. The guards are in on it. They get woopie and a piece of the action for looking the other way. The ladies who 'entertain' the guards get some prestige too because that's how everybody else gets their goodies."

Suddenly, I understood why Mama C. was so inflexible. She too was getting some benefit and didn't want it to end for her or anybody else.

I also knew there was a lot more going on in prison than the general public would imagine and I'd just seen the tip of the proverbial iceberg.

Several weeks later, my baby was kicking a lot more and all I was good at was peeing and farting. I continued to cling to the naïve notion that somebody, such as my former attorney, Alice Meer, would figure out that the courts were very, very wrong and I'd get a second chance of some type.

About that time, and out in the yard, Mary Ruth introduced me to an inmate named Trudy. "I thought you guys might like to meet each other," she said. "You have a lot in common."

Trudy and I traded glances. With several arm tatts and a ponytail, she looked a few years younger than me and quite a bit tougher. "Sure," I said, patting my plump tummy. "I'm not going anywhere for a while."

Niceties flowed between us, while we compared our backgrounds.

"I don't know about you," Trudy said, "but I've never been attracted to the intellectual guys or the stay-at-home men or the choir boys. I like the fun fellows. The ones who'll go dancing, and get tipsy, and make naughty love."

Thus far Mary Ruth was incorrect. Trudy and I had completely different backgrounds.

"Tell her about Mitch," Mary Ruth said.

Trudy nodded. "I met him at a bar. He'd been in jail for a couple minor things but nothing substantial. We liked drinking and smoking pot, but some dude owed him money and wouldn't pay up so Mitch wanted to go scare the guy."

"I know what you mean," I said. "Don was like that too, except for the drugs. He'd even been to prison for destroying private property and killing a dog. I loved him, but my life would have been infinitely better if we'd never met. So, what happened between you and Mitch? Did you get the money?"

"Just before we got to the guy's pad, Mitch told me I was going to hold a gun on the guy, just for show. But when the time came, Mitch and his buddy got into an angry screaming contest. Mitch grabbed the gun from me and blew a hole through the other guy's throat. I turned away from the gurgling and covered my ears, but Mitch grabbed the man's wallet - took twenty-two dollars."

Disgusted, but not particularly surprised, I turned to Mary Ruth. "You're right. This is a lot like my case. Don did something like that, too."

"Wait 'til you hear the rest."

"That's right," Trudy added. "The police said that since we took guns with us, we planned the whole crime in advance and I was just as guilty of first-degree murder as Mitch was, even though I didn't expect anybody to get shot or killed."

I nodded. "Trust me. I know that song."

Mary Ruth glanced at Trudy. "Tell Miranda about the sentencing."

"Sure. After I got a public defender, I discovered that good ole Mitch wasn't as innocent as he claimed to be. In fact, 'Mitch' wasn't even his real name. He was a suspect in another case where an elderly couple was murdered after they walked in on a burglary of their home. The police were sure that Mitch was responsible, but they needed more evidence so they offered me a deal. In exchange for my testimony against

Mitch, they lowered the charges against me to manslaughter and lowered the sentence to twelve years—"

"But she can get parole in half that time," Mary Ruth added.

Once again, the collar of injustice had wrapped itself around my neck. As Mary Ruth had suggested, Trudy and I had very similar cases. "Only I didn't have anything the police wanted," I said.

"That's right," Mary Ruth added. "We're talking forty-one years for Miranda versus six years for Trudy. That sucks."

Trudy rested her hand on my arm. "I'm really sorry for you, Miranda. Sometimes the courts can be so damn unfair."

I felt so low I couldn't even put a coherent thought together. All I knew was, if I had gotten a sentence like Trudy's, I could have had foster parents raise my baby until I was paroled, but there was no such option for inmate number 1516103-A.

14

As the days slowly dripped away, the combination of getting bigger and folding hundreds of towels every day brought a lot of unwanted back pain. Each day, I'd lie in my bunk and rue the job that everybody said I was lucky to get.

In one of those moments Mary Ruth and I were hanging out in her cell discussing aspirin and a few other things in the 7-Eleven that diminished some of my discomfort. "That's just one wing of our little mall," she said. "The other outlet is different. You put in an order and it gets delivered. Of course, contraband is technically illegal."

"You've mentioned that before."

"That's because I know that they'll be offering you all sorts of things after you have your baby. Some of it is downright dumb."

"Dumb? Like what?"

"Cigarettes, for example. Once a pack gets past the guards, somebody rips the cigs apart and rolls them into four 'bitty-sticks.' Those go for a buck each. That's where Lupe gets them."

I smirked. "Good ole Lupe offered to sell me two sticks for three bucks. What else can we get?"

"Lotsa things: little bottles of liquor, weapons, vibrators. Plus, all manner of drugs from pot to fentanyl or heroin. At the end of the day, you can get just about anything if you know who to talk with and have real cash."

"That's amazing," I said, "but can you stop right there for a minute? I gotta pee again. It seems all I do is pee and fart."

Mary Ruth smiled. "I remember those days. Go ahead, Honey. I ain't going nowhere."

Much less modest than I was in my previous life, I took my seat. "Where did we leave off?" I asked while the urine pinged off the steel toilet.

"I was just about to say don't rip off the suppliers. These people are running an entrepreneurial enterprise and have a lot of happy customers. If you stir that hornet's nest, you are going up against the vast majority of the inmates, and you'll get introduced to Solitary in a hurry. Trust me, you don't want that."

"Yuck! Have you ever gone there?"

"A few times," she said through a frown of pain. "That's why I'm trying to save you a few bruises."

I nodded. "Would you like a foot massage?"

In a split second her grimace faded. "Really? I'd love that, but I don't want to pester a guard. We'll just keep an eye out."

After she set her cane aside, we sat near the bars so that we could see guards coming from either direction. I slowly removed her socks and peered at black and blue ankles the size of large oranges. Above her ankles, a complete collection of multi-colored varicose veins looked as if they'd been tattooed to her legs. "I'm new at this," I said, "so I'm going to go slow. Let me know if I hurt you or you want me to apply more pressure."

After a few false starts, my ten little massagers slowly worked their way to just above the second ankle. By that time, she had oohed and aahed until she fell to sleep. I wondered if I could someday get a book about professional massages and do that for other ladies as a sugar-hustle of my own.

The next day I told Mary Ruth that we could repeat the routine whenever she wanted. She looked around, then hugged me like a loving mother. During her next trip to the 7-Eleven she bought me a gift and paid extra to get it wrapped. I'd opened other special gifts in my life, but none were as priceless as a simple bottle of lotion that she bought for us to share.

After that, Mary Ruth and I constantly sneaked hugs and cheek kisses and said, "I love you's." Some of the inmates assumed we were a couple, but it was more maternal than that, especially with my own pregnancy nearing its conclusion.

Eventually my breasts had swollen and my tummy had overtaken the waistline in my britches. I was introduced to Noel whose sugar had to do with sewing. She secured permission from one of the guards to sew a sling into my pants. Her fee for that welcome comfort was three 7-Eleven dollars.

Around that same time, I elected to stop torturing myself with impossible fantasies about being released early.

I'd also accumulated enough credits to snag a good pair of tennis shoes from the 7-Eleven. With what little I had left over, I bought a pen and some writing paper so I could make notes to myself, sort of like a diary. More boldly, one night Mary Ruth and I split a miniature bottle of pear brandy schnapps that she got from the contraband people.

Just as I was getting comfortable, a big fight broke out between two African American women in the cafeteria. In my pre-slammer days, I wouldn't have watched anything like that, but there's not a lot to do in the grey-bar building so I cheered for Alinda because she had a pretty smile.

As the battle escalated, other inmates went wild, climbing on the table and cheering wildly for blood. After a few very loud minutes, the guards restored order and the rest of us slowly mumbled our way back to our seats. As I sat down, I looked at my food tray where one thing was painfully obvious: Somebody had stolen my spoon.

15

"This is insane," I screamed at guard Roxy Padilla as she wrapped my wrists with plastic cuffs.

"Rules are rules," she said. "People can make that utensil into a dangerous weapon."

I scanned the cafeteria but had no idea who dealt me an automatic three days in solitary confinement, or "the vault," as some inmates called it.

"Get going," she said, pointing down the hall.

"But I'm pregnant. Are you blind?"

"No exceptions, Munchak. Now get going before you make things worse."

"This is stupid, stupid, stupid," I yelled.

In my pre-prison days, I never would have been so disrespectful of the rules, but I'd grown complacent about the spoon-weapon warnings. What a dumb butt I was. I should have lent that spoon the same importance that I would lend a purse or a child. I simply wouldn't have let those items out of my sight.

With the whistles and jeers behind us, Ms. Padilla revealed a more sympathetic side. "I wish I could cut you some slack, being pregnant and all, but I don't got no choice in the matter."

"Well then, find out who stole my damn spoon and tell her to shove it up her butt. Sorry. I don't usually talk like that."

"I've heard worse, but keep that kind of talk to yourself, or I'll have to add to your charges and I don't want to do that."

"Yeah. I shouldn't take this out on you."

"You ain't gonna like Solitary. Perhaps you can use the time to connect with your baby."

In an instant my anger morphed into self-pity. Any other expectant mom would have done just what she said, but Miranda Munchak didn't get to keep her baby, so special bonding would only make the scars deeper when the delivery was completed.

Scared out of my wits, I was guided down a very long hallway and finally into the Solitary area. Inside, a dark and shadowy corridor with a long row of heavy steel doors on either side reminded me of a creepy storage place where I once kept some furniture. "Keep a-going now," Padilla said.

We passed every door, sometimes enduring rude comments from inmates who were already cooped up behind glovebox-sized holes in the cell doors.

At the very last door on the left, I made a hopeless plea to escape the horrid punishment. "Is there anything I can do to get out of this? Please?"

"Sorry. It's a zero-tolerance matter." She slid the frigid heavy door open. "At least the bad people will leave you alone for a while. Step in there and push your hands through the hole in the door and I'll clip the cuffs."

A minute later, I was desperately alone in a frigid and remote dungeon with nothing but an exercise mat and a steel stool. I panicked. My knees buckled and I rolled to my side as I blacked out.

The next thing I knew, I was lying on a thick rug or something similar and rolling my head from side to side. I tried to recall where I was or what I was doing there, but nothing came to me. I opened my eyes.

Both my vision and thoughts were deeply clouded as I searched for answers to incomplete questions. I crawled to a nearby large steel bowl. It was bitter cold and contained water but what were we doing there? I leaned up against it for what seemed like days.

Then I awakened again, this time to a woman calling my name. "Ms. Munchak? Are you awake?"

Huh? I heard the words but didn't know what they meant.

"Are you okay, Ms. Munchak? You're all done. Time to join the others."

Who was that and what did she mean? Then the big door opened and a uniform stood over me. "You've made it," she said. "Can you get up?"

Huh? Get up? "Yeah, but--"

"Just get to your knees. Then you can do it."

I nodded, used the steel bowl for support and slowly rose to my feet.

"Good enough," she said. "Now hold out your hands while I cuff you."

Cuffs? Then things started to get clearer. Oh, yeah. I was in a bad-girl's place. And this woman was a boss. I held out my hands as instructed.

"Whew. You reek," she said. "It looks like you've wet your pants."

I felt around my big belly, then between my legs. She was right. When did I do that? Then I looked in the corner at a plate of garbage, and a crunched-up cup and two unopened bottles of water. I slowly rose to my feet. "Am I in jail?"

"Course you are. C'mon, now. I ain't got all day."

After a slow start, we walked down a couple long halls, and then stopped at the showers, where I was instructed to clean up. When the warm water hit me, I felt as if I were awakening from a sleepwalking episode.

And then it hit me. I'd just had a three-day blackout, a panic attack, like I had before my prison days, when Don killed those people. The more I concentrated the more I remembered: Some long minutes later I knew I was in Bakersfield Correction Facility for Women, near Delano, California and I'd been sent to solitary confinement for losing a spoon.

16

S OMEBODY ONCE SAID THAT four out of three people are bad with math. That's how dummy-me felt for losing a freaking spoon. My mistake was supposed to earn me three full days in god-awful solitary confinement, but fate had bizarre plans for good ole 1516103-A. My first gaze inside the steel box scared me so badly that my mind took a temporary vacation - just as it did some months back when I supposedly participated in my boyfriend's brutal crimes.

There was an obvious common thread between those two events: In both cases intense anxiety led to several days of lost consciousness.

As before, when the danger subsided, I slowly normalized. My only remaining memory involved the incredible mess that I had left behind. There was so much uneaten food lying around that it looked as if a bomb had landed in the city dump. Based on my filthy clothes and my general body odor I couldn't even guarantee that I'd used the toilet.

In any event, no sane person would live like that, even in Solitary, so I wondered if I could use the experience as proof that I could have been in the same mental condition when the murders for which I was convicted took place.

After I asked around, my peers convinced me that a colossal mess in a cell was not going to get me any sympathy with the authorities, let alone a new trial or reduced sentence. "Otherwise, everybody would do that," Lupe said.

Thereafter, I shifted my thoughts. Due to my pregnancy, my job became more challenging, but I did the best I could and used any spare time to wonder about the upcoming fate of my baby.

That basic routine brought me right up to the day of my first contraction. By that time, I had been residing in the Steel-Walls Motel for four-and-a-half months and my parole hearing was a mere forty-one years and three months off. But who was counting?

Then, just before lights out, there was some leaking and early contractions. This time, Lupe was quite helpful. She rhythmically banged on our cell door with her hairdryer and chanted "Lady in labor. Lady in labor."

Before I knew it, I found myself in the back of an ambulance with Ms. Pepperton. Our siren informed the world that a precious baby was on his way. I still didn't know what the gender would be but I'd decided if I had a girl, I'd think of her as Madeline. A boy would be Cody.

The delivery itself was normal by anybody else's standards, but the heavy breathing and contractions and incredible temporary pain paled compared to the agony in my heart for forfeiting my baby to strangers.

Eight hours later, cuffed to a bed, I knew that "Cody" was just down the hall with his new parents and they were destined for the Midwest. Alone in my room, with the lights out and a guard stationed outside my closed door, my regrets nauseated me. I rolled my head toward the window, but I didn't have any means to break it, let alone jump to my death.

Eventually, a soft-spoken 50-something Hispanic woman opened the door, and I could see a male guard sitting in a chair just outside my room. The woman closed the door behind her. "Hi, I'm Angela, your case manager," she said in a tender, calming tone. "I'm sorry you had to give up your baby. How are you doing otherwise?"

I could see compassion in her eyes and hear it in her words. "Thank you," I said in a subdued voice of my own. "To tell you the truth, I keep second-guessing my decision to have a no-contact delivery."

"I don't see it real often," she said nodding, "but I understand it. It's usually a matter of a clean break. Was that it?"

She hit the correct nerve. "A lot of me wishes I had held Cody, at least for an hour or so, but another part of me knows that looking into his eyes and hugging him would torment me further when I had to let go."

"Well, you obviously made the decision that was best for your baby and his new parents. That's one of the least selfish gestures I've ever seen in a while. May I hug you?"

I welcomed the embrace, pulled her to me and wept out loud. "You're the only person who understands me."

When we separated, her eyes were wet and red while makeup seeped down her cheeks.

She obviously didn't care that I was a societal outcast. Instead, at the very lowest time of my life, she was the gift from God that I desperately needed.

Eventually, she had to ask me a few more questions before she moved on. When the door clicked behind her, I wondered how one thanked somebody who restored your soul.

Incapable of answering my own question, I buzzed for a nurse to help me get to the bathroom. Minutes later, guard Stome freed me from my cuffs and a nurse helped me get to my feet and on into the restroom. Later that evening, my window boasted the first star-lit sky and a far-off sliver of the quarter moon I'd seen in nearly a half-year. I stared and stared knowing it could be generations before I'd see it again.

Two days later, the State wanted its daily pound of flesh from prisoner 1516103-A. I was returned to the prison infirmary where I spent three additional days recovering. Shortly thereafter I was called back to my job, where the other inmates were chiefly supportive.

A few days later my baby was old news to them, and the pre-birth paradigm resumed. From behind the folding station, I knew why guard Nick Stome had arrived. In the back of the building somewhere, a big truck was unloading food and supplies, plus a few mystery boxes, but since Stome was busy playing bellybutton tag with an inmate he wouldn't see those boxes and a good time was in store for all – at least for a while.

A couple weeks after that, Mama Christine called me to the side. "Your cakewalk is over," she said in a subtle but firm tone. "You're moving from the folding table to the machines."

A cakewalk? What cakewalk?

No longer "lucky," I was now required to move the heavy, water-soaked clothes as they came out of the washers to the dryers and load them. Most of those loads weighed 30 pounds or more and there were lots of them, which was why it was the most physically demanding job I'd ever had.

17

I'd been stoic and working the washer and dryer detail for over a month when another stunner landed in my lap. One Monday near the end of my shift, the all-powerful Mama C pulled me aside. "I take it you've figured out why Lucille and Breeta and Nonie are particularly appreciated around here," she said.

I sure did. They were the reason that contraband could come in the back door. "I try to mind my own business," I said.

"Good. It's best that way. That means you can be trusted." She looked over her shoulder before continuing. "You've noticed their necklaces and makeup, right? How would you like some of those things for yourself?"

Uh-oh. I may have been completely naive when I originally arrived at the cement jungle, but one can learn quite a bit in six months, and I didn't like where this conversation was headed. "If you're asking me to have sex with the guards, the answer is no. I don't want to do anything like that."

She immediately shook her head. "Don't be so hasty, Honey. It will usually only be once a month because you'll trade off with the other girls."

This woman had to be out of her mind. Naturally, I'd been intimate with a few men in my life, but I simply couldn't imagine taking on a stranger in a laundry room, especially with a group of cheerleaders egging me on. "No, thank you. I'd rather just do my work."

This time she lowered her voice to a whisper. "Trust me, Honey, you don't want to say no to those guys. They'll get somebody to stash a weapon in your cell and then they'll bust you for it. You'll spend so much time in Solitary that you'll do anything to get out of there."

I glanced around. Several sets of eyes pretended they weren't paying attention. "But that's like being raped," I objected.

"It's not rape. He's not going to force himself on you. If you have to label it, it's more like being a mistress and it's only for 20 minutes once a month. You gotta do this - for everybody's sake. You'll be a hero."

"No. No. No. There are lots of prostitutes around here. Get one of them."

"Can't do that. Since you ain't got no family or friends to sneak things in, this is your sugar."

Mary Ruth had warned me about sugar; she'd even said that it wouldn't come up until after my baby was born. "But I'm 36 years old and have stretch marks. Why don't they go for somebody younger?"

Mama C shrugged. "I don't know why they want you and I don't ask. They could just be ready for a clean-cut white woman. All I know is if they don't get what they want the shipments don't get in. That pisses off some very powerful ladies and a lot of their customers who count on those shipments. Trust me, you don't want to be in the crosshairs of that many angry people--"

"But I don't--"

"You'll get an extra twenty dollars in your commissary account and I can get you some hand lotion for Mary Ruth's feet."

"No. No. No. I don't care how much you give me. I can't do that."

She looked over my shoulder and back. "Don't give me that holier-than-thou bullshit, woman. Everybody around here knows that you had threesomes with twin brothers before you got busted."

What the hell? While she was technically wrong, she hit pretty close to home. "No, I didn't. I was never with them both at the same time, and I loved them both for different reasons."

"Don't care. You ain't calling the shots." Suddenly she softened her tone. "Lookie here, Munchak, we've all done a guy or two when we didn't want to. Rich or poor, black or white, single or married. We've all done it. Hell, I let my boyfriend climb aboard lotsa times when I wasn't in no mood, just to keep the peace. That's what you're gonna do. Keep the peace."

I didn't admit it, but she was correct again. When my ex started banging his employees, I felt like I'd failed him and tried to prove I loved him by being a good bed partner, even if I wasn't in the mood.

"Look, Honey," she added, "every woman does things she doesn't want to do, especially the ones in here - hell, the whole place is something we don't want to do - but sometimes you have to swallow your pride and focus on self-preservation and your friends. If you piss off these guards and they make things harder on the population, your life will turn into a living hell that you can't even imagine. You pretty much have to do it, for your own good."

"But there are real prostitutes in here. Young ones. Why don't they do it?"

"I already told you: I don't ask."

My fingers began to quiver. I sure as hell didn't want to become a twenty-dollar prostitute, but my brain told me Mama C was right. My life would become terminally worse if I were hated by all my peers and labeled a troublemaker. And yes, there were times that I had sex with a man when I didn't want to. But this was a lot different. How could I ever forgive myself if I were to go along with such an immoral concept? "But it's not right," I said in desperation.

Just then the outer door opened. Guard Pepperton was there to take me back to my cell.

Mama C leaned toward me. "You've got until Friday to make a decision. I hope you do the right thing - for all of our sakes."

18

God, how I hated prison. After the disgusting conversation with Mama C, I became dizzy and sought my bunk, where I could think more clearly. While I lay there, I considered ratting everybody out but that would be certain suicide. If I pissed off the guards, they could do exactly what Mama C said: frame me for something bogus just to make an example out of me. A trip to Solitary would surely follow. After that, they could do it again and again, after which the unhappy inmates would have their turn at me.

As the next couple days ticked away, inmates that I did not know smiled at me, or gave me a thumb's up or nodded their heads, doubtless to encourage me. But none of them knew how scared I was or how much I hated being in that situation. Then after one of my shifts and in my cell a shadow fell upon me. Guard Nick Stome stepped forward and eyed my breasts. "I hear you've got a decision to make. I'd hate to see you make the wrong one."

That man made me sick. In my heart, I wanted to rise up like Norma Rae or Erin Brockovich, but Stome had so much unchecked power it would be infinitely foolish to anger him so I kept my thought to myself.

Then, about an hour before dinner, Mary Ruth became very sick to her stomach and had to seek the infirmary. While she was away, several other friendly inmates approached me. I assumed they were picking my brain to find out which way the wind was blowing but I didn't have any idea what I was going to do. Common sense said to do it, but my heart was breaking because I thought myself more respectable.

Later that night I reached for my pillow and discovered a note beneath it that contained an ominous warning. "Your friend will be okay, but you won't be so lucky if you make the wrong choice." My knees buckled.

The next thing I knew, I was on the floor with a blanket draped over me, and a very young male guard whose name I did not know was tapping me on the shoulder. "This better not be some sort of game, Ms. Munchak, 'cause we got other things to do."

"I'll be okay," I said before lying down.

The next morning, I was a total wreck. Mary Ruth was still in the infirmary and I hadn't had any rest. I skipped breakfast but before long guard Roxy Padilla arrived to escort me to the laundry room. The last grains of sand had left my hourglass.

Padilla had barely left the laundry room before Mama Christine hustled right to me. "Mr. Huff is going to be here in fifteen minutes," she said, "and I have to have somebody ready. What's it going to be?"

I observed a number of workers watching me out of the corner of their eyes. I knew that I was too much of a basket case to help them. I wanted to back out or run away or, better yet, die, but I couldn't ignore what happened to Mary Ruth. While most of us were dealing with scumbags and pride and lust, she was fighting for her life. The same thing or worse could happen to me.

I looked into Mama Christine's impatient eyes and recalled one of Mary Ruth's lines: Sometimes, it's better to be smart than right. I nodded one time.

Surprised by my own impromptu gesture, I almost expected a round of applause, but instead I got turned heads from the workers and fresh orders from the woman who had just become my pimp.

"All right then," Mama C said. "Do something with your hair, then get to work at the machines. When I come get you, you'll walk quietly to the storage area. Once inside do what he tells you, but you don't have to do anything too kinky."

Too kinky? I tried to swallow, but my throat was too dry. "Too kinky?" I said.

Mama C groaned, "Lookie here, woman. We don't got no policy manuals. Use your common sense. Make sure he has a good time. Mix it up a little. As long as you do that, you don't gotta do nothin' painful. Got it?"

Yeah, I got it all right, but first Huff pulled me to him. I'd never had sex with an African American before, but he smelled of cheap cologne. "You're lucky," he said softly. "A lot of women around here would love to get away from their routines and have some physical pleasure once in a while."

"Uh-huh," I said before we played tongue tag until he reached for my blouse. I closed my eyes while he pawed me and groaned. I hated it even more than I expected, but I played along because I wanted it to end as quickly as possible.

By the time it was all over, he produced a condom and we'd visited the storage room floor where we adopted the missionary position with a stack of bath towels as padding.

The bargain-basement price to screw this particular once-per-month prostitute was a measly $20 and a bottle of hand lotion.

When it was all over, I quickly dressed and returned to the machines where fresh tears blended with the sticky humidity on my cheeks. Nobody said anything to me but one of the Hispanic women mouthed, "I'm sorry."

As for me, even though it had been over a year since I'd made love with a man, there was no pleasure to it. Zero, zilch, nada. Not even some sort of relief for having passed my initiation into the One-of-the-Gang Club.

19

AFTER MY FIRST EXPERIENCE AS A PROSTITUTE-in-a-box, I finished my shift and would have loved to expose the whole nauseating ritual, but the guards had stoolies that would cover for them. Instead, I sniffled and wiped my eyes with my sleeve.

Guard Roxy Padilla escorted me back to my cell. "I don't suppose we could stop by the showers," I asked.

She glanced at me like I'd just crawled out of a cave. "You know I can't make special accommodations for anybody. That includes you."

At my cell, I twice brushed my teeth and fought back a new storm of shame because Mary Ruth was in the infirmary because of me. I hadn't felt that disappointed in myself since the day Cody got away.

Fortunately, that afternoon, Mary Ruth was returned to her bunk. I immediately secured permission to massage her feet. "You don't know how glad I am to see you," I said in the understatement of the year.

She smiled at me. "The feeling is mutual. I haven't felt that bad since King Kong was a baby. They think I had a bout with food poising. Did anybody else get sick?"

I considered telling her about the note of threat, but I didn't want to rile her. "Not that I know of."

When dinner rolled around, we hobbled to the dining hall where I got a few head nods, presumably because word had spread that 1516103-A had boinked a guard so that everybody else could continue to receive their forbidden fruit.

After dinner, Mary Ruth and I slipped into one of the exercise rooms were I finally spoke of my get-together with Huff. "I don't know how I do it," I said through more tears, "but I keep making things worse."

"Don't be so hard on yourself, girl," she said in a welcome motherly tone. "We all do what we gotta do to survive around here."

"Mama C said it was like being a mistress, but I think it's closer to institutional rape because everybody allows it."

"I know what you mean, Miranda, and I'm really, really sorry about what happened to you, but you're trying to apply the rules of a civilized society to the war zone of a prison. It ain't the same, so do what you gotta do and forgive yourself because it isn't your fault."

Somehow, her wisdom and gentle tone enabled me to shed some of my shame. "I just hope the guards get tired of my ugly stretch marks."

"You never know. There are so many women rotating in and out of here that any one of them could bump you aside. In the meantime, the best way to prevent drowning is to avoid making waves. That's what I had to do."

I looked around and then kissed her on the cheek. "You make me feel better."

That night I thought of an appropriate nickname for Mr. Huff: From that point on, he became Huff & Puff to me. My highly sarcastic name for Nick Stome was St. Nick.

When another month had passed it was St. Nick's turn to disrespect me. "Okay, now," Mama C said when I entered the laundry area. "He's waiting for you right now. Take this tube of lipstick and put a lot on before you join him. He'll always want you to wear weird lipstick."

Weird lipstick, huh? I assumed that this was one of those

"not too kinky" things Mama Christine had mentioned previously. I reluctantly wandered to one of the nearby sinks where a scratched-up mirror reflected a haggard-looking woman who resembled my grandmother. A twist of the little gold cylinder produced a measure of coal black lipstick. I caked it on and slowly moved toward a door that hid my second customer.

Inside, St. Nick's prominently displayed badge intimidated me. "If we can get along in here," he said, "there's a good chance you'll get a few perks from time to time."

I nodded, indicating that I knew his rules.

"Okay, then," he added while mining his shirt pocket. "I've got a consent form for you to sign."

"A consent form? Why? I'm here, aren't I?"

"Yeah, but if anything goes wrong, I want to show that you approved. That way, I get transferred but I won't lose my pension."

Yeah, that was what I was worried about. A friggin' pervert's pension. Regardless, it was better to be smart than defiant, so I signed his stupid paper.

That done, he lifted my chin, kissed me, and slowly licked my blackened lips as if I were a lollipop. I wanted to gag. Like it or not, the sooner he got what he wanted, the sooner he'd leave me alone and I'd have another month before I'd have to do it all over again.

While holding the strange kiss, his hands washed down my backside and up again before he unsnapped my bra. For the next 15 minutes I suppressed my feelings and did what he wanted.

When he finished, he was breathing so hard I hoped he'd have a heart attack, but apparently all that good luck of my early days had clearly run out.

Two months later, when it was St. Nick's next turn to board the Miranda Express, he mined his front pocket for a small bottle of cologne. "It's cruelty-free," he said as if that was supposed to impress me.

I always hated being with those men, but at least Mama C's original claim was correct; there wasn't anything too kinky or physically painful involved.

Aside from the $20 and the lotion, about the only thing I got out of the experience was empathy for other women in society who were forced to forfeit chunks of their self-respect to get the other things they need to survive - be they drug-addicted, streetwalkers or everyday women in bad relationships. We were all backed into a similar corner.

Thereafter, I continued to do what I had to do and by the second anniversary, or should I say "crapiversary" of my first day in prison, I had swallowed my pride and come to see the visits as my monthly curse. Mary Ruth thought the occasion warranted a gift. She slipped me a one-ounce bottle of coconut cream liqueur.

After lights out, I had a half-hour or so to kill while I waited for Lupe to fall asleep. At the first snore, I twisted off the lid and ever so gently tapped my lips with a quick swig of the thick sweetness. For nearly an hour I savored my voluntary mischief knowing that if I were busted, I could spend a week in Solitary.

20

By the middle of my third year, Lupe had been released and Mary Ruth and I shared kisses and tenderness akin to what a couple sisters of drastically different ages might do. Fortunately, she'd gotten a wheelchair and the powers that be let us eat at the same table so I could help her get around.

Contrarywise, the ever-sickening appointments in the laundry room persisted. I tried to keep my emotions out of it but in the evenings preceding the get-togethers, I occasionally drifted into the familiar semi-conscious state that had been pestering me for years. Each time I woke up fuzzy-headed and sweating. It usually took a while to recall where I was, and then things normalized - that is, until something very different happened.

One evening in the dining room, I reached for a lowly napkin and a thunderous migraine bolted from the back of my right ear toward my right eye. I squealed as my vision went blurry.

"You okay, Honey?" Mary Ruth instantly asked.

"I don't know," I groaned. "It feels like somebody rammed an icepick through my head."

"Oh, my goodness," she said before signaling for St. Nick, who was leaning against a wall near the exit. He slowly strolled to our table. "What you guys want?"

"I gotta horrible migraine," I said, "and need to lie down."

He released a sarcastic sigh and motioned for Ms. Sarella Perry, a tall, young female guard, to take over.

She rushed to me and held my elbow. "Can you get to your feet?"

Even though there was gentle compassion in her tone, it felt as if she were yelling at me. "I dunno," I said being careful not to shake my head. "I'll try."

With her help, I slowly rose and steadied myself. "Come on," she said, guiding me toward the exit. "Let's get you to the infirmary."

As we passed through the door, each step sent reverberations up and down my neck like a rumbling train. I pressed my palms against my ears with all my might. Surprisingly, it was as if I'd flicked a switch. The train sensation lessened.

A few more steps and it was as if somebody were slowly removing the pick. I lifted my head. Additional slow walking brought a bit more relief.

By the time we got to the infirmary, I felt as though somebody had opened a release valve in my head and let out all the remaining pressure. Now what?

I considered leveling with Ms. Perry, but I was afraid that the pain would return. I rubbed my neck, faked a moan and slowly completed the last few steps to the infirmary.

Inside, two RNs and a nurse assistant tended to a couple dozen women in recliners or beds.

The petite nurse assistant, whose pigtails made her appear to be barely out of college, hustled over to us and spoke to Ms. Perry. "What can I do for you ladies?"

"Ms. Munchak has a bad headache."

"A migraine," I added while trying to look like I was still suffering. "I've had headaches before as well as dizziness and fainting spells but nothing like this."

She aimed me at a recliner and rushed off for meds.

"I think you'll be okay now," Ms. Perry said to me before walking off.

A short while later the nurse assistant brought a wet towel, a pill in a paper cup and a bottle of water. I hoped to palm the pill in case I needed later but the young assistant must have read my mind. "I have to watch you wash it down," she said.

While I tipped the cup to my lips, she studied me like a scientist would. I looked her in the eyes. "Can I have a few of these for later?"

"No. We can't hand out drugs of any kind. Now, I need you to stay put for twenty minutes to ensure there are no side effects."

And that was the extent of it, at least for a while.

A couple days later brought St. Nick another chance with the prostitute-in-the-box. It had all the appeal of the stomach flu. He was definitely ickier than Huff & Puff who went to those meetings with one thing in mind: to hump 1516103-A and get the hell back to work before somebody busted him. He also liked to do it doggie-style so I didn't have to look at him while he huffed along.

Don't get me wrong, I still hated every minute of it, but not as much as I hated being with the always-arrogant St. Nick. I would have loved to drive him directly to the nearest men's penitentiary where gangs made life especially unpleasant for authority figures gone bad.

21

IN THE WEEKS THAT FOLLOWED, the icepick-to-the-brain episodes became more frequent, and it became clear that whatever caused them was getting worse. One of the infirmary nurses found a doctor who agreed to come check me out the next week. Until then, I was to stay in the infirmary so the nurse assistant could administer some magnesium and vitamin B2 when necessary.

That week, while I waited for the doctor, I lived in "other-hand" hell: On one hand, I hoped my condition would flare up when the doctor arrived so he could understand what was going on and fix it; on the other hand, that damn icepick and the earsplitting noises held me forever at the precipice of another unwanted blackout.

Finally, on a Monday afternoon, and still in the infirmary, I was awakened by a man's voice. "Ms. Munchak," he said softly. "It's Dr. Burns. I'm here for our appointment."

I opened my eyes to see a white-coated man with gorgeous wavy black hair and striking green eyes. Since it had been over three years since I'd seen any eye candy, I didn't have to fake a smile.

"Hello," I said, sneaking a peek at his ring finger. After observing his gold band, I felt foolishly disappointed. "Thanks for coming to see me," I said softly.

"Certainly. There's a small dressing room over there. Can we have a private conversation?"

"I'd like that."

Minutes later, a handsome doctor who had everything to live for and a screwed-up prisoner with a faded cotton blouse and hundreds of split ends sat face to face. "I've examined your file," he said. "Can you tell me about your headaches?"

"Yes, sir," I said, "We're really talking about two different things, but they might be related." I told him the history of my blackouts going back to the high school play and the days just before my arrest. "When I get stressed out, I panic and fade into a semi-conscious state, like sleepwalking. I should also tell you that I have a twin brother who lives in a mental facility. He has rages and blackouts too."

"I take it the migraines that the nurse spoke of are another symptom?"

"Yes. That just started happening a couple months ago."

"Tell me about that."

"It's like somebody slamming an icepick through the back of my skull and all the way to my eye."

"Is it just one side?"

"Yes. The right side."

"Is it bothering you right now?"

"Not really. But my brain is usually a little numb."

"I see. When you have these episodes, does it sound like everybody is yelling?"

I nodded. "I have to cover my ears."

"Alright then," he said, reaching for his stethoscope. "Let's check out a few things."

After he checked my blood pressure and made me walk with my eyes closed to check my balance, he took a few notes. Then he said, "I think we should get an MRI. I can get us an appointment for next Monday at the hospital up the road a ways."

That actually sounded wonderful. As a woman who hadn't been outside the prison walls for three years, I would have sat in a front row seat at the city dump if he wanted. "Can I still work?" I asked. "I need the money."

"Based on what you've told me so far, I don't think your job is triggering your headaches. In fact, they appear to be random. I'm going to leave that up to you. Just be careful and if you have a flare-up, lie down for a while. If it gets unbearable, have a nurse give me a call."

He could count on that.

After we said our goodbyes, Ms. Pepperton escorted me out to the yard where I silently savored my meeting with the good-looking doctor.

Several days later when it was time for one of my fornication flings with St. Nick, I drew Mama Christine aside. "I don't know if you've heard but I've had to meet with a doctor to deal with my migraines. I'm supposed to take it easy until my meeting next week."

"Oh, yeah? Do you have one now?"

"No, but they come on without notice and if that happens—"

"Not my problem. Stome likes you and he don't like excuses. You'd best stick with the program and hope you get through it okay."

"But I was hoping you could get one of the other ladies to fill in for me."

She frowned. "This ain't no school. We don't got no substitutes. Case closed. Now, I gotta get back to work."

Disappointed, I slipped over to the mirror, applied a thick layer of the horrid black lipstick that St. Nick liked and hoped he'd choke on it. A short time later we met up as usual and I tried again.

"Can I ask you a favor before we have sex?"

He glared. "You're in no position to ask for favors."

"I know that, but you already know that I get splitting headaches and I was hoping we could take the day off, just this one time? I can make it up to you some other time."

"Who do you think you are? This place doesn't revolve around you. Now suck it up and do what you're supposed to do. Either that or we might find some contraband in your cell, and you'll spend a month in Solitary. Now, what's it gonna be?"

I'd never hated anybody as much as I hated that man, although Don was a close second...

22

Sᴜɴᴅᴀʏ ᴇᴠᴇɴɪɴɢ ᴀғᴛᴇʀ ᴅɪɴɴᴇʀ, my icepick returned with all its force. I plugged my ears and waited for the pain to subside as it always did. The next morning, I looked forward to seeing the doctor, so I fussed with my hair and artfully applied some of the new makeup I'd bought in the 7-Eleven. Ultimately, all of that beauty was offset when we boarded the prison van and my jewelry consisted of a single pair of stiff plastic bracelets. When Roxy Padilla belted me into my seat, I got a little kick out of it.

"What's the matter, Ms. Padilla," I said. "Is the State afraid it won't get its full forty years out of my hide?"

She grinned. "It sure seems like that sometimes, doesn't it?"

Huff & Puff drove the three of us a few dozen miles and past a few small towns to the hospital. All along I feasted my eyes on anything and everything I could, even things that would have been down-right ugly back in my pre-prison days. At one point, I fantasized about breaking out of prison. Why not, I thought. I had nothing to lose. Course, I had no shovel to dig my way out, nor a gun to shoot my way out, nor a ladder with which to leap over a wall with barbed wire on top. Then the thought-bubble popped.

As we drew close to the hospital, I'd hoped to see Dr. Burns but instead I was led, under armed guard, into the MRI room where a 3-D image of my brain was produced. A few hours later I was right back where the state wanted me – in the van and headed home.

Two days later, Dr. Burns returned with the results of the MRI. Once again, I dolled myself up the best I could and followed him into the dressing room.

"I don't know if this is good news or bad news," he said, "but we definitely found the source of your headaches."

That sounded promising. "Wonderful. Can you make me better?"

"I don't really know just yet. You have a golf ball-sized growth of some kind creating pressure inside your skull."

"What is it, a tumor?"

He nodded. "Potentially a very slow-growing tumor. That could be why it took so long to cause serious trouble. We're going to have to get a needle biopsy. Then we should have a better indication of exactly what it is and what to do about it."

"What's that?"

"It's fairly common. We make a small incision in your scalp and drill a tiny hole through your cranium. From there we'll insert a hollow needle through the hole and into the tumor to extract a small piece of the tissue for evaluation."

I smiled at him. "Is my head going to leak?"

He grinned. "The hole is inconsequential."

"Then what? Do I get radiation treatments or go on drugs or what?"

"It all depends on the lab results. I've made you an appointment for Wednesday morning. You'll be there a little longer this time. I want you to take it easy until then. We'll see if we can get you a couple days off."

"Okay. I'm all for that. Thank you."

"You're welcome. Do you have any other questions before I move on?"

I had a lot of questions alright, like, would he mind holding me in his arms and dancing for an hour or so. "No, I just hope my headaches go away."

"We'll do our best."

The next few days I was on pins and needles, but I made it to the hospital and went through the procedure before resting a bit and then scooting back to the big house until the doc could bring me the results.

I was taking it easy in the infirmary when he walked in and smiled that modest toothy grin of his.

"Hello, Ms. Munchak. Getting right to the point, we have some good news. Let's go to our little conference room and I'll fill you in."

"Fortunately," he began, "your tumor is benign, so that's a good thing. However, due to the fluids in your skull and the severe headaches I think we'll have to go in there and remove all the foreign matter."

I rolled my fingers into my palms. "That sounds dangerous."

"Surgery is always serious, but this is the most commonly performed operation for this type of condition. The recovery rate is very good. It's called a craniotomy. First, we'll have to shave a small area of your scalp. Next, we make an incision and remove a small plug from the skull. That provides access to the unwanted matter. After the bad stuff gets sucked out, we put the plug back and stitch up the scalp. The whole procedure will take about four hours."

"Then what?"

"We'll fit you with a helmet – it won't be much of a fashion statement, but it'll protect you just in case you reach for the itchy spot while you're sleeping. Anyway, if all goes as expected, you'll have a couple days of observation, then you can return to the infirmary for a few additional days. You should be back to work six to eight days from now."

"Yippee," I said with as much sarcasm as I could muster.

He smiled. "I'm certain you'll feel a lot better with all of that pressure out of your head."

"Will the blackouts stop?"

He cocked his head. "We're just going to have to wait and see. The important thing is, the migraines should go bye-bye."

"I hope so. I don't know how to thank you."

"Just get better. That's what we all want."

The next week, right on schedule, Dr. Burns removed my gooey golf ball, and I began the recovery process.

With a prison guard posted outside my room, I was cuffed to the side of my headboard. My new wardrobe consisted of a mummy's worth of bandages and a biker's helmet, but at least I could look forward to better days.

23

ON THE SECOND DAY IN THE HOSPITAL following the craniotomy, my door swung inward. "Good morning," a middle-aged white woman said. "My name is Diana Fisher. I'm here to see how you're doing."

She handed me a clip board. "Can you write down your full name, date of birth and which state we're in?"

"Sure." I sat up and immediately forgot what she'd said. "Can you say that again?"

"Certainly. I'd like you to write your full name, date of birth and which state we're in."

"Okay," I said before I slowly wrote my first name. "Now what?"

"Your last name, please."

From there, we worked through a series of simple questions designed to test my memory.

"You're doing fine," she said after I finally wrote down most of the letters in the word California. "Do you remember my name?"

"Hmm. I think it's Debra, but I didn't pay that much attention to your last name."

"Close. It's Diana Fisher."

"Oh, sorry."

"No problem. If you don't mind, I'd like you to tell me one of your earliest memories."

My first thought was of my twin brother, Mickey. I had to concentrate but eventually, I remembered a few things.

"I loved him a lot," I finally said.

From there, we talked about my life, working our way closer to the present. I couldn't always think of what to say but if she asked me a specific question, such as who was my favorite teacher, I could usually recall some relevant information.

Then she asked if I had any children.

I sat motionless for several seconds. "I think so, but it makes me sad."

"Well, we don't want that. It appears as if you're recovering nicely."

I pointed at my temple. "Yeah, but I forgot your name."

"Do you remember it, now?"

"Uh-oh. I'm really sorry, I only remember your first name. It's Debra."

"Well, it's actually Diana, but you're close and that will give us something to talk about next time I see you. If you don't have any additional questions for me, I have to scoot."

"Okay," I said, waiting for her to leave so I could grab her business card and memorize her name.

Although the meeting was brief, what's-her-name made me feel pretty good. Later that same day, my mind was clearing up when Roxy Padilla, the guard on duty, poked her head in my room.

"Dr. Burns is here."

I always liked being with the doctor, but as silly as it was, I wished I would have looked nicer. "Could you do me a favor, Ms. Padilla? Could you remove the bracelets while he's here? I'm too weak to cause trouble."

She hesitated for a moment before answering, "They go back on as soon as he leaves. Got it?"

"Yes. Of course. Thank you."

Once freed, I rubbed my naked wrists, fluffed my hair and smoothed a few wrinkles out of my sheets.

When Dr. Burns entered my room, a comforting warmth soothed me. "How are you feeling?" he asked with a depth of compassion that I rarely heard from anybody else.

"A little tired, and I have trouble remembering names."

"That's normal," he said, scooting to the head of my bed. "Let's remove your headgear so I can examine your incision. Have you had any migraines or headaches?"

"No, not really."

"What about your memory?"

I nodded proudly. "Debra Finley was here. She said I'm doing pretty well."

"Do you mean Diana Fisher?"

I paused a moment, then smiled. "Crap. I guess I'm not doing as well as I thought."

"I wouldn't worry about it. It's probably just a short-term issue. Do you remember where you live?"

"If you mean the prison, I couldn't forget that."

He nodded.

"Okay then, I'll schedule your release for the day after tomorrow. I'd like you to take it easy for a few more days. I'm also going to set up an appointment for new glasses. They can cut down on headaches. Keep wearing the helmet and drop by the infirmary every other day for the nurses to change your bandages. In a couple days you may discontinue use of the helmet, except at work for a week or so."

I watched both his eyes and lips as he continued.

"When will I see you again?" I asked, trying not to sound like a moony middle schooler.

"I'll drop by tomorrow and then again a few days after that at the infirmary."

"But you think I'm going to be okay. Right?"

"We extracted a lot of foreign material from your brain, so it will take a little time for everything to settle, but it appears that way."

Moments later Dr. Burns vanished and Ms. Padilla instantly chained my left wrist back to the bedpost as promised.

That evening it was St. Nick's turn to guard the door and I asked to see him. A little later he came into my room. "The nurse said you want something?"

"Yes, sir. A long time ago you said if I would be with you in the laundry room I could get a few perks, so I'm hoping you can do a big favor for me."

"What is it?"

"I haven't been outside at night for three years. I was hoping that you could wheel me outdoors tonight so I can look at the stars and moon for a while. It would mean a lot to me."

He rolled his eyes and shook his head before simply walking away.

Frustrated, but not willing to give up, that night I persuaded a nurse to scoot my bed closer to the window where a thousand stars twinkled just for me. I smiled and wept while I thought about Mickey and Cody and Dr. Burns and how the bottom had fallen out of my life.

24

HEADACHE-FREE AT LAST, I was returned to my cage. My cute little helmet would have gone over well at the Tour de France.

When I was able to go back to work, Mama C assigned me to the folding table where I wouldn't be exposed to heavy lifting or the possibility of bumping my head while loading and unloading machines. "Thanks for the concern," I said to her. "Can I ask you something else?"

"Hurry, 'cause I don't got no time to chat."

"When Friday rolls around, I hope you don't expect me to screw one of the guards."

She looked over her shoulder as if the guard-in-the-box activities were a big secret.

"I might be able to get somebody to switch weeks with you, but no promises."

"Well, I'd appreciate it, big time."

"It's not up to me. Don't you get that?"

"Yeah. We're all at the mercy of somebody else, but there must be a woman around here who would like the attention or some extra money."

"I already told ya, it ain't up to me. Now get to work."

I pivoted and moved toward the table. "Step aside ladies," I said. "The psycho is back to dazzle you."

Most of them smiled, but one of my Hispanic co-workers

made finger circles at her temple. I didn't give a darn because I had a cool helmet and my headaches were long gone and thus far, there was no sign of hazy blackouts.

It took a little time to regain the fast-folding pace, but I was more focused on Mama C in hopes she'd find somebody else to take on the storage room duties come Friday.

When my four-hour shift finally ended, I was one pooped woman, but at least I'd earned six additional dollars in my 7-Eleven account.

Later that afternoon, Guard Sarella Perry caught me napping in my bunk. "Hey, Munchak, I've got something for ya."

Huh? I rolled to my side and received a pair of glasses. I liked the more dignified look and decided to get some clip-on sunglasses, so there went my six bucks.

Anyway, as that week wound down, guard-humping day arrived, and Konie was called upon to pleasure St. Nick. Thereafter, Mama C made it perfectly clear that I would be back on screwing detail the following month, but neither of us knew that I was about to develop a wild idea that would get me out of the laundry room and the sex cave, once and for all.

It all started when I was getting used to my new glasses. Everything looked clearer, but also dingier and faded. With that revelation I asked a few friends if they thought their cells looked as gloomy as I thought mine. Some did, some didn't give a damn. I needed to do more investigating.

That afternoon, my therapist returned. "Hello, Diana Fisher," I said with extra emphasis so she knew I finally remembered her name.

We traded smiles and slipped into the dressing room near the back of the infirmary. I glanced at the dull corner of the small room. It too needed a paint job. "So, how are you doing?" she asked.

"Wonderful," I said. "After hosting that tumor for so long, I got used to the chronic headaches. I didn't really know just how bad they were until they went away."

"That's good to know. What about your emotions?"

"Well, now that I've got new glasses and a better outlook, I've noticed that my cell is gloomy. So are a lot of the others and some of the common areas. They could all use a good coat of paint."

"Sounds like when the headaches went away, your mind became free to think about new things."

Indeed, it was.

Thereafter, she asked the same questions, in the same order, as the last time we'd talked, beginning with my earliest memories and right up to the present. Then, "Is there anything else bothering you?" she asked.

"Well, I feel sad when I think about my stay in the hospital."

"How so?"

"It has to do with nighttime. From my bed, I looked out my window and saw stars and the moon. I'd forgotten how beautiful they were. But there are very few windows around here and we aren't allowed outside at night. I really, really miss being outdoors at night."

"Yeah. I can see why that would sadden a person. Would it help if you were to get you a poster of the night sky?"

"I don't know, but I can tell you this: Up 'til now, whenever the other ladies have talked about breaking out of here, I've dismissed the concept as hopeless silliness, but after seeing that gorgeous sky I've had daydreams about it."

"Yeah, I can understand that, too. But, like you said, those thoughts are probably very common."

"I also miss my brother, Mickey. Once in a while, his caregivers send me pictures of him. Some of it makes me smile. Other times it makes me cry because I can't be with him or comfort him or afford to send him to a better facility."

"That must be very frustrating."

"It's even worse regarding my son. He's three years old now and I've never even seen a picture of him. He and Mickey are my only family."

"I'm deeply sorry about your situation, Miranda, but I am

pleased to hear that you're experiencing complete thoughts and emotions. At least that's one good thing. Is anything else troubling you?"

"Thank you for asking that because I do have something else on my mind. It's not as serious though."

"Of course. I still have a few more minutes."

"This is going to sound bizarre, but I've been wondering about prostitutes."

She looked puzzled. "Prostitutes? Really? What about them?"

"A friend's daughter has started turning tricks," I lied, "and I'm wondering if you know of any books or articles designed to help women like that deal with their internal conflicts. You know. They don't want to do something like that, but they have to. How do they forgive themselves?"

Diana paused a moment and eyed me as if she knew my comment was more personal, but fortunately she kept it professional.

"Well, yes, I'm certain there are materials like that. In fact, I think I've seen a piece in Psychology Today. I'll see if I can find it so you can pass it on to her."

"Could you? I think she'd appreciate that."

25

THE REMOVAL OF MY BENIGN TUMOR proved to be liberating. Instead of obsessing about headaches and blackouts I was free to live my life without feeling like I was on the verge of the next disaster.

All of that, coupled with the visual ugliness in so many places, inspired me to put together a proposal for the warden. The idea was to create a crew of painters who would spruce up drab cells for those who wanted it.

While most of the inmates were simply serving out their sentences and doing the least they could to get by, another faction displayed some pride.

They weren't difficult to find. They tended to have more years to serve and could appreciate a better environment. That was the group I targeted.

There would be a reasonable fee to paint the clients' cells, which could be transferred from their 7-Eleven account to mine and I could pass it along to the workers. On a more selfish level, since I had a new way to earn money, I wouldn't need the job in the laundry room and that meant no more visits to the storage room with St. Nick and Huff & Puff.

I showed my proposal to Roxy Padilla, who agreed to pass it along to the warden. At first, I felt pretty good about my idea; after all, the entire place needed a face-lift and all the cost would be borne by the clients.

But months passed with no reply and I'd come to think the idea had died on the vine. That is, until one day when I was wondering what it would be like to see my brother again and another guard, Marcus Rudd, came by to escort me to the warden's office.

It was the first time I'd seen Warden Naples. The combination of a few excess pounds and her subtle but nice jewelry lent her a majestic look.

"I've given some thought to your proposal," she said from behind her huge desk. "I had to run your idea up the flagpole to see if my superiors would salute it. We decided to give it a try if you still want to do it."

I tried not to look like a gleeful youngster on Christmas morning. "Yes, ma'am. It'll spruce up some eyesores and give people jobs."

"That's what we liked about it. We can provide the paint. That way you can keep the costs down. As you requested, I'm going to put you in charge of all of it. Therefore, this will be your primary job. Your helpers may do this as an aside, until we see how things work out. Is that how you perceive it?"

Happily stunned, I nodded. "Yes, ma'am. That'll be fine."

"Okay then, we have an agreement, but let me make something clear; if this little project of yours presents extra problems for the guards or me, we'll shut it down. Agreed?"

"Yes, ma'am. If any problems arise, I'll take care of them myself."

"Alright. Carry on as usual until I can push the buttons. Then I'll tell Christine what's up."

So that was it. After countless months of hibernation, one lone cub escaped the dark cave in the laundry room.

The next morning, I wanted to flip off Mama C and everybody else who benefited from my misfortune, but that kind of thing created enemies with long memories, so I held my mud. Later that afternoon I got a message from the warden's office. She'd notified Mama C that I had taken on a new job.

From that moment forward I held the same sergeant-like status as Mama C, only there weren't any degrading activities in dark closets. With a much better form of sugar, Mary Ruth and I posted some Help Wanted information on the Opportunity Board. In the days that followed we interviewed dozens of potential painters. A fair number had painted rooms in their own homes, so they were put at the top of our list.

Before long we had three crews of two painters each, and a healthy waiting list. That was half the battle.

While we waited for the paint and supplies to arrive, we needed to line up some customers, so we posted hand-made signs offering to paint the two-bunk cells for a flat fee of $49. A few people jumped at the deal, while others took a wait-and-see approach.

Predictably, some of the guards grumbled because they had to watch over everything, but other guards such as Roxy Padilla thought it was a great idea.

After the first cells were painted, the clients added decorations like faux candles and posters on the walls that they got from the 7-Eleven. We immediately referred to the newly decorated cells as suites.

By the end of the first month, we'd transformed over a dozen cells to suites and everybody was happy, with one exception.

One day in the yard, while I was huddled with Mary Ruth and a couple others, Gerry Leah Yates, a tall thin brunette who had applied to be on the painting team but was skipped over because of her combative personality, wandered our way. "Hey, Munchak," she butted in, "I need a favor."

I turned her way. "A favor? What's up?"

"I want to paint my cage."

"Sure. If you have enough credits, we can get to you in about two weeks."

"Naw. Why would I pay for something that I can do myself?"

"I don't know what you mean."

"Simple. I want you to get me a gallon of hot pink and loan me your supplies. Then I'll do the work myself and reimburse you for the paint."

Everybody looked my direction. I shook my head. "Wish I could, Gerry, but it's not my paint and that's not how I set things up with the warden."

"It's no big deal. If anybody asks questions, just say that I'm an alternate on your crew."

Yeah, right. "There are several reasons I can't do that Gerry, but I'm not going to debate with you. If you can get the credits, we'll paint your place for you. Otherwise, I can't help you. And just so you know, pink is not an approved color."

Then, "Screw you, Munchak. You're just a power-hungry bitch, but I won't forget this."

True to her word, a few days later Carol Arlington, one of the ladies on the painting crew, kicked over a bucket of paint in one of the cells, making a big mess and pissing off the client and guards.

Since I had to replace the paint out of my own pocket, I was pretty upset about it too. Then, I found out that Gerry Leah had made Carol do it.

Before I knew it, we were all in the warden's office, where Carol and Gerry Leah got five days in Solitary for deliberately defacing State property. I got a warning, even though I had no role in the mischief.

Things went reasonably well for nearly two years but by then the prison population had ballooned to the popping stage. Some of the cells had taken on three inmates. Additional guards were hired. The cafeteria, yard and all the common areas were always packed while new prisoners were continually wedged into the mix.

Out of the blue, Mary Ruth got summoned to the warden's

office. I hoped she wasn't in trouble because it would be pure hell for somebody in a wheelchair to get by in Solitary on her own.

Later, I was commiserating with fellow inmates in the yard, when we saw her wheeling toward us. "Guess what, ladies?" she said waving a sheet of paper in her wrinkled hand. "This ole cripple has got her walking papers."

We all lit up. "No kidding, Honey?" I said, sneaking in a hug. "That's wonderful. What happened?"

She bounced back and forth in her wheelchair. "Apparently the Department of Corrections ordered the warden to issue some early releases to ease the crowding, and this old girl is one of them."

I had to grin. "And when does our mother bird get to fly away?"

"Next week, after the paperwork is finalized."

Over the ensuing days, Mary Ruth and I hugged dozens of times, knowing we'd never be together again as long as she was on parole. Finally the guards escorted her out the front gate and into the arms of her son.

Meanwhile, her newly emptied bunk made room for somebody else.

26

Over the next few years, various cellmates came and went, but then somebody special came into my life. "I'm Candice Carmichael," my new pixie-like partner said. "What should I expect around here?"

Based on how she behaved a few minutes earlier, when one of the guards dropped her off at my cell door, she reeked of innocence and ignorance and over-confidence - all at the same time. In fact, after five and a half years in the cement jungle, I'd never seen any other newbies smile on their first day.

I immediately knew that if I didn't administer a crash course in prison etiquette, similar to what Mary Ruth did for me, somebody would knock the smile off her face even if it meant a few days in Solitary.

Thus, I decided to be a tough guy, which wouldn't be difficult because I'd lived among a ton of them over the years. "It ain't too bad," I said. "Can you open your mouth wide, without showing your teeth?"

She quizzically looked at me. "Sure," she said before she dropped her lower jaw like a puppet and draped her lips to cover her teeth.

"Great," I said. "The guards have something that'll fit in there perfectly."

She recoiled and her eyes widened. "Do you mean what I think you mean?"

"Trust me, Honey. You're going to get fucked, one way or the other. And I sure don't mean in a fun way."

She tilted her head to the side. "They don't really do that, do they?"

"Hell, yes, they do. We're talking your prison virginity here. It's a symbolic victory to them. There ain't no romance to it. It ain't even fun, like a one-nighter."

"But I went to orientation," she whined. "They never said anything about that."

Her innocence was charming. "What the hell would you expect? And the guards ain't the only ones who'll screw ya. Have you ever been forced to have sex with a woman?"

Candice looked in my dead-serious face. "Not forced, but one night in college, my roommate and I went bar hopping. When we got back, we were tipsy and in a good mood, so we experimented until...well, until we both got off, but we never did it again because there were always guys around."

"Well, if you've never been assaulted by a lady lover, it's just as demeaning and scary as what the men do."

No longer sporting a grin, she asked, "Did they do that to you?"

"Not exactly, but just as bad. Five years back when I arrived, I was pregnant and fit a certain profile, kinda like you: good girl, raw, and young enough to still be shapely. I was teased unmercifully, told that a hot babe in her sexual peak was just the kind of love doll that the guards and certain inmates liked to take for test drives. The only thing that saved me was the pregnancy. Even the most incorrigible inmates have a soft spot for a new mom. Other than that, most of us gotta submit whenever we get the call. Otherwise, we get roughed up or thrown in Solitary."

"But my counselor didn't say anything about that."

"Course not. Those counselors don't know shit. Who would tell 'em? Not me."

The worried look in her eyes convinced me that I was finally getting through, but I didn't stop. "When I first arrived, I was older than you are now. I was 35. How old are you, anyway?"

"I'm 31."

"You don't look it, so you're still very desirable. Ever had any kids?"

"No. I was on the Pill."

"Good. That means no stretchmarks. The guards will like that, too."

Her slightly rounded eyes shot down the corridor and back. "They're not really going to do anything to me, are they?"

I smugly shook my head. "Aren't you listening? Course they are. If you're lucky they might settle for watching you undress or take a shower, but if they decide to bang ya, they got ways and places to do it and it ain't like being with a boyfriend. It's scary as hell. And we ain't even talked about sugar, yet."

"Sugar? What's that?"

"Another screw job. Everybody makes some sort of sacrifice for the good of the group. If the families learn that you're rich, you might be forced to hit your relatives up for some protection money. And there are plenty of enforcers around here to make sure you do it."

"Oh, my gosh. Have those things happened to you?"

"None of those exact things because I didn't have any relatives that I could tap, but after my baby was taken away, I got my share of the action."

"I'm so sorry. Do they still do that to you?"

I shook my head. "What would they want with an old cow like me when young ladies with perky tits, such as yourself, are available?"

Her worried eyes suggested that my message was getting through. "That's awful," she said.

"You got that right. Now that we understand each other, what you in for anyway?"

"My crime? My boyfriend stole a lady's purse. We used her credit cards and I wrote some bad checks, a lot of them actually."

"That doesn't sound very tough. Just how long is your sentence anyway?"

"Nine years, but my attorney said I can get out in four."

"Not if you make waves. If you piss off the wrong people, they'll frame you and you'll lose your chance at parole. So, you gotta ask yourself a question."

"What question?"

"Easy. Would you prefer to play ball for four years and get a good report card at a parole hearing or do you wanna become a punching bag and get a reputation as a troublemaker, in which case the parole board will send you back into the pit for more of the same?"

"I see what you mean."

"For now, try to stay close to me 'cause I don't have many enemies. Don't look cocky or meek. Either one will set somebody off."

She swallowed and nodded. "Okay, thank you for telling me all this."

Just then the dinner buzzer interrupted us, so I had one last piece of advice. "Lookie here, Candice. Whenever a new lady shows up, her suitemate gets to give her a nickname. Some of the names are pretty bad. We've got a Bed Toy, a Fat Ass and a Big Schnoz," I lied. "How would you like to be called Nookie Rookie?"

Candice's scowl damn near broke the bridge of her nose, causing me to giggle. "Relax. I was just messing with you. Earlier you said something about a roommate. What would you say to being called Roomie? That ought to keep you out of trouble."

Candice gently nodded. "Whew! For a minute there—"

"Good. Roomie it is. After dinner, I'll tell you about the three people I killed."

27

THE NEXT MORNING, while I was busy with the painting crew, Candice, aka Roomie, was ushered to the commissary so she could gather some essentials.

When I returned, she was in our cell fiddling with her footlocker. "I'm glad you're back," she said while holding up some earphones, shorts and a blouse, meaning she wouldn't have to wear the usual jumpsuit that most of the newbies wore until they could save up some money. "I also got some nail polish and cookies. Want one?"

"But that stuff cost a lot of credits," I said.

"I know, but my sister transferred some money into my account and I had to have some comfort items."

Obviously, she'd completely disregarded my previous warnings to remain humble. "Shh," I whispered. "You don't want people to hear you talk like that."

"It's okay. Nobody heard me. By the way, I was assigned to work in the kitchen, but I don't know much about cooking."

"Trust me, you won't be a cook. You're gonna do the dishes or mop the floor—things like that."

"But those things will be hard on my nails."

I sat on her bed. "Listen, Honey, I don't think you understand how dangerous this place is. When I first got here, I was poor and pregnant. It took weeks before I could buy one measly candy bar."

Roomie raised her head. "I'm sorry, Miranda. That must have been rough."

"That's not all. To make a token amount of extra money, I was assigned to the laundry room where I folded hundreds of towels per day. Everybody kept telling me how lucky I was. I thought they were teasing me, but they weren't. Then I had my baby and everything got worse."

"Really? How could it be any worse?"

"Aside from moving heavy loads of wet clothes from washing machines to dryers, let's just say that a couple of guards got very close and personal because I was vulnerable."

"That's what you were talking about yesterday."

"You gotta believe me: A new inmate such as yourself should lie low. If you make it appear that you're from a rich family, certain ladies will target you, figure out how to redistribute your funds."

"For real? How could they do that?"

"Easy. For instance, you just mentioned your sister."

"Yeah, her name's Naomi."

"Does Naomi have a family?"

"Sure. Hubby and two daughters. Why?"

"What if somebody sinister showed up at her door and threatened her or one of her daughters? Would Naomi send a couple hundred extra dollars per month into your account to keep everybody safe?"

"I guess she'd have to."

"Now you've got it. And another thing, when you're in the general population, try not to be so perky and cute."

"Cute? Me?"

"I mean it. There are ladies who'll slap the smile off your face just for fun. You gotta be humble, low-key - but not weak. That's bad too. Just don't draw attention to yourself. For now, I suggest you hide the nail polish and let your hair down. Then, over time you can do your nails or share a bag of cookies. It'll look like you had to save up some money for those things and bad people might leave you alone."

"Thanks, Miranda," she said before wrapping her arms around my neck.

"And that's another thing," I said, looking for guards. "We're not supposed to touch each other. I know it's stupid, but they can throw you in Solitary if you don't follow the rules."

"That's going to be hard for me, Miranda. I'm an affectionate person and need my hugs."

"I get it. I like hugs too, but we gotta be discreet. Now I gotta do some paperwork so I can pay my painters."

"Okay, I think a guard is going to take me to the kitchen to meet whoever is in charge."

"That's Lori Lane. You'd better kiss her butt, because she has a ton of power."

"Okay. Thanks for the advice. I'll try to restrain myself."

Finally. At that moment it sounded as if Roomie got the message, but a few days later I was out in the yard gabbing with Donella from the painting crew, when Roomie proved me wrong. "You gonna put your new cellmate on the painting crew?" Donella asked.

"No. That wouldn't be fair to the others who are in line."

"Good idea. What's she in for?"

"Bad checks and stolen credit cards. Seventy-thousand dollars worth. Got nine years."

Donella whistled. "She must have lived high on the hog for a while."

"Hi Miranda," I heard and turned to see Roomie, with a bleached streak in her hair. "Guess what?" she said, with a toothy grin. "They figured out that I'm creative so they asked me if I could do manicures because the usual lady got released."

I almost screamed. "I hope you didn't take it because inmates with more seniority want that job."

"No prob. I told them I didn't need the money."

I cringed. As likeable as she was, she didn't know when to keep her lips tight. All I could do was hope that whatever she said in the parlor stayed in the parlor...but sadly, it didn't.

In the following days, she kept up the cheerful stuff, almost like at a sorority house. Nearly everybody liked her. Adding to that, her classy sister came by with some nice underwear. They might as well have painted a target on one of Roomie's nice blouses. Then the medicine came out.

On a sunny Friday afternoon, she got lured toward one of the benches in the yard where a half-dozen women stood more or less side to side in front of a bench, thereby blocking the guards from seeing that Roomie had been taken down behind the bench.

A little later, I was checking the progress on the day's painting jobs when I got word that Roomie was taken to the infirmary. It had to be horrible, but all I could do was wait and worry. Then at dinner, I was informed she wouldn't be returned to our cell until the next morning, if then.

The next day, after the painting crews were in place, I was granted permission to return to my cell where Roomie had returned. From a few steps away, I heard her sobbing. "Roomie? It's me, Honey. Are you okay?"

From under her blanket, a mummy emerged. The ugliness made me want to throw up. Her entire face puffed like a bubble. A gash with several stitches tracked across her right eyebrow. But worse, I'd never seen a mouth so swollen and damaged. Huge, bloated lips were adorned by nearly a dozen stitches. Her frightened black eyes dug into mine and on into my heart.

As I'd warned, somebody in the kitchen didn't like her happy mouth and it caught up to her in the yard.

"You were so right, Miranda. They taped my mouth so I wouldn't scream and beat me up. Then they told me to say I fell off the bleachers."

"I know what you mean, Honey. I've been bullied too."

She shook her head. "I'm not talking about me. They're going to do something awful to my sister."

Oddly, as it turned out, she was correct, but many months passed before I finally knew what she meant.

28

Six Months Later

At medium height and weight, with glasses and curly, dark hair, Naomi Grant wasn't the type to stick out in a crowd. In the lady's room of a breakfast restaurant near San Francisco, the 37-year-old mother of two reached deep into the trash and retrieved a package the size of a small tube of toothpaste that she believed to be powdered cocaine.

Up until a few months ago, the deeply religious Naomi had never broken the law, let alone become a reliable drug mule for a prison group at the Bakersfield Correction Facility for Women. But all that innocence evaporated when Naomi's kid sister, Candice Carmichael, was sent to that particular prison for a slew of financial crimes.

It wasn't long before Candice and Naomi got dragged into an extortion plot in which there was no way out. As nervous about the monthly exercise as she always was, Naomi nabbed the taped-up baggie and hustled home, where she rolled the product into a manageable shape. The next stop was her church where her preacher made sure she could get in a side door and be alone with God when engaged in yet another unholy transaction.

Inside the church, Naomi stood behind the back pew. She clasped her hands together, closed her eyes and reminded herself why she was doing this.

When Candice first landed in prison, she accidently drew the attention of the wrong people. To make a point, certain bad ladies beat Candice to a pulp just a couple days before Visitor's Day. Then, Naomi came for a visit.

The bandages, cuts and stitches were bad enough, but the terror in Candice's eyes reached for Naomi's heart, which was precisely what the extortionists wanted.

From that day forward, the only way Candice could avoid another beat-down, or worse, was if Naomi performed a monthly, no-cost ritual. Unfortunately, Naomi had no choice.

During the early stages of the agreement, she got a call from a friendly-sounding man who called himself Maurice. "All you have to do," he said, "is get a small package of powder past the guards in the registration area."

"But how am I supposed to do that?" she asked, hoping that the answer was something other than what she suspected.

"The guards aren't allowed to do cavity searches unless they have some reason to be suspicious," Maurice said. "You're not the type they go after."

Naomi went silent.

"It's either that," Maurice reminded her, "or we ugly-up Candice again – worse this time. You wouldn't want that, would you?"

"No, no. Don't hurt her. I'll do it."

"Okay then, tomorrow is visiting day," Maurice had said, "I'll call you in the morning, at exactly nine o'clock. Be sure you answer the phone and be sure you're alone. I'll tell you where to pick up the package and what to do with it."

"Okay. Just don't hurt Candice, okay?"

"That's up to you, Naomi," he said in a sickening, saccharine tone.

As promised, that next morning Maurice directed Naomi to a trashcan in a lady's room of a nearby Home Depot where a miniature baggy with a small dose of powder would be waiting.

Three hours later Naomi arrived at the prison, hid the packet inside her and worked her way to the registration desk where she nervously traded her cell phone and purse for a faded yellow jumpsuit, indicating she was a visitor.

In a changing room, a smallish blonde female guard drew a privacy curtain around the two of them. The guard watched Naomi remove her clothes except for her underwear. Then, "Hands out to the side please," the guard said. "And slowly turn around."

After one short twirl the guard held out her hand and said "You got the package?"

Humiliated and scared, Naomi retrieved the package and the very first transaction of its kind was completed. A few minutes later Naomi and Candice met in the visitor's room where they sat across from each other and thanked God that their little scam was over – but it surely wasn't.

A few weeks later, Maurice unexpectedly called Naomi again. "It's time for the next delivery," he said.

Stunned, Naomi said, "You don't understand. I already did my part."

"I'm afraid you're the one who doesn't understand," Maurice said. "That last run was just a trial."

"But I don't want to do that again."

"You've done a good job so far and we've left your sister alone, right?"

"Yes, but I'd rather not—"

"Be quiet and listen carefully to me." His voice had taken on a more sinister tone. "We have that last package that you handled. It's full of your fingerprints and your DNA."

Naomi almost threw up.

"We'd hate to see that bag end up in the warden's office with a note advising them who to look for. The DA would be called in and you could expect to do a minimum of five years and your poor little sister could forget about parole. You wouldn't want that, would you?"

Trapped again, Naomi swallowed, then asked another question to which she didn't really want to hear the answer. "What do I have to do?"

"It's easy. You're just going to carry a little more product with you."

From that moment on Naomi was forced to sneak a package of cocaine into the prison on a monthly basis. She'd been doing it successfully for the better part of six months.

If nothing went wrong, Candice would be released a few years later and the nightmare within a nightmare would be over. But that was a lot to ask of just one God.

29

When I originally met Roomie, I tried to help her avoid some of the prison demons, but I wasn't very successful. I don't know if I was a poor communicator or if she mistakenly believed that she could sweet-talk her way through her sentence, but after she'd been there for the better part of her first year, she revealed that I had a couple blind spots of my own.

One night, just as the lights went out, she asked me if I ever thought of escaping. "What have you got to lose?" she said. "By the time you're eligible for parole you could be dead from a disease or something."

"They call that being 'in the wind,'" I said. "I have to admit that I've thought of it, but it's impossible so it just makes me feel bad."

"Yeah, that sucks. If it makes you feel any better, I know that you're not a killer." She lowered her voice to a whisper. "Would you mind if I join you on your bunk for a little while? I have something else to tell you."

"I guess so," I said, "but if we get caught, it could mean a trip to Solitary."

"I know, but the guards won't make their rounds again for at least another hour."

She was correct about that. It was common for inmates

to use that quiet time to satisfy their physical needs, either independently or by cuddling with their cellmates. Since we'd never had that kind of relationship, she had to have something else in mind.

"Okay, but we gotta whisper."

She scooted next to me. "You know that tomorrow is Visitor's Day, right?"

"Yeah, but I don't pay much attention because nobody ever visits me."

"I wish I could say that."

"What are you talking about? Your sister comes to see you a lot and you always look forward to it."

"Not entirely. Remember that time that I got beat up?"

"How can I forget? I still feel guilty about that."

"I should have listened. Remember when I said I could never tell you everything that happened? Now, I'm willing to tell you, but you have to promise that you'll never tell anybody else."

I lowered my voice further. "Alright, you know you can trust me."

"You were right," she added with a soft shiver in her voice. "You told me to act like I was from a poor family, but I wanted to be a big shot so I bought a lot of things from the 7-Eleven."

"I remember that."

"So did somebody else. After I opened my big mouth, I was out in the yard and got dragged into a conversation with a couple lifers who tricked me into revealing my sister's church."

"Her church? Why?"

"You'll never believe this, but they found her and forced her to be a drug mule."

Stunned, I looked into her now-wet eyes. "Are you saying that Naomi has been sneaking in hard drugs?"

"All I can say is it's very dangerous, and they've threatened to kill us if either one of us says anything. That's why they had people beat me up, to prove that they mean business."

I grabbed her hand. "You poor thing."

"Yeah. I know you understand because of your laundry room situation."

"Why are you telling me this now?"

"Because I'm tired of being a victim."

"I know what you mean but the deck is stacked against us."

"That's true, but some of this is our fault because we don't take advantage of our opportunities."

"Like what?"

"Like conjugal visits."

"But those are for married people."

"And that's the problem. The married women are having all the fun, and I want to do something about it."

"Such as?"

"I got a male friend who can visit me regularly. After that we'll trade some text messages and email. Then, as soon as it looks like we're boyfriend and girlfriend we can get married, which makes us eligible for conjugal visits. You can do the same thing."

"What?" I said a little louder than before. "You're crazy."

She lifted a finger to her lips. "I know, but other ladies have already done that. At least they're having some fun once in a while."

"I get that, but I don't know anybody like that."

"I can see if my guy can bring a friend."

"No thanks. There's no love to it and I don't want some stranger mounting me just because I'm desperate."

"So you admit that you're desperate?"

"I guess so, but I ain't no cougar. I don't want to screw some young stud just for kicks."

"I don't see why not, but there's one other thing we can do," she said while gently turning my head toward her. She gazed into my eyes and leaned in. "That is, if you want to."

Startled, I pulled back, but not a whole lot. "What are you doing?"

"Simple," she said softly. "You just said that physical pleasure isn't as good without love and we love each other, so let's test your theory."

"I know what I said, but I meant a different kind of love - like sisters."

"Best friends can love each other too, Miranda, and you're a normal human being. We both have needs. We all do. Don't let the damn penal system take that away from you over some crimes you didn't even commit. You deserve some love, and we can pleasure each other better than that silly little vibrator of yours."

Oops! "Oh, you know about that, huh?"

"Sure, I do. These cells are small with horrible acoustics." She tilted her head. "Listen to me. Toys are okay, but we both need real love."

"But I've never done anything like that."

"Well, I have. Do you remember me mentioning my college roommate?"

"Yes. You said you experimented with her one time."

"That's what I said, but I lied. It was more than that. Whenever one of us needed affection, we just took care of each other. That way we weren't so darn frustrated. You can understand that, can't you?"

"Yes of course. It's just that—"

"Good. You and me can do the same thing."

"But I've always considered myself to be 100% hetero."

"Understandable, but the circumstances are different. What would you say to an experiment?"

"I don't know."

"I'm just talking about a little making out. All we gotta do is close our eyes and clear our minds of past prejudices. From there, we'll just have to follow our hearts. If the chemistry is there, we'll know it. If there is no chemistry, it only cost us a few measly kisses to find out. I think we ought to try it. After all, we deserve romance just as much as the married women do."

"Just kissing, huh?"

"Not just a sister kiss. I'm talking about a genuinely affectionate kiss."

I thought about the seven-second kisses I'd given Lupe and how she benefited from them. "Okay. I guess it won't hurt anything."

That night, one single kiss lit a flame inside me that I'd basically snuffed out. For the first time in years, I knew that I deserved to be loved and Roomie was the one to do it. The seven-second kiss went on and on. I genuinely loved her more than anyone ever before.

30

I NEVER WOULD HAVE GUESSED that I'd have a physical relationship with another woman, but after Roomie and I made love that first time, we grew closer than ever. More importantly, whenever either one of us needed emotional or physical attention, it was freely given.

The two years that followed were the best of my prison days, largely because Roomie made me feel like I was worthy of love. But there were other reasons, too.

For instance, the painting teams were a big success, and my headaches were very rare and easily treatable with aspirin. So those were the pleasant things, but every time the sun comes up, it casts some shadows.

One day I turned down breakfast and opted not to go out to the yard, so Roomie figured out something was out of whack. "You seem awfully gloomy today," she said. "Is something wrong?"

Her tender heart was one of the things I most loved about her. I wiped at the corner of my eye. "It's Cody's birthday today. I'm so sad that I'm not there when he needs me."

Predictably, loving Roomie ignored the "no-touching" rule, wrapped her arms around me and whispered, "You would have been a fantastic mom."

Just knowing that she understood me made me feel better. But then I noticed guard Angelina Perry trekking toward us.

"Uh-oh," I said. "I think we're going to get a reprimand. I'll promise her we won't hug anymore."

"I got a letter for you, Munchak," Ms. Perry said, while glancing at my reddened eyes. "It's from your brother's caregivers."

That was strange. The guards rarely delivered mail in person. I cautiously slid the letter from within the envelope. My twin brother, Mickey, had died a few days earlier.

The flood gates broke wide open. It had been seven years since I'd seen him. I would have given anything to have been with him one last time, but it was not possible.

The next few days were extremely rough. Everybody expressed their condolences and quite a few women ignored the no-touching rule to gently tap me on the shoulder or arm for support. The guards even seemed to look away. Aside from my relationship with Roomie, I hadn't felt that much love since before my prison days.

About a week later I was still disconsolate, lying in my bed and praying that Mickey's death had been peaceful when I heard somebody coming. I landed eyes on St. Nick.

He curled a finger in my direction. "Come with me," he said in a gentler tone than I expected.

I really didn't want to go anywhere with the man because I hated everything about him, but I rose from my bunk as he pointed toward a door at the end of the row of cells.

I doubted that he wanted to bang me because we hadn't spoken in quite a while and there was a plethora of younger, firmer women around there who would love to play house with a powerful guard. "Where are we going?" I asked.

"Out in the yard."

When outside he directed me to a back corner where we had the area to ourselves.

"I'm sorry about your brother," he said from a few feet

away. "I have a brother too. It would hurt like hell to lose him."

I dunno, maybe I should have thanked him, but I was eternally suspicious of anything and everything about him. I glared at him. "Is that it?"

"No. It's not the reason I brought you out here, if that's what you mean. I wanted to talk about something else, off the record."

"Such as?"

He looked me in the eyes. "Have you been wondering why I've avoided you so much lately?"

"Really? I thought I was the one avoiding you."

"Well, I've been giving you more space and treating you better."

"I hadn't noticed."

"I know that I've never been a very nice person around here, but I met a special woman about six months ago. After a while I joined her church and then went to confession. Our priest suggested I apologize to you for what we did in the laundry room. Therefore, that's what I want to do. I apologize for what we did."

"We? Why the hell would you include me in that sin of yours? I didn't want any part of it."

"Come on now, Munchak, I've been around the block a few times. I can tell when a woman is having a good time. You enjoyed yourself more than you'd like to admit."

"You're full of crap and your apology isn't worth a damn because you're only saying this so you won't have to feel so guilty."

He straightened up. "I don't like your tone."

"Oh, I get it. If I forgive you, you get the best of both worlds. You get to screw anybody you want and then wash away the guilt with a few insincere words. Maybe God will forgive you, but I never will. You'll always be a disgusting asshole to me. Now take me to Solitary or to my cell or wherever the hell you want."

While I was as angry as a rattler, he wasn't done. "I said we're off the record and I meant it," he said. "I have one more score to settle with you. Do you remember six or seven years ago when you lost a spoon and ended up in Solitary?"

I was already seething but an anticipatory bolt of anger shot up my spine. There was no way I could forget those three ghastly days of excruciating fear and squalor. I tightened my fist. "Don't tell me you had something to do with that."

He nodded. "I apologize for that too."

31

MERE DAYS AFTER MICKEY DIED, I was contacted by some medical experts who reminded me that I had previously signed papers authorizing them to examine his brain. They already had him on ice and wanted to confirm that I was still of the same mind. I almost told them to leave him alone, but Mickey was a big-hearted man and would have authorized the procedure if there was any chance it could help somebody else; so, I did what he would have done and authorized the examination.

I never did hear the results of the procedure, but I did get a few nice letters about Mickey and his contribution to science.

I wish that was where the misery would have ended, but months later another prisoner informed me that in cases like that, the heads are severed from the bodies and sent to a cryogenics lab for young doctors to study. When I learned that Mickey's frozen head was probably on a platter somewhere in a medical school, I got sick to my stomach and prayed that he'd forgive me.

Moving on, I'd eventually reached the threshold of my 45th birthday, which meant I'd squandered nine years of my life. The woman in my tin mirror had taken on wrinkles in her forehead, eyes and lips, not to mention unwelcomed bags and sags in all the wrong places. It would be three additional decades before I'd be eligible for parole.

If I learned anything from those early years, it was that close relationships were fleeting. Whenever one of my prison friends served her sentence or earned her parole, she bolted for her alternate life, and a new hole bore its way into the heart of prisoner 1516103-A. Sooner or later, Roomie would be added to that list.

Eventually, she had her first hearing. Since her elder sister, Naomi, had been sneaking in drugs the whole time, the bad guys watched over Roomie, so it appeared as if she had been a model prisoner; thus, her odds of gaining parole were very good. In a mean, devilish twist, the best scenario for Roomie was the worst case for me.

Then on one particular Visitor's Day, Roomie returned from another successful visit with her sister. "Your eyes are red," she said. "Have you been crying?"

"Maybe a little. I miss my brother and my son and Mary Ruth, and sooner or later, you'll be gone too."

"I'm sorry. Do you want to be alone?"

"No. I want to be with you as much as I can before you get released."

"If it makes you feel any better, when I get out of here, I'm going to get a job and hire an attorney so you can get another trial."

"On what grounds? I appreciate the sentiment, Sweetie, but we both know that I'm not going to get out of here until I'm an old woman, if then. You'd be wiser to save your money and enjoy your freedom."

"Nonsense. I've heard you say a hundred times that you'd like to meet your son someday. He's worth fighting for and he might make you a grandma someday. We need an attorney to review your case. You can't ignore all of that."

"I know, but the best way to avoid disappointment is--"

"That's another thing I'm going to do. I'm going to hire

somebody who can find your boy and get you some pictures of him."

"The courts aren't going to allow that, Honey. I agreed to a sealed adoption and I don't know who his parents are or where they live."

"That doesn't count. You had a tumor in your head. That's why you had blackouts. You didn't know what you were doing. An attorney can look into that. And talk with the boy's parents. They may be willing to get you some pictures."

"Thanks, anyway. I'm extra depressed right now because you're going to get away too. I'll miss everything about you: the late-night whispers, your contagious smile, even the elaborate conversations we've had about escaping."

"Yeah. For a while there, I thought we were on to something."

"You know what else I'm going to miss? The intimacy. You always seemed to know when I needed that."

Roomie went silent and her eyes filled with tears. She scooted across the cell, sat right next to me and took my hand. "I've got something to tell you, Miranda, and you're not going to like it. I'm very, very sorry, but I couldn't tell you this sooner, because Naomi and I decided to keep it quiet so that the lifers wouldn't get wind and pull off a last-minute stunt to blackmail us again."

"Huh? I don't like the sound of this."

She looked down the hall before whispering, "I get released at noon tomorrow."

My entire body went limp and my head fell into my hands. "That means we won't be able to speak to each other until your parole is over."

"I know, but it's just five years. I can come see you then, and I surely will. I promise."

"I doubt it. You could be married, have kids. I'll never know any of it."

Once again Roomie glanced down the hall. Then she said, "We may not be allowed to talk with each other directly, but we can both talk to my sister and you're entitled to receive a phone call every once in a while. I've already talked with Naomi about it. She agreed to be our middle lady. She can keep us both posted about how the other one is doing."

"That's not the same."

"No, but it's better than nothing. I also want you to memorize Naomi's number. If you ever have an emergency, the prison might make a call for you. I want to know how you're doing."

"You mean I'm going to die someday and you'll want to know about it when it happens."

"Stop talking like that. I just want to have as many options as possible on the table."

Yeah, right. Everybody had options but me.

32

ONE DAY AFTER ROOMIE LEFT, St. Nick slithered up to me and pulled his cuffs from his belt. "Put out your hands."

"Sure," I said trying not to sound apprehensive. "What's up?"

"Warden wants to talk with you. There's some kind of meeting. In the meantime, I still think you should accept my apologies for the things we did in private."

Yeah, right. I'd already popped that balloon, which might be the point of this meeting. Maybe Nick let it be known that I'd been disrespectful and some sort of discipline was in my future. I elected to hold my peace while we walked through a series of hallways and surveillance cameras to an elevator.

At the third floor, another hall led to the office of Warden Keith Stedman, who had replaced Glenda Naples about a year back. All I really knew about him was he was younger than me and trying to make a name for himself.

"Stop here," Nick instructed just before knocking on the warden's door. Suddenly the voices went silent and the door opened upon the balding warden and several well-dressed people, who sat surrounding his desk. Warden Stedman rose to meet me.

"I think we can remove the jewelry," he said to St. Nick.

"Ms. Munchak isn't going to cause us any problems." He turned his head my way. "Are you, ma'am?"

Still confused, I shook my head. "No, sir. That wouldn't do any good."

"Glad to hear it." He waited for Nick to remove my cuffs and leave before he spoke in the general direction of everybody else. "This is Ms. Munchak, the lady I told you about." He then turned toward me, "May we call you Miranda?"

If the man was trying to earn my respect he'd already done so. "Sure. Thank you for asking."

"This is Dr. Ellerbrook," the Warden added, "and his nurse assistant, Lacy Morgan. Over here we have Ms. Erin Prague and Mr. Mark Killmer. They're both attorneys."

What the heck was going on? Why were doctors and attorneys present?

Warden Stedman gestured to a stuffed leather chair at the side of his desk and urged me to sit down. The luxurious soft swoosh beneath my rear end felt naughty.

Warden Stedman looked right at me. "I imagine you're wondering why you're here."

"Yes, sir. But it's nice to see some new faces."

He nodded. "I'll let the attorneys explain it to you."

Erin Prague leaned forward from the center of the large sofa. "First off, Miranda, Mr. Killmer and I represent clients who need a human liver or at least part of one. That's where you come in."

Huh? I glanced to the warden and then back to the attorney. "You caught me off guard. Do you want me to be a donor or something?"

"Perhaps I can help," Dr. Ellerbrook said from the end of the sofa. "Livers are usually mendable. That is, if a patient needs a partial liver for some reason, all we usually have to do is attach a piece of a healthy liver from a compatible donor to the patient. Neither gender nor race plays a role. So, most of the time, both patients grow new tissue and recover without difficulty. It happens quite frequently."

"Why are you telling me this? Are you mining organs or something--'cause that's kinda morbid."

"Not really. We can usually get livers from cadavers if nothing else."

"I don't get it. You're saying it's a common procedure, and you can get livers elsewhere, yet you're talking to a nobody like me. Are you speaking to any other inmates about this?"

"No, ma'am," the doc added. "We have our reasons for focusing on you in particular."

"So, you want a chunk of my liver for some reason. What do I get out of it?"

"Nothing, really," Warden Stedman said. "Except a chance to help out."

"I'd like to cooperate, Warden, but a while back some doctors climbed around in my brother's brain and it made me sick to my stomach. I don't want to give up my body parts. I think you should ask somebody younger."

With that definitive answer everybody went quiet; glimpses swept from attorneys to doctors and the warden and back around to me. Finally, the warden took over. "Alright, then, Ms. Munchak, I can appreciate your position. I'm going to let the doctor level with you."

Dr. Ellerbrook continued. "We have a patient who's been having acute liver problems. As we said, ordinarily a transplant is successful, but this is one of those rare situations where our patient's body has rejected two different healthy donor livers."

"Yeah? I'm sorry to hear that, but I still don't get it."

"When the customary procedures aren't working, we try to secure the tissue of a more compatible donor."

"Me? Compatible? I think you people have made a mistake. I don't--"

The warden leaned toward me. "We're talking about your son, Miranda. He's the one who needs a compatible liver."

Cody? I almost didn't believe my ears, but these weren't the type of people to be cavalier. It had to be true. "Is Cody nearby?" I asked.

"No, he's not," Attorney Mark Killmer said. "Our clients are your son's adoptive parents. When this 'compatible donor' idea arose, we had to locate one of the boy's closest blood relatives, so we obtained a court order to open the adoption file. It appeared that the father has passed away and you are the only known relative. Is that true?"

Still trying to come to grips with this craziness, I nodded. "My parents could be alive, but they're in their 70's and I haven't spoken with them in twenty-five years. Other than that, there might be some cousins from his father's side, but I wouldn't know."

The doctor shook his head. "You're a better match."

Then I recalled the hospital where I had my tumor removed. If this procedure were carried out in that hospital, I might be able to meet my son, or at least see him.

"So, what's your position, Ms. Munchak? Will you do it or not?"

There was no doubt in my mind, but I felt like I could get some more information out of them before answering. "Will I get to see my son, Warden?"

"Afraid not. That's the kind of thing that causes birds to spread their wings. You'll be in two separate surgery suites in the same hospital."

The nurse nodded.

I turned to the doctor. "What would happen to my son if I say no?"

"We'd probably try again, but he's very frail. This is his best chance. That's why we hoped you'd help us."

"So, I'd be saving his life?"

"Possibly, but we don't know that either. His body might reject your tissue too."

"What about me? How long will it take to recover?"

"About ten days before you can resume ordinary activities."

In the meantime, I could get away from all the steel and cement. That alone was worth the trip. "If I agree, what do we do next?"

"That's why the nurse is here. We'll do some basic tests right now - blood pressure and blood samples to see if you have any medical conditions that we need to know about. If everything checks out, you'll be contacted tomorrow. The procedure will be soon after that."

I turned to the female attorney. "If I can see a picture of him, I'll do it."

"We'll have to ask his parents, but no guarantees."

Excited, I sprang to my feet. "Okay then, if I'm his best hope. I'll do it."

33

With my liver tucked safely under my ribcage, and my wrists cuffed to a waist chain, I stepped into the prison van.

As I shuffled down the van's aisle, I had a very good feeling about saving Cody's life. "Take the seat on your right," Guard Marcus Rudd said. A moment later he buckled me in and I seized the opportunity to look out the dark van windows to a packed parking lot. Even that was a welcome sight.

After Rudd sat behind me, Roxy Padilla climbed into the driver's seat, and off we went.

Immediately after escaping the shadows of the prison, Mr. Rudd moved forward into the shotgun seat. "What's a-matter?" I asked. "Do I stink or something?"

He looked at me. "I figured you'd feel better without me looking over your shoulder."

That was pure b.s. I'd seen those two trade flirty glances several times before — even though they were each married. Oh well, I had my own thoughts to ponder. I relaxed and enjoyed the sights.

Before long, I also missed Roomie. I smiled when I recalled the day that she made me memorize her sister's phone number. Then it occurred to me that there might be a phone in my hospital room and I might be able to call her. All those happy thoughts made me understand something that the warden said: Prisoners get ideas when they whiff non-prison air.

I became mesmerized by the wild grasses and sage that wrestled with the wind. A road sign indicated there was a Dairy Queen and a 7-Eleven ahead. "Hey," I said to the now-giddy guards. "Will Mommy and Daddy get their little girl a chocolate dipped ice-cream cone?" A minute later we blew past the exit and my thoughts returned to the primary issue.

I already knew that the officials weren't going to place my room close to Cody's, but I took some comfort in knowing we'd be on the same floor of the hospital, especially during the recovery period.

I imagined that I could get close to Cody by watching the corridors for husband-and-wife teams who might be his other parents. If I were to see potential candidates, perhaps I could somehow draw them into my room and beg them to let me see Cody, or at least get me some pictures of him.

Of course, I knew that all of those thoughts were nothing more than fantasy-bubbles because the whole time I was in the hospital the door to my room would be closed and a guard would be posted outside.

Back in the van, we eventually came upon a roadside rest area, complete with bathrooms and a half-dozen steel picnic tables spread about. A click from behind the van's steering wheel activated the van's turn indicator. "Potty break," Mr. Rudd announced.

I felt like a family dog at walk-time. Padilla slowly rolled past all the other vehicles before she parked the van near the end of the lot and next to some tall bushes. If I had a tail, it surely would have wagged.

Minutes later, with me still shackled, we all shuffled toward the restrooms. Mr. Rudd dropped off first, leaving Roxy Padilla and me to wait until he finished his business.

Next, the three of us moved toward the other side of the building and the lady's room. While Rudd and I waited, Roxy went on in to do her thing and to scope out the room for any potential escape routes that a double-cuffed con might utilize.

When she returned, she addressed Rudd. "You stand where you can make sure nobody else enters the room. I'll go with Munchak while she takes her turn."

Inside the room, Ms. Padilla removed my handcuffs so I could deal with my clothes and attend to the rest of it without unnecessary awkwardness. After I washed my hands, her cuffs were returned to my wrists. Back outside, and drawing closer to our van, Rudd tapped the top of the last picnic table. "Have a seat, Munchak, while I have a private talk with Ms. Padilla."

I had no idea what was going on, but I certainly liked the change of scenery and the relative peace and quiet, so I gladly parked my rear-end.

"Okay, Munchak." Rudd said. "You're going to stay here for a bit while Ms. Padilla and I take care of some paperwork." Surprised, I glanced to Padilla for an explanation.

"We'll have to cuff you to the table," she said, "and we'll have our eyes on you the whole time, so don't get any dumb ideas."

Hmm. I had a pretty good idea what that "paperwork" was, but I'd spent a whole lot of time behind walls in recent years and wasn't in a hurry to get into my hospital room.

The next thing I knew, Rudd cuffed me to the frame of the steel picnic table while Roxy Padilla walked the remaining 50 feet to the van, opened the side door and climbed inside. Predictably, Rudd quickly followed and closed the door. Clearly, Hanky and Panky were about to have a party.

34

WHILE THE GUARDS CARRIED OUT their lust-fest in the back of the prison van, inmate 1516103-A sat alone and cuffed to a picnic table while she watched other people turnstile themselves in and out of the restrooms.

Before long, a fancy SUV pulled in. A mother and her seventeenish daughter sprang out and hustled toward the ladies room. Then a long-haired kid, perhaps 13, dragged himself out of the back seat while texting somebody or playing a video game. When he moved toward the restrooms, I had an idea.

"Hey, there," I said, careful not to reveal that I was cuffed to the table, "how would you like to help a friend?"

He looked at me and then over his shoulder, then back again. "Are you talking to me?"

"Yes," I said, hooking the index finger of my free hand, "Come over here for a minute. I need to ask you something."

He scooted closer "What do you want?"

"Could you lend me your cellphone? I really need to make a call."

"Don't you have one of your own?"

"No. They won't let me have one, but it's an emergency."

"Who's they?"

I spun in my seat, aimed my bracelets at him and directed

my thumb toward the van. "The people in that truck. They're taking me to a hospital for a surgery, but I need to call somebody before it's too late."

Caught off-guard and stunned by the cuffs, he scoped the van. "Are you a prisoner?"

It wasn't going to do any good to lie. "Yep. My name's Miranda. They want some of my liver, but I need to call somebody first. How about being my hero? I'd really appreciate it."

He grinned like he'd just won a video game. "Okay, if you'll let me take a selfie with you."

A selfie? I'd seen some of those, but I'd never been in one. "What do I gotta do?"

Unexpectedly, he slid right next to me and extended his arm. "Nothing, just hold up your wrists so my friends can see the handcuffs. I'm Jay.'

"I'm pleased to meet you, Jay."

After he snapped a couple pics, he handed me his iPhone. "It's all yours."

The only number I knew was that of Roomie's sister, Naomi. Technically speaking, it wasn't against any rules for me to talk with Naomi because she wasn't a criminal, but I was supposed to get permission so that my call could be monitored. Oh, well.

After a couple rings, Naomi took the call. "Hello?"

"Naomi. This is Roomie's... er, I mean Candice's friend, Miranda Munchak, from the DOC."

"Oh, my goodness. What do you want? She's not in any trouble, is she?"

"No. No. It's nothing like that. They're taking me to a hospital so I can donate a piece of my liver to my son. I might save his life. I only have a few minutes, so I hoped you could tell your sweet sister that I called and how much I miss her."

"Oh, really? She's right here, with Randal. I'll put her on."

OMG!!! Suddenly a new wave of vulnerability washed over me. Other than jumping in St. Nick's face a while back and making this particular phone call without permission, I hadn't broken any rules in years, but this was a big, big, biggie. If Roomie and I were to get caught talking with each other, we could both get reamed. I could get time added to my sentence or spend a month in Solitary or lose my elevated status and privileges for another decade, but Roomie would surely be charged with a parole violation, which could send her right back to prison.

Suddenly I heard, "Miranda? Is that really you? I thought I'd never hear from you again."

My heart jumped. Rules or no rules, I loved her and wasn't about to hang up. "Yes, Honey. I'm on my way to the hospital so I can give a piece of my liver to Cody in the morning, but I don't have much time."

"Oh, no. Cody? How did you find him? Is he going to be okay?"

"I think so. He needs a liver transplant and I'm the only one who had a compatible one so his parents reached out to me." I glanced at Jay, whose buggy eyes suggested he was listening to one side of the most important call in history. "Right now," I added, "I'm cuffed to a picnic table at a rest stop. A heroic young friend named Jay loaned me his phone so I could tell you how much I miss you."

"I miss you too," Roomie said.

"Naomi mentioned somebody named Randal?"

"Yeah. He's my boyfriend. How long are you going to be in the hospital?"

"Four days of recovery and then I get transferred to a different place for a few more days before going back to the cages."

"Maybe I can come by and see you."

"No way. I would love that, but I'll have a guard around me at all times. If they caught us together, they could revoke your parole."

"Oh, yeah. Hey, I have another idea; why don't I wear a disguise? At least we can trade smiles from a distance."

"No, listen to me; that's way too risky."

"Not if I bring Randal. He can be a lookout and text me when it's clear."

"No. No. No. Don't do that either. We don't want to drag him into this. Promise me you won't do that."

It took several seconds before she sighed. "Okay. Okay. I promise."

Suddenly, from behind me I heard the van door open, indicating that the naughty guards had completed their mission. I only had a few more seconds.

"I gotta go now. I just wanted to say I love you."

Apparently, Jay got the urgency better than Roomie did because he snagged his phone from my sweaty palm. "That was cool, lady. I'm outta here," he said, before he bolted down the sidewalk.

By that time the guards had reached me. "We saw what you were doing, Munchak," Rudd said. "Who the hell was that kid?"

My pulse quickened. "I dunno. Honest. I just borrowed his phone."

"You know that's against the rules. You'll get a least two weeks in Solitary for this."

Then something obvious popped into my head. "I don't think so. Any charges like that would lead to a conference in the warden's office and questions would arise regarding how I got the phone in the first place. I'd have to say I was cuffed to a table while two married guards were rocking the van."

Roxy Padilla cupped her hand over her mouth and I knew I had them. "So why don't we just declare a truce?" I added.

Rudd paused and then nodded, and I'd successfully blackmailed somebody for the first time in my life.

Just then, Jay's sister and mom came from the restroom. His sister glanced at her own cell phone and pointed toward the far end of the lot. Apparently, my young hero had texted her and told them where to pick him up.

35

HAVING JUST HUNG UP HER sister's hardline phone, Candice plopped next to her bearded boyfriend on the couch.

"Miranda, huh?" Randal Biskitt said to happy-faced Candice. "What did that jailbird want?"

"I'm so excited," she replied. "I literally thought I'd never speak to her again."

"I don't know, sis." Naomi said from off to the side, "To be honest with you, I'm regretting that I told her you were here."

Randal twisted his beard. "That figures."

Tensions between Naomi and Randal had been brewing ever since Roomie first introduced them. As far as Naomi was concerned, there wasn't much to like about the man. He was unemployed, vulgar, 12 years older than Candice and had that ugly, scraggly beard. But worst of all, he had to be fornicating with Candice.

When Naomi suggested that the guy was downright dangerous, Candice insisted that she and Randal were merely friends with benefits and she could get away from him anytime she wanted. Predictably, that cavalier attitude didn't make religious Naomi feel any better, because Candice always had a tendency to disregard the consequences of her actions.

"Chill out," Candice said to her sister. "You know that Miranda saved my butt in the early days of prison and I love her."

"You don't have to remind me. I'm the one that nearly had a nervous breakdown from sneaking drugs into that place. Or have you forgotten that?"

Candice clucked her tongue. "Of course not. If it weren't for you, I might not have lasted that long. That's why I've thanked you at least a hundred times."

Randal raised a finger. "That's right, Naomi. I've heard her thank you a dozen times, so cut her some slack."

"Stay out of this, Randal," Naomi said. "It's none of your business."

Randal tossed his hair from side to side. "Who are you: the Gestapo?"

Naomi returned her attention to Candice. "I know that you like Miranda, but if your parole officer discovers that you were talking to her, they can throw you right back in prison, and Holy Jesus knows that neither one of us could handle that."

Randal glanced at Candice and rolled his eyes. "That ain't going to happen."

Frustrated, Naomi sighed and continued to speak with her sister. "If that kid tells the wrong person that he loaned his phone to a prisoner, the authorities could check his cellphone records and they'd see that the call came to my house and I don't like that."

"So what?" Candice said. "It's okay for you to talk with inmates and nobody would know whether I was on the call."

"You're wrong again, Naomi," Randal said.

"Don't you get it, Sweetie? Miranda's not supposed to do that unless her calls are monitored and you're not supposed to talk to her at all."

Randal shook his head. "Big fucking deal. You're the only one who gives a shit."

Naomi raised both her voice and a wagging finger. "You

know something, Randal? I've had it with you. I don't like your language or the disrespect. I want you out of my home, right now."

"Gladly," he said, rising and eyeing Candice. "You coming with me, Candy Cane?"

"Yeah. I'm coming," she said before making one final comment. "Look, Sis, he's got a point. You worry too much."

"Maybe so, but we'd both be better off if you kept better company."

"Fuck you, bitch."

* * *

"I gotta talk to you," Roomie said as she and Randal climbed into his van and pulled away from Naomi's home.

"If it's about your holier-than-thou sister, I ain't gonna put up with her bullshit and I don't like how she talks down to you."

"Naw, it ain't that. I know she's uptight."

"No shit. Hey, do you know what was hot? The whole time you were on the phone with that Miranda babe, I kept thinking about the two of you getting it on at night."

"We weren't the only ones. We just did what we did because of the situation. She'd gone seven or eight years without making love to anybody so she needed some love - I did too."

"I don't see any problem with jumping in the rack with people you like."

"Neither do I, most of the time. That's why I think of us as friends with benefits, but it wouldn't hurt you to be romantic once in a while."

"I dunno. That kind of stalling just makes me hornier."

"Yeah, but when there's an emotional connection, it makes the physical part more enjoyable."

Randal grinned and looked right at her. "So, who was the aggressor?"

144

"Back and forth. Now get your mind out of the gutter and listen to me. Miranda has never seen her son or even a picture of him. She doesn't even know his real name. Could you help me scope out the hospital? Maybe we can get some information for her."

"Interesting. What you got in mind?"

"I don't know exactly. I'd like to at least get his name. Maybe a picture. We'd have to do it in the morning on the day of the operation, when they're all out of their rooms."

"I might be persuaded to give it a try, but what's in it for good ole Randal?"

"I dunno. What do you want?"

"If your girlfriend was here, I'd suggest a three-way, but I've got a pipe from a swing set at my house that I can hang from the ceiling and you can be a hot pole dancer named Candy Cane, and I'll be a rich customer who pays big money for Ms. Cane's attention."

"I guess we could do that," she said tapping him on the nose, "but Candy Cane don't need no pole. She can just give her customer one hell of a lap dance."

Randal smiled. "I'm in!!!"

36

AFTER A BEDROOM ROMP FOR THE RECORD BOOKS, Roomie and Randal began a three-hour trek to the hospital where Miranda and her son were. At dinner time, they pulled into the lot. From the rider's side Roomie tucked the last of her hair under a dark wig and donned an old pair of eyeglasses. "How do I look?"

Randal snickered. "Those baggy jeans make me want to laugh because you've got the skinny legs of a fashion model."

"Good. If we get near the guards, I don't want them to recognize me."

"Alright then, what's first?"

"Simple. I'm going to ask the receptionist for the room number of a 10-year-old boy who is getting a liver transplant from a prisoner."

"Oh, you naïve young thing. You said your parole could be revoked if you get caught aligning with a prisoner, so that idea is too risky. Besides, Miranda is probably registered under an alias so that the receptionist doesn't even know what's going on."

"Okay, Smarty Pants. What would you do?"

"I say we look for the vultures."

"What?"

"I'm talking about human vultures, baby. The prison will

make sure that guards are circling your buddy the whole time she's here. They're the vultures. When we find them, the carcass can't be far away."

"Oh, I get it, but I don't like you talking about her like that."

"Relax, it's just a metaphor. If we're going to find the kid, we gotta find Miranda first. I'll talk to the receptionist. If that doesn't work, we'll methodically work our way up the hallways, looking for the vultures. It should be easy. The guards will probably cuff Miranda to her bed and sit out in the hall so they don't have to be hooked directly to her 24-7."

"You know something, Randal? You're pretty smart. What about Cody? How are we going to find him?"

"That's a little trickier. Since the kid and Miranda ultimately have to be in the same operating area at the exact same time, I bet they'll keep both patients in the same basic area, but not so close that Miranda can see him."

"I see what you mean."

"We'll just have to figure that out when we get there. For now, grab that bottle of meds from your purse."

"Okay, let's go for it."

Once in the main lobby, Randal approached the young receptionist. "Hi, can you tell me where my brother is? He's a guard from the ladies' prison. He asked me to bring his meds."

"Try the fourth floor."

As Randal and Roomie moved toward the elevators, Roomie giggled. "It worked."

"Yeah, but that was the easy part."

"I hope I can see her."

"I know you do, but if the guards figure out what's going on, your whole house of cards could crumble down. Just remember, if we see guards walking around or a chair in the hall, just stroll on past, looking instead for any clues where the kid might be. Maybe we'll get lucky."

On the fourth floor, the main doors led to a dual hallway, separated by a nurses' station.

"Which way?" Roomie asked.

Randal glanced both ways then heard a male's voice down the corridor on their right. "This way is as good as any. Now remember, if we see any guards, don't stare at them. Just walk on by."

"Got it."

"And if you get to peek into any of the rooms, look for signs that a youngster might be in there."

They bypassed the nurses' station and got their first glimpse down the long corridor, where Randal's previous comment was proven correct. In addition to a couple carts in the hall, a uniformed female guard sat in a padded chair reading a magazine outside a room half-way down the hall. "Oh, my God," Candice whispered. "That must be Miranda's room."

"Yeah. Do you recognize the guard?"

"No. They had well over a hundred of them and there's a lot of turnover, so I only knew a fraction of them."

"Well, that's one good thing. Remember what we said; just walk on by."

Candice's heart pounded so hard she could almost hear it. "My hands are shaking."

Randal grinned. "Give me your hand and don't walk too fast."

After passing a handful of rooms, and then the guard, they came to the end of the hall where it turned toward the left, and then left again up the other bank of rooms. "Let's go all the way around," Randal said. "Keep your eyes open for a sign of the kid."

"Will do."

Ultimately, they made it to the seating area of the second bank of rooms. "Nobody's in here," he said, tugging Candice toward two padded chairs in the corner. "We can wait here and watch the hall for anybody who might be here to visit the kid."

"What if that doesn't work?"

Randal flashed a grin. "I found Miranda, didn't I?'

"Yeah. You nailed it."

"You do realize that you're going to owe me a lot when this is over, right?"

"Maybe so, but I don't have anything else I can give you."

He gave her a lopsided grin. "Oh, yes you do. When this is over, we're going on a weekend trip to Reno where we're gonna hire a classy call girl for a three-way. We'll put it all on your credit card."

Candice's hands snapped to her hip. "Really? A prostitute? You've said things like that before but I thought you were just joking."

"Oh, I ain't joking. We're going to hire a high-class expert and you're going to pay the bill."

"Really? A three-way? I don't think--"

"Now you're sounding like your sister. There are a ton of hookers in those towns and you've already told me you've made love with Miranda--"

"Yeah, but that was different. We didn't have any other options."

"Boo hoo. The point stands: You've been with at least one woman before, so you can do it again. It'll be fun. I promise."

"How many times have you been with a prostitute?"

"I dunno. Maybe five or six. Trust me. It's erotic as hell and you'll love it."

"But that must be expensive and my cards are always maxed out. I can't afford anything like that."

"I think you should borrow the money from your sister. That would serve her right."

"But I can't tell her that I need money for a prostitute."

"No, but you can tell her that you're looking for your own apartment. She'll be so happy she'll gladly throw a thousand bucks your way."

"I dunno. Can't I thank you some other way?"

"Nope. You're the one asking me to put my head in a noose

to help your girlfriend. If I get us in that kid's room and
get some useful information for Miranda, that's my price.
Besides, you just might learn a thing or two."

37

HAVING ASSUMED THAT CODY was in one of the nearby rooms, Randal and Candice spent several hours watching a slipshod parade of visitors come and go, paying special attention to anybody who might be carrying anything a 10-year-old kid would like.

Whenever somebody promising walked by, one or the other followed the newcomers in hopes of getting a peek inside the room. Just before the sun dropped out of the sky three additional visitors walked by. Randal tapped Candice's knee.

"Your turn to tail 'em."

Candice followed them around the corridor and to the other hallway where the guard was. When a dozen rooms from where Miranda was, the trio stepped inside one of the rooms and Candice's eyes shot to the foot of a bed where a couple dancing helium balloons were tied to the footrail. "Okay, Trev," the lone male said, "Mama and Daddy are going back to our hotel and get cleaned up and get something to eat."

"Aunt Jenn is going too, Honey," the more elderly woman said, "but we'll all be back a little later and stay with you as long as we can. Then tomorrow is your big day."

Bingo. That had to be Cody's room and his family - presumably a mother, father and aunt.

"Okay, Auntie," the patient said softly. "I'm sleepy anyways."

Candice wanted to get a better look at Miranda's son but tore herself away to return to Randal, who was still in the waiting area. "You found him, didn't you?" he said.

"Yeah. How'd you know?"

"Let's just say you'd make a lousy poker player."

After Candice filled Randal in, he pursed his lips. "Are you sure they said they were going to their hotel and dinner?" he asked.

"Yeah, and the dad called the kid Trev."

"How many beds were in there?"

"Just one, as far as I could tell."

"Good, then this shouldn't be too difficult. We need to wait 15 minutes or so, until the kid is asleep, then we can sneak in and do our thing."

"Sounds good. Do we need anything besides our cell phones?"

"Dunno, but let's take a small plastic bag."

"For what? You're not going to steal anything, are you?"

"It depends on what's in there."

After walking around a bit, Candice and Randal made their way to Cody's room. "Are you ready?" Randal whispered.

Candice looked over her shoulder and up the hall. Nobody was there. She nodded.

Inside the boy's room, the drawn curtains lent a cave-like darkness. The frail youngster's head was buried in his pillow and facing them. Randal pointed to Candice's cell and mouthed, "Go ahead."

She snapped a few pix of the lad and noticed some framed pictures and some mail on a bedside table. A red envelope addressed to a Trevor Montgomery topped the heap. That had to be his name. Candice snapped a picture of the table and its contents.

Suddenly, down the hall somebody knocked on a door. "Dinner," the person said to some other patient.

"We gotta get out of here," Randal whispered.

Candice nodded. Seconds later they were walking down the hall and Candice scanned her pictures. "Cool beans," Randal whispered. "You got your pictures and I earned my free three-way."

"I don't think so," Candice said softly. "This picture isn't good enough. None of them are very good. It was too dark. You can't tell what the boy looks like. Besides, I saw his name on a red card, but all I remember is the name Trevor and an M of this last name. We gotta try again."

Randal stepped back. "No friggin' way. That kid is getting his dinner now and his family will be back any minute."

"We can't give up now," Candice said, frustrated. "We gotta get a better picture somehow."

Just then the guard in front of Miranda's room rose and strolled into the public restroom. "Oh, my God," Candice said to Randal. "If I hurry, I can see Miranda. Go keep the guard busy."

Inside the room Miranda sat near the window with her feet cuffed together and one arm cuffed to a three-foot chain that was cuffed to the headboard. Miranda turned her head and scrunched her brows.

Candice put a finger to her lips. "It's me, Roomie." she said, removing her glasses. "The guard went to the restroom, so I only have a couple minutes."

Shocked, Miranda's hand shot to cover her own mouth.

Candice rushed to Miranda for a quick hug. "Look what I've got," she said revealing the picture she'd just taken. "It's not very clear but they're pictures of Cody. His real name is Trevor."

Caught off-guard, Miranda glanced from Candice to the picture and back again.

"Hurry up," Randal whispered from just outside the door. "Find out what time her procedure is."

"Who's that?" Miranda asked Candice.

"Randal. What time is your procedure tomorrow?"

"Eight o'clock. Why?"

"I dunno. I learned not to question him."

"After that I get four days to recover and look out this window. Then it's back to hell for me."

"I heard the toilet flush," Randal whispered loudly. "Get out now."

"I gotta go," Candice said. "I'll mail a picture to the prison. I love you."

"You too," Miranda said, reaching with her free hand.

Barely back in the hall, Candice heard the bathroom door close, indicating the guard had damn near caught them. She tapped Randal's arm. "Why'd you want to know the time of the procedure?"

"Simple," he said. "We can come back when everybody is preoccupied and get better pictures in that kid's room."

* * *

That night, Candice paid for a cheap motel in which they made enough late-night animal noises to get a warning from the manager.

The next morning, they got up early and drove to the hospital. At 8:15, when the operation had just begun, they waddled their way to the fourth floor. This time a female guard was perched outside Miranda's room. They walked past, sneaked into Cody's room and flicked on the overhead light. On the table beside the bed were a couple of small, framed pictures including one of the boy and a pet dachshund. Near the framed pictures, a stack of get-well cards was topped by the red envelope that Candice had seen the day before. This time she could clearly see that it was addressed to Trevor Montgomery.

"Here's something," Randal said, pointing to an information sheet that contained the boy's address and his parents' names. Candice snapped close-up pictures of most of it. Then she said, "I have enough. Let's go."

A couple minutes later on the elevator, Randal reached into his shirt and handed Candice the picture of the boy with his dog. "Here you go."

Shocked, Candice stopped. It would have been crazy to take it back, so she did the next best thing. "Miranda's going to love this," she said with a huge toothy grin.

"Good," Randal said, "and that means you and me are headed to Reno."

Candice sighed and went silent. "You know something, Randal? I know how Miranda feels. I miss her just as much as she misses her son. I'd give anything to see the expression on her face when she sees this picture."

"In that case, I have a better idea. Let's break her out of here."

Stunned, Candice stared into his eyes. "Are you insane?"

"Not really. We just have to wait a few days for her to recover. Then we can come back. I know what to do from there."

38

THE NIGHT BEFORE THE SURGERY I tried to make sense out of Candice's crazy visit. Apparently, her disguise had enabled her to squirt past a careless guard who wasn't paying much attention. Additionally, somehow she sneaked into Cody's room and grabbed a picture of him sleeping. It wasn't a great picture, but I hoped she'd find a way to get a copy of it to me. All of that rammed a double-edged knife into my heart. Part of me wanted to know as much as I could about my son; a bigger part knew the deck was stacked to keep Cody and me apart forever and that meant more regrets.

Eventually a counselor dropped by to verify that I still wanted to go through with the procedure and to see if I had any last-minute questions. After assuring me that the surgeon was highly talented, she repeated some of the things they'd said before. Specifically, I could expect the doctor to make an incision just under the ribs on both sides of my belly. The incisions were to extend straight up for a short distance over the breastbone.

She proceeded to say that the recovery period was slow and painful partly because there were so many stitches and bandages. That information didn't matter very much because I would have endured any pain to help my son.

After the surgery I'd be taken to ICU for observation and if all went well, I'd return to my room where I'd rest for several days before being transferred to a more home-like facility for a few more days of recovery.

After I gave my final signature of approval, all that was left to do was get a good night's sleep and implement the strategy the following morning.

Quite honestly, I don't recall a lot about the morning of the surgery, but I do recall a flush of euphoria when they began streaming my body with drugs.

A more objective person might say that in a best-case scenario, both halves of my liver - one in Cody's body and one in mine - would survive the surgery and regenerate into a full liver within a month. In the worst case, his body would also reject my liver and that would probably mean a tragic outcome for him and more lifelong regrets for me. But none of that stuff mattered to me because my maternal instincts were off the chart and I just knew I would save Cody's life.

Aside from that, I prayed with all my heart and reminded God that Cody's life was infinitely more valuable than mine because he had a long future before him while my future was severely limited. "If you can only spare one of us," I begged, "please spare Cody."

Eventually, I was given some knockout drugs, which was the last thing I remember until I awakened in the intensive care unit. About all I remember about those woozy moments is how stiff I was from all the stitches and bandages.

Late the next morning I was moved from the recovery room to my own room for more recovery and found myself cuffed to the side of the headboard.

Meanwhile, Guard Roxy Padilla had taken a post on the other side of the door just in case I sprang to my feet, wielded a butter knife, and pulled off the most infamous female escape in history.

When I asked Ms. Padilla about Cody she had no news,

but I wasn't sure if I could believe her, given the tiff I'd had at the picnic table with her and Rudd.

The next time a nurse came in she told me that I could expect to be shuffling my feet on my own within a couple days, but that wasn't my biggest concern. I again asked how Cody was, but she didn't know either. In fact, that's what everybody said every time I asked. I assumed that had to do with the original sealed adoption concept that I ordered 10 years earlier when I was basically forced to give Cody away. But once I knew that we were all in the same building, and I had become a critical de-facto part of his life, it was as if God wanted me to be more involved with him and I had a change of heart.

Unfortunately, nobody gave a damn about my change of heart and I was in no condition to force the matter. All I could do was get more rest and hope somebody would be more forthcoming soon.

39

Second Day Following the Surgery

When Randal floated the idea of breaking Miranda out of the hospital, Candice thought he was out of his mind, but after hours and hours of conversation in his living room, he convinced her. And now they were running low on time.

If everything went as planned at the hospital, Miranda had been in surgery the day before and was in recovery. "Can we go over everything again?" Candice asked.

"Sure," he said, fondling his beard, "but you worry too much. We just have to be smart about it."

Candice looked deep into his eyes. "But what if we get caught? Jails are full of risk-takers. I've seen lots of them and I don't want to go back there."

"And a lot of people get away with crimes. Hell, only half the murders get solved. And those are the easy ones. The cops don't have a lot of resources so they prefer to go after the low-hanging fruit. Thus, it ain't the risk-taking that fills the jails; it's carelessness."

"I guess that makes sense."

"Think about it. You wrote all those bad checks because you were impulsive. There was no way to get away with what you did."

"Oh, no," she said, leaning forward. "I just thought of something. Miranda won't be completely recovered for over a week. We'll have to take her someplace clean and quiet until she gets better, and we don't got any—"

"Relax," Randal interrupted with a big smirk. "I got it handled. I hope she likes Utah."

"Utah? Who's in Utah?"

"One of my Navy buddies, but they won't be there. They're going on a vacation and won't be back for nearly two weeks. Dude already said we can crash there if we want to."

"Oh, my God. That's perfect."

"Somebody has to think of these things." He leaned toward her. "Listen to me, now. It's time for us to shit or get off the pot. If we're going to spring Miranda, we have to be smart about it. They don't like patients to take up the beds any longer than necessary, so they're probably going to transfer her somewhere after a few days. We need to get in there just before that.

"Okay, that makes sense."

"And we have to do it at night when there are fewer people to get in the way. Once she's out, the cops will suspect her prison friends, so you have to have an impenetrable alibi. That's why we gotta send both of our cell phones to my cousin in Houston. I'll have him place a few calls with our phones to his local businesses at just the right time. Then, if the cops ever do question you and check your phone records, the logs will back that up. So will my cuz. With that kind of alibi, we're home free."

Candice relaxed. "I wish I had thought of alibis when I wrote all those bad checks."

"I know. That's why I keep telling you we have to deflect any suspicions before they get started."

"You know what? My parole officer likes to hear from me twice a month. I think I'll give her a call now. That way she won't be calling me for a while."

"Now you're thinking."

"Just lucky, but I got another question. We know that Miranda is cuffed to her bed. How do we cut the chains?"

He grinned. "The cops might as well use toy cuffs. Anybody can pick the locks on their cuffs with a paperclip in thirty seconds. You just have to know what you're doing."

"Are you sure, Randal? That sounds way too simple."

"If you don't believe me, we can look at videos online right now."

She tilted her head. "If you don't mind, I'd like to do that 'cause I don't want anything to go wrong."

"Go ahead. Ain't gonna bother me none."

She grabbed her phone and a very short time later lifted her head. "Wow. That really was simple."

"Told ya," he said, picking up his plate and moving toward the trash. "Course, when all this is done, you're gonna owe me another big favor."

"Oh, really?" she said, her hands on her hips. "Last time we had this conversation you wanted me to hire a prostitute for a three-way. What else could I possibly give you?"

"I've been thinking about that. Why don't you and Miranda make love in front of me and let me video it? That'll be really hot."

"Are you kidding me? I wouldn't want to do that and I doubt that she would either, especially if you want to get a video of it."

"Oh, bullshit. She's been locked up for ten years and she loves you. She'll probably be all for it. Furthermore, you've told me that when you were her cellmate, you both did things that fit the circumstances. What did you call it, 'circumstantial' sex?"

"No. Its 'situational' sex."

"Yeah. That's it. If you want my help, I have to get something out of it too and that is what the 'situation' calls for."

Candice sighed. "All I can say is, if we get her out of there, I'll ask her, but don't blame me if she says no."

"Okay, then, we have a deal. Now, give me your cell

phone. After I send it to my cousin, we'll get a temporary burner phone and get back to that hospital to scope things out. I wanna see if we can find any weaknesses or danger zones. Oh, by the way, I need you to get as much cash as possible."

"But I don't have much money."

"You can get a cash advance from your credit card now or better yet, borrow from your sister. I can kick in a couple hundred."

"Why do we need to do that?"

"Good question. When we get Miranda out of there, the cops will automatically suspect you. They'll check your credit card activity and your cell phone activity to see if you were in the area when the escape went down. We already agreed to send the cell phones to my cousin in Houston. So that's our cover and we don't want a poorly timed credit card transaction to contradict the phone records."

"So, I should get as much as I can right now and stop using the card for a while?"

"Or borrow from your sister."

40

By the time the third recovery day presented itself, I was stiff and sore and my left wrist had been cuffed to my headboard for so long I was looking forward to a walk down the hall.

At about 9:00 a.m. an African American nurse named Brenda arrived to get my vitals and help me stretch and take me for that much needed walk. Roxy Padilla removed my cuffs and shackles.

The three of us slowly shuffled down the hall and back. Roxy allowed me to stretch a little more before she locked me down again and took her position in the hall. Alone with Brenda I had an idea.

"I see your wedding ring," I said. "Are you a mom?"

"Yeah. Two teenage girls. Sometimes they scare the heck out of me."

"I wish I was that lucky. I've asked several people how my son is doing, but nobody wants to talk about it. Can you get any information for me?"

She smiled. "We're not supposed to talk about other patients."

"I know, but you just said that you're a mom. I just gave

half my liver to my son. If you were in my situation, wouldn't you at least like to know if your child was on the mend?"

Brenda rested a compassionate hand on my forearm. "Yes, I would, but I still can't talk about it."

I would have screamed if it would have done any good, but I knew what it was like to be held back by unfriendly rules.

After I'd gotten some more sleep, both Roxy Padilla and Brenda returned. "Alright, Miranda," Brenda said, "we gotta loosen you up and take you for another walk. A little farther this time."

A quick stop at the restroom was followed by some stretching exercises plus a longer walk and a return trip to my bed where Padilla removed her cuff keys from her belt. "Do you have to restrain me?" I asked, "'Cause I couldn't get ten feet without falling over."

"'Fraid so," she said with no hint of sympathy.

"Please reconsider," I begged. "I promise, I can't get away. Honest."

"Right. Anybody who says 'honest' after a statement couldn't possibly be lying."

Her harsh tongue suggested she was harboring a grudge regarding the dirt I had on her and Rudd. "Well, you don't have to be so rude."

"You just worry about your own business, inmate. Now I'm gonna take my station and I best not hear a peep unless it's a medical emergency."

After Padilla stormed out, Brenda tapped my forearm. "You didn't hear this from me," she whispered, "but your son is going to be okay."

Delightfully stunned, I looked her in the eye. "Really? Are you sure?"

She put her finger to her lips. "He's tired but doing fine."

I thanked God.

***

After Candice got a loan from her sister, Randal mailed his and Candice's cell phones to his cousin in Houston. He slid behind the wheel of his van. "Now we gotta check out the hospital again."

"I brought a notebook and pen," Candice said while reaching in the glovebox. "I know we've got to look for surveillance cameras, but what else do we need?"

"I've been thinking about that. To begin with I'll need a hat. You can wear what you wore last time – baggy clothes and a wig. In addition, we'll need surgical gloves so we don't leave any prints anywhere."

"This is good," Candice said. "What else?"

"We're also going to need two vehicles."

"Why? Your van will be perfect. We can put a mattress in the cargo area until we can get her to Utah."

"You may be the sweetest person I've ever known, but you're incredibly naïve. If we use either one of our vehicles, surveillance cameras will get our tags and we'll be cooked before we light the oven."

"Couldn't you just remove the plates?"

"No. They'd still know what kind of car we're in and they'd notice any stickers or dents and put out a BOLO."

"What's that?"

"Be On Look Out. All cops use it. We don't want any part of that."

"Alright, then. What are we going to do?"

"Simple. We're going to leave my van somewhere close by that has lots of vehicles and no surveillance cameras. Then, we'll use a different vehicle to get to the lot."

"But not my car?"

"Right. You're supposed to be in Houston. If your car shows up on surveillance, there goes your alibi. Instead, I can borrow a very common-looking SUV to use while we're on the hospital lot. Then after we get Miranda into the SUV, we head for my van, make the switch, and we're all clear."

"But what about the first vehicle? Won't the surveillance camera get those plates?"

"You know something? You worry too much. I'll put some stolen tags on it. When we make the switch, I'll remove the hot plates and call my buddy and tell him where he can find his SUV. Nobody will know the difference."

"Wow, you really have thought this through."

"Of course, I have. That's what it takes to beat the cops."

"Okay. I can get some clothes for Miranda."

"Good. While she's recovering, we can't take her into any restaurants or stores or even a public restroom. It would be too obvious, so you gotta get some adult diapers and wipes. While you're at it, get me a white button-down shirt so I look official."

41

Early the next morning, Candice dropped Randal off at the home of one of his friends, so he could borrow a car and steal some bogus license plates from the nearby used car lot.

When back at Randal's place, she methodically packed his van with the things that they could need after the escape.

As Candice placed a stack of her own clothes in the back of the van, a benign white SUV came toward her with Randal smiling from behind the wheel. After inspecting the spotless cargo area, Candice said, "I don't know if Miranda will need to lie down in here but I'll throw in some blankets and a pillow on the floor so it'll be a little more comfortable."

"Okay," he said, "but keep those things to a minimum. When we make the switch, we don't want to draw attention to ourselves."

"Got it," she said while admiring his command of the endless details.

Randal looked up the street and back again. "Did you get everything we talked about?"

"No, but we've got the most important things, and we can get whatever else we need from any Wal-Mart along the way."

"Good enough," he said pulling her to him and pointing to the mattress on the floor of his van. "That means we've got some time before we go. How would you like to christen our adventure?"

After a fair amount of adult entertainment and the gathering of the last few items, Randal led his van away from the curb and Candice followed in the white SUV. It would take a long two hours to get to the Sunshine Apartments, which were a few miles from the hospital and boasted tall bushes but no surveillance cameras.

During the drive, they spoke via burner phones. Candice reminded herself that Randal had thought of everything and all he asked in return was to get some naughty videos.

Very reasonable, she thought. After all, she'd had firsthand conversations with inmates and most of them would screw Quasimodo himself if that would get them out of prison a week earlier.

Therefore, if Randal really did bring a premature end to the remaining thirty-one years of Miranda's sentence, that would be an extraordinary accomplishment, worthy of much, much more than the teeny tiny token he'd requested. Surely, Miranda would agree.

* * *

When my final evening at the hospital was winding down, I'd regained at least half of my strength. I could sit in a chair beside my bed or stand up, but I couldn't go anywhere because I was always attached to chains and cuffs. So, when a young male guard and a nurse named Rita came in for one of my scheduled exercise routines, I could have kissed them both.

"It's time for your walk down the hall," the nurse said.

As people go, I liked her because she usually knew what mattered to me at the moment. "Of course, we'll use your restroom first," she added.

With that resolved the guard named Gary Furr unlocked my ankle jewelry and then freed me from the wrist cuff.

Completely unshackled for the first time in hours I repeatedly raised both hands above my head and brought them back to my side for a little exercise. "You guys don't know how good it is to have full range of your arms," I said, rubbing my sore wrists.

Rita smiled slightly. "Your feet have been restricted too, so walk slowly until you loosen up a little bit."

Predictably, I was all for the privacy of that little bathroom. After all, I'd been in prison for ten years and seclusion was impossible. Ultimately Rita and I waddled down the hall to the elevators and then back.

"Can you do another lap or two?" she asked. "If so, tomorrow we'll transfer you to an offsite facility where it's more comfortable."

The idea of a recovery house was appealing, especially compared to the sterile hospital room. For that matter anything was better than returning to prison for 31 more years. "Let's give it a try," I said, knowing that I'd do whatever it took to move on.

Eventually, 7:00 p.m. rolled around and I heard a tap at my door. Before I could say, "come in," my least favorite person of all time, St. Nick, entered. "Hey, Munchak," he said, "just thought I'd let you know that Furr has gone home and it's my turn to babysit you until morning."

God, how I loathed that man. I merely grunted.

He took a step back, checked out the hallway and then leaned back into my room. "Look, Munchak," he said, "I know that you hate me, and you're probably tired of me saying I'm sorry for the past, but God is guiding me and I'm genuinely anxious to make peace. I'd do anything to take away what I did if I could, but I can't, so, I'm hoping you'll take the higher path and forgive me. I am sincerely sorry. Really."

He sounded like he actually meant it, but I still thought the "I got religion" bit was b.s. It would take a bigger person than me to forgive what he did. I didn't reply, but he failed to get the hint.

"I know it doesn't count much to you," he continued, "but I wish I could do something to make it up to you."

I almost screamed at him but just then nurse Rita returned with my nightly sleeping pill and rescued me.

42

WELL AFTER SUNSET, Randal and Candice dropped off Randal's van at the Sunshine Apartments. While there, they donned their disguises and grabbed a bag of clothes that Candice had assembled for Miranda. With their primary escape vehicle ready for a long drive, they climbed into the white SUV and drove to the hospital.

"Okay," Randal said while he parked the SUV as close as he could to the hospital's cafeteria. "We'll want to move swiftly so don't lock the doors."

"It's almost nine o'clock," Candice said while they removed their surgical gloves. "There should only be one guard near Miranda's room."

They walked around the building and into the main entrance, where they spotted an unmanned wheelchair.

"Bring this with us," Randal said. "We might need it- and don't leave your prints on it."

"I need to pee," Candice said while wishing she were as confident as her boyfriend.

Randal grinned. "Alright, while you do that, I'm gonna call my cousin in Houston and have him place a few calls with our cellphones so it'll look like we were down there when Miranda gets away."

After a brief pit stop, Candice and Randal hustled to a

vending machine for a couple cups of coffee. "We gotta use napkins and a cardboard carrying tray," Randal insisted, "so that we won't leave any prints."

In the elevator, they popped the lid of one of the cups and added some sleeping pills. "Put a lot of them in there," Randal said, "in case the guard only takes a few sips."

"Got it," Candice said just as the elevator pinged.

"Leave the wheelchair in that little hallway," Randal whispered, "just in case we need it."

"Will do. I'll leave Miranda's change of clothes here too."

A lack of action at the nurses' station inspired quiet glances down the hall. As expected, one lone guard was posted in an armchair just outside the door. "That's Nick Stome," Candice whispered. "He's the one who forced Miranda to screw him."

Randal nodded. "Too bad we don't have time to kick his ass."

"Miranda hated that creep. I hope he gets in a shit-ton of trouble for this."

"I get it," he whispered, "but keep that kind of emotion out of it. We need to concentrate on our plans."

Candice checked her wig. "How do I look?"

"Ugly. I doubt he'll recognize you."

"Okay, then. Here goes."

"Remember, stay friendly."

On her own, with spiked coffee in a tray, Candice walked nervously past the nurses' station, then not too fast, not too slow and past the janitor's closet. When just a few paces from Miranda's room, her motion caught St. Nick's attention. She slowed, then stopped right in front of him and went into her act.

"Thank God!" she said, feigning a smile. "I bought this coffee for my sister and me, but she left while I was downstairs. I'd hate myself if I wasted it. Would you like it? Nobody has touched it."

The hated guard eyed her briefly, then tilted his head.

"Yeah. It's gonna be a long night. I could use a hot cup of coffee. What do I owe you?"

"Nothing," she said, extending the tray so he'd take the spiked cup. "I'm just glad I don't have to waste it."

"Alright. That's very nice of you. Thanks a lot."

"You're welcome." As she walked off, she grinned like a happy clown at the circus.

When she caught up to Randal he rose from his chair. "It went well, didn't it?"

"Just as you said it would, but I was nervous as hell and need to pee again."

Randal patted her shoulder. "All we gotta do now is wait for the pills to take effect."

After forty-five slow-moving minutes in the lounge area on the second floor, Randal whispered to Candice, "That should do it. If our boy drank any of that coffee, he should be zonked out. Let's get on up there."

At the fourth floor, Randal held up a hand indicating Candice should stay back while he peeked down the hall toward St. Nick and Miranda's room. "His head is leaning back against the wall," he soon whispered to Candice. "I think he's out."

More confident now, Randal and Candice held hands and quietly strolled past the guard just to be certain he was asleep.

He didn't move.

"Let's walk by again," Randal said taking Candice's hand. As before, Nick didn't move.

After taking one last look up and down the hall, Randal slipped to the side of St. Nick and on into Miranda's room. He hooked a finger, urging Candice to follow him.

Inside the room, Miranda was asleep. Candice eased to Miranda's side and jiggled her lightly while Randal wiggled a bent paperclip into Miranda's wrist cuffs.

"Miranda, wake up," Candice said as quietly as possible. "We're going to get you out of here."

Miranda stirred just as the wrist cuff clicked open. Randal grinned and shifted his attention to Miranda's ankle cuffs.

"C'mon, Honey," Candice urged her former cellmate.

"Shake her harder," Randal said softly. "They must have given her a sleeping pill."

Candice gently gripped Miranda's jaw and aggressively moved her head back and forth causing Miranda's eyelids to part slightly.

"C'mon, Honey," Candice insisted. "Wake up. You're getting out of here."

The click at the other end of the bed indicated that Randal had sprung one of the ankle cuffs.

"One more to go," he whispered proudly.

Miranda opened her eyes wider and rolled her head from side to side, confused.

Once again Candice whispered in her friend's ear. "It's Roomie. You gotta sit up so we can get you out of here."

Less groggy, Miranda stared into Candice's eyes, then mumbled, "No. You'll get in trouble."

"Shh. You gotta trust me." Roomie tugged Miranda to a sitting position.

"Got it," Randal said as the last cuff was released from Miranda's feet."

Candice whispered to him, "Get me a wet towel, for Miranda's neck. It'll help her to wake up."

Candice helped Miranda to her feet. "C'mon, Honey, we gotta go."

They inched to the door and cracked it slightly to see St. Nick's head still propped against the wall. Randal waved his hand in a "hurry-up" motion.

Seconds later the ladies followed Randal out the door. When just past the doorframe, they turned toward the elevators.

One more shuffle of their feet brought extremely weak Miranda right past St. Nick, who lifted his head ever so slightly.

"Good luck," he whispered loudly enough for them all to hear. "I'm giving you fifteen minutes, then I gotta turn you all in."

43

The evening of the break-out I was too sluggish from my nightly sleeping pill to know exactly what was going on, but later I learned that Roomie was totally stunned by St. Nick's comment. Randal, on the other hand, used the opportunity to run for the wheelchair, near the elevators.

In the elevator, before hitting the down button, Roomie helped me put on an oversized pair of blue jeans and a sweatshirt. At ground level, the elevator pinged.

"Don't rush," Randal said to Roomie as they wheeled me in the direction of the cafeteria.

She gladly followed her leader.

When just outside the cafeteria, Randal said, "Okay. Hold her head up so it looks like she's alert."

"C'mon, Honey," Roomie said, tapping me behind my ears. "You gotta hold your head up."

Even though I was barely ambulatory, I sensed the urgency and followed my friend's orders as best I could.

We rolled into the cafeteria. There were only a few people in there and none of them were paying any attention to us. Behind a counter, the lone worker was busy wiping down his cabinets.

Randal calmly went straight for the exit door and held it open like he might do for a sister. Almost on cue, Roomie leaned forward and whispered in my ear, "We're going outside, Honey."

It was all like a dream, but I think I instinctively nodded.

Outside, Randal said to Roomie, "There's our SUV. I'll go open the tailgate."

The exit door closed behind us and Roomie guided me slowly down the sidewalk as if I was merely a slow-moving visitor, not an escaping con.

A few feet from their white vehicle, Randal handed Roomie a pair of surgical gloves and smiled. "So far so good, but we gotta hurry. If that guard was telling the truth, we've only got ten more minutes before he blows the whistle."

"Listen to me, Honey," Roomie said to me. "You've got to help us get you in the back end of this SUV. Then we can get out of here."

Even in my half-conscious state, I knew that I wanted to get away. A rush of adrenaline countered the sleeping pill for a few brief seconds. I nodded and stood as erect as I could, which caused my bandages to tug at the stitched-up incision on my stomach. I cringed but kept trying to follow instructions.

Seconds later, the tailgate dropped. "Scoot toward me. Get closer. Lean in. I'll help with your feet."

Finally, I was lying on my side in the cargo area holding my stomach. Randal piloted us out of there.

We drove about ten painful minutes and pulled into the parking lot of an apartment building with tall bushes. Randal parked the SUV next to a blue van at the back of the lot.

"We're changing vehicles, Honey," Roomie said to me.

I have to admit that the sleeping pill made it impossible for me to think clearly, but I definitely knew that I was nearly free from prison life.

My anxious partners shuffled me from the nice SUV to the side cargo door of the blue van.

"In here," Roomie said while Randal slid the side door back, revealing a very inviting mattress.

I backed in as best I could, and Roomie lifted my legs and pivoted me onto the mattress.

"Let's get out of here," Randal said, rushing around to the driver's door and starting the van. Seconds later, Roomie had wiped down the area of the SUV where I had been and we were headed for the interstate. For the first time, I felt a warmth under my bandages, indicating that some bleeding had taken place.

"I'm coming back there," Roomie said, climbing over the console and reaching for a blanket and pillow and bottle of water that she'd placed in there earlier. "Let's get you comfortable."

Still fighting both adrenaline and a sleeping pill, I drank some water while Roomie removed my baggy jeans. "Can you look at my bandages?" I asked.

"Sure, Honey," she said in a tender, motherly tone. She gently lifted the sweatshirt she'd given me in the elevator.

"There's a little blood on your bra, Baby, but it doesn't look bad. We'll stop a little later and change your bandages and get you some better clothes."

With a blanket on top of me and the whirr of tires beneath me, all I knew for certain was prisoner 1516103-A was "in the wind."

I obeyed my eyes and closed them.

44

NICK STOME MAY NOT HAVE BEEN the brightest headlight on the highway, but he had a pretty good idea what Munchak's buddies were up to, which meant that he'd just entered one of life's unexpected inflection points.

Certain that he was under surveillance, Stome pretended to be asleep for the designated time before he rose and acted as if he were checking on his prisoner. A moment later he rushed out of the room and called the sheriff's office to report the escape.

"That coffee lady must have given me some knockout pills," he said. "I couldn't help it."

Sheriff Vincent ignored the excuse. "You didn't get a sense of whether there were any other accomplices, did you?"

"No, I was zonked out, but I checked the room and the handcuffs have all been sprung. No way Munchak could have done that."

"Alright then. We're on our way. In the meantime, there are surveillance cameras all over the hospital and grounds. I'll see when we can view them."

"Good idea. What would you like me to do?"

"Stay where you are until I can get there."

Thereafter, Stome placed a call to the warden's office with the same basic objective—to report the escape. He left a message with an answering service that would immediately forward the bad news to the warden.

He waited outside Munchak's vacant room and caught a wave of second thoughts for what he'd done. But then he had third thoughts that washed away the second thoughts.

In the ten years he'd known Munchak she'd never crossed a soul and wasn't the criminal type, making it obvious that she got railroaded by a zealous prosecutor.

To add fuel to the devil's fire he'd constructed a long road of bad choices. He shouldn't have taken any women into the closet of the laundry room, but Munchak was among those who deserved it the least. Now he was fighting for her freedom and his very soul.

He wondered if he should tell his new and righteous wife that he had wedged himself between two awful sins: namely, he could either fess up to everything and face the music, which would surely send him to prison and drive a stake into her heart; or, he could deceive her forever, just as he had done to so many others, and live with the hot coals of guilt.

Suddenly, his quagmire was interrupted. The Warden was calling back.

45

EXCITING THINGS RARELY HAPPENED to prisoners, especially at midnight, but after several hours of deep sleep, I sensed that I was riding in the back of a noisy vehicle. Then I barely heard a woman's voice.

Still groggy, I forced myself awake and glanced toward the driver. All I could see was a dark beard. Beside him sat a woman.

"Roomie? Zat you?" I asked in a near whisper.

She perked up and swiveled toward me. "Hi, Sweetie. How you feeling?"

"I dunno," I mumbled while scratching my bandages. "What's going on?"

"It's almost midnight. We're near the state line."

"What?"

"Nevada. We're almost to Nevada. This is Randal. You can thank him for getting you out of that nasty hospital."

"Pleased to meet you," the scraggly-haired driver said. "How's it feel to be in the wind?"

I rolled my head back and forth. "You guys shouldn't have done this."

Roomie smiled. "Too late now. It's already done."

"But they'll revoke your parole."

"Nobody is going to know," Randal said. "Cause I thought of everything."

Roomie clucked her tongue. "Not everything, Smarty Pants. I brought some things that Miranda needs to get better."

I tugged at my bandage and sighed. "You got any pain meds?"

"Told ya so," Roomie said to her boyfriend.

After washing down three Tylenol, I began to understand the situation but still had lots of questions. Based on our cruising speed, the hospital had to be way behind us.

"Not that I'm complaining, but what made you two think you could get away with this?"

"It was my idea," Roomie said, proudly.

"But how'd you get me outta there?"

"Randal picked your cuffs just like he said he could."

"Yep. Picked all three in a minute flat," he bragged.

"But how'd you get past the guard?"

"Simple," Roomie said. "The guard was that Stome guy. We gave him some knock-out coffee."

Randal nodded. "We waited for the pills to do their thing, then slipped right passed him to get in your room."

"Now, here's the strange part," Roomie offered. "After we got you on your feet and shuffled past him, the fucker said, 'Good luck.' He was conscious! I couldn't believe it, but then he said he was gonna wait a few minutes before blowing the whistle."

My tired jaw dropped. "That animal has been trying to apologize to me for all the bad things he did to me. He must have been serious."

Roomie shook her head. "The important thing is we got you outta there."

"By now," Randal said while changing lanes, "the cops are probably looking at the hospital's surveillance videos to see what kind of vehicle we were driving. Even if they find it, they won't know who we are or what we really look like because we had disguises."

"And we switched vehicles," Roomie injected. "That was another one of Randal's ideas."

"Really? I remember that other car, but I don't remember getting into this one."

"Doesn't matter now," Randal said. "They only know about the other car."

"Besides, Randal's friend has probably picked up the car and replaced the stolen plates with his real ones and the cops won't have no reason to pull him over."

"Another brilliant move on my part."

"That reminds me," Roomie said to her boyfriend. "You have to call your cousin in Houston--"

Randal grinned and raised a hand to stop her in mid-sentence. "It's already been handled, ma dear."

Roomie laughed out loud, reached over and put her hand high up on the inside of his thigh. "Like I said, you're the smartest man I know." She returned her attention to me. "So, how does it feel to be free for the first time in ten years?"

"It's hard to believe, but all I know at the moment is I gotta pee. I might need you to help me."

"Me and Randal already talked about that. You can't go in public places for now. You'll draw too much attention so we'll find a place where we can pull over."

"There's an exit in three miles," Randal said. "We'll find a side road."

He was correct. Within mere minutes I eased out of the van and took my first step on free land in a very long time.

"I'm still a little shaky, so I'll need to lean against the van and have you guys hold me up."

Not long thereafter, I returned to the back of the van. "I still think you guys should drop me off somewhere and get away before it's too late."

Roomie shook her head. "We ain't doin' that. Now get some sleep."

Comforted and worn-out, I curled up on the mattress, scrunched the pillow and closed my eyes.

"You know something?" Randal said to my former cellmate. "I'm gonna start calling you Roomie, too."

"Really? I like that."

46

Following Nick Stome's call to the sheriff's office, and very near midnight, three detectives and several uniformed officers popped off the fourth-floor elevator.

While the cops taped off the area, the detectives moved briskly toward Stome. The lead detective, a chubby 50ish female, spoke first. "Are you Nick Stome?" she asked sternly.

"Yes. I'm ashamed to say I fell asleep in my chair."

"We're with the Fugitive Apprehension Team of the California Department of Corrections and Rehabilitation. I'm Captain Phyllis Manny. These are Detectives Lisa Argyle and Lieutenant Cristobel Woodson. Additional officers are searching the building and the grounds for anybody suspicious. What's our inmate's name?"

Lieutenant Woodson smoothed his mustache and readied his cell phone.

"Her name is Miranda Munchak. She was a model prisoner until now."

"Does she have any aliases?"

"None that I know of."

"Is she armed or otherwise dangerous?"

"Hell, no. She's been in the hospital."

"There were accomplices, weren't there?"

"Yes. I've already told the sheriff and warden that."

"Then they could be dangerous, couldn't they?"

"I guess so."

"Alright then. What was she in for?"

"A couple murders, but as I heard it, there were no weapons and she got dragged into the crimes by her boyfriend."

Manny smirked. "Can you describe her?"

"Of course. White. Mid-forties. Five-foot five or so. About a hundred and thirty pounds, cropped, dark blonde hair."

Manny turned to her younger counterpart. "Get that description out to all agencies."

Detective Lisa Argyle snagged her cellphone from her suit pocket. "One BOLO coming up."

"Can we assume she's in a hospital gown?" Manny continued.

Nick Stome shook his head. "Like I said, I was asleep. I didn't see her get away."

"Can we assume that she was cuffed to her bed before that?"

"Damn right, but somebody picked the lock."

"Interesting. What happened before that?"

"Well, the inmate was given a sleeping pill by a nurse before nine. When I checked on her, she was zonked out, still cuffed to the bed and her ankles chained together."

"Then what?"

"A little later, out in the hall, a young woman offered me a cup of coffee that was supposed to be for her sister, who had left the building. The damn thing must have been spiked." He pointed to the side of his chair. "That's it on the floor. You might be able to lift some prints off it."

"We'll check that out. Can you describe that woman?"

"Sure. White. Mid- to late thirties, hundred and fifty pounds. Blue Jeans. Glasses. Pink blouse."

"Was she alone?"

"Yeah," he lied, "but I'm betting there was at least one accomplice."

"Oh, yeah, why's that?"

"There are a lot of crime-savvy women behind bars, but I haven't known many who could pick cuffs. In addition, Munchak may have needed some help getting out of here, so I'm guessing there's at least one additional accomplice, probably a male."

Manny and Woodson traded glances.

"Alright, we're just about finished for now," the captain said, "but I would like you to come down to the station tomorrow morning. We should have surveillance footage by then. Maybe that will trigger more of your memory."

"Of course. Anything I can do to help," he said as Detective Lisa Argyle returned to the huddle.

"Update that BOLO," Manny said. "Our escapee has at least one accomplice, but probably two and one is a male. Mr. Stome can give you descriptions."

While Argyle and Stome traded information, the others stepped aside.

"Are you buying this guy's story?" Woodson asked of his superior.

"I'm not sure, but a few of his answers sounded as if he had sympathy for her. A guard wouldn't usually be that way."

"I wouldn't think so. What now?"

I want to check the background on Stome and our bird. I'd like you to call the warden and the prison counselor. Ask if Stome has ever shown any excessive fondness for any of the prisoners; and while you're at it, get me a list of everybody who has called or visited this Munchak woman, going back to her first day. I also want a list of the current prisoners, and any others who have been released in the last year. And don't forget the staff and vendors."

"That could be a thousand names."

"True, but if this job were easy, we wouldn't need smart fellows like you, would we?"

"No, ma'am. I'll get right on it."

47

In the very early morning and no longer under the influence of a sleeping pill, I awoke to the sounds of whirling tires and country music on the speakers. It took a moment before I recalled that I'd become a prisoner "in the wind" and we'd been on the road for quite a while.

Part of me was sure that we'd get caught and I'd be responsible for drawing Roomie and her friend into committing crimes that could land them in prison. More selfishly, I didn't have much to lose.

"Good morning, you two," I said toward the front seats. "Where the heck are we now?"

Roomie pivoted to speak over her shoulder. "Good morning, Sweetie. We took a little nap, but now we're on our way to Utah. Randal found us a place to stay until you get better. Thank God, he has lots of connections."

"Speaking of connections," Randal said, drawing a burner phone from his pocket, "it's time to remind my cousin to make some calls on our cellphones."

While Randal made his call, Roomie spoke to me. "So how you feeling, Honey?"

"Not real bad. I'm still sore but at least I'm not chained to a bed."

"That's good. We're gonna pull over pretty soon for gas

and food. You'll have to stay out of view, so we'll get take-out. Later, we'll get you a toothbrush and some hair dye and decent clothes from Wal-Mart."

"Are you sure you don't want to drop me off someplace? You really don't need this."

"Stop saying that. As soon as you can walk without drawing attention to yourself, we'll get you a new identity. It's all Randal's idea."

"Why bother? We'll probably get caught and sent right back to prison."

"Ain't gonna happen," Randal said, joining the conversation. "Before you know it, you'll have a new name, Social Security number, a birth certificate, and a driver's license."

From what I'd seen of Randal to that point, I had my doubts. "I heard of people doing things like that, but I never knew how it worked."

"It's like anything else. You have to know the right people and do things in the correct order. For now, all you gotta do is recover so that you can enjoy your freedom."

"That's right, Honey," Roomie said, "We didn't do all this just to get busted again." She turned toward Randal. "What crime would we be charged with?"

"Oh hell, cops can think up a bunch of them. Things like Kidnapping. Conspiracy, Endangerment, Harboring a Wanted Felon — not to mention that crossing a state line is a parole violation."

"Well, I don't care," Roomie said. "Miranda is innocent and deserves to get out of that place."

My brain may not have been operating on all burners, but I felt like a slice of burnt toast: cooked and headed for the trash.

"I wasn't actually innocent, Honey," I reminded her. "As far as I know, I didn't commit those murders, but--"

"Miranda had blackouts." Roomie said to Randal, "but there weren't any witnesses, just dead people."

"Yeah, but I was willing to steal money from an elderly woman."

"Maybe you were willing, but you never actually did it, and you had no other way to pay your brother's medical bills."

"But conspiracy to commit insurance fraud is wrong too, and I hoped that her insurance company would cover the loss."

"There we go," Randal said, pointing ahead to a McDonalds. "Roomie and me will go inside to get some food and take a leak while you stay out of sight. After we get back on the road, we'll look for a place where you can relieve yourself too."

Precautions like that made me suspect that he may have actually served time. "Got it," I said. "Can you leave the radio on? I hope I'm not on the news."

When we pulled into the lot, I hunkered down under a blanket in the back of the van. When my nostrils sniffed the air, it occurred to me that I used to hate McDonalds and other drive-through places, but this time, I couldn't wait to get at an Egg McMuffin and a few french fries.

After I wolfed down my breakfast, we pulled into the lot of a combo convenience store and gas station. Once again, I stayed out of sight while Randal and Roomie gathered near the gas door at the back of the van. They must not have realized that I could hear everything they were saying, but it was fairly clear.

"We need to conserve our cash," he said.

"No prob," Roomie said.

"Good," Randal added. "Another thing: Don't forget when we get to Utah and your friend is better, we have a deal. Right?"

"That again? Sometimes you have a one-track mind. D'you know that?"

"Yeah, but we all deserve some special fun."

"I'll try, but right now I want to find some oatmeal-raisin cookies."

After gorging ourselves, we pulled over so I could take care of my business. "Sorry to be so crude," I said, "but this time I gotta poop."

48

As we proceeded eastward, the rising sun was another one of those first-time-in-ten-years things.

"You squirming back there?" Roomie asked.

"Yeah, I'm trying to get comfortable. Where are we, anyway?"

"Utah state line," Randal said. "How you feeling?"

"I'm rested, but I'm still stiff from not moving very much."

"Do you need another Tylenol?" Roomie asked.

"Not really, but I need to change my bandages; and let me remind you that you can drop me off anytime you want."

"No way," Randal said. "We've got you covered."

"But the police are going to catch us sooner or later. They always do."

Roomie turned my way. "You hush that talk. We can do this."

I sighed. "Well then, thank you both."

Roomie reached into a paper sack. "For now, we can celebrate with this bottle of champagne."

"Oh, my God," I said, propping myself up. "I haven't had a good glass of wine--"

Randal turned slightly. "I thought you guys could get wine in prison?"

"Once in a while somebody will share some crappy

homemade wine that they made God-knows-how, or a bottle of liqueur someone sneaks in through the back docks."

"Well, you deserve some of this good stuff," Roomie said, "because we've got something else to tell you."

"Really?" I said reaching for a glass she'd poured for me. "What you got up your sleeve now?"

Smiling, she handed me a sheet of paper. "Simple. When you and your son were in surgery, Randal and I found the boy's room. This has all his contact info on it."

Suddenly the champagne was irrelevant. I anxiously shivered as I examined the form. "Oh my God, his real name is Trevor Montgomery. He lives in Cincinnati." I pulled the paper to my chest.

"Here's something else," Roomie said, smiling and handing me one of Cody's get-well cards. Inside, there were good wishes and a comment about his church paying for his airfare to the hospital. I wanted to scold Roomie for stealing my son's precious card, but it touched me deeply too. Tears crowded into the corners of my eyes.

"I saved the best for last," Roomie said, handing me a framed picture. "Looks like it was from a few years ago," she added.

A good picture? A wave of chills spread up and down my back. A beautiful young boy, perhaps seven or eight, stood next to a bicycle with a tawny brown dachshund at his side.

Tears gushed down my cheeks. "He's perfect," I said to Roomie in a cracking voice. "I can never repay you for this."

Randal winked at Roomie and then spoke to me. "We'll think of something," he said with a mischievous tone.

I'd never loved anybody in my entire life like I loved Cody and Roomie and Randal at that moment, except maybe my brother, Mickey. I clung to the photo while we drew closer to our destination and I wondered if I should start calling my son Trevor.

During the final stretch, we cruised past a large truck stop. "Just a few more miles to the house," Randal said.

I sat up. I hadn't been in a normal neighborhood for a long time. I admired the lawns and trees. "There it is," Randal said. "The one with the blue trim."

I eased back down so nobody would see that a slow-moving escaped con had arrived.

Randal parked the van. Then, "They're not home so you guys stay here for a couple minutes. I gotta go round back and get the key."

"This place is going to be nice," Roomie said turning around. "I'm so happy for you, Miranda. I just can't quit smiling."

"Me too, but I'd sure like to change my bandages."

"We'll do that as soon as we unload and pee. I gotta get rid of some champagne."

I looked out the van window. "You and Randal seem to get along real well. How'd you meet him?"

"You know me. I'm always trying to have a good time. One night I went to a bar and he asked me to dance. He was sexy as hell and single. We went outside to this van and did it right there on that same mattress. It was hot."

"Sounds like it."

Just then Roomie pointed toward the rising garage door. "Looks like he got in the back door," she said.

A tired Toyota took up one stall, but the other was empty. Randal motioned for Roomie to pull the van into the vacant spot. Excited, I clutched my picture of Cody and waited until Randal tapped the button that brought the door down.

"Everybody out," Randal said before helping me out of the van. We wandered through a normal-sized door which led to the laundry room and then to the kitchen.

Randal pointed toward the central hallway. "Roomie and I get the master bedroom 'cause it has a private bath. Miranda, you get the girl's bedroom and the central bathroom."

I felt like I should have been toting some luggage, but I

was wearing everything I owned. I inched down the hall and into a real bedroom of my very own, where I rested Cody's picture on the bed stand.

"Good news," Roomie shouted from back in the kitchen. "We've got some frozen food."

49

WHEN ROOMIE ANNOUNCED that she found some food, it seemed presumptuous to me. "Are you sure it's okay to eat their food?" I asked.

"Sure. They told Randal we could help ourselves."

"That's right," Randal said, having rejoined the conversation, "We'll leave them some money or replace anything we eat before we leave."

"Alright, then. After we eat, I desperately need a shower and some clean clothes. I've been wearing the same underwear for days."

"There are some undies in the master bedroom dresser." Randal said. "Help yourself. Helena won't care."

"I can't do that, Randal. It's too personal."

"No prob," Roomie said. "I have a tee shirt and some sweats you can wear until we get you something else."

"I'd rather do that. I'll wash our clothes a little later, that is if you guys think it would be okay to use the washer and dryer?"

"Course it is," Randal said, turning on a TV in the living room.

Happier than a puppy dog, I rushed into my bathroom, gently dropped some bath crystals in the tub and eased into a tiny sea of solitude where I savored the miracle of a private bath.

Warmed both in body and spirit, I closed my eyes and wondered how Cody was doing.

Then, I heard the floor creak outside the door. I noted a shadow underneath the door. Roomie wouldn't eavesdrop on me, so I knew who it was. "Do you need something, Randal?"

"No. Sorry. You were so quiet, I wanted to make sure you're okay."

Yeah, right. This wasn't the first time that his dirty mind had undressed me, but it would have been unwise to alienate him. I forced a kind voice.

"Thanks for worrying about me, Randal, but I'm okay."

I soaked until my fingertips shriveled. Then, I smelled something incredible. I toweled off and donned Roomie's mismatched jogging outfit, which was surprisingly comfortable. In the kitchen, she had managed to nuke some frozen lasagna.

While we ate, Roomie told me that after she went to prison her sister, Naomi, almost disowned her, especially when Naomi was forced to sneak drugs to a guard.

"She said not to call her if I ever get arrested again," Roomie said.

Yikes! Another wave of guilt swooshed through me. "That is what I was trying to say before. This is way too risky for you guys. You should drop me off in town somewhere and get back home before the police catch us all. I'm probably going back to prison sooner or later for the rest of my life anyway, but you guys don't need this."

"We already plowed that ground," Randal said, staring at my braless breasts.

Suddenly a TV report came on about the escape. A very old picture of me filled the screen.

"The escapee is Miranda Munchak," the announcer said. "She's 45, has dark blonde hair and has at least two accomplices. They are expected to be in a white SUV."

"What a bunch of dumb-fucks," Randal said with a prideful grin.

Roomie had a more pragmatic idea. "This proves we gotta get you a new look, ASAP: clothes, hair, eyeglasses."

After the report, Randal hit the mute button on the TV remote.

"After Roomie and me get cleaned up we'll take the Toyota for some wine and groceries."

"Can you get some bandages and antiseptic too?" I asked.

***

A short time later and on their way to the liquor store, Roomie tapped her boyfriend's shoulder. "I've been meaning to ask you, how'd you know about Helena's panties?"

"Huh? Panties?"

"You told Miranda that she could get some panties out of Helena's dresser."

"Oh that. Easy. When I first got into the house, I scoped things out."

"So that's what took you so long."

"Yep, had to do it when Miranda didn't see me. The master bedroom has some jewelry and a few guns that we can pawn. In the other bedroom, I found a box of checks that we can use to get gas and food and clothes for Miranda."

Surprised, Roomie tilted her head. "I don't get it. Why would you steal from a friend? It makes me think you'd steal from me too, and--"

Randal raised his hand to stop her. "One of the things I've always loved about you is your naiveté."

"What's that supposed to mean?"

"Simple. I don't really know the owners of that place. I just saw two women jawing on Facebook. One of them said she and her family had booked a 17-day trip to Europe. The timing fit perfectly for what we wanted to do...so, I did a search and found out where she lived. In the meantime, I've been checking Facebook regularly. That dumb bitch is posting pictures and comments about her whole itinerary.

Bottom line is Miranda owes her comfort to an unknown woman with a big mouth."

Roomie raised her hand to her mouth. "Wow. That's so weird I don't know what to say."

"Not only that; you remember that SUV I borrowed?"

"Of course. What of it?"

"I stole it off a used-car lot. The dummies had keys in several vehicles."

"No way. You said you borrowed it from a friend."

"I know. That's what makes it so funny. Damn thing is hotter than Tabasco sauce in August."

She cupped her hands over her mouth. "Now you're scaring me. What about the phones? Do you really have a cousin in Houston or is that a sham too?"

"That one is real. If the cops ever get to us and check the calling logs, they'll see we were in Houston during the jail break."

"Whew!!! That's good to know."

"You don't got to sweat it. You only got one more thing to worry about. You gotta pay your debt and get Miranda into the bedroom with us. I bet she's hornier than a nest of rabbits in heat."

50

After the sheriff called the California Department of Corrections & Rehabilitation (CDCR), they put Stome on temporary leave with instructions to remain close by.

By mid-morning, Captain Phyllis Manny of the Fugitive Apprehension Team (FAT) had interviewed Stome and contacted the National Crime Information Center (NCIC), with all of Miranda Munchak's identifiers.

Not long after that, Manny and her team got hold of the hospital's surveillance videos and prepared for a follow-up chat with Stome.

Toward that reunion, Stome drove slowly and rehashed the how-what-and-why of it all. Ultimately, he literally asked himself what Jesus would want, and the answer was clear; he had to aid in Munchak's pardon.

Of course, that gave rise to a problem of his own. If he couldn't find some way to wiggle out of the legal mess that he'd created, he could expect to do a lot of hard time. Worse, male cons had no sympathy for incarcerated authority figures, so he would be kept away from the basic prison population, which could drive a man insane.

To avoid that web, Stome's best chance was to stick with the "I fell asleep" defense and hope they'd buy it. In that case, he might get off with a short leave of absence, with pay.

With all his secrets tucked into the back alleys of his mind, he reached the police building, where a desk cop escorted him to a room in the back of the building. Captain Manny and Lieutenant Cristobel Woodson had already set up a viewing station.

"Take this spot," Manny said to Stome, resting her hand on the nearest chair. Stome's butt had barely hit the seat when Lieutenant Woodson sat next to him, leaving the end chair for Manny, where she could watch both the videos and Stome's reaction to them.

Woodson began with a video of a suspect coming off the elevator with a tray of coffee. Manny pointed to the screen. "There's our lady. Do you recognize her?"

"No. She was fairly ordinary."

"Are you sure? The warden tells us that Ms. Munchak never has any visitors. Therefore, the vast majority of her contacts have been with other prisoners. That's why we think this lady could be a former inmate or a friend of an inmate. Does that make sense?"

Stome could feel Manny's cold eyes glaring at him. "Yeah. I guess so, but I don't recognize her."

"Could it have been a man in a disguise?"

"I don't think so. I heard her speak enough to know that."

"Take another look. This is important."

Stome feigned a stare, noticed the woman's dark hair and chubby build. He genuinely didn't recognize her. "I don't know. She had bangs. Is overweight, but millions of women fit that description."

Manny nodded to Woodson. "Fast forward."

In the next scene, a nurse walked past Stome in his chair. "Stop right there," Manny said. "See there, Mr. Stome? Your head is leaning against the wall. It appears you were asleep at this point."

He lowered his head. "Yeah. That's exactly what happened."

Manny urged her partner to proceed, and a moment later a woman and a bearded man wearing a baseball cap appeared on the monitor. "That looks like your coffee friend," Manny said. "What about the gentleman? Did you recognize him?"

"How could I? I was asleep."

"But you're not sleeping now. Look closer. Does he look familiar or not?"

After the obligatory glare, Stome raised his eyebrows. "Not really. I guess his beard could be part of a disguise. I'm afraid I can't help you."

"Next," Manny said to Woodson.

This time, the characters in the video slipped past the sleeping guard and inside Munchak's room.

Manny seemed to be staring right through Stome, who remained as calm as he could and until the moment when Munchak and her accomplices slipped past him.

"Stop it right there," Manny said to Woodson. "See that, Mr. Stome?"

"See what? I didn't see anything."

"Just as the bearded gentleman passed by you, he turned back toward you as if to say something. Why would he do that?"

"I really have no idea."

"Could it be because he was responding to something you said to him?"

"How could I? I was asleep."

"Maybe. Okay Cristobel," Manny said to her subordinate, "Let's follow our perps to the exit."

Scanning a series of camera angles, they watched the Munchak gang work their way through the hospital halls and eventually out the cafeteria doors and onto the sidewalk.

"What about that white SUV?" Manny eventually asked Stome. "Do you recognize it?"

"It looks like a Ford Explorer, but there's nothing distinguishable about it."

"Are you sure you don't know somebody with a vehicle like that, because if we can trace it back to you—"

"Sorry. No connection."

"Then you won't mind if we scan your computers, cell phone records, and bank accounts to see if there is any suspicious activity."

Thankfully, Stome's records were as clean as a whistle. "Of course," he said, "but it'll be a waste of your time."

"Good. If you're clean, you won't mind taking a poly this afternoon, would you?"

He hesitated, then noticed Manny and Woodson trading glances.

51

AFTER SUNDOWN, Randal called his cousin in Houston to log in some additional calls on his and Roomie's primary phones. While he did that, Roomie asked if I'd like to go dancing with them to celebrate the escape. But I wasn't strong enough for that — and I was afraid somebody might recognize me.

"Better not," I said. "Believe it or not, I'd rather load the dishwasher, watch TV and walk around a little. I saw a box cake in one of the cabinets. Do you think it would be okay for me to make a cake?"

"Sure, it would. That's a great idea."

They were barely out the door when I turned on the TV. Even a simple thing like that held forgotten value. Back in prison, the TV room was a place of constant conflict. There were only a handful of approved channels to choose from and nobody could agree on what to watch. Bloody fights were followed by forty-eight hours of solitary confinement.

But there in Utah, I had so many choices I couldn't decide what to watch. There were game shows, movies, music videos and everything else. They all deserved my attention. I settled on a real estate show in which a couple had to remodel their home and decide whether to keep it or sell it. While that little puzzle played out, I skipped into the kitchen and whipped up that lemon cake that had my name on it. Throughout that wonderful time, my mind had room to wander.

At one point, I looked into Roomie and Randal's room where a dressing mirror stood upright in the corner. I couldn't resist the urge to take an honest inventory of my body. I removed the sweatshirt, sweatpants and Wal-Mart panties that Roomie had bought me. I stood naked before that damn tattletale mirror.

While my eyes examined my body it was embarrassingly obvious that prison had not been kind to me. In addition to tiny wrinkles at my lips and the bags under my eyes, my boobs sagged. So did my butt. On top of everything else, there was now an ugly scar on my tummy that kept my stretchmarks company. I doubted whether I would ever be attractive to a normal man.

Back in the living room the couple on the TV had decided that a completely remodeled home was not good enough for them and yet I was thrilled with a single bedroom. With that mystery solved, I changed the TV to a crime-drama movie. I felt naughty because such programs were forbidden where I'd been living.

Sometime after midnight, I heard the car pull into the driveway and then into the garage. Roomie and Randal and I stayed up at least another hour, which was another forbidden thing I hadn't done for years. Eventually, I couldn't keep my eyes open and sought the privacy of my very own bed. This time there would be no breakfast-bell or nurse to awaken me.

I smile now, because the peace didn't last very long. A combination of Randal's shamelessly loud bedroom profanities and Roomie's record-setting screams of ecstasy caused me to wrap my pillow around my ears until I fell to sleep.

The next morning, I heard squirrels playing tag on the roof. That too was something I'd forgotten. While I lay there, I marveled at how my liver had unexpectedly morphed into a ticket to freedom. Then, my thoughts were drawn to some mumbling on the other side of the wall. A moment later Roomie and Randal were at it again, like a couple newlyweds. I'd never imagined anybody making that much noise in a bedroom, but it was genuinely erotic contrasted to prison sex of any kind.

This time I didn't cover my ears, but rather I closed my eyes, slowly slid my hands over my body and imagined that I was in a similar situation with a lover of my own.

52

LATER THAT MORNING I made some coffee and did some stretching exercises. A short time later, Randal emerged from his room, clad in tight blue jeans and a wrinkled, pink polo shirt. He pointed his chin at me. "You seem to be moving better."

"Yeah, I've been walking back and forth a lot, sometimes with food cans in plastic bags. It feels good to get around on my own again."

"If you want to go for a walk, there's a park just up the street. They have some walking trails that go all the way to a truck stop that we passed on the way in."

"I have to admit that I'd love the open space, but that TV bulletin advised viewers that I'd just had surgery and to watch for somebody who is gingerly scooting along so I'm not quite ready for that."

"Probably a good idea, but when you're back to normal Roomie and I have a surprise for you."

"Really. You've already done too much for me."

As usual his eyes trickled down my front. "I'm sure you'll have your chance to repay us," he said with too much confidence for my comfort.

Just then, Roomie ventured out of the master bedroom and nodded to Randal, "It's all yours."

"Great. I always love a hot shower."

Alone with Roomie, she addressed me. "How you feeling?"

"Noticeably better now that I can walk around without clinging to a nurse."

"Glad to hear it. I hope Randal and I didn't make too much noise in bed. I'm a little embarrassed but he likes it loud when we make love."

"So I heard, but it don't matter to me. I'm glad you have somebody to love. I just wish there was some way I could repay you for what you've done for me."

She looked over her shoulder and then whispered, "Now that you mentioned it, there is something I want to discuss with you, but I'm not sure what you'll think."

"Really? I don't have anything I can give you, but I can do all the cooking and—"

"That's not it. I'm a little uncomfortable to ask this, but I'm just going to come out with it. Would you like to take a shower together and then make love?"

I probably should have been surprised by the proposal, but I wasn't. I assumed that she was simply offering to comfort me like the old days.

"I'm flattered that you'd consider my needs, Honey, but it'll probably be quite a while before I do something like that — and as much as I love you, it wouldn't be with a woman. So, let's think of something else that I can do. Okay?"

Roomie's eyebrows pressed downward. "I don't think you understand me, Miranda. I'm not just talking about you and me. Randal wants to be in on it, too. You know, a three-way."

Noggin, meet palm. Of course, he did. Randal oozed more testosterone than a battleship full of Navy SEALs, and he'd been scanning my body like a radar operator all along. Those masculine vibes had to be one of the reasons Roomie loved him. That didn't shock me either. I knew from our prison chats that she'd been with quite a few men and she was free-spirited when we were cellmates. In fact, a fair number of our peers were like that. They talked openly about participating in threesomes and everybody knew about open marriages and clubs in which couples exchanged partners. So, I wasn't shocked by the concept or that Roomie was willing to participate. But I preferred a typical monogamous relationship with men who drove decent cars and liked a little romance.

I'd fallen for men like that several times - my ex being the greatest example. Ed could be very charming when he wanted to, but he proved to be a cheater and refused to fix it. Anyway, none of that candlelight romance activity fit Randal. He was about as debonair as a drooling, 200-pound St. Bernard administering stud services.

Suddenly, "Ah, that's a lot better," Randal said, having rejoined us. At that moment, with his hair pulled back, a towel resting on his shoulder and wearing nothing more than a pair of frayed boxer shorts, the man didn't look half-bad. Throw in a six-pack that rippled from his waist to his muscular chest and it was easy to see why Roomie was drawn to his body.

"After I get dressed," he said to me, "Roomie and I have to get some cash and run a couple errands. When we get back, you can go to Wal-Mart with us if you'd like."

Hmm. I was never a Wal-Mart type, but that was then, and this was ten years later when nearly everything was new.

"I wouldn't want to draw attention to any of us."

"There has to be a first time," he said while he tugged his towel off his shoulder, revealing his hardened nipples. For some reason, I doubted he'd been circumcised. "We'll park toward the back of the lot," he continued. "That way you can easily get in and out of the car. Once we get inside you can hang on to the buggy for support if you need to."

"That might work," I said, turning to Roomie. "Do you suppose that I could borrow that wig of yours until I can dye my hair?"

"You got it, Honey."

53

"I TAKE IT WE'RE GOING TO A PAWNSHOP NOW," Roomie said to Randal as they backed Helena's Toyota out of the garage.

Randal nodded. "Got to. We're running out of cash. That jewelry box I lifted is behind your seat. See what you think."

Roomie recovered the box, lifted the lid and grabbed a dainty crucifix on a golden chain. "I don't think we should pawn this. It just wouldn't feel right."

"Fine with me. Why don't we give it to Miranda? It might give her comfort."

"Good idea. She hasn't had any new jewelry for a long time."

"I'm just hoping we can get a grand for the rest of those items."

"I'm no expert on these things," Roomie said while scoping out the cross, "but I can't imagine a woman leaving valuable jewelry in plain sight."

"I guess we'll soon find out," he said as the pawn shop came into view.

A short time later he returned to the Toyota, threw $250 on the dashboard and banged his fists on the steering wheel. "That bastard knew we were desperate, so he took advantage of us."

"We could try somewhere else."

"Naw. Those jerks are all alike. They know that people don't give up their valuables unless they have to. Now all we got left to sell are three guns and we can't do that at a pawnshop because they want an ID. We gotta find a private party or a swap meet and we gotta go easy on spending money."

"Okay, but I gotta get Miranda some dye and Tylenol."

"I'll take you to Wal-Mart. Hopefully, you can steal those things."

Roomie sucked air through her teeth. "I don't like that idea. If we get busted it could ruin everything."

"They wouldn't do much for such a small amount but I guess that means it's best to just buy what we need – along with some wine for our threesome."

"But I already told you she didn't go for the idea. She's got a lot of heavy shit on her mind."

"It shouldn't be a big deal."

"I don't know, Baby. She's got a lot of heavy shit on her mind."

"Look. We both know there's no better way to work off pent-up anxiety than to have a couple drinks and fuck each other's socks off. Now, what kind of wine do you want?"

* * *

While R & R ran errands, I stuffed my sweats in the washing machine by the back door. Wrapped in Helena's robe, I bagged my canned goods and walked briskly around the house in longer and quicker spurts than before.

A short time later, slightly winded, I moved the clothes from the washing machine to the dryer where some movement at the window caught my attention. A closer look revealed a large slit in the screen. It seemed odd considering how well the home was kept, but it was none of my business so I resumed my exercises and actually looked forward to my upcoming jaunt to Wal-Mart.

210

At that point, I'd been wearing drab prison garb for so long I would have loved any colorful new clothes, even if they came from lowly Wal-Mart. Eventually, the duo returned with some spicy food, a bottle of wine and some hair dye. I almost jumped for joy, but a frown on their faces suggested something was wrong.

"Randal's account is messed up," Roomie said, "so we won't be able to take you to Wal-Mart."

"She's right. The bank's computer is fucked up. I'm gonna call those bastards and make them apologize."

You'd think that after a decade of setbacks I would have rolled with the bad news, but I lowered my head. "I understand."

Roomie sat on the couch and patted it so I'd sit next to her. "I know you're disappointed, Miranda, but Randal said we can still get you some decent clothes from Goodwill tomorrow. For now, why don't we enjoy this Mexican food? I can assure you it's better than what you're used to."

Goodwill, huh? I was the kind of person who gave things to Goodwill, but I'd never bought anything there. I almost cried, but a glass of wine and an awesome meal took some of the sting away.

"We can't stay here forever," Randal said while dipping some chips in salsa. "So, we have to work on getting you a new identity."

I would have never imagined doing something like that, but I knew he was correct. "How do we do that?"

"We'll go to a big cemetery and find a handful of women about your age, who died three to five years ago, but not the most recent year because survivors could still be transacting business in that person's name."

"Why do we need so many?" I wondered out loud.

"We need somebody who worked for a small employer. Then we can get the Social Security number, and presto, you'll become that person."

I wasn't entirely ready for something like that, but I knew I couldn't keep my name much longer.

"Eventually," he continued, "we'll need to get you a place where you can receive mail. Cheap motels and homeless shelters will do that. With an address, a Social Security number and Date of Birth, which we already have, you can get a Replacement Driver's License on line. Then you can use the driver's license to get a birth certificate. After that you can get a job and save some money."

"I'd really like that. I know a little about painting. Maybe I could be a salesclerk."

He shook his head. "I have a better idea. What would you say to dancing in a strip bar?"

Roomie slapped his arm. "What's the matter with you? She's not going to do that."

"Besides," I said. "Nobody wants to see my ugly scar or sagging body."

"I was just kidding," Randal said while eyeballing the front of my sweatshirt. "It's been a long time since you've been laid. How would you like to do something about that?"

Roomie slapped him again. "Stop talking like that."

That yucky trait of his was mildly irritating but I held back because I still needed him and Roomie. "Well, thanks, but I've been looking forward to dyeing my hair."

54

Meanwhile, Nick Stome agreed to meet with a polygrapher for a lie-detector exam, which was riskier than letting the Fugitive Apprehension Team peruse his personal records. After he finished the test, he held mixed feelings about the outcome.

"So, how'd I do?" Stome asked the detectives with cautious optimism.

Captain Manny shook her head. "Not real well."

"Oh, bullshit," he said with feigned confidence. "Why are you guys acting like a bunch of buzzards?"

"Easy. Our investigations employ the 'pebble in the pool' concept. Most of the time, the mischief maker is right in the middle of it, and that means you."

"I get it, but you better move on to some other ripple in that pool of yours, because you're wasting your time and mine."

"Perhaps, but if we find any evidence that you're entangled with Munchak's captors, then we'll arrest the lot of you. Now answer my questions and we can all get out of here."

Stome took note of Manny's choice of words. If she was looking forward to "getting out of here," then they must already believe that he had not conspired with anybody about the escape and was therefore only guilty of nodding off, which he could pin on the sleeping pills. For the moment, all he had to do was stick with his story. "Alright. What do you want to know that I haven't already told you?"

"For starters, the test was inconclusive about you having anything to do with the escape. How do you explain that?"

"How would I know? That's your department."

"Yes, it is, and I'm telling you that you had a couple of blips regarding the time between when you accepted the coffee and the actual escape, so I'm asking again, why is the test inconclusive?"

"I dunno. It might have something to do with my daily duties."

The Captain glanced at Woodson and then back to Stome. "Explain that."

"Sure. Guards are constantly on patrol inside and outside of the prison. We regularly pass the cells and scope them out to see if everything is as it ought to be – no contraband, beds made, personal items stowed in the footlocker, things like that."

"Yeah? So?"

"Once in a while, when we walk by, an inmate is on the pot, or changing her underwear. Most of the time, they look down the hall before they do that, but other times they forget or don't give a damn."

"Alright, I'll bite; what does that have to do with what we're talking about?"

"Simple. I've seen Munchak in her most vulnerable moments and she doesn't like it."

"So, you've ogled her?"

"Of course not, but part of my job is to visually examine the cells whenever I walk by and that can lead to some compromising moments for the more reserved inmates and I feel bad about invading her privacy. Besides that, Captain, we both know that poly's aren't reliable. That's why the results are not admissible in court. So, if that's the only thing that bothers you, we both know that I passed your test with flying colors, and the only thing I did wrong was fall asleep on duty, and I've already acknowledged how careless that was."

A gentle knock interrupted the moment. Detective Lisa Argyle poked her head into the room and spoke to her boss, "You said you have a job for me?"

Manny nodded before returning her attention to Stome. "We're done for now, Mr. Stome, but you're not off the hook."

"Alright then; let me know if you need anything else."

After Stome departed, Manny and her subordinates gathered around the table. "So, what did you think?" Detective Woodson asked of his superior.

Manny sneered. "Something about that guy bugs me, but the warden told me he's not the type to show sympathy for inmates."

"Well then, when we add that to what we just heard it sounds like we should look elsewhere for now."

"It sounds like it, but I want to try one more thing, before we put him in our rearview mirror."

"What's that?"

"I'd like you two to take turns tailing him for 48 hours. He knows we're bugging his cell phone and emails, so if he has any nefarious cohorts, he's got to talk with them face to face. Keep me posted and we'll have another powwow, day after tomorrow. After that, I want to chase down Munchak's ex. He might know if she has any other relatives or old friends that may have been involved in the escape."

55

I'D NEVER DYED MY HAIR BEFORE, but Roomie had some experience with the procedure so we stayed up late. She began by giving me a major haircut. I actually like it. Next, we hid my natural color behind a shade called Espresso Brown.

Meanwhile, Randal was messing around on his iPad. "I found something interesting. Do you guys know about Zillow?"

I hadn't heard of it, but Roomie had the right idea. "You can look up house prices. Right?"

"It's more than that. It has pictures of every neighborhood and home." Then he looked right at me. "You know what that means, don't you?"

"No, what?"

"You've got your kid's address on that paper we took from the hospital. You wanna see what it looks like?"

We scoped out Cody's home and neighborhood, near Cincinnati. I probably should have felt comforted by the exercise, but instead a wave of anxiety reminded me that I'd literally given him away.

After a restless night, Roomie and Randal and I met up in the kitchen. "How ya feeling?" Roomie asked.

"I'm definitely getting stronger. Now, I gotta get some different clothes, so I can give you your sweats back."

Roomie hugged me. "I'm excited for you. Randal and me can be ready in a little while."

"That's right," Randal said. "You can drive if you want to."

He might as well have spritzed my face with seltzer water. "I'd better not. It's been ten years since I've been in public and I'm nervous enough as it is. If somebody recognizes me as the escaped fugitive that they saw on TV, I might panic and screw up and crash into a building."

"That ain't gonna happen," Randal said. "That's why you cut and dyed your hair."

"You're probably right, but I'd better wait until I don't have the jitters."

"Up to you," he said sweetly.

After cereal, we piled into the Toyota with me in the shotgun seat because it was less challenging and nearly painless compared to getting in back. Predictably, I gawked at everything until we bypassed a Wal-Mart in favor of the parking lot at a Goodwill store. My stomach churned at the thought of somebody recognizing me.

"Can you get me a pair of shorts and a blouse first?" I asked Roomie. "I'll feel less conspicuous if I wear some normal clothes when I go in there."

Some minutes later Roomie returned with a colorful, long-sleeved plaid blouse and coveralls. "This is cute," I said. "It reminds me of a farm girl."

"True, but they don't have many other things in your size. The clerk said anything nice in your size goes right out the door, but I think we can get you a couple decent items."

"Well, I gotta wear something other than your sweat suit."

Inside the store I quickly learned that Goodwill had some better-quality items than Wal-Mart. I scored a near-new pair of tennis shoes and a black bra, some sunglasses and enough additional clothes that I could wash one outfit and still have something else of my own to wear around the house besides underwear.

"We'll come again in a few days," Roomie said while we all returned to Helena's car.

"Now, we've got a date with death," Randal said as we drove up the road.

At a very old cemetery on the outskirts of town, we spread out and marched up and down rows of headstones, paying special attention to the death date of deceased women. Nearly everybody was way older than our target group, but we still nabbed a couple names. Then we noticed some newer foliage up a hill a ways. It took a while but we eventually found names of five additional women who were roughly my age.

"All we gotta do now," Randal said as we drove back to Helena's home, "is review their obituaries and find the ones who worked for small companies."

Back home, that was exactly what he did. He eliminated anybody who worked for governmental entities or large companies because most employees there were too organized and knew not to give out Social Security numbers.

Instead, one of the deceased women, named Eunice Waxman, had been dead for over a year. Her obituary said she worked at a local Gym and Fitness Club. Randal searched for clubs near Eunice's residence and got their numbers. A few calls later a young woman took his call.

He asked her if she knew Eunice and then pretended to be her husband.

"As you may have heard," he said, "she passed away last year. We're trying to deal with the damn IRS for her final tax return. They keep saying she owes a bunch of money, but you guys didn't pay her enough to owe that much money. Our attorney thinks that they've got Eunice's Social Security number mixed up with someone else's. Could you please look in her file and see what number you folks used on her W-2 form? It should only take a minute."

I listened in awe. Sure enough, Randal pulled it off. A moment later the woman returned with Eunice's Social Security number and Eunice became my benefactor.

Randal ended the call with a mile-wide grin aimed right at me. "How do you like your new name?"

"I dunno. It'll take a little while to get used to it."

"Well, you might as well start right now by memorizing your new Social Security number. After that, Roomie has a proposal for ya."

56

I'D NEVER KNOWN A MORE EXPLOITIVE MAN than Randal Biskitt. After pulling off a truly impressive accomplishment for my benefit, he immediately sent Roomie after me in another attempt to draw me into a threesome. But the idea of that was too much like my laundry room days, when I was nothing more than a meaningless tool to get somebody else off.

Roomie understood me so she was more pragmatic about the idea. "It wouldn't take very long and nobody else will know," she said at one point.

"I'm not passing judgment on anybody else," I replied, "but I'm not interested in doing anything like that right now."

She lowered her voice to a whisper and tried again. "It's been a long time since you've willingly been with a man, so it might not be so bad."

Logically, she may have been correct, but I was more concerned with regaining my strength and repairing my dignity than adhering to somebody else's logic. "That's not the point," I said.

"What is it then? Would it help if he used a condom or turned the lights off or didn't take video? Maybe I could get him to—"

"It's none of those things, and it's all of those things, Roomie. I know this is hard to understand, but when those guards took me into that laundry room, month after month, I vowed to myself that if I ever got out of there, I would never cheapen myself again and that's what a three-way is to me. It has nothing to do with you or Randal. In fact, I'm glad he makes you happy, but my self-esteem is already bruised so meaningless sex of any kind would only make things worse."

Her jaw tightened and she left the room, defeated. I knew she'd have to give Randal the bad news, but I didn't know how Randal would take the rejection.

To avoid any immediate tension, I grabbed Cody's picture and stepped outside and onto the little porch where I actually considered two opposing concepts: running away and turning myself in. At first it was scary, but a cool breeze inched me forward and I gathered enough courage to go for a walk all by myself.

On the way to the nearby park, my thoughts shifted away from my trouble with Randal and toward the flowers and trees and birds. Odd how therapeutic Mother Nature could be.

At the park, I walked around a long asphalt track that encircled the perimeter. I admired the sunshine, the clouds and the people.

Then a female jogger came from the other direction. I recalled the news flash on TV wherein they showed me hanging all over Roomie and Randal as we scooted down a hospital sidewalk. The video of that get-away wasn't very clear, but I was paranoid and suspected that the jogger would automatically recognize me anyway. I crossed my fingers and feigned a smile as she passed.

She simply said, "Hello," and kept on going.

Genuinely optimistic, I increased my pace and within mere minutes I passed several other folks coming from the opposite direction. They too were friendly and oblivious to my identity. I felt like a normal person and silently thanked Roomie and even Randal for my dyed hair, different clothes and the care that eventually enabled me to walk without assistance. For a brief moment there, I felt guilty for denying Randal the one simple thing that he wanted for all that he'd done.

Temporarily conflicted, I made it to the backside of the park where another woman, this one with a cellphone to her ear and a perky boxer on a leash, were walking toward me. It occurred to me that everybody took simple things for granted, including their freedom and health. While they were traipsing around the park to their hearts' content, prioner 1516103-A was still recovering from liver surgery and had clearly walked too far.

57

IT TOOK NEARLY AN HOUR to slog my way back to Helena's home. The entire lap around the park would have been a masterful cathartic cleansing were it not for my other lingering hurdles, such as becoming Eunice Waxman and what to do about the 160-pound penis that Roomie and I knew as Randal.

For one thing, there was no guarantee that he'd be content with a one-time event, so my life would revert right back to sex slave mode. It was all very disquieting, but at the same time it indicated that sooner or later, I'd need to break away from Randal and Roomie to reduce everybody's risk.

Anyway, as I wrestled with my predicament, I rounded a corner and observed a middle-aged couple walking toward me. For a moment there I thought they might be FBI agents, poised to take me into custody. My stomach tightened.

"Hi, there," the woman said while the man handed me a flier. "We're Chris and Christie. We're having a block party up the street a little later. We hope you can come."

Yikes. Trading "hellos" with a few strangers in the park was one thing but a party would require complete conversations where somebody might recognize me.

"I dunno," I replied.

"Well, we're gonna eat around five. Which house are you from?"

I pointed a nervous finger to the second house up. "That one, with the blue trim. The owner is letting us stay there for a while."

"Cool!" the women said. "If you decide to come, bring a dish of some kind if you can."

The fellow nodded. "We got a keg, but if you don't like beer, you'll have to bring your own drinks."

As I walked away, I let out a deep breath. Maybe the whole world wasn't focused on me after all. A few additional steps and I pushed in the door of our temporary home. Inside, shirtless Randal spun my way. "Where's Roomie?" I asked, just to avoid a more stressful topic.

His eyes penetrated mine as if we were having some sort of ocular intercourse.

"I know that you and my girlfriend have been slow-playing me," he said, "but you're running out of time. You know that, right?"

"I know what you want, but I'm still healing and I couldn't do anything like that right now, even if I wanted to."

Just then, like a godsend, Roomie came from the bedroom. "I saw you talking to those people outside. What did they want?"

"Oh, them? They're having a block party later today and invited us to come, but I don't think I'm ready to mingle with a bunch of strangers."

"That figures," Randal said, plopping in the recliner. "How the hell are you going to play with the big dogs if you pee pee like a puppy?"

As usual, he had a good point. "It's been a long time since I've done anything normal so everything feels awkward."

Roomie sat right next to me. "I've been there, done that, Honey, so I know what you mean, but you have to become that Eunice woman and get back in the game."

"I don't know how I'm going to do that, Roomie. Eunice worked in an exercise club, but I don't know anything about a place like that."

Randal shook his head. "What the fuck's the matter with you, Miranda? Do we have to put everything on a goddamn silver platter for you? When somebody asks you a question, act like they just threw a porcupine in your lap; give a short answer and throw the damn thing right back by asking them a question. Most people will gladly carry the conversation if you'll ask the questions."

I would have liked to yell in his face for hurting my feelings, but he was a perfect mentor for me in that moment. His blunt lessons were right on. I needed to stop thinking like a timid escapee and become Eunice Waxman. That party would be a good place to start. "All right. I'll go, if you guys will go too."

As the party drew closer, my confidence bounced back and forth. On the one hand, what if I accidentally told someone my real name? What if a real-life detective was invited to the party? Those people were trained to read the tea leaves. On the other hand, I had to get out in public sooner or later, otherwise I was still living in a cell.

I eventually slipped into my room, wrapped myself in a quilt and decided to go to that party with my chin up. If everything went well, I could get in and out of the party without seeming out of place. But more importantly, I'd be one step closer to functioning on my own. I reached for Cody's picture and wondered how he was doing.

58

IN THE OLD DAYS I had several things I could wear to most occasions, but all I had for the neighborhood party was the plaid blouse and coveralls that I got from Goodwill. "Are we going to take some wine?" I asked Randal and Roomie just before we departed.

"Hell, no," Randal said. "Why would we do that if the beer is free? We ain't going to take no food neither. There's always way too much food at these 'bring a dish' events."

Roomie pointed to the kitchen cabinets. "At the very least we should borrow a package of Helena's cookies."

A short walk later we reached the home of the party, where a rumble of voices, kids included, wafted from the back yard. At the side gate a handsome man with dark wavy hair scooted toward us. "Welcome. Welcome. Happy Friday to you folks. I'm Vince. Come on in."

While Randal and Vince shook hands, I nervously quick-eyed the yard where two dozen adults, mostly in their thirties and forties, loitered near the back of the home while a handful of kids were determined to break the decibel meter. "The keg-beer is free," Vince said.

"That's good," Randal said, "because I only like two kinds of beer; microbrews and anything that's free."

226

"Good enough," Vince said with a grin. "I see you brought your sisters."

My former cellmate smirked. "Call me Roomie. Randal and me are practically engaged."

"It's nice to meet you, both," he said, turning my way.

And there it was; my first opportunity to speak with a non-prison stranger in a typical social setting. "I'm Eunice," I said, holding up the cookies. "Sorry. We didn't have enough time to pick up something from the deli."

"No problem. We got plenty of food. Come on in and mingle."

Whew! I followed Roomie and Randal into the yard, where Randal turned my way. "You go drop off the cookies. Me and Roomie will meet you near the keg."

A chill tapped my backbone. There were at least a half-dozen people between the food tables and me. I had to wedge my way through a cluster of strangers and hope that none of them recognized me from the TV newsflash.

As I wiggled toward the table, one of the women took a step backward and bumped right into me. "My name is Eunice," I awkwardly blurted as she spun around and looked me in the eyes. "I mean, I'm sorry. I hope I didn't make you spill your drink?"

"Are you kidding me?" she said smiling, "I'm the one who backed into you. I'm the one who's sorry."

It wasn't exactly the smoothest moment, but with my first potential disaster averted, I said, "Okay, let's call it a tie."

I proceeded to the food table where I hid the cookies near a pan of thick homemade brownies. My assignment completed, I spotted Roomie and Randal near the back of the lot, talking with another couple. More or less on my own, I would have liked a glass of wine, but Randal had already nixed that idea. Instead, I eyed the keg.

"Hiya," a man said from my left and behind me. I turned to see if he was actually talking to me. "My name is Morris," he said. "I saw you and your friends when you came in. You weren't wearing a ring, so I thought I'd say hello."

I'd pretty much expected something like that, but I didn't expect to get drawn into a conversation that quickly. Grateful that prison-life hadn't made me completely repugnant, I looked again and noticed well-groomed grey hair and a little more girth than on most of other men in attendance.

"My name's Eunice."

Morris grinned and pointed to the keg. "Can I buy you a beer?"

The humor of a witty man was yet another thing I'd nearly lost. "I'd rather you gave me the money," I said, hoping I didn't sound too flirty.

"Okay, I'll go along with that if you'll lend me ten thousand dollars for my funeral."

"Let me guess. You'll pay me back right after the services?"

He grinned again. "I see we've both heard the same joke. Do you live nearby?"

A little less comfortable, I pointed up the block. "We're staying with friends."

We shuffled toward the keg, "so, what does Eunice do when she's not hanging out at block parties?"

Fortunately, I'd recalled Randal's porcupine concept. "Well, my ex and I used to run a small restaurant, but we got a divorce some months ago. So, I'll be looking for a job pretty soon. What about you? What do you do?" I asked, expecting him to say he was a detective and I was under arrest.

"I'm an engineer. The desk kind, not the choo choo kind."

Just then, a crackle came over a speaker. "Listen up, everybody. Listen up." The female voice bellowed from behind the food tables. A 35ish woman with an acoustic guitar draping her shoulder and a thin nine-year-old lad with unruly blonde hair, presumably her son, had something in mind. Predictably, a boy of that age caused me to think of Cody.

"Dexter here has decided that he likes singing," the lady

began, "so we've been practicing a few songs. We thought we'd play them for you now."

"Yeah, we call ourselves Dexter and Mom," her son said, earning a few giggles.

Morris and I maintained a dash of small talk, while the duo sang a few blockbusters such as "You Can't Rollerskate in a Buffalo Herd" and the ever-popular "On top of Spaghetti," a parody of "On Top of Old Smokey."

When they completed their short set of songs, Dexter and mom wandered toward Morris and me. "How'd you like us, Grandpa?" Dexter asked Morris.

Surprised, I smiled at Morris and suddenly yearned for a real and full relationship with a man.

"No doubt about it," he said to his offspring, "You're getting better."

Then Dexter looked at me, presumably for a supporting comment. I wanted to be honest with him, but the performance wasn't very good so I went with a different truthful answer. "You know something, Dexter? Your courage really inspired me. That kind of thing can take you places."

"I hate to be a party pooper," Dexter's mother said, mostly to Morris, "but I've got to meet somebody else so me and Dexter have to get going."

Morris nodded. "Okay. I'll be with you in a couple minutes," he said before addressing me.

"I've enjoyed your company, Eunice, and would like to see you again if you'll give me your number."

He seemed to be a nice guy, and he had helped me climb out of my shell to some extent, but that certainly wasn't going to happen. "I'm flattered, Morris. If things were different, I'd take you up on your offer, but I won't be dating for a few more months. Thanks, anyway."

After Morris disappeared, I felt more confident and traded benign conversations with several other people before drifting to the food table. Homemade cooking looked fantastic. I wanted one of everything but picked out small servings of a half-dozen different dishes.

While in mid-meal, Roomie approached me with teary red eyes. "Randal has been flirting with other women all night," she whimpered. "Right now, he's in the house hitting on a bimbo with big boobs. I'm going home."

I didn't know how Roomie could be shocked by Randal's behavior. The man had a one-track gutter for a mind. "Do you want me to go with you?"

"No," she said, shaking her head and walking off. "You need to stay here."

Another thing I needed to do was appease Mother Nature. Inside the home, the restroom was busy, so I waited in the hall and caught a glimpse of Randal talking to a large cleavage with a head of big hair and an ample amount of makeup. Surprisingly, he was bragging about how much he loved his wife. Maybe Roomie had misjudged him.

59

"We shadowed Stome," Detective Lisa Argyle said to Captain Phyllis Manny at the next meeting of the FAT team, "but he stayed home, unless he went out with his new wife."

"Oh, yeah, where'd they go?"

"Nowhere in particular: a couple stores, a gas station and to church. He never talked with anyone suspicious."

"That's right," Lieutenant Woodson said. "It was benign. If first impressions mean anything, his wife is a straight arrow."

"Good to know," Manny said. "You got anything else?"

"The coffee cup came back. No prints except Stome's."

"That's suspicious, too."

"How so?"

"The woman who gave him that coffee handled the cup, so her prints ought to be there."

"I see what you mean."

"Moving on, the warden got us a complete list of all the current prisoners, as well as all the parolees over the last year, plus anybody else of special interest. You're going to interview the bulk of those people to find out if any of them are tight with Mr. Stome or know anything about Munchak and the escape."

"I don't mean to whine," Woodson said, "but there must be over seven-hundred prisoners to interview—"

"Actually, it's closer to nine-hundred plus the other folks. I'll get a couple other detectives to help you. Also, it turns out that Munchak runs a painting crew. You can start by interviewing them."

"Painting? Pictures?"

"No. They paint individual cells. It's cheap labor for the prison and a few extra dollars for the inmates. Apparently, those ladies are quite fond of Ms. Munchak. They might know her secrets. Meanwhile, I've recruited Sergeant Bradburn to assist me in interviewing Munchak's former husband and a few others who might know where she would go. Let's all stay in touch."

That afternoon, during a two-hour drive, Captain Manny filled in some blanks for her current partner, Sgt. Daniel Bradburn, a well-dressed thirty-something African American with a sharp-looking goatee.

"I brought you along to brainstorm with me and because you're known as a body-language expert. I'd like you to watch for any indications that this guy might know more than he tells us."

"Got it," the sergeant said. "Didn't you say that our escapee was in the hospital when she got away?"

"Yeah, as a liver donor – for her son who was adopted."

"Maybe somebody in that group helped her get away - to thank her."

"Doubtful. She's never met that family and all the communications went through the warden, attorneys and doctors."

"You're probably right. What's your next angle?"

"The warden said Munchak has never had any visitors, except doctors when she had a benign brain tumor removed, but that was five years ago. Aside from that she had a very small circle of influence. We're going to start by talking with her ex."

"Good. Sometimes exes stay in touch. He may even be our male accomplice."

"Or, he might know how to find her parents or other people she's known."

"That too. What about any former prison pals? Cons talk to each other a lot. They could know a few things."

"The warden said the best bet would be two close friends who've been paroled. The first one is Mary Ruth Saines. She's north of seventy, can barely walk. The other one is a Candice Carmichael. Mid-thirties. Munchak's former cellmates. We'll get to them after we check out the ex."

After twenty additional minutes of bumper tag, Manny and Sgt. Bradburn found the home of Munchak's ex and rang the bell.

Manny flashed her badge at the curly-haired dude who answered the door. "Are you Ed Franklin?"

The man nodded. "What's this about?"

"Your ex. We need to ask you a few questions."

"Which ex? I have three of them."

"Miranda."

"Oh really, I heard she's in the big house for life. Is that true?"

"Could be. How long were you married to her?"

"About four years. We were not a good match – course, all my exes would say that."

"Oh, yeah? If you don't mind my asking, why did you split up?"

"Simple. I'm a player, but she's a boring 'straight arrow.'"

"Can you elaborate for us?"

"Sure. She's the kind of person who won't break the rules; drives below the speed limit; keeps her fork on the right; loyal as a service dog. I wasn't like that. Usually had a little action on the side. She couldn't handle it."

"Then why did you get married in the first place?"

"Same old shit. I kept my secrets and she was like all the other women on the planet – they think they can change us. After we split the sheets, she changed her name back to her maiden name."

"When was the last time you saw her?"

"A long time ago. After our divorce we didn't have any reason to get together."

"What about her family and friends?"

"She had a couple roommates before we got married. As far as I know, she never talked with them after that."

"Did she stay in touch with anybody else, like co-workers, classmates, clubs?"

"Not that I can think of."

"What about family?"

Ed Franklin grinned. "Now there's a strange group. Miranda loved her twin brother, Mickey, even with his issues, but she couldn't stand her parents."

"Why not?"

"Sad story. Mickey was a slow developer, then he got into some poison when he was a toddler and went completely cuckoo. The old peeps didn't want to deal with him, so they dropped him off at one of the government facilities like a bag of laundry. When Miranda was old enough to figure out what happened, it pissed her off. A couple years after high school, she took over his guardianship. Far as I know, she never spoke with her folks after that."

"You got their names and addresses?" Manny asked while Bradburn readied his cell phone.

"I don't have the exact address," Franklin said, "but they used to live on the northeast corner of Ferrell Blvd. and Edison Parkway in San Jose. Had a big hedge around the place."

"What about the brother? You know where we can find him?"

"Mickey won't be any help. He's got brain issues. Been institutionalized all his life."

"We'll have to verify that too. Where can we find him?"

"I don't know where he is now, but last I knew, he was at a place called Broadplace, or something like that. It's inland, somewhere."

"Alright, just one more question. Lots of people split up

and try to get back together. Did you and Ms. Munchak ever try to reconcile?"

Ed laughed. "No chance in hell. Why would a playboy want to wrestle with a chastity belt when there are so many free-spirited honeys to be had?"

Manny shrugged. "Thanks for the info. We might have more questions for you later."

"Yeah, sure. If you do catch Miranda, say hi to her for me."

"We didn't say we were trying to catch her."

"You wouldn't have asked all those questions unless you were trying to find her."

Back in the car, Manny spoke to her partner. "There's a gas station up here. While I refuel, see if you can confirm whether Mickey Munchak is capable of helping his sister escape, or if he remembers any relatives that we haven't heard about."

After a few taps at his cell, Bradburn found the facility that Ed Franklin mentioned and placed the call.

When Manny rejoined him, he had her answer. "Mickey Munchak couldn't have helped with the escape because he died three years ago."

"Oh. Alright then, that means our next stop is at her parents.'"

"Yeah, but they're on the other side of home base and five hours from here. Are you certain you don't want them to come to us?"

"I'm certain. I like to catch them off-guard so they don't have a chance to make up a phony story. Plus, I like to see them in their own environment. But you're right about the distance issue. We'll get back to home base for now and regroup in the morning."

60

Randal was correct again when he said I needed to go to that party. When I first arrived, I was paranoid that somebody might recognize me as the woman who had escaped from a California prison, but everybody appeared to be oblivious to the story, and that elevated my confidence.

When I returned to our place Roomie sat puffy-eyed in front of the TV. Randal was in their bedroom, arguing with somebody on his phone. "I know it's none of my business," I said, "but have you two patched things up?"

Roomie dabbed a tear. "He's a hypocrite. He flirts with anybody who has tits and then gets pissed off if I look at some dude."

"Well, I wouldn't be too shook-up about it. I've got some good news for you along those lines."

"Good,'cause we're due for some good news. We're running out of money and we gotta get home sometime next week so one of us can get a job."

I sat next to her. "I'm really sorry that you've spent all your money on me. I'll pay you back someday."

"That's okay. Breaking you out was my idea, and it was worth it, but I couldn't have done it without Randal."

"That's sorta what I wanted to say. After you left the party, I heard him talking to the woman you'd mentioned."

236

"Let me guess. He was trying to get in her pants."

"No. No. It's the opposite. He referred to you as his wife. Even said that he's crazy about you. And now, you're telling me he gets jealous when you look at other men. Don't you see? He loves you a lot more than you know."

She paused, cocked her head and gave a faint smile. "Maybe you're right. Thanks Miranda, er, Eunice. You've made me feel a lot better. What about you? Who was that snazzy gentleman? You seemed to like his attention."

"It's been a long time since I've had a normal conversation with a normal man in a normal situation, so it felt good, but I liked the boys who were about Cody's age the most."

"Don't you mean Trevor?"

"Yeah. I've been thinking about that. I've been referring to him as Cody for so long, it's not easy to think of him as somebody else."

"Well, I hope you don't have that same problem with your own new name."

"That's taking a little concentration, too. Anyway, I'm regaining my confidence and you guys made all that possible. No matter what happens after this, I'll literally never forget what you've done for me."

"And Randal. Don't forget Randal."

"Randal, too," I said. "You've both been remarkable."

Roomie glanced toward the hall and then back. "While we're being honest with each other, I have to tell you that he thinks you've healed more than you've indicated, and he's mad at me for not convincing you to go along with his proposal. To be perfectly honest, it seems like you could 'love' him for what he's done for you. That way it wouldn't be meaningless sex."

"She's right," Randal said from the hall and joining our conversation. "I've seen you moving around. You're doing just fine. I think we should do that three-way right now — and video it."

I wanted to scream. I knew that I owed them the world,

but I also knew that I could screw Randal every Friday for a year and that still wouldn't satisfy him. Besides, back in my laundry room days, I felt cheap and vowed that if I ever got out, I'd only have sex if it was meaningful and romantic to me, and there was nothing they could do to fit Randal in that mold.

"Look, Randal," I said, hoping to buy a little more time, "I know I owe you a lot, and I know that a lot of people do things like that these days, but after what I went through in the prison laundry room, I don't want to be pressured into anything like that."

He scoffed, "Stop pretending to be so damn righteous. Roomie told me what you guys did, so I ain't buying your bullshit."

Stunned, I eyed Roomie. "You agreed not to say anything--"

"I know. I'm sorry, but I didn't think I'd ever see you again."

"So how much does he know?"

"All of it," Randal said. "The naked hugs, the fingering and licking, and those tiny vibrators. She also said you had other girl-on-girl action before she got there - not to mention the guards. I bet you enjoyed some of that attention too."

Shocked and disappointed, I glared at Roomie. "No wonder he's so aggressive. He thinks I'm easy."

Roomie turned to Randal. "Look, Honey, I sorta exaggerated because it aroused you."

"Oh, bullshit. You're just covering for her."

"No, she isn't," I said before retuning my attention to Roomie. "Go ahead, tell him the whole thing."

Roomie sighed in Randal's direction. "If you must know, whenever we did those things, it was usually because I needed the affection. I was ordinarily the one who asked Miranda to hold me."

"I don't care who started it," he said, obviously irritated. "Either one of you could have said no and taken care of your own needs, but you didn't. Instead, you wrapped yourselves into knots and got each other off. That means you both liked it."

"Okay Randal. You're right," I said. "Either one of us could have backed off, but we didn't so I liked the affection too, but all of that was out of necessity. I knew I'd never be with a man again and Roomie and I loved each other so it was what the situation called for. But it's different now. You two love each other and I have new hope."

"That's right, Honey. When I met you and found out how hot you are, I lost interest in anybody else - man or woman. It's a different situation."

I nodded. "The important thing now is you guys love each other, and that's all that matters."

"Wrong," Randal said. "The important thing now is, you owe me and you've got twenty-four hours to change your mind, or you're going to regret it. I can guarantee that."

61

AFTER MY MOST RECENT STANDOFF with Randal, I sought refuge in the park where I could think more clearly.

It seemed to me that I could either engage in Randal's offbeat fantasies or find a way to take care of myself. But to climb that impossible mountain, I'd need a useable ID and maybe even a driver's license, not to mention the traditional necessities like food, clothing, shelter and a job. Regrettably, I had none of those things, nor a means to acquire them. Net result: I still needed Randal.

With my time running out, I returned home where Roomie grinned like a naughty coed and turned toward Randal. "Go ahead, tell her what you're going to do."

"You mean about the gun? I was just saying that we need some operating capital so I'm going to sell one of my favorite guns at the flea market in the morning. That'll solve our money problems for a week or so. You ladies can come with me if you'd like."

There he was, being all nice again. Things like that made me think that if I actually "appreciated" him one time, it might be barely, sorta, maybe, almost hold-your-nose tolerable. At least he hadn't forced himself on me like the guards did.

"Really?" I said. "That's very generous."

Temporarily pleased with himself, he went out to get us

some ice cream and wine. Before the night was over, we finished off the ice cream and wine but ignored the elephant in the room; my twenty-four hours were tick, tick, ticking away.

The next morning, I still hadn't made a final decision, but I was looking forward to the flea market.

Unfortunately, Randal was long gone and that brought things back into perspective. Randal may have said and done nice things from time to time, but he was so narcissistic, most of his good intentions were as fleeting as smoke in the wind.

I dragged myself into the bathroom and made eye contact with the woman in my mirror. She reminded me that Randal loved Roomie so much that he had risked everything to set her friend free. I genuinely appreciated that part of him. Then, I thought about the other side of the Randal coin and disliked him again. Back and forth I went. Randal was bad, Randal was good.

Just as I was about to pull my dyed hair out by the roots, Roomie knocked. "Hey. You okay in there? When you're done, I have something to discuss with you."

Moments later, with the house to ourselves, we sat together on the sofa.

"Yesterday," she began, "I noticed that you two were getting along pretty well, so I'm hoping you've decided to go along with his request?"

I sighed. "I admit that he has been more endearing lately, but that doesn't mean I want to let him mount me."

"But you and I have been together before so it wouldn't be that weird."

"I know, but that was different. What do you think he'll do if I just say no?"

She shrugged. "That's hard to say. I don't think he'd force himself on you because he hates men who do that, but he's real serious about this threesome idea. What would you say to some sort of compromise?"

"A compromise? How do you do half of a three-way? You

two should take me to a bus station and I'll go somewhere else."

"You can't do that. They might have your picture on a bulletin board. Besides, where would you go? What would you do?"

"I dunno. Randal mentioned homeless shelters."

"But that can't be very safe and I want us to stay together."

"I'd like that too, Roomie, at least until I can get an ID and maybe a job."

"That's why you still need him and why I think we should find a way to make him happy - some sort of compromise. What's your biggest concern about his proposal?"

"I have a ton of them. For starters I don't trust him."

"What? Why not?"

"He has no self-control. He could put the video on the internet, not to mention that he's an insatiable sex machine. We both know that he won't be content with a one-time fling. He'll expect me to do him anytime he wants until I'm completely on my own, and I don't want to do that. In fact, I'm surprised that you're willing to share your boyfriend."

"Why not? I've made love with both of you, and I want you both to be happy."

"No offense, but when I want to be happy, I don't think about boinking my best friend's boyfriend."

"Regardless, if we're going to work this out, we gotta come up with a compromise. Let's at least try?"

Common sense sucked sometimes. I paused, took a deep breath and sighed. "I guess I owe you that much."

Obviously encouraged, Roomie sat up and smiled. "Okay, what's the most important thing to you?"

"Alright. To begin with, if I do anything along those lines, there won't be a video. That way nobody else will ever know about any of it."

"I don't know if he'll accept that. What else?"

"I dunno. I'm sorta accustomed to communal showers. Would he settle for watching me take a shower?"

"Come on, Miranda. You're a nice-looking woman and I'm sure he'd enjoy that, but that's not the spirit of a three-way. At the very least I think you ought to give him a blow job or a hand job."

Yikes! As unpleasant as that sounded it was pretty much what I expected, but I meant what I said. "No way. I don't want to touch him and vice versa. That's final."

Roomie's eyes went blank as if she were in deep thought. Then. "I have an idea. Would you be willing to switch roles with him and film him and me while we do it? If he gets to show off, he might agree."

Hmm, that was less horrible and actually sounded like a workable idea. "If I do that, I want a full bottle of wine to get my mind off the whole friggin' exercise. And, one more thing: I want a whole day to change my mind."

"Now, we're getting off course."

"Too damn bad. This is supposed to be a compromise and I've made a huge sacrifices. He can take it or leave it."

"Okay, I'll ask him, but I don't think he's going to like this idea."

"Well, that's one thing we can agree on, because I don't like it either."

62

Eventually, Randal returned from the flea market. He immediately grabbed Roomie and lifted her off her feet. "I did it. I sold the gun."

Roomie held her hands together as if she was praying. "Now we can get Miranda a few things."

"Yeah, but we gotta go easy on the spending."

"Sure, and I've got some good news for you regarding your three-way idea."

Randal's eyes shot my way. "Great, when do we start?"

"I'm getting to that," Roomie said. "But first, we're all going to sit down and I'm going to speak for Miranda because this is very difficult for her."

"What's the big friggin' deal? I saved her ass and we all want to have some fun. It's about damn time."

"Not so fast. I want you to sit down and listen to me – really listen. This is important."

He glanced at me again. "Yeah, sure, I guess I can wait a few minutes." He plopped on the couch and I sat in the recliner.

Still standing, Roomie began. "We all know what you want, but Miranda can't do that right now because of some of the things she had to do in prison."

"Yeah. The laundry room capers, but that don't matter now. She's free to party."

"No, Randal. You don't know what it's like to have somebody exploit you. It's not a party. You can lose your faith in people and your self-respect. It's not easy to overcome something like that."

"Blah blah blah. What of it?"

"Well, I can tell you that we had a very long talk, just like this one. She respects your position. But we also want you to respect her position by going along with a compromise."

"A compromise? Really? That's high-schoolish."

"No, it's not. Miranda knows how much you've done for her, but she can't do what you want right now. Maybe later, but not right now."

He tilted his head and slowed down a bit. "All right, all right, I get it. She still hasn't put prison behind her, so what did you two nut-cases come up with?"

"Like I said, you both got to respect each other. She's come half-way. Now it's your turn."

"Half-way? Okay, I'm listening."

I almost applauded for Roomie, because it was the first time I'd seen her take control of him.

"There will be no video," she said, "and you won't get to touch Miranda in any way, but we'll do something just as exciting. Miranda will flip-flop with you and video me and you doing anything and everything you want. We'll talk dirty and she'll get close-ups and side views – all of it. And you can show the whole world what a great lover you are because you can do anything you want with the video, even put it on the internet. The best part is, it will still be like a three-way because we'll all be in the room at the same time."

With that Roomie quickly looked at me and then back to Randal. "If you want to know what I think, I think you should do it because I'm getting horny just talking about it."

It was all so bizarre, I expected Randal to laugh out loud, but instead he tilted his head to the side. "I guess that might be interesting."

Roomie wrapped her arms around his neck and kissed him, "This is why I love you. You always surprise me."

He nodded and smiled. "Well, we can always do a complete three-way the next time."

I looked right at Roomie and broke my silence. "See. I told you. He's already planning for the next time."

"Don't be crying on my shoulder," Randal said. "Your silly little plan takes a lot of meat off the bones, so it only buys you a few days. Besides, I'm betting that you'll loosen up after you see how fun I can be."

That was impossible, but there was no reason to elevate the tension. I'd just bought some time. I wasn't at all enthusiastic about the agreement, but I did have a debt to him and at least I had some say-so in the matter. Besides, previously Randal stated that our hosts would be coming home in less than a week so I might have an ID by then and that would be a short step away from a job, which would be the end of Randal's power over me.

Suddenly Roomie spread her arms. "Team hug!"

I didn't feel like hugging anybody, but "Ambassador" Roomie was so juiced up I went along with her gesture.

Predictably, Randal's hug included a low-hanging hand that stopped at my butt. I brushed it away, but Randal wasn't done.

The next time Roomie went to the restroom, he confronted me.

"So, we have a compromise, huh?"

"I guess so," I said, trying to step around him, "but I don't like those kinds of things."

"Bullshit, I'll bet you actually had a little fun when you got used to fucking those guards."

Exasperated, I felt like I could blow steam out my ears. "You don't have a clue. I only did that because I had no choice."

"More bullshit. You did it so everybody else would like you and leave you alone. The fact is you fucked those guards because you wanted to. You're no better than a crack-addicted whore. You both trade your pussies for the things you want."

I felt like a cornered rat.

63

AFTER OUR MINI-WAR Randal drove off to parts unknown. Roomie and I watched TV until Randal pulled into the garage and entered the kitchen area with a full haircut and a trimmed mustache. "Whaddya think?" he asked.

Roomie rushed for him. "I love it. Give me a big kiss."

"What about you, Miranda," he asked in a sickening tone. "Am I too pretty for ya?"

"I think you look better too."

"Good. It's unanimous. Now, what we gonna do for dinner?

"Miranda's making meatloaf," Roomie said. "You and I can go get some wine first."

"Sorry, Baby. I got a couple calls to make. Can you go by yourself this time?"

Yecch! Not wanting to be alone with Randal again, I cringed. But fortunately, the store was close by, so Roomie would likely return before he could get aggressive.

When Roomie drove off, Randal moved into the garage with his phone. Since the garage was on the other side of the wall, I could hear his conversation, and the angry tone.

"Uncle Mitch?" he said loudly to whomever he had called. "You don't got no Uncle Mitch, Honey. Go tell your mother I want to talk to her right now."

I knew that eavesdropping was rude, but something bizarre was going on and he was on my bad side again, so I kept listening.

"What the fuck's going on, Kristy?" he snapped at the next person. "Our daughter just told me that some dude named Uncle Mitch stayed overnight. If I find out that you've been fucking some other man, so help me God, I'll kill him and take our kids away. You're my wife, and I own you. You got that?"

My eyes must have been the size of golf balls. Neither Roomie nor Randal had ever said anything about him having another family. I knew that I had to tell Roomie even though it would break her heart. Then I got a wild idea and waited to implement it.

As the evening progressed and our dinner disappeared, I wanted to explode in Randal's face, but I restrained myself and waited for a chance to catch Roomie alone.

Finally, around eight, Randal wanted to watch a movie and I had my chance. "You know something?" I said to my friend. "I would love some fresh air and to gaze at the stars. How 'bout coming with me?"

Roomie glanced at Randal and then back to me. "Okay."

Once we were down the street, I slowed my pace. "I don't like to bring bad news, Honey…"

"You're okay, aren't you?"

"This isn't about me. I'm just wondering how well you really know Randal."

"I told you before. We've been going together for six months. Why?"

"What about his family? Have you ever met them?"

"No. He's kinda like you—doesn't have much family. Just a few folks in Oklahoma. But I've never met 'em. Why?"

"Are there times when he goes away for a couple days at a time?"

"Yeah. Every couple of weeks he likes to go camping. That's why he has a mattress in his van. He sleeps in it."

I exhaled. "When you went for wine, he slipped into the garage with his phone. I heard him yelling at a woman named Kristy. Do you know who that is?"

"Sure, his step-sister."

"Does she have kids?"

"Yeah. a couple of them. C'mon Miranda, what the heck are you getting at?"

"How about an Uncle Mitch? You ever hear of him?"

"No. Get to your point."

"I wish I didn't have to tell you this, but Randal clearly called that woman his wife and the little girl his daughter."

"Naw. She's his step-sister. That's all."

I shook my head violently. "No way. I heard him clear as a bell. He was super pissed off. Jealous about her sleeping with that Uncle Mitch dude. A brother wouldn't talk to a sister like that. Trust me, Honey, he's been cheating on you the whole time."

Roomie went silent and wobbled her head. "Are you sure?"

I looked her in the eyes and rested a hand on her shoulder. "You don't deserve this."

Tears formed in her eyes. "To tell you the truth you could be right. I've seen other clues along those lines, but I convinced myself I could trust him."

"I'm really sorry, Honey."

"That means when he was at the party and said he loved his wife, he didn't mean me. What should I do, Miranda?"

"I know what I'd do. I'd leave him."

"But he'd just find me again."

"Maybe so, but you can't condone his behavior. He'll just keep using you. I have another idea. We can walk to that truck stop up the road in an hour or so. If we're lucky we can hitch a ride."

"But where would we go?"

"I haven't gotten that far. Maybe to your sister's place. All I know is we have to leave before it's too late."

Roomie paused, then sniffled. "Nope. I ain't doing that.

I'm gonna confront him and give him a chance to explain himself, but if you're right, I'll do what you say."

"Okay, then. If we're going to leave him, we'll need a head start. If I'm right, let's plan to leave at four tomorrow morning and sneak away."

Roomie sighed. "I hope we don't got to do that."

"I know but he's a pathological liar and you'll always be his victim if you don't get away now."

She lowered her head and nodded, after which we returned to the house where the rest of evening was one of those deep-water situations. On the surface everything appeared calm, but below that a silent river raged.

I went to bed around eleven o'clock and set my alarm for a few hours later. Then I heard Roomie and Randal talking. Before long they got louder and louder and eventually went to the garage where Roomie yelled like a wild woman and that meant our plan was a go.

I didn't sleep well after that, but my alarm finally went off. I quickly shut it down and slowly eased into my lone pair of shorts and my only blouse.

When I opened my bedroom door, I heard a soft commotion in the kitchen and suspected that Roomie had just sneaked out of her bedroom too. Then I heard the garage door rising, which indicated that she wanted to take Helena's car, but I didn't want to do that.

Determined to convince her that we should walk rather than drive off, I tiptoed to the kitchen and then the laundry room in time to hear an engine start. I pushed the door inward where I saw Roomie backing out in Helena's car. Then the van moved, and Randal backed it out, too.

Oh, my God, they were leaving me.

I rushed toward them, but it was too late.

Dumbfounded, I quickly retreated into the garage where I tapped the button to lower the overhead door. As it descended, I rushed toward the center hall and looked inside their bedroom. They had taken all their things with them.

64

AFTER LOTS OF STOPS AND STARTS, Captain Phyllis Manny and her temporary assistant, Sergeant Daniel Bradburn, located the hedge that Ed Franklin had mentioned.

"Are you Mr. Munchak?" Manny asked the unshaven grey-haired man who opened the door.

"Could be. Who's asking?"

"I'm Captain Manny. This is Sergeant Bradburn. We're investigating the escape of a convict. Can we come in and ask you a few questions?"

"'Bout what?"

"Your daughter. It won't take long."

"We don't got no daughter."

"Are you saying that Miranda Munchak isn't your daughter, 'cause--"

"Oh, her? Haven't spoken with that fire plug for twenty-five years and good riddance."

"Twenty-seven years," a grey-haired woman said from behind him.

Daniel Bradburn addressed the woman. "Can I use your restroom, ma'am?"

"Let 'em in, Lawrence."

Inside the home, Bradburn went down the hall while the

captain focused on Mr. Munchak. "Why did you say good riddance when I mentioned your daughter's name?"

"First off, that Miranda person ain't our daughter no more."

"That's right," Mrs. Munchak said. "She was a know-it-all. When her brother got brain damage, we couldn't take care of him no more, so we turned him over to the state. Miss Smarty Pants didn't like that - but she didn't know how difficult it would have been for us to have that kid underfoot, so she had a hissy and we disowned her."

"I see. It must have been painful for you when he died."

Mrs. Munchak tilted her head. "Mickey died? When did that happen?"

"We heard it was a few years ago."

"Probably for the best."

"We're trying to find Miranda," Manny said, mostly to Lawrence. "Do you know where she is?"

"Don't you people listen? We ain't seen her in over twenty years."

"Twenty-seven years, Lawrence. I keep telling you it's twenty-seven years."

"Makes no difference. We don't even know if she's still in the country. Don't care, neither."

Bradburn returned and worked in a question. "What about cousins or old friends? Could she be in touch with them?"

Lawrence shook his head. "You guys just don't get it, do ya?"

"Just doing our job, sir. Would you mind if we checked your phone records for the past couple months?"

"Why the hell do you want that for?"

"To see if you're being straight with us."

"You callin' me a liar, mister? I don't take to that."

"No, sir, but we have to confirm everything."

"Well, you ain't gonna find nothin' so go ahead. Help yourself."

"Good. We'll need your contact information too - in case we have any additional questions."

Lawrence shook his head. "See what I mean. That girl has always been a pain in our ass."

Manny smiled at Mrs. Munchak. "Thanks for your time, ma'am. You've got a nice home here."

Back in the car, Manny addressed her partner. "That was revealing. If they didn't know that their own kid died, they probably don't know anything about our escapee, either."

"No wonder Munchak left home. Makes me want to call my own mom and tell her I love her."

"Good idea. Moms like that."

"Okay. What we doing next?"

"Tomorrow I'd like to look up those two parolees who used to be tight with Ms. Munchak. In the meantime, I want you to call their parole officers to get their contact numbers and any other info that might be useful."

"Will do."

"When you're done with that, I've got numbers for Munchak's former employers. I'd like you to check them out. See if anybody knows where she could be."

"No prob."

Manny tapped her phone. "While you're doing that, I'll check in with Argyle. She's still questioning inmates."

A minute later, Argyle took the call. "How are the interviews going?" Captain Manny asked.

"Typical," Argyle said. "Nobody knows anything. Quite frankly, I don't think they'd say anything that would help us."

"Yeah, inmates tend to be tight-lipped unless they can get something for their information. Have you spoken with her current cellmate?"

"Yeah. Name's Lenore Stevens. She wasn't any help either. When I asked her if she knew anybody who might have helped Munchak escape, she brushed me off."

"How nice of her," Manny added sarcastically.

"We've also asked the inmates if Stome could have purposely helped Munchak escape."

"Good. Any bites?"

"There appears to be bad blood between Stome and Munchak, but nobody would elaborate."

"How many people have you spoke with so far?"

"Let's put it this way. We've only talked with the paint crew, the guards and about forty additional inmates. There are hundreds more."

"Okay then, I'll get you some more help, ASAP."

65

AFTER ROOMIE AND RANDAL left Helena's house, they pointed both the van and Helena's Toyota toward California. At the first convenience store they pulled over for fuel. "How much money you got?" he asked her.

"Only two hundred dollars from overdraft protection at my bank."

"Alright I've got a little more than that from the gun we sold. That should be enough. While I gas up, I want you to go inside and buy a small amount of cooking oil and some baking soda. Also, get a large cup with nothing in it. You may have to pay for the cup, but that's okay. Got that?"

"Yeah. Cooking oil, baking soda, cup. Why do we need those?"

"I'll show you later. Let's keep moving. We've got a meeting to attend."

Thereafter, Roomie followed Randal nearly a hundred miles before he took an unexpected road toward some farms and country homes. She couldn't help herself and snagged her burner. "What the heck are you up to?"

"We're buying another car."

"What the heck are you talking about, Randal? We can't afford what we got now and who's gonna drive it?"

"Trust me. I got it covered."

Randal led her to a cute country home where a nearly identical, but wrecked, Toyota was facing the garage. When they pulled up to it, a gentleman with a cowboy hat slipped out of the house and addressed Randal.

"As I told ya on the phone, my kid got drunk and ran this thing into a tree. Now it's totaled."

Randal dipped his hand in his pocket and pulled out all his cash. "Well, thanks for saving it for me. Here's three hundred twenty bucks, just like I said."

"You got yourself a deal," the man said pulling an envelope from his back pocket, "you beat the other offer by a goodly amount."

Randal palmed the envelope. "I gotta do some work on it now. It'll probably take a couple hours."

"Since you paid in cash, you can take all the time you need."

"Okay, then. Thanks." Randal turned to Roomie. "I need you to round up the things we bought a while back."

Minutes later, Randal poured some cooking oil and baking soda into the cup. "Now stir this," he said, while opening the door to the crumpled Toyota and pointing to a sticker on the door frame. "I want you to dab this sticker with that solution until I'm done removing both dashboards. That should take us a couple hours or so."

"Okay, but why are we doing that?"

"I'll tell you later. Just keep that sticker damp. Now I gotta get my tools."

Nearly three hours later, Randal had switched the dashboards and checked Roomie's sticker. It was fairly soft so he made a phone call before he used a razor blade to remove both stickers and replaced the one in Helena's car with the other one. "All we gotta do now," he said wiping away the excess glue, "is put away our tools and wait."

"Okay then. Can you finally tell me what that was all about?" she asked.

"Yeah. All cars have Vehicle Identification Numbers

plastered all over the place. But if a driver gets pulled over, the cops only look at the dashboard version and the sticker in the door frame. If the numbers match the numbers on the title, they can't tell that the car is stolen."

"But we're driving carefully. We're not going to get pulled over."

"Probably not, but look over there. See that tow truck and trailer coming this way?"

"Yeah. What of it?"

"You'll see."

Sure enough, the driver parked right next to them. He looked over the destroyed Toyota and handed Randal two hundred bucks. A few minutes later, the driver pulled the Toyota up on the trailer and drove off.

"We're done too," Randal said to Roomie. "Let's get out of here."

Confused, Roomie asked one last question. "Well, at least tell me why you paid more for a junk car than you got back for selling it just a few hours later."

"If you must know, when I found out that the tow truck guy was only willing to pay $200 for that car, I topped the offer so that the farmer guy would gladly sell it to me instead."

"But why? Just so you could switch dashboards?"

"Actually, it was all for this," he said, holding up the envelope that the car owner gave him earlier.

"What is it?"

"A title and a bill of sale that says I paid 4K for his car. That way it looks like any other transaction between two private parties."

"Huh?"

"It's simple. Everybody wins. The owner makes an extra hundred twenty bucks or so for selling to me. The tow truck guy works for a junkyard. Those people will sell the tires and battery and any other things they can and then they'll haul the carcass off to a salvage yard where they'll smash it for melt-down and get their money back for the metal. And you and me get some priceless papers. All I had to do was switch the VIN and presto; now, we ain't driving Helena's stolen car no more."

Roomie laughed. "That's ingenious. You never stop amazing me."

"Thanks, but here's the best part. We can sell the damn thing on Craigslist to a private party for $5,000 or so. At that price it'll fly off the shelf."

"That's very, very clever. How did you figure all that out?"

"Think back. Just before we left, Helena's house I was on the phone a lot."

"Yeah. I noticed that."

"That's when I put it together. All we gotta do now is get a motel and find our buyer. Then we're on our way to Reno."

"And you'll finally get your threesome."

"Why not? We earned it."

66

When Roomie and Randal abandoned me, my heart pounded and my mind filled with regrets.

If I had agreed to do what Randal wanted in the first place, I would have bought enough time to get an ID, go elsewhere, and land some sort of job. But NO!!! I was too stubborn.

To compound my woes, when I heard Randal's phone conversation with his wife and kids, I should have minded my own business. I also should have known that Roomie would pick Randal over me if she were forced to make a decision along those lines.

That's clearly what happened. I had absolutely nothing to offer her; he, on the other hand, brought a lot of things to the table, including the fact that he had taken on an enormous risk for her. Regardless of the man's shortcomings, that was an extraordinarily romantic gesture on his part. And, obviously, the feelings were mutual. Why the hell didn't I see that?

While shaking my empty head, I took several deep breaths and rejected some immediate thoughts regarding turning myself in. Then I reminded myself that Randal had been checking the internet to keep track of Helena, and the police said they didn't have any idea where we were. That meant I had some time to get my act together.

I looked around the house and observed that a few things

were missing. The master bedroom had forfeited a TV, a pair of lamps, and some of Helena's better clothes, all of which were likely destined to end up in a pawn shop somewhere. Then, I peeked in the master bathroom, where I spotted a note taped to the mirror. It was a last-minute comment from Roomie.

Dear Miranda, by now you realize that Randal and me are gone. I'm sorry that things ended like this, but what can I say? I love him and he loves me. Like Bonnie and Clyde. LOL!

By the way, Helena is supposed to be back tomorrow night, so you better bolt too.

Good luck, to you and Eunice. I really, really, really love you.

Roomie.

p.s. When Randal agreed to help you escape, I promised him I'd hire a prostitute for the both of us. I don't got no more money, but he knows how to pay for it so he's gonna get his 3-way, anyhow. Reno, here we come. LOL again!

In spite of my anger and anxiety, I understood my friend's choice. After all, I'd been telling them to get away from me since day one.

Panicky and filled with adrenaline, I was tempted to jog to the truck stop several miles up the road, but I forced myself to calm down and play it smart for a change. I figured I had time to wipe away all of our fingerprints so that all three of us had a better chance of getting away with all the shenanigans.

I located the rubber gloves and window cleaner in the laundry room. I'll borrow these, I said to myself as we'd all been saying for over a week. Then it occurred to me that nearly everything we'd used or eaten in that home amounted to stealing. It was also possible that the guns that Randal sold at the flea market weren't really his. I felt sorry for our host.

"Somehow, Helena," I said to her spirit, "I'll find a way to pay you back for all of it."

I began a cleanup phase by rounding up the bedding and towels. As I stuffed a load in the washing machine, I observed the screen on the window again. This time, the tear in it had more significance. Unmistakably, Randal had pried the window open when we first arrived. I vowed to replace that too.

While the laundry bounced around, I quickly visited the master bedroom. On the far side of the bed, I observed a pair of panties that Roomie had left on the floor. Since I had so few clothes, I set the undies aside for later.

Before I began wiping things down, I reminded myself to be thorough because Helena would call the police and I sure didn't want the forensic people to figure out who was behind all the losses. I dutifully wiped away our prints from ceiling to floor and ultimately assumed that was the cleanest those rooms had been in a while.

By early afternoon, I'd cleaned everything except the laundry room and was ready to take on the final few tasks. I'd peeked in the dressing mirror behind the bedroom door. I looked like a filthy and sweaty disaster. I couldn't go out in public like that; it would draw too much attention. I added the bulk of my meager clothes to the next laundry load.

Wearing nothing but a tee-shirt and Roomie's freshly washed panties, I vacuumed the carpets and mopped the other floors. In between, I bagged my pictures of Cody and my toothbrush.

When nearly finished, I took a very necessary shower then wiped the room clean, packed the dryer with a final load, made the beds, and returned the towels to their original spots.

Finally, exhausted, I attended to a few final odds and ends

and glanced around to see if I'd forgotten anything. In the central closet a shelf hosted a camera that Roomie and Randal must have overlooked. I probably could have traded it for a burger or something, but that would be more stealing and there had already been enough of that.

It was time to head for that truck stop while I still had a chunk of time before Helena would return and call the police.

After one last visit to the restroom, I donned my farmgirl outfit and grabbed a bag of trash. If I were lucky the cops would think some kids or dopers broke in, stole what they could, including the Toyota, and disappeared. According to Randal, the loss barely qualified as a felony so the police would put together their initial reports and check out any obvious leads, but after that they wouldn't put much time or effort into catching the people who were responsible.

Finally, being careful not to leave any new prints, I stepped outside and closed the door behind me. I hoped Helena had enough insurance to cover her losses.

Due to my previous trips to the park, I knew they had a few trash barrels there, so I toted the trash along with my plastic grocery sack of clothes and Cody's picture up the street. At the park, I ditched the trash and briskly headed for the truck stop. Then a cruel thought visited me. I might have to screw a truck driver to hitch a ride.

I could almost hear Randal laughing and saying, "I told you so."

67

I DIDN'T KNOW EXACTLY HOW FAR it was to the truckstop but I did know from the treadmills in the exercise room at the prison that I could cover three miles an hour without getting too sweaty.

I began my trek and wished I could call Roomie to tell her there were no hard feelings. After all I knew hundreds of ladies who would have loved to trade places with me.

It took an hour and a half to spot the truck stop; therefore, I'd walked about four miles. Both hungry and thirsty, I had to get the heck out of the area. I reminded myself that I had a new name and kept moving.

When I finally arrived, I saw a wide variety of vehicles - trucks, campers, cars, and motorcycles. The first thing I did was scoot to the restroom where I found a much-needed mini-treasure: an empty water bottle. I filled it up, gulped down the whole bottle and filled it again.

After a personal pep talk, I wrapped the handles of my plastic bag around my palm and looked in the mirror. Eunice summoned her courage.

Out in the lot, I glanced around, took a sip from my water bottle and approached a well-groomed man about my age leaving the café and walking toward a row of trucks. I hustled toward him.

"Hey, can I talk to you for a minute?"

He stopped and faced me. "I guess so. 'Sup?"

"I need a ride east. Any chance you can give me a lift?"

He shook his head. "Can't. My cab only has room for two."

"Well, you're one person and I make two."

"Sorry, I already got a partner. My wife is in the bunk now."

"Well then, I hate to be a moocher but can you spare a couple dollars so I can get a burger?"

"I only got a buck," he said, "but I suppose I could give you that."

That wasn't even enough to buy a burger, but I took it anyway. "Thank you," I said, stuffing the bill in my front pocket. "I need this."

I eyed another cluster of big-rigs and approached a pudgy, whisker-faced driver with a dirty baseball cap. Extremely apprehensive, I moved slowly.

"Well now," he said through small yellow teeth, "what would you want?"

I could see a chewing tobacco bulge beneath his lower lip. Grossed out or not, I still had to get out of there.

"Would you be able to give me a ride?"

"A ride, huh? What's your name, Honey?"

"Eunice. I'm heading east."

"I dunno. I can tell by your looks that you got a lot of miles on your back."

"Does that mean you'll take me?"

"No, it means I might be able to help you out. I like bodacious ta-ta's. Show me your girls. If I like 'em, I 'might' try you out – that is, if the price is right."

"No. You've got it all wrong--"

"Well then, I'll tell ya what. If I can't find somebody hotter, I guess I could take a swing at the mark-down bin. But I ain't paying more than twenty bucks and I ain't using no condom."

Completely grossed out, I almost, sorta considered it, but

at that rate, I'd have to put out for several guys to afford a cheap motel down the road somewhere.

"You've got me all wrong," I said. "I'm not a hooker. I just need a ride or some spare change for something to eat."

He snickered. "You ain't getting no free ride outta me. Now get out of my face afore I kick ya in the ass."

As I stepped back, I empathized with some of the prostitutes I'd met in prison. Their lives had to be a lot tougher than I'd imagined. I also understood that when it came to slithering about in society's shadows, Randal was a lot wiser than I'd realized.

My next prey was a stocky single woman. I was surprised that she would ride alone, but she said she couldn't take riders due to insurance regulations - just as Randal had suggested. I don't know what her problem was, but she became pretty huffy when she turned down my request for a couple dollars.

Frustrated, but still strongly motivated, I approached others. Most were nice, ordinary people who said that their companies or insurance company wouldn't allow them to take riders. A smaller group consisted of nonaffiliated drivers who had more flexibility. The few that I met were more arrogant and wouldn't help me unless there was money or a sexual component for them. I thought about Randal and Roomie again. At least a three-way, or even a string of them, would have been safe.

Eventually, a huge moving van pulled in. I hustled toward the parking area and met the red-shirted driver as his feet hit the ground.

"Excuse me," I said from ten feet off. "Can I ask you a favor?"

He turned and nodded. "What kind of favor?"

"Well, I could use a ride, if you're going east."

"Possible. What's in it for me?"

"I'd be real grateful."

"How much to make me totally happy?"

It was a lot like being with Randal. Every benefit had strings that led to the inside of my pants. This whole conversation made me sick to my empty stomach, but I needed to get out of there and this fellow wasn't nasty.

"How does a hundred sound?" I floated.

He laughed in my face. "It's sounds like you're a fucking moron. That's how it sounds. I got twenty bucks. Take it or leave it."

That was the same basic price I got from doing Stome in the laundry room. "No, thanks." I turned around just as a woman approached me, wearing a shirt emblazoned with the name of the truck stop.

"I know what you're doing," she said to me, "and I don't like it. We look the other way when it comes to solicitation, but our customers don't like panhandlers. You need to move along. Got it?"

I got it alright: It was okay to screw the drivers, but it wasn't okay to be hungry and ask for a dollar.

68

After speaking with Miranda's ex and parents, Captain Phyllis Manny determined that none of them was involved in the escape. With that group in the rearview mirror, the path forward involved chasing down two parolees who had once been very tight with Munchak.

First on the list was Mary Ruth Saines, who had been released some five years back. When Manny's team contacted Mary Ruth's parole officer, they learned that Saines spent most of her time in a wheelchair in Florida, where she lived with her son.

Manny would have preferred to interview Saines in person, but given the circumstances, she opted instead to have an initial conversation with the woman via Facetime or Skype and go from there.

Meanwhile, Argyle and Woodson continued to interview the rank-and-file inmates in the prison, so Manny asked for Sergeant Daniel Bradburn's assistance.

After Saines's son wheeled her in front of a computer monitor, Manny broke the ice. "Thanks for talking with us, Ms. Saines. I'm Captain Manny and this is Sergeant Bradburn."

"Did I have a choice?"

"Yes, but to tell you the truth, the optics wouldn't be good."

"Optics? What's this all about, anyway?"

"How long has it been since you've spoken with Miranda Munchak?"

"Miranda? Is she getting a new trial, 'cause she got railroaded. I'll do anything I can to help her."

"Good. Can you describe your relationship with Ms. Munchak?"

"Sure. When she first arrived, we had adjoining cells. She was sweet and naïve and I was a cripple. I taught her the ropes and she helped me get around. Eventually we were allowed to be cellmates. We were like sisters."

"So, are you saying you haven't heard from her?"

"You got it. She wouldn't even know where I'm at."

"She could have called you." Just then, Manny's iPhone announced an incoming text. She tapped her partner.

"I gotta make a call. Go ahead and finish up with Ms. Saines."

Manny slipped out of the room and Sergeant Bradburn adjusted the monitor before asking Mary Ruth his first question. "So, just to be clear, Ms. Saines, exactly when was the last time you spoke with Ms. Munchak?"

"I thought we just buried that bone. I told you guys that I hadn't jawed with her since the day I got released."

Bradburn leaned in. "We can get your phone records, you know."

"Be my guest, Junior, but you know that the terms of my parole forbid me from having contact with Miranda or any other cons. You people could put me in another cage and throw away the key. I only got a few years left in this world and I sure as hell don't want to spend them crippled in the big house, so I ain't gonna bullshit ya."

"Alright then," Bradburn continued. "Did Munchak ever speak of old friends or family members? Maybe a favorite cousin or a childhood acquaintance or an old roommate?"

"As I understood it, that well was shallow. She had a retarded brother but couldn't visit him and vice versa."

"We know about him. Did she ever get messages or money from home or from her husband?"

"Naw. She'd lost touch with her folks; and her ex was a two-timer."

"Do you know of anybody else who she communicated with?"

"Just the twins," Mary Ruth said while raising her eyebrows. "That was one hell of a story. One of them figured out how they could steal some money to help her brother, but before it was all over, both of them was dead and dumb-ass cops like you said she was involved, but I doubt that."

"Doubt what specifically?"

"I doubt she killed them. She insisted that she didn't know what happened 'cause she had blackouts and I believe her, she wasn't the type to hurt nobody or to lie about it."

Some movement caught Bradburn's eye.

"Alright, Sergeant," Captain Manny said. "We can check in with Ms. Saines a little later if we have any additional questions."

"There ya go, Junior," Mary Ruth said. "Your mommy has spoken."

After they terminated the call, Manny had some news for her subordinate.

"Looks like we've got the get-away vehicle. It's a white SUV at an apartment building."

"That could be helpful."

"Not sure about that. They tell me there's no surveillance footage and it looks like it got wiped clean of prints."

"Well, that vehicle had to drive past other surveillance cameras to get there from the hospital. Maybe we can look at them."

"We'll give it a look, but we've spoken with scores of inmates plus painting teams and Munchak's little family. We only have one more lead. If Candice Carmichael doesn't pan out, we'll have to shelve the whole case until we can get some other leads."

69

DULY INFORMED, I CONTINUED MY QUEST. I talked with a very thin dude who offered to "do me" for free, but I wasn't trying to get laid. I wanted to get food or to get out of there.

Next up, I was offered $17 for a missionary ride. The John said it was all he had. I doubted that part, but just then, the worst possible thing happened. A police car, complete with red flashers, wedged me between his vehicle and that same trucker, who calmly put his vehicle in gear and inched away.

I considered running away, but it was a long way to the next building and I couldn't out-run a police car. I turned toward the officer, whose window was already rolled down.

"What's your name, ma'am?" he asked.

It was time for the best show of my life and perhaps my reckoning. I instructed myself to be respectful. "Eunice Waxman," I said in the most confident tone I could muster.

"You got an ID?"

Uh-oh. "Not really, but here's a paper with my name and social security number on it."

"What you got in that plastic bag?"

"Nothing, really. One change of clothes, underwear and a picture. I'll show them to you, if you want."

He took the paper and quickly scanned it. "What are you doing out here, Ms. Waxman?"

He surely suspected I was a prostitute, but I thought I needed something different to get him off my back. "Well, to tell you the truth, I'm getting away from my boyfriend. He gets drunk and beats me."

"If he's that abusive, do you want to press charges?"

"No, sir. The sooner I get away from that creep, the better."

"Where you headed?"

"Minnesota. I have a cousin there. I can work for her."

He unlocked the rear door of his car.

"Slide in here and across the seat where I can see you while I check on something."

I almost swallowed my tongue, but I was in too deep to do anything other than stay in character. He looked at me through his mirror then grabbed a mic and called his home base. After he checked in, he gave them Eunice's name and date of birth.

While we waited endlessly for a reply, he said something that I'd already figured out. "Most of these truckers are nice guys, but I can't vouch for all of them."

Just then an emergency call came back at him and more codes bounced back and forth. He immediately returned my paper.

"All right, Ms. Waxman. There's been an accident up the road a bit, so I gotta take you at your word. Be careful, now."

"Yes, sir," I said, feeling like I'd just landed on a mattress full of four-leaf clovers. "I'll be okay."

He activated his siren and light, but I knew that he would likely come back after he attended to the auto accident. With my very survival on the line, my pride be damned. I desperately needed to move on, by any means necessary. But I also needed to find some food — even an apple core or some cold french-fries.

I peeked in a trashcan, hoping I could find something to eat without having to spend my only dollar. Just then I heard a low rumble coming from the other side of the main building.

A gigantic, dark blue, three-wheeled motorcycle with a matching trailer coasted toward me.

The tan, clean-cut driver appeared to be in his mid-thirties. He had a round baby-face. He stopped right next to me and smiled. "Hey," he said. "Would you like to share a burger with Killer?"

"Huh?"

He pointed his thumb over his shoulder.

There was a carrying case behind him that housed a very small, hairy dog.

"Oh, my goodness, he's adorable. What breed is he?"

"Shih Tzu, only Killer is a lady. She only weighs eight pounds and she's very dangerous. She just might try to lick you to death. By the way, my name is Phillip—not Phil, but Phillip. She likes you," he said. "She also gets tired of my tales. We could both use somebody else to talk with. So, how 'bout joining us for a while?"

Phillip and his four-legged sidekick had only been there a minute and they'd almost melted me, but I didn't want to sound as desperate as I really was.

"I've ridden on a bike before. Where you going?"

He shrugged. "Overall, we're flexible," he said, "but I've got a reservation at a campsite for tonight. It's about a hundred and fifty miles east."

Some of that sounded very good, but a campsite could be secluded and potentially dangerous.

"If you're worried," he said right on cue, "it's a KOA campground with a little convenience store and dozens of people around. Besides, we'll have Killer to protect us."

I felt like I'd been touched by an angel. "Okay, 'Not Phil,' you and Killer have got yourselves a traveling partner. My name is Eunice."

"Alrighty, then. Before we blast off, you should know it'll be a little chilly dressed like that. Would you like to borrow a hoodie?"

I definitely did.

He dismounted, flicked a couple buckles and moved Killer's little house to the pavement. While he opened the cargo lid, I got a pretty good look at Killer and the back of her little home. A thick-wired screen door reminded me of a prison cell and her little body appeared to be contorted or out of proportion.

"Here ya go," Phillip said, handing me a plush, dark-blue hoodie. "It might be big, but it'll keep you nice and warm. I also have some sweatpants if you want them."

Considering the chill, I surely did. He removed a helmet from the cargo area and filled that spot with my meager plastic grocery bag. "Here's your helmet," he said. "It has earphones and a microphone so we can talk back and forth while we ride, that is, if you won't mind Killer eavesdropping on us."

I had to grin. "I'd like that."

While he returned Killer to her rightful spot, I slid into the comfy sweats and strapped on my helmet. After we mounted, he drove around the building and entered the drive-through lane where a couple vehicles were ahead of us. Neither of us spoke until it was our turn to order. "Burger or chicken or something else?" he asked.

I was so hungry I might have eaten a worm. "A chicken sandwich would be nice."

"What to drink?"

"Do they have iced tea?"

He leaned toward the order board. "We need a chicken basket," he said to the order-taker, "with fries and an iced tea."

My stomach growled in approval.

"Aren't you eating?" I asked.

"Already did," he said, snagging a twenty from his wallet.

Moments later, he traded the bill for a bag of food. "Here ya go, Eunice. It's all yours. Would you rather eat on the patio or take it with us?"

Duh!

70

WHILE GULPING DOWN THE BULK of my delicious sandwich, I observed a small screen on the dashboard of the trike. Killer was in her little home behind me and wagging her rear-end. I literally knew the feeling.

"How you doing back there?" Phillip asked via the helmet's sound system.

"If you don't mind my saying so, I'm concerned about your dog."

"What about her?"

"Well, I noticed her huge nipples and her belly sags way too much."

"That's because she was over-bred. She should have been restricted to four litters over her lifetime, but a backyard breeder forced her to have twice that many."

"That's awful. What's the matter with people?"

"I was told that she was cooped up in a three-by-three cage until she was six years old. She never went anywhere, not even for walks. Her sole job was to make puppies that were taken away from her as soon as they could be sold."

"And you rescued her. That's very noble of you."

"I don't know about that, but she's my little princess. Gets to see all sorts of things now."

"What about the wind? Doesn't it hurt her ears?"

"I wondered about that too, so before I bought the carrier, I put a lit candle in there and went for a ride around the block. When I got back the wick was still burning so I knew she would be safe. Now, I talk to her and play her favorite songs, which just happen to be my favorites, too."

Satisfied that both Killer and I were safe for the time being, I worked my way through the remainder of my sandwich and a few fries.

"So," Phillip said, "would Eunice like to tell me something about herself?"

I'd been so engrossed in my sandwich that he caught me off-guard. I paused to collect my thoughts. "Would you prefer that I tell you a little bit about me?" he asked. "Then you can tell me anything you wish about you."

"That would be great."

"Well then, when I was born my maternal grandmother insisted that everybody call me Phillip, not Phil, because Phillip Pilday sounded more regal. I'm 32. Most people think of me as a tech nerd. I can thank my father for that. After law school he met some other brainiacs who got involved with multi-million-dollar medical devices. They created billions of dollars out of the air. Now, he's on the board of directors for a large law firm. He intimidates some people, but he's actually a pussycat, especially with my sister. Speaking of my sister, she and I were home schooled by our mother, who was a natural-born teacher. It was a shame not to share her with public schools, but she didn't have a certificate. In addition to the book lessons, she taught us about the pleasures of sharing and kindness. That was probably why I felt compelled to talk to you in the first place. Corny as it is, I still love my parents and sister. Oh, yeah, I play the piano, and I pray every night. So that's my story and I'm sticking to it. How 'bout you?"

I already liked how this was going. "For starters, I'm older than you are, but not old enough to be your mother. My favorite flower is a white rose because they are so pure. My favorite person of all time was my twin brother, Mickey. He had special needs, but he gave a lot more than he got. I loved Mickey until the day he died four years ago. My parents weren't as kind as your parents. They basically brushed Mickey aside. Then they brushed me aside for calling them out. I never spoke to them after that."

From there a blend of benign conversations led us, via I-80, deep into Wyoming where the sun was casting longer shadows. We turned onto a dirt road where we quickly arrived at a KOA campground. Just as Phillip said, there were several dozen groups, each with their own designated areas, complete with firepits.

Inside, a modest convenience store held framed pictures of old cars and campers of years earlier. The restroom was spotless and even had a first-come-first-served private shower.

After registering, Phillip glided his trike to our spot. On one side of us, an expensive, polished black Rover was attached to a typical house trailer.

The other site hosted a white pickup with one of those slide-on campers. Each group was huddled around a campfire drinking beer.

"If you'll deal with Killer," Philip said," I'll set up our campsite."

I nodded and removed his tiny dog from her home and held her for the first time. Considering her disfigured belly, I wondered how vulnerable she was. Just then she kissed me.

Phillip shifted his trike into low gear and slowly inched toward the rear of our spot. There, he disconnected his trailer from the trike. "Now, I'm gonna do the Hokey Pokey," he said with a grin, "and turn myself around." A couple minutes later, both the trike and the trailer faced the other way. He held up both arms in feigned celebration. "And that's what it's all about."

I loved his playful nature.

Within minutes, he pulled a dozen pieces of a mobile campsite out of his trailer - like a magician with a rabbit and a hat. I smiled again and grabbed Killer's little leash. "Can I take her for a walk?"

"Sure. Just be careful."

I held her in my arms and wandered through the campground. I felt like I was cuddling a baby and a few tears found my eyes. Then two teenage girls commented on the "cute little doggie," which enabled me to talk about normal things like bad dog breeders, funny dog names and puppies.

By the time Killer and I turned around, a half-hour had evaporated. Then I saw a car pulled over near the big Rover next to our site. Beyond that, Phillip appeared to be arguing with a man in a uniform, perhaps a ranger or security guard. "Of course, I have a gun," Phillip said to the man, just before spotting me. "There they are now. Come on over, Eunice. This man doesn't believe me."

This didn't sound good, but I strolled toward the officer as a non-con would. Phillip reached for Killer's collar. "It's right on her tags," he said to the ranger. Look here. Her name really is Killer."

The man looked at the tag and then chuckled. "I guess you're right. Sorry about that."

"What's going on?" I asked, turning my back on the officer so he wouldn't get a good look at my face.

Phillip shook his head. "Somebody heard us using the word killer and got nervous."

"That's ridiculous," I said, cuddling my little friend.

Thankfully, nobody knew that Phillip's other traveling partner was an escaped prisoner who had been convicted of three actual killings.

71

AFTER THE TWO "KILLERS" REJOINED PHILLIP, the taller one glanced at the gear he had spread out. "I'm embarrassed to ask this," I said, "but where do we sleep?"

He pointed his thumb over his shoulder. "The tent is by the front wheel of the trike."

I turned to see a green nylon bag slightly larger than a backpack. "That little bundle? Is this a joke?"

"I'll show ya."

He, unzipped the bag, removed the outer casing, then clutched the remainder of the package, and stood up.

"Are you ready?"

"Go ahead, impress me."

He quickly lobbed the package into the air where it immediately sprang in several directions and morphed into a small tent that landed on the ground.

Before I could comment, Killer bolted for the center of the little tent. "Our home for tonight," Phillip said with a huge grin. "Killer loves it."

I chuckled. "That's one of the cutest things I've seen in a long time."

"The brochure says it'll sleep four, but they would have to be very small and very friendly people."

"That's all very interesting, but what about—"

"Trouble is, I only have one sleeping bag and one air-mattress," he said. "If you'll let me wear the sweats, you and Killer can have the tent and the sleeping bag. I'll sleep under the stars."

"You don't have to do that," I said. "We can share the tent. We'll all be warmer that way."

"Take a closer look," he said pointing to the opening in the tent.

I moved toward the waist-high tent and peeked inside. A lone twin-sized air mattress would consume nearly all the floor space. Since I'd been sleeping in a prison bunk for so long, the close quarters didn't particularly spook me, but if we were both in there at the same time, we would literally be sleeping together and that was another one of those awkward moments I preferred to avoid.

"See what I mean?" Phillip said. "I'd rather put my iPad and other items in the tent and sleep outside than the other way around."

"Okay, you convinced me but I feel guilty."

He waved off the comment. "No need for that. For now, we can make a campfire."

The mere mention of a campfire warmed me. "I'd love that."

Phillip enthusiastically scooped up a few pieces of paper trash and some twigs into a miniature pile. "Can I help?" I asked.

"Not necessary. I'll have this fire rumbling in a couple minutes," he said while making a teepee out of wood that he'd bought in the store. A quick click of a lighter produced one tiny flame that went right to work.

"Were you a Boy Scout?" I asked, as his fire grew right before my eyes.

"As a matter of fact, I'm an Eagle Scout. You should have seen my grandmother when I got my award."

"Must be the same grandmother who insisted that everybody call you Phillip, not Phil."

"Yep, same one."

Feeling more at ease than I had in quite a while, I allowed my thoughts to dance in and out of the flames while my eyes sought pleasant sights such as the star-filled sky plus a nice man and his dog.

With the fire going nicely, Phillip broke the silence. "I don't know about you, Eunice," he said, "but I'd like to know a little more about you. I can tell you a few things about me first, then you can say whatever you want after that."

I knew that this little game of I'll Tell You Mine if You'll Tell Me Yours was a tad juvenile, but it enabled me to side-step specific questions such as my living arrangements for the past ten years. "Sure," I said. "I'd like to hear more about Not Phil."

"Okay then, I've had my fair share of blessings. I was raised in California and have never lived anywhere else. As I told you before, I was home schooled so I didn't get to interact with other people my age very much. Rather than play baseball with the neighborhood kids, I played chess with my dad and grandpa. My other grandma – my father's mother - taught me how to memorize and recite long poems. That was a helpful skill for a student, so I earned a business degree just after my twentieth birthday.

"In my private life, I've always been more sheltered and naïve than other people my age. That is one reason why I decided to travel. I wanted to learn about the south and New York and the Midwest. My most recent thoughts are about New Orleans. It seems like everybody but me has been to Mardi Gras.

"When my maternal grandma heard I wanted to ride a motorcycle across the country, she said that I should get a trike instead of a two-wheeler because they are safer, and I could always have a loyal companion with me. Obviously, she was correct on both counts.

"Anyway, I want to visit all of those places and meet other people – not just read about them, but to actually live among them. That may have been why I was drawn to you. I've never met anybody who hitchhikes.

"Maybe later, I'll rent an apartment or a small house for a while. There are so many possibilities, I catch myself thinking about the future and forgetting to live in the moment, but not now. Right now, I'm truly enjoying your company and looking forward to learning whatever you want me to know about you."

I loved his enthusiasm and looked forward to learning more about him too, but he'd handed me the reins.

"Well, that's all very interesting," I began. "I've always liked to travel. What else? Oh, yeah. I'm a good painter: rooms, not pictures. I like to talk with other people. One of my strengths is also a weakness. I have high hopes for people and make friends of both genders easily so that's good, but I also trust the wrong people sometimes. My ex-husband included. Ditto a boyfriend or two. That sounds like I'm promiscuous, but I'm not.

"Anyway, I've had to start over a couple times and that's why I'm out here right now. I'm not particularly afraid because I know that God is looking out for me as evidenced by an interesting man that has a priceless little dog. When I'm riding on that man's motor-trike, the fresh air makes me feel like I own the whole world, but I feel sorry for his little doggie because her name doesn't fit her. She seems more like a 'Lilly' to me."

"You know something, Eunice?" Phillip said, "It sounds like we're both pretty selfish."

"Selfish? Why?"

"Yeah, we yearn for all the pleasures of a home and family, yet we also like to wander and meet new people."

He didn't know the half of it.

At about that time, Phillip and I were tired for different reasons. I'd had a very, very long and stressful day while he endured the wind in his face and did nearly all of the camp chores. We decided to call it a night.

"Can I ask you something?" I said at the last minute. "If I hugged you, would you promise not to take it the wrong way?"

As it turned out, that relatively benign embrace was both the end of the beginning and the beginning of the end.

Once inside the tent, Killer pawed me. I lifted all eight pounds of her onto my scarred tummy and petted her little back until we both fell to sleep.

72

Since Mary Ruth Saines wasn't in California when the Munchak escape went down, Captain Phyllis Manny was down to her last decent lead. Based on a conversation that Manny had with Candice Carmichael's parole officer, Candice had declared that she was primarily living with her sister, Naomi Grant, in Riverside, California.

"If we don't learn anything here," Manny said to her partner, Daniel Bradburn, as they stepped onto the porch of Naomi Grant's home, "we'll drop back and help the others interview inmates at the prison."

Bradburn nodded and hit the buzzer. "Sometimes police work is tedious."

"Yes? Can I help you?" a middle-aged woman said a moment later.

Manny flashed her badge at the resident. "My name is Captain Phyllis Manny of the Fugitive Apprehension Team of California. This is Sergeant Bradburn. We'd like to speak with Candice Carmichael if she's in."

"She's my sister, but she's not here."

"Well then, you must be Naomi Grant. May we come in and ask you a few questions?"

"I guess so. We can sit in the living room."

Seconds later, in an armchair with a crucifix on the wall

behind him, Sergeant Bradburn spoke. "When do you expect Candice?"

"I don't know. We haven't talked for a while. Is she okay?"

"As far as we know. We were told by her parole officer that this is where she stays."

"It's the closest thing she has to a permanent address, but she stays other places too."

"But you didn't report her as missing, did you?"

"No. Why would I? She bounces around so it's common for her to be absent for a while."

"How long has it been since you've spoken with her?"

"I don't know exactly. I'd say eight to ten days. She usually calls when she's gone this long, but she hasn't been in touch lately."

"Have you spoken with her parole officer?"

"No. Candice does that twice a month. There's no reason for me to call unless she's in trouble."

"What about Miranda Munchak? Have you seen or heard from her in the past few weeks?"

"I should have known this was about her. She's a bad influence."

"Really? How so?"

"She and Candice were cellmates. My sister said they actually had sex from time to time, against God's will. I blame that Miranda woman. She was ten years older and should have known better."

"You don't suppose they're together right now, do you?"

"I don't know. Did Miranda get released?"

Manny leaned in. "We want to eliminate your sister as a suspect. Are you sure you don't know where we can find her?"

"I don't know where she is, honest."

"Who is she with?"

"I don't know that either. She doesn't come around as much as she used to. She goes to bars, meets people. She could be anywhere with anybody. Last I knew she was with a man named Randal, but she could have moved on from him."

"Do you have Randal's contact information?"

"No. I don't like him either."

"You got any pictures of them together?"

"No. I have some current pictures of my sister, but I wouldn't want any pictures of that man."

"Okay then, what about her work? Does she have a job?"

"Not that I know of. She's a free spirit. Has a poor work history, spends the night with men she barely knows."

"Besides Randal, do you know any of these men?"

"No."

"We have some video of a man and woman helping Munchak escape from a hospital. We'd like you to take a look at it."

"Okay, I guess so."

The sergeant tapped at his cellphone and produced a short piece from the surveillance camera that they'd watched earlier. "Does this look like Randal and your sister?"

Naomi's hand shot to her mouth. "Oh, my God."

"Is that them?" Manny prodded.

"The woman is too heavy to be my sister, but that guy has a beard and so does Randal."

"Is it them or not?"

"I can't be certain."

"Has this Randal person ever called you? His number could be in your phone logs."

"No. He and I barely get along."

"What about a vehicle? You must know what he drives."

"I know that he has a faded blue van."

Bradburn delivered the next question, "Are you sure it isn't a white SUV?"

Naomi shook her head. "Naw. He couldn't afford one of those."

"Alright, Ms. Grant," Manny said. "We'd like permission to look at your phone records just to verify that you haven't been speaking with your sister."

"Sure."

"We also want your sister's number if you have it."

"Sure. I just hope she's not in more trouble because I won't help her if she goes back to jail."

"One more thing. If you hear from her, you'll let us know. Right?"

"Yes, of course."

"Alright then, we'll be in touch."

When back in the car, Manny called her underling, Lieutenant Cristobel Woodson, who was busy interviewing inmates along with Lisa Argyle and other detectives.

"How are you guys doing?" she asked.

"Slow, but steady," Woodson said. "Detective Argyle checked Munchak's commissary account to see if she's been transferring large sums of money but no luck."

"I'm not surprised," Manny said.

"I guess not but something else arose. When Munchak first arrived in prison she was pregnant, and she gave up her newborn son for adoption."

"We already knew that from other interviews. She calls him Cody."

"But did you know that over the years she's made multiple comments that she regretted that she sealed the file."

"Meaning?"

"Meaning, it was a closed adoption. She was totally cut off from him. Now that she's out, maybe she'll try to find her boy."

"Maybe. The maternal instinct can be very powerful. We'll look into it. Good job. I'll get back to you later on."

73

AFTER SPENDING THE NIGHT IN A TINY TENT with a tiny, saggy-bellied dog, I opened my eyes and thought about Helena, the owner of the Utah home. I felt sorry for her and imagined what she'd been through.

When she reached her house, tired and toting dirty laundry, she would have noticed her absent Toyota fairly quickly. Curious and scared, she may have fled the house, fearing an intruder, and waited from a safe distance until the police arrived and could ensure the house was empty.

More exhausted than before, she would have gone inside and discovered that most of her nicer belongings had been stolen. If Randal was correct, the police would have taken a report and looked for any easy clues or leads. Absent that, they wouldn't put a lot of resources into the matter because the loss wasn't catastrophic. Instead, they would encourage Helena to file a claim with her insurance company. Ironically, I'd relied upon that same reasoning when Mickey needed medical treatments and my whole life flushed down the drain because of it.

After I reminded myself to pay her back someday, I thought of the relationships I'd had with men during my lifetime. I envied the women who could have "friends with benefits" or one-night stands while I preferred more affectionate relationships, which had a tendency to blow up in my face.

That was why I held so much angst over the laundry room episodes and Randal's three-way plan and the idea of boinking my way across the country in the back of huge trucks. There was no affection, no love, no appeal. After a generation of disappointing relationships, I came to suppose that I'd never have the kind of bond that I wanted.

But then I met Phillip. He'd made a pretty good first impression. Of course, our fragile relationship could go south in the blink of an eye. He'd certainly figured out that I was vulnerable in some way. If I were to anger him for any reason, he could threaten to call the police or simply leave me somewhere, and I'd be on my own again. I already knew how awful that was.

I also disliked the most probable scenario: specifically, if I were to stay with Phillip for very long, sooner or later, he would likely seek to get much closer. But I didn't want to do anything like that unless I absolutely had to.

Suddenly, a whiff of coffee caught my attention and I heard a gentle shuffle outside the tent. I unzipped the sleeping bag and crawled out the door flap.

Outside, with his doggie at his feet, Phillip sat peaceably at our picnic table while he pecked away at his iPad. He'd obviously taken a shower. In addition, he'd managed to set the table with one plastic plate, one paper plate, some plastic silverware and a tiny bowl, presumably for Killer's breakfast.

"Good morning, team," I said.

Killer instantly sprang from beneath the table, raced toward me and lifted herself until her short legs reached my kneecaps. Her active rear-end and a loving whimper warmed my heart. I reached for her.

Phillip grinned. "I'm jealous," he said, setting his iPad aside. "How did Eunice sleep?"

That impressed me. While I had spent the night on his airbed, he'd slept on a few towels and under the stars.

"Well, a sleeping bag and air mattress don't beat a canopy bed, but I'm so sorry you had to sleep on the ground."

"No problem. I love watching the sun come up," he said, gesturing toward the east.

Maybe I was emotionally vulnerable or something, but I loved how he appreciated the simple things. I hadn't met a man like that since one of the doctors visited me in the prison hospital several years back. "It's been a long time since I've watched the sun rise," I said.

"That's why Killer and I spend half our nights at campsites."

"Half the nights? What do you do the other times?"

"Mostly motels, but we sprinkle in an airbnb every once in a while."

"I've heard of those but I've never used one."

"The difficult thing is finding places that will accept Killer."

I patted her little head. "Don't worry, Honey, 'cause your Daddy will always take care of you."

"Anyway," he said, "we ordinarily alternate: spending one night in a campsite and the next night in a motel or one of those other places. That way, we can relax more. You know, better beds, fewer chores, morning meals." He pointed toward my thighs. "And a chance to wash our clothes."

That was pretty blunt and I might have been offended if it weren't true.

"So, if you don't throw me overboard sometime today, does that mean you plan to stay in one of those places tonight, 'cause—"

He smirked and giggled at the same time.

"What's so funny?"

"While you were wondering if I would 'throw you overboard' I was actually hoping you weren't going to ask me to drop you off somewhere."

"I guess that means we're both willing to give this situation another twenty-four hours."

"Or more. To answer your other question, I have a motel booked for tonight."

What an enigma. I'd just learned that I'd get to stay in a motel, which was comforting, but it brought new problems, too.

"I might like that," I said, "but I don't have any money to pay my share."

"I figured that, Eunice, from the moment I saw you at the truck stop. So, don't worry, I can cover it."

Whew! "You don't know how much that means to me. Now I have one more question—"

"It's easy," he said without hearing me out. "We can either get two beds or you can have your own room. That way you can sleep in peace."

74

AFTER PHILLIP AND I AGREED to stick together for the time being, he poured a cup of hot water into a food pouch and a short time later we ate instant biscuits and gravy. It wasn't the best breakfast I'd ever eaten, but compared to digging around for morsels in trashcans, it was a banquet.

We remained at the campsite until mid-morning before we headed east again. We traded non-threatening small talk via the speaker system in our helmets until a little after lunchtime, when we slow-rolled into the parking lot of a grocery store in Cheyenne, Wyoming.

"What about Killer?" I asked Phillip as soon as he parked. "Most food stores don't allow dogs."

He smiled knowingly, lifted the trunk lid and retrieved a small padlock. "That's why I lock the carrier to the trunk and lock the little door on the carrier. Killer likes watching people; they like her too."

I didn't doubt it. I would have loved a window in my cell.

We made our way to the bakery where I picked out a beautiful lemon crème donut. At a small table we agreed to engage in another round of I'll Tell You Mine if You'll Tell Me Yours. That little game, while silly, was beneficial because I could talk about the 34 years before prison and avoid conversations about the past ten.

"Do you want me to go first?" Phillip asked.

"I'd like that."

"Well, I've been working out of my parents' basement, designing a software program. When it's done, it'll speed up huge computer systems for governments, tech giants and the military. I'm not sure if I really want to help the military, given all the dumb wars they get us into."

I wanted to interrupt him and hear more about his family, but that would have meant that he could ask me personal questions too and I wasn't ready to lie or tell the whole truth.

"I can understand that," I said before chomping on my pastry. "What else?"

"My sister is interesting," he went on. "She likes to say that if we don't shake things up once in a while, our lives remain unlived."

I nodded. "I can relate to that."

"Four years ago, she inspired me to go to Alaska in the winter when it was dark for nearly twenty-four hours a day. While I was there, I met a woman in church whose grandparents were Eskimos. She told me about nose kissing. They call it a kunik. The funny thing was she insisted on showing me how it worked and when I finally got it, she kissed me on the mouth. I gotta tell ya, she was a really good kisser."

I chuckled and noticed a middle-aged female employee coming from behind him. "Aren't you guys the ones riding that big motorcycle out front?"

Phillip nodded. "Yes. Why?"

"Somebody is out there trying to steal that cargo crate on top."

"Killer!" We both raced outside, in time to see a woman watching her boyfriend break Killer's little home away from the trike.

The man grabbed the handle of the carrier and hustled away while Phillip and I raced toward them.

"Hey, you guys," Phillip shouted, "that's our dog."

The couple slowed at an SUV, where the woman went for the tailgate. We'd just about caught up when the man lifted the carrier, spun around like a wobbly dancer and smashed the cage, Killer and all, into Phillip's face. From inside the cage, Killer yelped while the lady lifted the tailgate and screamed at her partner.

"In here, Chuck. Put the dog in here."

Phillip wiped a stream of blood from his nose and regained his feet. He reached for the cage, but that man dropped it and squared up with Phillip. That left the lady and me to fight over Killer and the cage. Unfortunately for her, she didn't have the rage that I had been building up in me for years, nor had she seen as many prison fights as I had. The trick was to get in the first blow, so I grabbed a large hank of her hair and snapped it with all my might, ripping out hundreds of strands and some of her scalp.

"That's our dog, you bitch," I screamed. "You can't have her."

She slapped at the new bald spot on her crown and shrieked. I threw her hair at her, bloody roots and all.

"Chuck, come on," she yelled. "I'm hurt."

Fortunately, the bad guy ran to his whimpering partner.

While they raced out of the parking lot, I knelt before woozy Phillip and heard little Killer sobbing in her carrier.

"Are you gonna be okay?" I asked.

"Forget about me. What about Killer?"

I rose, righted her cage and brought her to him. "She might be sore but she's moving around."

"Here's the key. She'll want us to hold her."

By that time the woman who told us of the potential theft arrived with a cell phone.

"You guys want me to call the police?"

"No," I said emphatically while I unlocked the gate to Killer's cage. "They won't do anything and we'll be okay."

The whole ordeal only lasted a minute.

After washing up, we put all the pieces back in their proper places and packed toilet paper in Phillip's nostril.

"Thanks, Eunice," he said, "I don't know if those two wanted Killer or the carrier, but I couldn't have saved Killer without your help."

I wasn't sure about that, but it felt good to have made a meaningful contribution to the group.

75

WE NEVER DID FIGURE OUT if those thieves were after the carrying case or Killer, but either way, Phillip got the worst of the deal. While we waited for his nose to stop bleeding, he found some new scratches on the deck of the cargo area. He was definitely pissed off about it, but he controlled his temper, which said a lot for him.

"You know something," I said as we pulled back on the highway, "I think we can get by with one motel room, provided it has two beds."

"I'm glad," he said, "'cause Killer and I like your company."

A half-dozen highway hours later, we glided into a charming Gingerbread Motel in the middle of Nebraska. "I booked this place the other day," Phillip said. "The tricky part was finding a place that would take Killer."

"I think it's cute," I said, looking forward to a real bed, a shower, and to washing my meager clothes.

When we entered our room, Phillip immediately lifted Killer's carrier onto one of the beds and let her out. She crawled around in little circles before plopping on the pillow and sighing. By that time, I'd observed several sealed boxes stacked in the corner plus a vase holding two white roses on a bedstand. Stoked, by the flowers, I grabbed the little vase and stole several deep whiffs.

"You must have paid attention when I told you of my favorite flower."

"The other things are yours too - a very special friend who helped me and Killer. Go ahead. Open the boxes."

Gifts! It was like Christmas, a birthday and a wedding all rolled into one. Unable to hide my smile I pulled a very classy backpack from the first box. Given that the backpack was more valuable than everything else I owned combined, I began to tear up and pulled it to me.

"Thank you, Phillip. No matter what happens to us from here, I will always cherish this."

"Now you won't have to carry your things in a dumb ole plastic grocery sack," he said with a toothy grin. "Look inside."

I discovered a stylish black jogging outfit.

"I could have gotten you a small suitcase," he said while I shook my head in disbelief, "but this backpack will be more practical. Now, you won't have to borrow my clothes or wrap yourself in a blanket while you do your laundry. I also bought another air mattress and sleeping bag for the tent. This way, nobody has to sleep on the ground."

"Really? How'd you get all these things?"

"Amazon. All you need is a place that'll hold packages for you. Now I have a question for you. I hate to be so personal, but would you like to get a couple other things? How about a pair of jeans or some shoes? I could get them to a Starbucks the day after tomorrow."

I hesitated because I didn't want to amass a debt that could lead to uncomfortable expectations such as the ones I had with Randal. At the same time, his comment suggested we'd be together at least a couple more days and I liked that idea.

"Oh no, I couldn't ask you to do that," I said.

"You didn't ask. I offered and it's no big deal."

"Well, if you're sure it's okay, we both know I could use a couple things."

"Great. We can wash our clothes while we're shopping."

After I donned my new jogging outfit and loaded our other clothes in the motel's washing machine, Phillip and I gathered at a desk with his iPad and he showed me what Amazon was all about. Before I knew it, he bought me some tennis shoes, some socks and my first fanny pack. Then he finalized an order and turned my way.

"Killer and I are hoping you're not in a big hurry. We like traveling with you."

A warm feeling raced up my neck. It was as if he'd read my mind. "I'm glad to hear that," I said, "because I like you both and don't have to be anywhere else for a while."

Then, something else occurred to me. It had to do with Helena.

"I know you don't know me very well, but would you be willing to lend me a thousand dollars?"

He stopped in his tracks. "What for?"

"I owe some people for room and board. I know you've already done a lot of nice things for me, so I wouldn't blame you if you said no, but I can find a way to pay you back."

"I see. So, you'd be willing to work it off?"

"Well, yeah, but only to a point."

"In that case, you could pay me back by hanging around with Killer and me for a whole nother week. I want to find out what a normal person thinks of some of my whacky technology ideas."

"But I'd do that for free."

"I know. That's how I know you'll tell me the truth."

"You do realize that's almost $150 a day, right?"

"Actually, it's $142.86 to be exact."

I paused for a moment. "Well, then, would you mind making it the full $150 per day?"

He chuckled. "Why?"

"A girl has to have a little spending money."

"Okay, but if I'm gonna throw in all that extra money, you better have some good stories to tell me."

"In that case, you have to pay for all our room and board for the week."

"I thought I was already doing that."

"You were, but this makes it official."

"Okay, then you've got a deal."

We shook hands and I almost wished he'd pulled me to him.

76

Following a fun-filled trip to Reno, Randal and Candice were nearing Randal's home in Riverside, California.

"We're real close to the Post Office," he said. I want to swing by because my cousin should have returned our primary phones by now. After that, we're going to soak the burners in a bowl of Pepsi overnight, then we'll dump 'em somewhere."

"Why would we do that?"

"Pepsi or Coke. They both have enough acid in them to destroy these cheap phones. After that, nobody can trace them back to us or figure out that we weren't really in Houston."

"I'll be glad to have my other phone back. My sister is probably worrying about me."

Not long thereafter, Randal handed Candice her original cell phone. She immediately called her sister and apologized for not being responsive.

"We went out of state and didn't want to be bothered. Most of the time we just turned the phones off."

"I can understand that," Naomi said. "I'm just glad you're okay because there's something else you need to know. Don't get alarmed, but I've been talking with the police. Miranda broke out of jail - well actually, she was in a hospital."

Having been tutored by Randal, Candice knew to keep her comments brief.

"Miranda? Hospital? Is she okay?"

"They think so, but they're trying to figure out who helped her. For a while there, they thought you might be involved, but they checked your phone records and discovered that you were in Texas when the escape took place."

"Randal has a cousin down there."

"That's another thing. They know that you were out of state without permission. They said they can revoke your parole. Also, they told me to call them as soon as I heard from you. All they want is to find out if you know anybody else who might have helped Miranda escape."

"Just tell them you talked with me and I don't know anybody like that."

"You don't understand. They want to meet you in person and you should do it so that they don't hold these other things against you."

"Well, we just got back in town. Haven't even been to Randal's place. We gotta clean the van and stuff."

"I guess an hour or so won't matter, but promise me you'll call right after that."

"Okay. If it makes you feel any better, I'll call you after I speak with them."

"Thank you, thank you, thank you. I just wish you'd move in with me and start going to church. You might meet a nice man with a good job."

"Now you're being our mother. I gotta go now. We're pulling into Randal's driveway."

"Before you go, what's Randal's last name? They asked that too."

"Biskitt. Like 'biscuits and gravy,' but he was with me the whole time – in Texas."

"I know, but I want to be as cooperative as possible, so they'll leave us all alone."

After disconnecting, Candice spoke to her boyfriend.

"You were right again. The cops checked my cell phone records and cleared me. They still want to talk to me in person, but I'd rather not."

"You'll do fine," he said as the van came to a halt. "They'll want to talk with both of us. We just gotta keep our story straight."

"I'm just glad to be home." She grabbed a bag of trash, hopped out of the van and scooted toward the cans at the side of the home. When she returned to the van, Randal had plopped their cooler and clothes and a bunch of other things onto the driveway.

"Can you put this shit away?" he asked. "I have to go somewhere else and I'm late. I'll catch up to you a little later."

Surprised, she put her hands on her hips. "I've been with you nonstop for three days, and I haven't heard you make any appointments. Can't you help for a little while?"

He lowered his voice to a slow, soft whisper.

"You're gonna like what I gotta do. I promise."

She recalled the troubling conversation he'd had in the Utah garage. "This doesn't have anything to do with your wife does it because—"

"That cunt?" he scoffed. "Why would I want to be with her when I've got the world's best lover right here?"

"Are you sure, Randal, because you've said things like that before--"

He, pulled her to him, dropped his hands to her butt. "Did I tell you my favorite part about our stay in Reno?"

"Not really, but you were sure excited when we were all licking each other."

"Yeah, that was hot, alright, but the best part was when you turned me on more than that whore did. You were so hot, I almost threw her out so I could finish up with you."

She grinned and pulled back. "I didn't know that."

"You got all three of us off. That makes you a better lover than the pros and a guy has to appreciate something like that, which is why I've decided to tell Kristy that we're through."

Candice's eyebrows lifted, "Really, Randal? So, you're really going to tell her it's over?"

"That's what I just said, isn't it?"

"Oh, my God. This is great. I want to go with you."

"Better not. That could lead to some ugly yelling in front of the kids, but me and you can celebrate tonight. Now I gotta get out of here."

As Randal drove off, he thought, you may be a great piece of ass, Candy Cane, but you're one gullible bitch.

* * *

A couple blocks from the home that he and his wife had bought seven years earlier, Randal was eager to settle a score. For one thing, Kristy hadn't laid him in four weeks, nor had she invited him to drop by for that purpose. After all, they'd made a "separated, with benefits," agreement that he expected her to uphold.

And then there was the financial matter: "If that bitch gets to live in my home," he said out loud and to himself, "then she owes me rent for using my part of the home."

Angry, horny and under-appreciated, he hurried around the last corner and observed an unfamiliar car parked in front of his home.

As he drew closer, the dirty windshield suggested that the car had been there for a while.

"You'd better not be fucking somebody else, Kristy," he said as he parked.

The other fellow was there alright. The fight began in the living room and lasted but five minutes. That was all Randal needed.

No matter how Kristy screamed and pleaded, Randal wouldn't put the base of the lamp down. Like a baseball bat hitting grounders to the infield, each swing of the lamp landed in Kristy's boyfriend's groaning face until it looked like hamburger - with bits of bones still in it.

Snarling like a crazed wolf, red-faced Randal stomped on the man's balls with all his might, producing an eerie moan that would make any man wince. With blood splatter on all the walls and furniture, Randal pointed his finger in his wife's face.

"See what you made me do, Kristy? This is all your fucking fault."

He kicked the already smashed face of the dude on the floor one last time, then trudged to his van and began making up a story for his ever-trusting Candy Cane.

77

Two days had passed since the FAT team interviewed Naomi Grant about her sister's relationship with Miranda Munchak. In the original conversation, Ms. Grant appeared to be nervous but cooperative. Of course, detectives didn't take all the information they gathered at face value.

Therefore, the FAT team examined Candice's cell phone records. Candice was five states away when the escape took place. Thus Ms. Carmichael was no longer a suspect, although she wasn't entirely out of the woods.

In the meantime, new-found information contradicted a couple minor things that Ms. Grant had said, and it was time for Captain Manny and Sergeant Daniel Bradbury to iron out those wrinkles.

"I want to squeeze this woman and see if she's hiding anything that could help us find Munchak," Manny said.

Bradbury reached for Grant's doorbell. "I get it," he said. "Everybody lies occasionally, even righteous people."

"As you know, Mrs. Grant," began Manny, "your sister's parole officer wants to talk with her and we're trying to eliminate her as a suspect regarding Ms. Munchak's escape."

"But I told you everything I know."

"Maybe, maybe not. We want to go over a few things, but

before we begin, have you tried to reach Ms. Carmichael since we were here last?"

"She called and I told her to call you guys, but she put it off. I never know what she's up to."

"That's why we put out a BOLO on her - and her boyfriend."

"A BOLO? What's that?"

"Be On the Look Out. We still think that your sister might have some useful information about Ms. Munchak's escape."

"I hope not, but I wouldn't know."

"Would you do us a favor and call her right now?"

"I guess so. Why?"

"Because we want to see if she'll pick up. That's all."

"Sure. I'll put it on speaker."

A handful of rings later, Naomi Grant shook her head. "See what I mean? Her phone could be turned off, for all I know."

"How often does your sister use her alias?"

"Alias? What alias?"

"Our people say that she goes by Roomie from time to time. Is that right?"

Naomi shook her head. "Miranda gave her that awful nickname."

"Who does she know in Houston?"

"Houston, Texas? I don't know anybody there. Don't think she does either."

"What would you say if I told you that her cell phone was down in Houston when the escape took place?"

Naomi's eyes widened. "That's good news, right? She couldn't be in two places at the same time."

"But, she's on parole and she's not supposed to leave the state without permission of her parole officer. If she can't explain herself, her parole could be revoked, sending her right back to prison to finish her original sentence."

Naomi sighed. "That girl can be incredibly hasty sometimes."

"What about you? We found some suspicious activity in your phone records."

"My records? No way?"

"You received a stray call just a couple days before Munchak's medical procedure. We chased it down. A teenage boy said a prisoner borrowed his phone at a rest area. That call landed right here in your living room and you didn't tell us about it, even though we asked you directly if you'd spoken with Munchak."

"But—"

"But nothing, Mrs. Grant. Do you remember saying that?"

"Yes, but this is a misunderstand—"

"Now, we have reason to believe that Munchak could be in another state. That might cause us to ask the U.S. Marshal to help with our investigation. They'll want to talk with you too, only they're not as gentle as we are, so you better have a good explanation for why you neglected to tell us about your contact with Munchak."

"When you were here, I answered your questions but sometimes you asked two questions in one breath."

"But you still knew that we were looking for Munchak and withheld that information right up to now."

"Not intentionally. It's intimidating to talk with you people."

"That doesn't give you the right to withhold information, ma'am. You could be charged with obstruction."

Naomi sighed "I'm very sorry, but try to understand; Miranda called here. I didn't recognize the Caller ID so I took the call."

"I believe that part, but the other day you told us you don't like Munchak, yet that call went on for over five minutes. Why didn't you cut her off?"

"Simple. Candice and Randal were here. I gave the phone to Candice."

Captain Manny shook her head. "In doing so, you helped your sister commit another parole violation. She's not supposed to have contact with felons. Did you know that?"

"Yes, but it wasn't planned. I was caught off-guard and it

didn't occur to me. It all happened so fast. Please don't use this against my sister. There wasn't anything devious going on."

"In that phone call, did Munchak and your sister conspire to spring Munchak?"

"No. I could only hear one side of the call, but it wasn't like that. All I know is Candice was happy to talk with her friend."

"What about Munchak's son? Did she say anything about finding him?"

"I don't think so. They only had a few minutes."

"Alright. What did Candice do when the call was over?"

"Nothing special. She just ran off with that disgusting boyfriend of hers."

"And now all three of those people are missing. Doesn't that sound suspicious to you?"

"Not really. You just said that Candice was in Houston when Miranda broke out."

"Alright, Ms. Grant. We've got to check on some other things, but—"

"Don't worry. I get it. If I talk with Candice, or Miranda I'll be sure to tell you. I'm just happy that she wasn't in the state when the escape took place."

"Regardless," Manny said while she and Bradburn rose, "Candice should contact her parole officer about her trek to Texas."

"I'm sure she just forgot. That's all."

"I hope so."

As the detectives walked away, Manny's phone interrupted her. "It's Argyle," she said to her partner. "Hi. Detective. What's up?"

"The warden just gave us some of Miranda's old emails. The only people she's spoken to were at a painting store about opening a credit account. Very benign."

"Alright. Anything else?"

"There were a couple exchanges with a counselor after her

brother died. She regretted that she couldn't be with him at the end. She felt like she'd abandoned him and was having similar concerns about her son, but no talk about an escape."

"This is consistent with some of our earlier findings, but she sure as hell had accomplices. If we don't get some decent leads, we'll have to shut down until we get some new information. For now, I'll call Cincinnati and give them a heads-up."

78

I HADN'T FELT COMFORTABLE WITH A MAN in quite a while, so I was surprised when Phillip's non-threatening demeanor actually awakened my libido. I wasn't going to jump him or anything like that, but it was nice to have normal impulses again. That alone made for a peaceful night's sleep in the Gingerbread Motel.

When I awakened, I had a little partner at the foot of my bed and Phillip was asleep in the other bed. I recalled many years earlier, when my ex and I lay in bed every morning before facing our days. Now I imagined being with Phillip in that way. I smiled at the prospect of being a cougar. I rolled toward the nightstand, found my roses, and welcomed the gentle fragrance.

I quietly slipped into the bathroom for another luxury - a private shower. Undressed, I noticed the ugly scar from my surgery. Worth it, I thought, before sliding into the inviting spray of very warm water. At ease, I washed my hair and allowed the soap bubbles to trickle over my nipples as if they were urging me to come to life.

I wiped a fresh bar of soap onto a thick washcloth and closed my eyes. I slowly eased the gentle cloth over the scar and then down my tummy while my free hand reached down to my vagina. With my eyes still closed, three gentle fingers tapped the area as if to wake it up. I wondered if I'd ever fall in love again. I wondered if I'd ever make love again. I wondered if Phillip would get close to me. Would he hold me and talk softly, and kiss me and remove my clothes? God, how I needed to be loved.

With tears of self-pity forming, I turned off the water and sought refuge in a fluffy towel.

A short time later, my travel partners and I packed up, sans the old air mattress, which Phillip stuffed in the motel's recycle bin. "Now, to a bank," he said.

Phillip kept his previous promise and I mailed Helena one thousand dollars in cash with no note. With my self-imposed debt settled, I felt like the wind rather than a tumbleweed for a change.

I hugged Phillip.

Back in the wind, we rolled past the state line and well into Iowa. "I booked something a little different for tonight," Phillip said with enthusiasm. "Shaker's campground is before Des Moines. It has two areas. The first one is more or less typical, but I'm more interested in the other one. It's supposed to be more rustic and it's farther from other campers."

For the remainder of the drive, wild thoughts and feelings rushed through me - Would wild cows stick their snotty noses in our tent? Would I have to poop in the weeds?

When we entered the main lot, my heart dropped. The last thing I wanted to see was a police car and two local officers talking with a half-dozen campers. Unfortunately, a trike with a trailer and a doggie carrier managed to catch the eye of nearly every head in that group. We dismounted and bypassed the parking lot gossipers in favor of the combination store and sign-in station, where a bearded man with a ponytail was stocking some shelves.

"Hi. I'm Phillip Pilday. I have a reservation for one of the rustic sites."

"You got it, dude," the laid-back clerk said en route to the register. "You'll need mosquito repellent. It's four bucks for a large can. If you want to get anything else, bring it on over here and I'll ring everything up at the same time."

While Phillip scouted the shelves, I wanted to ease a few jitters. "What's going on out there?" I asked Ponytail Man.

"Not a whole lot. A couple hours ago we heard some loud pops over the ridge; could be gun shots or fire crackers. Mostly they're worried about brush fires."

Mostly?

"Okay," Phillip said returning to the register with a bottle of wine, some hotdogs and a bundle of firewood. "This ought to do us."

The manager rang up the order. "Your campsite is a half-mile up the dirt road. Look for the outhouse on your left. Park there and follow the split rail fence about thirty yards. You'll hear frogs near the pond. There's a fire pit with some stumps for chairs."

To a former inmate, frogs, a pond and a private campfire were much more alluring than a couple officers. "This'll be fun," I said.

After traveling a long, rut-filled dirt road on which I couldn't stop thinking about guns, we finally saw the infamous outhouse. With the skill of a professional trucker in a huge parking lot, Phillip circled the trike around and stopped a short distance from the split rail fence. We slapped on a layer of insect repellent and elected to check out the fire pit area.

Then, from off in the distance, I heard a loud pop.

"Guns make me nervous," I said to Phillip. "My ex had guns, but I didn't like them."

"Listen closer, Eunice," he said while he unloaded Killer's carrier. Those shots are coming one at a time, about a half-minute apart. It's a pattern. Bad guys wouldn't do that. I think somebody is practicing. But it's gonna be dark in an hour, so they should stop by then."

"I hope so," I said while I pulled Killer from her little home and hooked a leash to her collar. "Daddy made us feel better, huh, Baby. Now, all we gotta worry about is a stray bullet."

Meanwhile, the sun was looking for a place to hide; we built a fire, opened a bottle of wine and made an appropriate dinner of hot dogs and beans. I thought of my prison friends. Most of them would give up their entire 7-Eleven account for an evening like this.

When the fire got to crackling, Phillip said, "How would you like to listen to the earth?"

79

Phillip had a knack for reintroducing me to the wonderful things that I had to give up when I became prisoner 1516103-A. Consequently, I wanted to know what he meant by "listen to the earth."

We found a level spot about half-way between the tent and the fire pit where we unzipped a sleeping bag and spread it out like a thick blanket and laid down on our backs, side by side, with him holding Killer.

"Now just be as quiet as possible," he whispered. Before long, we heard the soft swish of tall grasses, a chorus of crickets, the crackling fire, a high-flying jet, and faint laughter way back at the main campsite.

As the star-packed sky twinkled, a bright half-moon refused to surrender to the darkness.

The mood was soothing and romantic. I came to peace with being Eunice Waxman, the friend of an unlikely triker. In fact, if Phillip had reached for me in that moment, I likely would have melted in his arms.

Then he gently took my hand and broke the silence. "I have something to tell you," he whispered. "Then you might be able to help me with something."

"I'll do my best," I said.

"Okay, then," he began. "As I've said, I'm grateful for

my upbringing. I learned a lot about things like history and technology and business, but I was sheltered more than most people.

"I didn't really have a peer group so when I became interested in girls, I didn't know where to meet them or how to go about it. I was bashful, so I held back. Over time, I got my information from television and internet porn. I was 27 the first time I went all the way, but it wasn't too successful. I still didn't know anything.

"When my grandmother heard me talking about Eskimo kisses, she realized I'd never had a real girlfriend, so she urged me to join one of those online dating clubs, but that hasn't worked out either. Most of the ladies I've met say they just want to have fun, which appears to be code for sex without commitment.

"Since then, I've had casual sex a handful of times, usually when somebody was drunk or at least tipsy, but I'm not sure if any of the women had any fun. I hear that a lot of them fake orgasms, so I don't know how to tell. And if they don't have orgasms, why do they bother going through the motions? So anyway, I wonder how people get past all of that superficial stuff and into fulfilling relationships. Maybe you can explain it to me."

"Interesting," I said, thinking that Phillip had a dilemma similar to my own. He was concerned about the mechanics of what made women tick and I was disgusted by the men who exploited women, but neither of us got very much out of one-night stands.

"I'm not exactly a relationship expert myself," I said. "I can relate to some of what you say, Phillip, but it sounds like you're looking for a one-size-fits-all explanation for relationships. I can tell you this: It's a lot easier for the reserved ladies to let go when they like and trust their partners."

He paused for a moment. "Maybe I should stop talking with women who say they just want to have fun."

I had to chuckle. "To tell you the truth, Phillip, I suspect that the women who would appeal to you would also use that exact same line to indicate they don't want to get too serious too quickly."

"I don't get it. You're telling me both that all women are the same and that all women are unique."

"Yep, Phillip. That is precisely what I'm saying. That's why men think we're fickle."

He shook his head and we both chuckled.

"I think you should be patient," I said, "and just let things happen naturally."

"Alright, I'll try. Now, what would you say to the three of us taking a side trip?"

That perked me up because I'd had thoughts of my own along those lines. Thus far, we were a long way from the California hospital from which I'd escaped and I liked that, but we were also well within a day's drive to Cody's home in Ohio. I had imagined spinning by there and seeing if I could make contact with him, but it would be awfully brazen of me to ask Phillip to participate in anything like that, especially since he'd paid for everything.

"Where to?" I asked.

"I was thinking about going to New Orleans or some other places down south. As I said before, I've never been there. Have you?"

"Yes, but it was 15 years ago. It was pretty fun."

"Great. We wouldn't leave for a couple of days. But before we do that, I have another surprise for you."

"A surprise for me? I don't know. You've already bought me a backpack and clothes. I don't need anything else."

He grinned. "It's not that kind of surprise, but I think you'll like it."

For the next couple hours, we chatted like a couple of college roommates at a reunion, and then things got awkward again.

At bedtime, in the tent he set up the new air mattress, which was a little bigger than the other one and rolled up around the edges. After that he and Killer drifted outside while I donned my jogging outfit. A younger me couldn't have imagined sharing a bed with a man without being intimate, but this was different.

Then he returned with the unzipped sleeping bag, which was like a fluffy quilt. He laid down beside me and pulled it over us.

"If you're worried—"

"I'm not," I interrupted.

"Not what? You haven't even heard what I was going to say."

"I'm not worried about you, Phillip." Almost on cue, our four-legged buddy leapt between us. "And now I have a dangerous killer to defend me."

The next thing I knew Killer jumped to her feet and growled for all she was worth.

80

"WHAT'S GOING ON?" I asked.

"Probably an animal," Phillip said. He crawled across the tent floor to the door flap and peeked out.

"What kind of animal? It's not dangerous, is it?"

"Don't know, but they learn that campers leave food scraps lying around. Oh, wait a minute. There it is. Not real big. I can see his eyes sparkling. Come over here, Eunice. See for yourself."

The scaredy-cat in me wanted to stay back, but I was also curious. I scooted toward the tent opening and gazed into the dimly lit night.

"I can't see very well," I whispered. "It's too dark."

Phillip placed his hands on my head and redirected it more to the right. "Look for a pair of eyes, low to the ground. I think it's a raccoon."

Sure enough, there it was, maybe 20 feet away and staring right back at us. "What does it want?"

"Probably just table scraps."

Suddenly, Killer growled and tried to get after the larger animal. I shrieked, and held her tight, while the critter instinctively rose to its haunches, snarled and flaunted wolf-sized teeth.

In protective mode, Killer barked and bared her ultra-tiny

teeth, causing the coon to lazily run off. Phillip laughed and patted her little head. "What a great protector."

With the half-moon as a poor flashlight, I said, "That animal could have killed our little friend."

"Yes and no," Phillip said. "Coons don't like to fight, but if they get backed into a corner, they can be deadly."

"Really? I didn't know that."

"Well, we all know different things, especially when we travel."

After we returned to our one lone bed, I felt enormous comfort in our little makeshift family. Eventually, the adrenaline and conversations subsided and I could sleep in peace, but that too was short-lived.

The next thing I knew, the alarm on Phillip's phone broke the silence.

"What's going on?"

He picked up Killer and held her just below his waist. "You said it's been a long time since you've watched the sun come up," he said. "Now's your chance. Hurry, It's after five o'clock."

I couldn't contain my grin.

"What's so amusing?" he said, still holding Killer below his waist.

"Oh nothing," I said hoping he wouldn't press the matter.

"Don't give me that. You're smiling for a reason."

"Oh, alright, I guess I can tell you. As I've said before, I've been married and had boyfriends."

"Yeah. So?"

"So, I've seen men get up in the morning. Your soldier was standing at attention. And you were trying to hide it. I thought that was funny. That's all."

He laughed out loud and I did too. God, how I needed a good laugh like that.

A short time later we watched in awe as the darkened sky transformed into a light blue morning blanket. I took a few pictures with Phillip's phone while he opened his iPad and pecked away.

"What's so important?" I wondered out loud.

"Just following up on that surprise I told you about."

By that time, it really didn't matter what the surprise was. I cherished the memories that Phillip and Killer had created for me.

After another breakfast from a pouch, I took the back seat of the trike and watched the highway signs for clues regarding Phillip's surprise. He'd previous said that he wanted to go to New Orleans, but we weren't going in that direction so I presumed he was taking us to Chicago instead.

That too was wrong.

Eventually we ended up in Dubuque, Iowa just across the Mississippi River from Wisconsin and Illinois. As we zigzagged through the town, I marveled at the century-old stone and brick buildings and imagined the area in its heyday - before the railroads and highways - when countless ships moved goods up and down that well-known river.

Eventually, we cruised a ridge on the southern side of the little city where a few dozen multi-leveled mini-mansions overlooked the water in which a potpourri of boats were on parade. It was all so beautiful and peaceful that I thanked God and Roomie and Randal for making it possible.

Then we pulled onto a cobblestone driveway of one of the gorgeous mansions. Atop the eaves, two gargoyles appeared to be looking down on us with suspicious eyes. I grinned at Phillip.

"Do you know the owners of this place?"

"Nope. It's an airbnb. I found it online and we've got it all to ourselves for the weekend."

81

I DON'T KNOW HOW TO EXPLAIN IT, but Phillip made me feel like I mattered again. "I've heard of airbnb's," I said after we parked. Aren't they similar to a bed and breakfast?"

"Except you deal with the owners and there is no food," he said, grabbing Killer's carrier. "We can go out, or have somebody deliver to us or make our own. Let's check this place out first. It's got spectacular reviews and an incredible full-family bed."

"What's that?'

"I don't know exactly. That's why I want to see it."

"I'm sure it'll be very nice," I said, "but are you certain you can afford this?"

He smirked. "Don't worry about it, Eunice. It's already done."

I might have doubted him but thus far he hadn't been prone to hyperbole. "All right. I just want you to know that I'm grateful."

A large, heavy wooden entrance door presented a tall-ceilinged foyer and a huge, wooden staircase. All of it reeked of money. We dropped our gear and let Killer out of her carrier.

"Let's tour the ground floor first," Phillip said, walking toward the living room.

Not surprisingly, the living room was bigger than a condo I once rented. The vaulted ceiling was topped with a beautiful antique chandelier. Off to my right, a plush sitting area hid behind two cherry wood pillars. In the center of that wall, a massive stone fireplace climbed to the ceiling. Between the fireplace and the sidewalls, lead-glass windows protected shelves of antique books.

"Now I know why they wanted a three-thousand-dollar damage deposit," Phillip said.

I agreed and gently shook my head. "It's like we're in the movies."

Beyond the living room a modern kitchen butted up to a plush formal dining room. The lavish wood cabinets, marble counters and stainless-steel fixtures were to die for. "It's got two refrigerators," Phillip said, while I noticed a service window through which the kitchen workers could pass food to the dining room.

"I don't think so," I said. "I saw a kitchen like this in a magazine one time. One is a refrigerator. The other is a freezer," I said, walking toward the window above the sink. Outside, a perfect view of the magic river and a procession of boats, both large and small, would have made for an excellent opening scene in a movie.

"Let's go upstairs," Phillip said in an excited tone. Back at the foot of the main staircase it was obvious that Killer's legs were too short to climb the mountain of steps, so I carried her while we climbed wide stairs adorned with a thick green runner that reminded me of fresh-laid sod. On the upper landing, a church-sized stained-glass window splashed a rainbow of colors upon the walls.

In the original master bedroom, rich, baby-blue curtains and a matching carpet served as a soothing background for a king-sized canopy bed, an open sitting area and a spotless bathroom adorned with golden fixtures.

"I see what you mean," I said, putting Killer down so she could roam too. "This place is a sea of wealth."

Phillip nodded. "If the website pictures are correct, this is the second-best bedroom. The other is a super-master suite."

I'd never heard of such a thing.

"Okay. You've got my interest. Let's have a look."

At the other end of the hall, Phillip pressed a massive door inward, revealing the first glimpse of the super-master suite, which was actually two large bedrooms combined. My stunned eyes ping-ponged back and forth between the biggest bed I'd ever seen and a spotless copper hot tub beneath an extra-large stained-glass window in the corner.

"This bed is a double-king," Phillip said with a huge grin. "It's got fourteen pillows. It sleeps eight people and still has room for the family dog."

Still stunned, I looked over my shoulder and noticed a huge and well-placed TV screen that practically begged a handful of people to lie down on that bed and watch a movie in the most luxurious home theater imaginable.

"Did they scoot two king-size beds together?" I asked.

"No. It's supposed to be one large mattress with custom frame and custom sheets."

I recalled the cot-like bed I'd been using for the past ten years and pursed my lips.

"Look over here, Eunice," Phillip said from behind me. Seconds later we slid into an ultra-luxurious master bathroom with a walk-in shower, big enough to accommodate that whole clan of movie watchers at the same time. "Look at all these shower heads," he added. "You can set it like a rain shower or try them one at a time."

I could have told him of a larger communal shower that accommodated a dozen naked inmates of various sizes, shapes and colors at the same time, but I kept that little secret to myself. Nor did I point out that the abundance of large strategically-placed mirrors throughout the suite seemed to be designed for swingers. A handful of horny friends could easily pile onto that bed at the same time and follow that up with gang showers if they were inclined.

"It's all very interesting," I said, "but to be honest with you Phillip, you're making me nervous."

He paused a moment. Then, "Oh, I get it. You're thinking that I'm being presumptuous."

"Well, yeah. That's a good way to put it. This place is like a honeymoon castle and we don't have that kind of relationship."

"That's true, but we've already shared a bed a few times with no problems. Besides if you were here with an old high school girlfriend or somebody like that, you'd probably both soak it all in, so that's what we should do. Right?"

He had a point, but he also confused me. I'd been fighting unwanted advances for years. Then Phillip came along. He clearly liked me for who I was right from the moment he scooped me out of the gutter. You'd think that I would have welcomed a benign relationship like that, but quite frankly, the woman I'd once placed in hibernation was waking up.

I grabbed his hand. "Let's look at the hot tub," I said, leading him to the corner, where the classy window invited any tub users to peer through the kaleidoscope of rich colors to the mighty river and beyond.

"I'm very impressed." I said, "but I could use a burger or something for dinner."

"Me, too," Phillip said. "Would you rather go someplace nice or have Doordash bring us something?"

An hour later, we left a department store and I had new slacks, a pink silk blouse, a sweater, and leather loafers to wear to dinner. "I'll try to repay you some day," I said, holding back tears of gratitude.

"Forget it. I'm just happy to be in public with such an attractive woman. It'll make the other guys jealous."

I knew he was simply flirting, but a love-starved woman needs to hear things like that from time to time and I was way overdue. I kissed his cheek. "Thank you."

82

As IT TURNED OUT, Phillip booked dinner reservations on a boat called Mr. Twain's Riverboat Dining. The two-hour trip down and back was scheduled to depart at 6:30 p.m. but we got there a bit early.

While there, another fellow got to talking with Phillip about the trike and before I knew it, they decided to take a quick ride, which left me with the other man's wife, who was younger than me and fidgeting with her cellphone.

After a little small talk, I recalled something I'd done once before and had an idea. "Guys sure like the bikes," I said.

"Yeah. Craig has always wanted one of those three-wheelers, but we never could afford it.'

"That can be a problem all right. Would you mind if I ask you a favor? I didn't bring my cellphone with me and would like to call a friend while we're waiting. I don't suppose you'd let me use yours?"

"Oh, sure," she said sliding it toward me. "I need to go to the ladies room, anyway."

"I appreciate it."

"Hello?" Roomie said after a couple of rings. "Who is this?"

"Hi, Roomie. It's me, Miranda. Can you talk in private?"

"Oh, my God! Yeah! Just a minute. I'm at Randal's place

and can step outside. I can't believe this," she soon added excitedly. "Are you okay? Where are you?"

"Yeah. I'm safe, but it was close there for a while."

"I'm so sorry for leaving you behind in Utah, but Randal was pissed. I hope you can forgive me."

"Of course, I do."

"How are you doing? How'd you get away?"

"I don't want to say too much, but I hitched a ride and found a nice guy. I think he'll help me get my ID and things. How about you?"

"You know me. I'm always knee-deep in drama. After we got back from Reno, where Randal got his three-way, which was actually pretty fun, we came back home. But I've barely been talking with him since then."

"Why? What's wrong now?"

She paused for a second then lowered her voice. "I suppose I can tell you. The truth is you were right about him. He's got a wife, and I think he still loves her."

"You poor thing. Why haven't you left him?"

"What can I say? I'm a hopeless romantic. He keeps telling me he's going to get a divorce and I pretend to believe him."

"But you can get somebody better," I said, just as the woman who lent me her phone came toward me. "I gotta go now, Roomie. I'll call you later. You be careful. Okay?"

"Oh, I get it," Roomie said. "Call me again as soon as you can. I want to know if you've found your son. I love you, Miranda. You've always been a great friend."

***

Neither Phillip nor I had ever been on a river cruise, so we stood on the back deck of our boat as we pulled away from the dock. Shortly thereafter, we were seated in a charming, darkened booth with electric candles.

We sipped wine and talked more about the future than the past. That was one of the many things I liked about Phillip. He enabled me to ostrich my past and embrace brighter thoughts, such as whether I might be able to meet Cody someday.

After we drifted down the river awhile, a fabulous catfish dinner added to the peace and romance. The time was right to test other waters.

"Can I ask you a question? How long do you expect to be touring around?"

He grinned. "What do you mean? Are we talking about tonight or in the broader sense?"

"Yeah, that. Where does this journey end?"

"Well, I can tell you that Killer and I like our company of late and we still like to see new things."

"But don't you miss your home and your work and friends?"

"Well. My laptop keeps me connected with my people and I can do most of my work on it, so I don't have to go home if I don't want to - but eventually I gotta get back to Silicon Valley to work on my software program."

"What about getting a house or apartment? Have you ever considered that?

"Not really. Why would I? The point of this trip is to see new things and meet new people. If I would have been confined to an apartment, I never would have met you and that's been a priceless blessing that I'll never forget."

Comments like that separated Phillip from nearly every other man I'd ever met. It tempted me to remove a shoe and foot-rub his leg under the table, but I wasn't certain how he'd react. "Are you still thinking about going to New Orleans?" I asked.

"It'll take a couple days to get there, but I'm game if you are."

"I dunno. I was wondering how far it is to Ohio."

"Three hundred miles, more or less, depending on where you want to go. Why?"

I couldn't ask him to help me find Cody because that would require me to admit my past.

"Just curious, that's all."

83

After dinner, Phillip ordered some raspberry sherbet and more wine. The remainder of the return trip may have been nothing more than a boat ride, but it certainly had a romantic quality to it. We arrived at the airbnb a little before ten. After we took Killer for a necessary walk, we returned to our one-of-a-kind mini-mansion.

"What would Eunice say to soaking in the hot tub for a while?" Phillip asked.

Naturally, my feelings ran mixed. In one regard, that super-suite complimented the evening perfectly, but I also harbored other reservations.

"I'm not sure," I said.

"Really? Why not? What if I promise not to gawk at you? Better yet, you can wear your undies if you want to."

"It's not only that, but there's something more personal—something cosmetic."

"What are you talking about?"

I hesitated for a moment and then sighed. "I've got an ugly scar from a surgery, when I was an organ donor. I think it's disgusting."

"Wow. Are you kidding me, Eunice? That's a scar of honor. My God. That's one of the least selfish things I've ever heard of. I'm not the only one who would respect you for that."

Respect? It had been a million years since a man said that to me, but on the other hand Phillip had been treating me with respect from the first day I'd met him, when I was literally scavenging for food in a trash can. For the first time in years, I caught a tingly feeling. I knew that I loved him on some level. If it weren't for the fact that I was an escaped con, he might have been a perfect fit for me.

"If it'll make you feel any better," he said, "we have to shower before we get in the tub so we can go one at a time. That way, you don't have to feel self-conscious. Surely you want to try out the shower of rain. We may never have another chance like this."

He made an incredibly powerful point. I'd just endured thousands of days in prison. Every one of those days was a lost opportunity. "Okay. You convinced me, but you go first."

He grinned and bolted for the showers. I don't know if it was intentional or not, but he failed to close the door completely, which caused my tingly feeling to become more pronounced. I looked again. It was the first time in over ten years that I genuinely wanted to be intimate with a man. I looked at the sliver of light behind the door and wondered if I dared open it.

I went for it.

Inside the bathroom, Phillip was facing away. I admired his blemish-free butt, then flicked the light to draw his attention. I slowly undressed for him, unconcerned about my visible flaws. I closed the space between us. We embraced under the imitation rain.

"I want you to know that you are a genuinely kind person and I really, really love that about you."

He squeezed me tighter. "I think I love you too, Eunice,"

We kissed gently and pressed our naked bodies together. While our tongues gently tasted each other, our torsos rubbed together and I could feel his soldier taking up what little space there was between us. We moaned while our hands explored each other's backs and rear ends until we couldn't take it any longer. "I think it's time," he said. "Don't you?"

It surely was.

We dried each other off before we walked hand-in-hand toward the most incredible bed in the world. Near the foot of the bed, we embraced again then moved into the center of the gigantic mattress. The time was right. I looked in his eyes and laid back to welcome him. He eased on top of me and I guided his penis to the moisture. A few exploratory pushes yielded to deeper thrusts. I moaned my approval and wanted that moment to last as long as possible, but we were both way too turned on for restraint. Within minutes Phillip's thrusts became erratic and more powerful. His choppy breaths aroused me too. His eyes were open but empty. His deep groans indicated he was nearing climax. I wanted him to cum in me. I grabbed his butt cheeks and pulled him into me. "Go for it. Go for it." I urged.

Suddenly, he raised his head and arched his back. "Yes. Yes," I encouraged. He exploded inside me and continued to thrust until he finally collapsed beside me and rolled onto his back.

We both drew long deep breaths until I grabbed his hand and rested my head on his shoulder while we calmed down.

I closed my eyes, feeling incredibly peaceful.

Phillip wasn't the most skilled lover I'd ever been with, but he was kind and unbelievably appreciative. In that regard Phillip was an unmatched lover and I knew there would soon be additional opportunities for me to have powerful orgasms of my own. Surprisingly, that moment arrived sooner than I expected.

After we cuddled and rested and hydrated, we found the strength to do it again, this time in a cloud of fourteen fluffy pillows. On that occasion, Phillip lasted longer, and I taught him what I liked. Shortly thereafter, I got the intense orgasm that I craved.

That time, we fell to sleep while holding hands, and never got to the great copper hot tub.

* * *

The next morning, I felt married in spirit: not legally, not physically, not even age-wise, but spiritually. I found my picture of Cody and held it to my chest and sniveled. If life hadn't been so cruel to me, I would not have gone to prison, and Cody would have been part of my life.

Perhaps I would have married a nice man like Phillip and had another child or two. If so, Cody would have a half-brother or half-sister and God only knows where that family would have lived and how it would have worked out. I teared up for the life that never was, but I also understood that Phillip gave me new reason to live; reason to do new things; reason to be happy; reason to love; and reason to enjoy every free minute while I had a chance - which was precisely why I felt like the worst hypocrite on earth.

All along, I rejected men with shallow agendas. I'd been forever convincing myself that I had to have respect and feelings for somebody before I'd get intimate with them, yet when I finally discovered a man worthy of my affections, I was the one living a big lie. I was the one who wouldn't unveil her past. That was just as devious as anything those men did. I felt sick to my stomach. The hypocrite inside me knew that Phillip deserved the truth, no matter the consequences.

I decided I'd look for the right moment and then share my story. But how do you tell a kind and decent man that he's been sleeping with a thrice-convicted murderer?

I simply didn't know.

84

Randal Biskitt had lied when he told Candice he was going to tell his wife he wanted a divorce. Instead, Randal beat the snot out of his wife's boyfriend and returned home.

Candice wrapped her arms around his neck. "I'm so proud of you, Randal."

"Well, what would you expect? I just had to wait for the right time to tell her. That's all."

"That must have been difficult for both of you. I hope she wasn't too sad."

"Well, she wasn't happy, especially when I told her that you and me have become very, very close and might just do something official about it."

Warm and excited, she rose to her toes and squeezed him as hard as she could. "Oh, Sweetie. I'm so happy to hear all this."

The next few days, thinking she was on a track to matrimony, Candice beamed. She contacted her parole officer with the good news and comments about stability. She gladly made arrangements to come in for a last-chance discussion about such things as leaving the state without permission.

With her head still in the clouds and back at Randal's home, they heard car doors slamming outside.

Candice looked through the drapes and saw two local cops

and several suits approaching. Her heart sank. Her stomach tightened. "Oh, shit, it's the police. I hope they haven't figured out that we sprang Miranda."

Randal took a look of his own. "No sweat. Play it cool. They can't prove anything."

She reached for the knob. "Can I help you?" she asked the front man.

"Yes, ma'am. I'm City Detective Koontz. We'd like to ask you a few questions. Would you come out on the porch please?"

"No problem," she said, feigning confidence and moving through the door frame.

"Thank you, ma'am. Now I need you to step toward the two uniformed officers please."

"What's going on?" she asked as she followed orders.

Koontz banged on the door.

"Randal Biskitt, we know you're in there. You've been under surveillance. Now, I need you to come out of there so nobody gets hurt. Hurry up now, before we get nervous."

Following a short pause, Randal muttered, "Alright, alright, I'm coming." Candice watched him step to the porch, but something was amiss.

The scenario was playing out differently from what she expected. She looked into her boyfriend's eyes.

"What's going on, Randal? What do they want?"

"I dunno. Must be some sort of mistake."

Detective Koontz spoke to one of the uniformed officers. "Make sure she's out of the way so she doesn't get hurt."

The officer grabbed Candice's arm just above the elbow and tugged. "You heard him, ma'am. Step back, please."

"Turn around," Koontz said to Randal. "You're under arrest for felony assault of Frederick Martin."

Randal's head reared back. "I don't know what the hell you're talking about."

"I'm not going to tell you again, Mr. Biskitt," Koontz insisted. "You won't like it if we have to use force."

Two other officers took a step forward to indicate they were prepared to take Randal down if needed. With a face full of anger, Randal looked toward Koontz. "This is bullshit."

Shocked, Candice faced her boyfriend. "What do they mean, Randal? What did you do?"

"I didn't do nothing. They got the wrong guy."

As the cuffs clicked around Randal's wrists, Detective Koontz addressed Candice. "I'll tell you what he did. He broke into his wife's house and damn near killed an innocent man. That's what he did."

Her eyes darted from one guy to the other. "Oh, my God. Is that true, Randal?"

Randal ignored her and yelled in Koontz's face instead. "What the fuck would you guys do if the woman you loved threw you out of her house and some other bastard was fucking her?"

"I don't know, sir, but I certainly wouldn't bludgeon a man half to death."

Koontz signaled one of the other officers who stepped toward Randal. "You have the right to remain silent..."

"Okay, I admit it," Randal said hurriedly, "I got carried away, but I had to prove that I loved her so she'd take me back."

Take him back? Candice heard it clearly. He'd been lying to her again. Words like fool and final straw came to her mind.

She probably should have felt as if she'd been shot in the heart, but she'd been-there, done-that too many times and was numb from ignoring all his lies.

The end had arrived.

She relaxed before speaking to him one last time. "You know something, Randal? I hope God forgives you for what you did, cause I sure as hell won't."

"Shut the fuck up, Candice. I don't care what you think."

"Too bad for you, Randal 'cause nobody else will ever love you like I did."

The officers released their grip on her and Randal got a ride in the back seat of a patrol car.

After they all drove off, Candice returned to Randal's apartment and called her sister. "Naomi, it's me. I need a place to stay. Can you come get me?"

85

On the way to the police building Randal nearly panicked because he knew that they'd submit his prints to the data bases and discover that his real name was Richard Charles, and that he had been using an alias for a dozen years because he had a two-page rap sheet full of burglaries, embezzlement, identity theft, forgeries, and selling illegal guns.

His only hope was to bluff his way out. "Listen, you guys," he said from the back seat, "how about taking me over to my wife's place? She'll tell you that you're making a bigger deal out of this than it really is. She'll vouch for me."

"Not likely," Koontz said from shotgun. "She's the one who called us when the ambulance picked up her boyfriend."

"Don't call him that," Randal snapped. "She's married to me. She can't have a boyfriend."

"You've got bigger things to worry about," Koontz said. "If your victim dies, you'll be charged with murder. You could end up behind bars for the rest of your life."

"Alright, alright. I get it, I really do. I shouldn't have smacked on that dude like I did, but I lost my cool. If you'll just listen to me, you'll see that it was self-defense. That asshole was sleeping with my wife and it just ain't right. I had to stick up for what's mine. You get that, don't ya?"

"We're going to be at the station in a few minutes. You can tell us all about it when we get there."

Thereafter, they took his prints and dragged him into an interrogation room. "While we're checking for any outstanding warrants," Koontz said, "I want to get a few things straight. When you went over to your wife's home, what did you do? Did you knock, or let yourself in, or what?"

"I don't remember. I just wanted to be with her."

"That's interesting because when I was over there, I saw some splintered wood in the door frame. Not only that, your wife tells us you kicked the door in. Are you going to call her a liar?"

"No. But I still think you should let me go. You can understand my situation, right?"

"We understand perfectly. After breaking and entering you ripped the lampshade off the lamp and nearly beat that man to death. Now why don't you tell me if I'm going to find any warrants for your arrest?"

"A guy has to protect what's his, so you should let me go and I'll promise to stay clean. I can't handle jail, dude. I'm claustrophobic."

"Nice try, but you screwed up and now you gotta face the consequences."

Randal paused for a moment, then played his final card. "Okay, okay. I get it. You guys gotta do a job. I get that, but I have some information to trade. No shit. It's huge."

"Oh, yeah? Information? How do I know this isn't another one of your desperate lies?"

"I ain't lying. Honest. You know that Munchak chick? The one who escaped from a hospital?"

"Yeah. We're familiar with the case. What about it?"

"I know how she did it, man, and where she's going and who her accomplice was. I'll tell you everything if you'll let me outta here."

"I know one thing. You've been saying all of this was about your wife, but the truth is you don't want to go to jail. I'm guessing you've been there before and it didn't work out so good."

"Whaddya say? Do we got a deal?"

The cops paused, traded glances. Then Koontz faced Randal. "You've caught my interest, Biskitt. You stay here for now while I go check on something."

"Yeah, you do that. I got big news. no shit."

Not long thereafter Koontz returned with his cellphone in hand and spoke to Randal. "Alright, Biskitt, I've got Captain Phyllis Manny of the Fugitive Apprehension Team on the line. She's been looking for that woman. If it's okay with you, we'll put this call on speaker and you can answer a couple of her questions. How's that sound?"

"Will it get me out of here?"

"I don't know what we can work out until you tell me what you've got. You ready?"

"Okay. Sure."

Koontz spoke to Manny. "Did you hear that, Captain?"

"Yes, I did, Mr. Koontz. First off, Mr. Biskitt. I understand that Officer Koontz read you your Miranda rights; is that correct?"

"Yeah. They did that earlier."

"And you're speaking of your own free will and none of us have offered you anything of value for your information. Is that right, sir?"

"Not yet, but I won't tell you what I know without some benefits for me."

"We'll see about that. Just to be clear, we're talking about the escape of prisoner Miranda Munchak. Is that your understanding, sir?"

"Yes, yes. I know her real well."

"Okay then, just what do you know about the matter?"

"Like I said before, I know who helped her, and how they got away and where they stayed and where she might be going."

"How do we know that you didn't just get your information from the television, cause if that's all you've got—"

"I know that there were two getaway vehicles. The first one was a white SUV. It was a decoy with stolen plates. They drove to a place where there were no surveillance cameras: the Sunshine Apartments. There's a real tall fence at the back of the parking lot. That's where they dumped the white one and picked up their real getaway vehicle."

The captain hesitated before going for more information. Then she said, "And exactly where will we find Munchak right now?"

"No way. I ain't stupid and I ain't saying any more unless I got an attorney and you're gonna cut me a sweet deal."

"Hold for a moment, please," Captain Manny said while she had a brief chat with somebody else who was with her. Then she said, "Alright Mr. Biskitt. We can get there in a few hours. By that time, you'll have an attorney, and we can discuss the matter further. Is that okay with you?"

"As long as I get a deal."

"We'll see what you have first."

"Good. Hurry. I don't want to stay here any longer than I have to. It stinks in here."

86

AFTER SPEAKING WITH DETECTIVE KOONTZ and listening to Randal Biskitt's comments about Munchak, Captain Manny knew it was highly likely that the woman who was with Biskitt when he was apprehended was Candice Carmichael.

With a hot lead like that, she had the police stake out both Biskitt's home and the home of Carmichael's sister, Naomi Grant, until the FAT unit could get there and talk with Carmichael.

"If you have to," Manny said to Koontz, "hold Mrs. Grant for suspicion of aiding a fugitive."

A half dozen hours later, and with the bright half-moon as a witness, detectives at both homes banged on the doors and a somewhat nonchalant Carmichael was located at her sister's home. From there she was undramatically escorted to a back room of the police building.

Furious with Biskitt, Candice was ready, willing and able to redden the ears of her inquisitors. Then a man and woman added themselves to the conference room, shut the door, and seated themselves.

"I'm Captain Manny of the Fugitive Apprehension Team," the woman said. "This is Lieutenant Woodson. He is going to read you your Miranda rights, then we're going to ask you some questions, mostly about Ms. Munchak. Do you understand that?"

"Yes. I've heard them before."

After the rights were stated, Manny got right to it.

"To begin with, we've spoken with your parole officer and you're going back to prison, so from here on out, you're going to answer the questions honestly because that will determine just how long you're going to be locked up. Got it?"

"I already told my sister I'm going to face this on my own, so I'll tell you anything you want to know, just so long as you promise me that you're going to send Randal to the worst prison you can."

"That's up to somebody else. I trust that you know hospitals are full of surveillance cameras. We saw you and your lover boy escort Ms. Munchak through the halls and out the building. You don't deny that, do you?"

"I deny that he's my lover boy. I'll just call him Asshole."

"But you don't deny that you and he helped Munchak get away?"

"Of course not."

"Good. And you don't deny that you and Munchak planned everything, including the escape, and where you could hide out, and the dual getaway cars and that clever idea to send your cell phones to Houston; and then you blackmailed Mr. Biskitt into helping you. Didn't you?"

"That's ridiculous. Did Asshole tell you that? I asked him to help me see Miranda and he knew all the ins and outs. Miranda didn't know anything about it until we wheeled her out of there."

"That's not what Biskitt said. He claims you threatened to tell his wife that he was having an affair and that that information would end his marriage, so he was basically forced to help you and Munchak."

"Oh, yeah? Well, assholes are known to fart, you know? The dude is lying."

"Alright then, let me ask you something else: Is Munchak using an alias?"

"Not that I know of."

Manny glared at her young opponent. "Now, you're the one who's farting, Ms. Carmichael. We happen to know that you helped Munchak obtain the name Eunice Waxman. If you keep lying to me—"

"I didn't lie. Asshole was the one who knew how to get an alias. But Miranda was recovering and not interacting with anybody, so I never heard her use the name, except maybe one or two times."

"That's just a technicality. What about her kid? Could she be looking for him?"

"Don't know, she mentioned him a couple times. That's all I know about that."

From there, Manny pushed and tugged until she got to the point when Miranda refused to participate in a three-way. "And that's when you split up?" Manny asked. "Where did Munchak go from there?"

"I don't know that part. Asshole was pissed off and wanted to leave her behind, so we took the car from the garage and his van. We sold the car, then went to Reno and then back to California."

"Where was Munchak after that?"

"I already told you, I don't know. That's the God's honest truth, but I do know something else that will please you vultures."

"Oh? And what does that mean?"

"It means that Asshole killed a man a long time ago. He said it's a cold case now."

Manny glanced at Woodson and then returned her attentions to Candice. "Details. I need details."

Candice shook her head. "I may be stupid, but I'm not that stupid. I want an attorney."

Manny stared at Carmichael for a few seconds. "Alright, she said, we'll have somebody take you to a cell until you can get that attorney."

Next, in the hall, Manny spoke with Lieutenant Woodson. "So Biskitt killed somebody. That puts a fly in our ointment."

"Yeah. It explains why he's been singing."

"True, but it doesn't move us closer to the goal line. Both Carmichael and Biskitt said they don't know where Munchak went and they sounded believable."

"And we already knew that she could look up her kid. That was why we put out the BOLO in Cincinnati."

Manny nodded. "Bottom line, Munchak is still in the wind and she could have left the country by now. We need a bigger break. A witness or something. If we don't catch a break of some kind pretty soon, I'm afraid we're going to have set the file aside and put our time into other cases."

"What now?"

"I want to play one more card before we move the case to the back burner."

"Utah?"

"Yeah, I want to check out the home that they stayed in. Maybe the neighbors will know where Munchak went."

"The words long shot come to mind."

"Yeah, but it's all we've got."

87

AFTER MY SHARE OF SEX-CRAVED MEN, I'd come to believe that I'd never be with a good man again. But Phillip Pilday proved me wrong. In a way that saddened me.

Phillip was interesting in his own way, but no doubt his greatest strength was his kindness and decency toward both people and critters. A man of that character deserved friends and lovers of similar values and that was the genesis of my sorrow.

I'd completely flunked the integrity test because I hadn't made a meaningful attempt to reveal who I really was. Phillip deserved the whole truth. Lacking that, I needed to step aside so he could meet somebody whose future did not include a prison cell.

Before deciding whether I should finally fess up, I asked myself a key question: Why was I still with him? Was it because I had no other options or did I genuinely like, or even, love him?

Being honest, when I first met Phillip, he was nothing more to me than an escape hatch from a sewer. He more or less rescued me, just like he had done with Killer.

But the cherry on my Phillip sundae came from the airbnb. Just booking it was a sweet and wacky idea; but it was much more than that. When we originally toured the quirky place, his child-like enthusiasm was contagious. He brought that out of me and had become much more to me than a ticket out of town. We genuinely wanted to be together, and that special connection of the hearts could only be maintained if I'd come clean about my past – but how does one dump a king-sized diaper of bad news in the lap of somebody she loves?

With so much to lose, I decided to employ a phased-in confession. The idea was to wait for the right moment and then feed him individual bites of my elephant as opposed to shoving the whole animal down his throat at once.

With my strategy in place, I waited for him to finish his shower so we could enjoy the copper hot tub and go from there.

While in the tub, we decided to stay in paradise one more night and then scoot toward New Orleans the next day. That'd enable us to visit a western club that we'd seen across the river.

That night, on the steps of the first bar I been to in a decade, I assumed that any normal person could easily see the age marks in my face and would simply let Phillip and me walk right in, but we came across a bouncer who'd lost touch with his common sense. "This is no ID," he said while examining my pathetic piece of identity paper. "Anybody could make up something like this. It's no good."

"Look at me," I said, while tapping at my face. "Do you see these wrinkles and the crow's feet at my eyes? Do I really look like a minor to you?"

"Not the point. If I let you in—"

"I can vouch for her," Phillip said, slipping the bouncer a folded-over bill. "She's my sister. I thought she might like this place, but we can go someplace else if we need to."

The bouncer glanced at the bill, nodded and suddenly had a change of heart. "All right. You folks convinced me. Go on in."

We moved toward a table that was near a small stage, which contained a piano. "What did you give him?" I asked

Phillip while I took a chair that faced away from as many people as possible to limit my exposure.

"I don't know what you're talking about, ma'am," he said with a schoolboy grin.

I assumed it was at least a twenty.

A waitress arrived and we ordered beer from a local micro-brewery.

"A Yamaha," Phillip said while pointing his thumb toward the piano. "They're pretty good. Has Eunice ever played a musical instrument?"

"No. Not me. I can't sing or play an instrument, but I like most music. What about you?"

He grinned. "When I was a kid, my ever-present grandmother insisted that I play piano. Naturally, we had two different opinions of what kind of music I should play. After eight years I was okay, but I sorta phased out."

"Really? Why don't you play something?"

"I dunno. Some owners don't like that."

"Two brews," our waitress said, setting down our drinks. I posed the obvious question and seconds later Phillip had permission to play around with the Yamaha.

"Not before I visit the boy's room," he said.

While he was gone, it was absurdly clear to me that I still had to get an ID. Just then a curly-haired dude with a ten-day beard wandered toward me.

"I saw you at the door. You looked uncomfortable."

"Not really."

"Your partner looks too young for you."

"I don't mean to be rude, but I don't want to talk to you."

"Why not? Are you a snob or something?"

"No, I'm just not interested."

A few minutes later another man, this one wearing a baseball cap, approached and offered to buy me a drink.

"No, thanks," I said, feeling like I had a target on my back.

Phillip returned and immediately grasped the situation.

346

"Hey, pal, do us all a favor and leave the lady alone, okay?" he said.

The guy hesitated for a moment, then backed off, "Sorry, man," he said, and walked away.

Apparently emboldened by his act of chivalry, Phillip rose and moved to the piano. Some fifteen minutes later, he'd played four or five songs from various genres and earned enthusiastic applause and two more beers – on the house.

In the end, the evening was a perfect microcosm of our relationship. Phillip's kindness and creativity constantly reminded me of why I had to level with him.

88

I COULD HAVE STAYED AT THE AIRB&B for months or even years, but the final morning began with a shower and another dip in the hot tub. All the nudity and closeness sparked an extra trip to the middle of the giant bed. That time, when we made love, we were more familiar and shared tender whispers.

Ultimately, Phillip booked our next campsite. We packed up, locked Killer down and aimed for New Orleans. With the better part of three days to reveal who I really was, I decided to stick with the elephant metaphor: one bite at a time.

It didn't take long to open up just a bit.

"Can I ask you something?" I said. "Why haven't you asked me anything about my past?"

"Several reasons. One is, my parents and my grandmother taught my sister and me to mind our own business."

"Ah yes, your loving grandmother. Anything else?"

"Yeah. Your actions spoke for you."

"What does that mean?"

"It's a smoke and fire thing. A person who is looking for a ride, but only has one plastic grocery bag for luggage, has to be in a predicament of some kind. I observed how you treated Killer and learned that you have a very gentle soul and wouldn't purposely hurt anybody. My best guess was that you were having an affair with a powerful married man who would do anything to keep you quiet, so you had to run away. That's about as far as I've gotten."

He may not have been totally correct, but he wasn't totally wrong either.

"I can see why you think that," I said. "Maybe we can talk more about it later."

"Suit yourself, because it's none of my business."

So far, so good. I'd essentially admitted that I had some kind of nefarious secret, but more importantly, I hadn't shocked him enough to chase him off.

The next bite at the elephant came right after a noon break. This time the idea was to find out how he would respond to a theoretical situation that was vaguely similar to my own.

I began, "What would you say if I told you I've been in a little trouble?"

"I don't know. What kind of trouble?"

"I'm just talking hypothetically, but what if I said I was an alcoholic who had a horrible car accident and ended up serving 12 months in a county jail?"

"Is that what you're saying, Eunice? Did you kill somebody in a car crash or something?"

"No," I said, "but I just wanted to know what you'd think."

"Well, that would be very serious, but we've had a few drinks, yet you've never been out of control, so I doubt that you're a dangerous alcoholic. I'd be inclined to extend you the benefit of the doubt and let you tell me more."

That was one of things I liked about Phillip. He was a positive person with nice things to say – just like Roomie. "That's good to know," I said, hinting that we were on the right track. Additionally, I could infer that he wasn't likely to go running to a sheriff or police officer if he knew my situation.

That night we pitched the tent and sat on opposite sides of a little campfire.

"You're sweating," I said. "Don't you get tired of all the work?"

"Not particularly. There's a lot of peaceful time too. That reminds me," he said while standing and moving toward his trike, "I got you a birthday present."

"What? I'm sorry to disappoint you, Phillip, but it's not my birthday."

"Well then, it's a belated birthday present," he said, while mining around in the trunk, "so that's good enough. Ah, yes, here it is. Close your eyes."

"You've already gotten me too many things," I said, pretending that I'd received all the gifts I could ever enjoy.

"Here we go," he said. "Take a look."

The first thing I saw was a ring box in his hand. "Don't get the wrong idea," he said. "I'm not asking you to marry me, or anything like that, but this box contains something you could use. Go ahead and open it."

I grinned. "Well, I have to admit you have my attention." Inside the box, there were indeed two beautiful rings—both an engagement ring and a wedding ring.

"They're not expensive," he said, "but they'll be good dude repellant."

I actually laughed, "What a great idea. Would you mind if I wear them all the time?" He nodded and looked as if he wanted to say something special — perhaps that he loved me — but he kept his powder dry. Regardless, it was a tender moment and a good opportunity to dine on our elephant.

"Well, thank you. I think by now you know that I have something important to tell you."

"Yeah, but you don't have to say anything if you don't want to, Eunice. We all have our secrets."

"I know that. You've been wonderful in that regard, but I have some very dirty laundry to air and you deserve to know the truth."

"Sounds serious."

"I've been trying to come clean, but it's very difficult. Can I just ask you a couple questions? Maybe that'll make it easier.

"Certainly. Anything you wish."

89

THAT EVENING, WE ATE DINNER at a restaurant with outdoor tables, and spent the better part of an hour talking about New Orleans. When we finished, a couple of middle-aged police officers rolled in and were checking out the trike and Killer. By that time, I was used to the admirers but the authority figures always made me nervous.

I thought about hiding in the restroom, but Phillip marched right up to them.

"Hi, officers," Phillip said. "Do you need something?"

"No," the taller one said while flipping his thumb toward the trike. "Your getup caught my eye. How do you like it?"

"The trike? We like it a lot, but the basic storage area is too small if you're carrying a tent and typical camping gear."

"I like how you added the doggie compartment. My wife would like that for our dog."

At that moment, the shorter officer faced me, indicating that he wasn't as intrigued by the trike as his partner was. "How long you folks been on the road?" he asked.

Trying not to soil myself, I brushed some hair out of my eyes so that I looked more like a wife than a convict. "Several weeks," I said with a pounding heart, "but we still have more to see."

"When I bought it," Phillip said of the carrier, "the salesman said it was windless inside, so I put a lit candle in there and took a test ride up the highway. The flame never went out."

"Impressive. Would you mind opening the storage compartments?"

Yikes!!! A minute earlier that same officer had implied that this was not a police matter, but that last question sounded to me like a sneaky way to search us for some reason. I balled my hands into fists.

"Not at all," Phillip said, before unhooking Killer's carrier.

"Do you guys have fishing gear?" my cop asked. "That's what I would like."

Hmm. In a game of good cop/curious cop, the officers had us engaged in two completely different conversations.

With so many probing questions, I assumed that one of them would ask for my identification. I swallowed hard and waited for the hammer to strike.

"Well, it's been nice meeting you folks," tall cop suddenly said. "We'd better grab our dinner now."

A moment later they disappeared into the restaurant and Phillip closed the trunk.

"That was nice," Phillip said.

Apparently, I had the only heart that was pounding like a freight train. "Mmhmm."

***

The next day, en route to New Orleans, my brain had been juggling several issues. One had me anxiously looking forward to the jazz clubs on Frenchman Street, not to mention the fabulous food and maybe a little dancing with Phillip - all while wearing my dude-repellant rings.

At other times I couldn't shake a powerful urge to locate Cody. I yearned to go back and find him and hug him and tell him that I'd always love him.

Suddenly, a thunder of loud music on our left overwhelmed the rumble of the trike. In an instant a maroon convertible full of drunken 20-somethings pulled alongside us. With beer bottles in hand, they yelled the kind of profanities that you hear in prison. I grasped Phillip's belt.

"Ignore them," he said via the helmet mic.

But it didn't matter. The driver swerved uncomfortably close to our rolling trike, enabling three of his trouble-makers to simultaneously chuck beer-bottle grenades at us. Phillip clamped at the brakes and I ducked my head while one of the bottles bounced off the handlebars. Another dinged off Phillip's helmet, causing the attackers to cheer.

I glanced to see if they were pulling away, but the driver stayed abreast of us and nudged dangerously closer, causing Phillip to swerve clear to the shoulder where the right wheel ran out of asphalt and dropped several inches. The trike nearly tipped over and Killer yelped. At that moment another round of beer bottle bombs were launched. One flew under the tires. Another thumped off the trunk and one more smashed solidly into my face. I'd never been hit that hard. I grunted and squeezed Phillip's belt so I wouldn't fall off the trike.

This time the driver hit the gas and his happy warriors screamed like a bunch of crazed sports fans who had just won a championship. Phillip stopped the trike. "You okay, Eunice? Are you okay?"

Aside from being soaked in beer, my face throbbed in several places. "Not really," I said, gingerly feeling my face. I discovered blood from a deep cut on my lower lip.

"Those assholes," Phillip said looking me over. It was the first time I'd heard him curse.

I bent down to look in the mirror and almost didn't recognize myself.

Just then, a delivery truck pulled over and a young Black man hustled toward us. "I saw it all," he said. "My truck won't go fast enough to catch them, but I can call the cops."

"Hell, yes," Phillip said, while checking on Killer. "Jail's too good for those bastards."

"No," I said immediately. "I'll be okay. No need to call anybody."

Our new buddy looked at me again. "You gotta be kidding me, ma'am. You're bleeding bad. We gotta call the police and you should get to a doctor. Your lip needs a couple stitches, at least."

I vigorously shook my head, "Nope. Ain't doing none of that. You've been real nice. Thank you, but I'm going to be okay. Honest."

Phillip looked directly at me. "Are you sure, Eunice? I think he's right. You need some attention."

"I can't do that."

He paused for a moment and must have gotten the hint. "On second thought, she's right. We don't have any insurance and it would cost way too much. We'll just buy a few bandages at the next pharmacy."

"Yeah," I said past my torn lip. "That's all the doctors would do, anyway."

"But what about those guys who hurt you? What if they come back?"

"Don't worry," Phillip said in a very determined voice. "I gotta gun and this time I'll be watching for them."

Our friend shrugged. "All right, then. Sounds like you folks know what you're doin'. I guess I'll get back to work."

"Yeah. Thanks again," Phillip added, just before I literally spit blood.

90

THE BEER BOTTLE EPISODE represented a huge turning point. As Phillip and I worked the trike back up on the shoulder I knew that my house of cards would always be aflutter, and he didn't need the risk of being involved with an escaped felon.

As we re-entered the traffic, I silently wept and watched for a decent place to come clean. Finally, "Look for a place to pull over," I said into my helmet mic.

"You okay, Eunice?" he asked. "Do we need a doctor?"

I tongued my split lip. "No. No. I just need to tell you something."

The next exit was within sight so he took the ramp and settled behind a gas station with a field behind it.

When we dismounted, he glanced at my wounds and handed me a Kleenex. "Oh my gosh, Eunice, are you in pain?"

I shook my head vigorously.

"No, it's way more important than that, but before I tell you, I'd like you to take Killer out of her carrier so I can hold her while I talk."

"Sure, Eunice, sure. Just remember that I'm here for you."

With more than enough tears for two people I waited until the kindest man I'd ever known handed me his tail-wagging buddy. I stroked her head and back, then raised my head.

"You'd better sit down, Phillip. This isn't going to be easy."

He leaned against the trunk. "Okay, Eunice, what is it?"

With a cuddly security blanket in my arms, I wiped at my tears and took a deep breath.

"This is the most difficult thing I've ever had to say to anybody."

"Go ahead, Eunice. I'm listening."

I paused until the first rush of words finally forced their way out of my mouth.

"I'm sorry to tell you this Phillip, but I'm an escaped convict, and you have to get away from me. The cops can arrest you too. I'm so sorry I put you in this situation. I was in a hospital, donating some of my liver to a son I'd never met. One of my former cellmates helped me escape the hospital, but I didn't know what they were up to. Once I got out, I didn't want to go back--"

He raised his eyebrows and his hand.

"Whoa there, Eunice. That's a whole lot to take in and you're not making sense."

I shook my head. "It doesn't matter, Phillip. I'm the worst person in the whole world."

"Baloney. I know you very well and you're a very good person, so the first thing you should do is stop demeaning yourself. Okay?"

"You're wrong, Phillip. You don't know the real me. My real name is Miranda Munchak. Ten years ago my boyfriend dragged me into a series of crimes, including murder, and I got sent to prison."

"Wow, Eunice—"

"I'm not Eunice. My name is Miranda."

"Sorry. That's an incredible statement, er, Miranda and way too much information all at once. I'm sure you have good explanation, but let's not go down that rabbit hole just yet."

"You don't get it, Phillip. You have to get away from me or they can arrest you too."

"Let me be the judge of that. Here's one thing I do know. There's a good way to deal with complicated topics like this, like they do in court. So just give me the bullet points for now. Then, we can discuss one issue at a time and decide what to do."

"Okay, but everything about me is a lie."

"Stop that. You've told me lots of truthful things, too. So, I know you've been in prison and I know you escaped. Is that right?"

More grateful than surprised, I sighed. "Yes, but from a hospital, not the actual prison. Now I'm in the wind."

"Okay, now we're getting somewhere. When I first saw you at that truck stop, you were carrying a small bag. Was that right after you escaped?"

"No. The prison and hospital were in California, not Utah."

"Okay then, how'd you get to Utah?"

"Roomie—she's my former cellmate—and Randal, her boyfriend. They had it all planned."

"Alright, that fills in one of the blanks. But for some reason you guys split up and you wanted to get farther away so they dropped you off at the truck stop?"

"Not exactly, but that's close enough."

"Okay, I know everything from there, and why I'm in danger, but I'm telling you one thing before we go on. I'm not leaving you. We love each other. We're a family and families don't walk away from each other. I'll stick with you forever. You got that?"

I looked him in the eyes. He was as steady as a rock.

"But, what if—"

"Simple, if I get arrested for being with you, they'll go easy on me, 'cause I've never been in trouble and we haven't committed any additional crimes or hurt anybody so I'm willing to hang in there. For now, tell me how a kind and decent woman could have landed in prison in the first place. I'm betting that it wasn't your fault."

I rushed to him, grabbed ahold and cried on his shoulder.

"You're my guardian angel. I love you too, Phillip Pilday. Thank you. Thank you. Thank you."

"You can thank me later, Eunice or Miranda or whatever your name is. Now tell me how you got into this mess."

It took nearly an hour to explain everything, beginning when my brother's mental condition got worse and ending with three dead people and the police claims that I was involved even though I'd always had blackouts in high-stress situations and didn't know what happened.

Eventually, I added the part about the worst day in my life.

"Since I didn't have any family or friends who could raise my baby," I said. "I had to put him up for adoption. I only saw him for a few seconds on the delivery table. That was ten years ago and I've always regretted that day. I've been in prison ever since and the only good thing that has happened to me, prior to meeting you, was some years back when I had a brain tumor removed. That put an end to my blackouts and headaches."

Finally, with all of that baggage off my chest, I felt better and lifted my head just a bit to measure Phillip's reaction.

"I thought it was something like that," he said. "Not the specifics, but you've been trying to tell me something colossal for days. It had to be big, especially considering that you had absolutely nothing when I first met you."

"So, you're not giving up on me?"

"Hell, no. I already told you that I love you."

I grabbed him and cried and squeezed and cried and squeezed some more.

"In that case, I have to ask you for another huge favor. This lifestyle is dangerous. The walls can cave in on me at any minute. I want to find and meet Cody since I will probably never have another chance to see him. It's hard to explain but it's the most important thing in the world to me."

Phillip nodded "My grandmother always said there's no love stronger than that of a mother's love for her children."

"I know where Cody lives, only his real name is Trevor.

He's back in Ohio. If you just get me close to him, maybe I can see him come home after school. If you'll help me do that, I'll do anything you want as long as we're together and I'll never ask you for anything else. I promise."

91

AFTER HEARING THE CONFESSION that I'd been trying to get out for days and my heart-felt dream about seeing Cody, the ever-reliable Phillip truly "got" me. For one thing, he was instinctively more convinced than I was that I hadn't killed anybody. And he agreed to help me see Cody.

Basically in harmony, we scooted to the nearest Walgreens for bandages and salve. "You'd better stay here," Phillip said. "If somebody sees your wounds, they might get the wrong idea and alert the police."

"Okay, I'll hold Killer while I wait." To be totally honest, while I waited it occurred to me that he might call the police. If so, there was nothing I could do about it, so I mentally shrugged and waited him out.

Per usual, he eventually returned with the items I needed. I used the trike mirror to soothe my wounds before we scooted north on the same road that we'd taken toward New Orleans the day before.

Two uneventful yet exhausting days later, at sunset we rolled into a Super 8 Motel about forty minutes south of Cincinnati.

"This'll do," Phillip said, while we slipped off the trike. "They take pets, and we can get to your son's place in a reasonable time."

I'd never felt so connected with a man. I waited for him to sign us in, then asked a selfish question. "When can we go find Cody?"

"Not tonight. I'm beat and we couldn't see much in the dark anyway. But we should be able to get by there tomorrow, that is, if I don't have to leave town for a few days."

Leave town? Mildly embarrassed, I'd grown so engulfed in my own desires that I'd more or less forgotten that Phillip had a life elsewhere. "Of course," I said. "You have other important things to worry about."

That night, we walked Killer, then Phillip tapped at his iPad while I turned channels in search of something that could hold my attention. Ultimately, I was exhausted and should have slept straight through the night, but I wanted to see Cody so badly that I didn't get much rest.

Finally, some daylight found the edge of the sky and a new Sunday was born. "If we're lucky," Phillip said, "we might roll past Cody's home when they're going to church or out to breakfast."

"I can't wait," I said.

"I can tell you this," he said. "We shouldn't stop in front of his house, or even slow down. For all we know, the authorities have alerted his family that you're on the loose, so if we rubberneck that particular home, we might draw their attention."

"I hope he's playing in the yard with friends. I might recognize his chin."

Phillip shook his head. "I know you're anxious, Eunice …I mean Miranda, but we have to be extra careful. I think we should only go by the house one time for now. After we do that, I want to find the school. We might be able to figure out if he walks to school or takes a bus."

I nodded enthusiastically. "You're probably right. I'm too excited to think straight."

We waited a couple hours before we locked down Killer's carrier and idled out of the motel's parking lot. As we approached the outskirts of Cody's neighborhood, my heart filled with love and my fingers quivered.

Phillip lifted one hand off the handlebars. "We're just a couple blocks away now. Remember, no matter what, don't stare at the home or anybody. Just stay nonchalant and gather as much information as we can. Then we can regroup."

Seconds later the GPS directed us to turn left and onto a block of typical middle-class brick houses. Cody's home was the fourth one on the right. The curtains were drawn and nobody was moving around in the yard, but I saw a silver bicycle leaning up against the side of the home. That had to be his. I warmed and then chilled as we proceeded with our plan.

Up the block, several young girls were playing in the street, but there was no sign of my precious son. Regardless, just seeing his charming home and his neighbors and his bicycle made me feel closer to him. I was already looking forward to the next day when I'd have another chance to see him.

As planned, we found the closest grade school, figuring it would be his, and Phillip agreed to bring me back the next afternoon, in hopes we'd see Cody come home from school. At least that was the plan, but things didn't work out that way.

We'd barely gotten back to our motel room when Phillip got a call from home. Something important was going on. He stepped out of our room to talk with his caller. Eventually, "I'm really sorry, Miranda," he said, "but I warned you. I have to go home for a couple days."

I teared up. "To California? When? Why? What about our plans?"

"Gotta leave right away. I can't tell you any more just now, but I'll get back as soon as I can. Can you watch Killer, or should I take her to a kennel?"

"No. No. I'll take care of her," I said all teary-eyed. I don't know exactly what to call my feelings, but it was a combination of impatience, self-pity and fear of being alone again, just like when Roomie and Randal left me behind.

I needed to cuddle with Killer.

92

Later that day, Phillip's plane landed at LAX Airport. Due to the time zone differences there was still plenty of time to attend the butt-chewing that his maternal grandmother, the family matriarch, had scheduled regarding his recent wild spending. At least that was how she couched it, but Phillip knew her as well as anybody and whenever she played the tough guy for a while, she always softened up. She would likely do the same thing now.

He planned to listen respectfully to his grandmother and take whatever medicine she had in mind. Afterwards, he'd be free to focus on the other appointment that he'd secretly made when he was in the Walgreens store buying Miranda's ointments and bandages.

At the curb of the passenger pick-up area, Phillip saw his grandmother's Mercedes coming his way. He grabbed his backpack, threw it in her trunk, and rushed to the driver's door, where he reached through the open window and gave her a big heart-felt hug. Her real name was Julie, but he'd always called her JuJu.

The woman may have been a bit officious, but she had her strong points, too. For one thing she always looked perfect when in public. More than one person had assumed her to be 20 years beneath her actual age of 72.

"Hi, JuJu," he said as he buckled himself in. "I couldn't wait to see you."

"The feeling's mutual, Sweetie, and how's our little dog?"

"Killer? She's doing great. She's with my friend right now."

"I wish you wouldn't have named her that."

"I know. You've said that before. But after what she went through, she deserved a tough-guy name."

JuJu snickered. "That poor little critter only weighs ten pounds. I doubt she puts the fear of God into a kitten, and who is this friend anyway? That Eunice woman you keep talking about in your emails? You're not sleeping in the same bed, are you?"

"Come on, JuJu, I'm almost 33. Do you expect me to tell her that my grandma is not comfortable with our sleeping arrangement?"

"Well, in my day, things were different. You didn't do things like that unless you were married or at least in love. When I first met Pops—"

"You've already told me all this, JuJu. Let's talk about something else. Okay?"

"Fine with me. I suppose you know why I asked you to come back home, don't you?"

"It has to do with money, right?"

"You nailed it, lover boy. You've spent twelve thousand dollars in just two weeks. What the heck is the matter with you? Did you forget that I get the statements?"

"I know all that, JuJu, but I had to make an executive decision."

"An executive decision? You don't mean that hitch-hiker, do you? Didn't you say she's ten years older than you? Why don't you stick with ladies your age? They'd love a guy like you and could give you a bunch of babies."

"I know what it looks like, but this woman is special."

"Baloney. Pops and I worked hard for your trust money, but you were supposed to make it last and stay in low-cost motels and camp sites, but you stayed in a high-priced airb&b. It looked like—"

"I know, but—"

"Don't interrupt me, Phillip. That mansion cost you two thousand dollars for a long weekend – probably with this Eunice woman. Don't you know what she's after?"

"She's not like that."

"Then how do you explain this reckless behavior of yours?"

Phillip smiled. "I couldn't help myself, JuJu. I fell in love. I wanted to take her places and buy her nice things, just like Pops did for you."

"That was different. We'd known each other for a long time."

"That's not the point. I love her and she loves me."

"And, just what does she do to help pay the bills?"

"She's in-between jobs right now."

"Oh, yeah? And just how long has she been unemployed?"

Phillip shrugged. "I don't know exactly, JuJu, and I don't care."

JuJu clucked her tongue. "Sounds to me like she loves your money, not you."

"You wouldn't say that if you met her or saw how she treats Killer and children, like her son. Cody."

"A son? Now, that's rich. Can't you see what she's after, Phillip? Somebody to raise her kid."

"You're wrong, JuJu. She's special and I'm not letting you say otherwise. Now I need some more of my trust money. How about five thousand dollars? I'll be more careful this time."

JuJu scoffed.

"Fat chance, mister. You can't be trusted with that much money all at once so we're going in the other direction. You're going to have to get by on a hundred dollars a day. That'll cover gas, food and shelter. If you can handle that for a while I might consider returning to the old rules, but you've gotta learn to respect money and I'm going to make sure you do that. Now, how's that for changing the subject?"

93

Very early the next morning, Phillip took an Uber to the law offices of Breanne Hize, a long-time family attorney and dear friend. As feisty as she was smart, Breanne was with Phillip's mother the day Phillip was born and became his godmother. Professionally, the attractive brunette knew the ropes, especially in corporate crime.

When it came to attorneys, Phillip wouldn't have called anybody else.

In a large office building, Phillip entered the greeting area, too early for a receptionist. Instead, he heard a gleeful voice trotting up the hall.

"I hope that's my Phillip out there." Seconds later, she rushed him and hugged him. Dressed in a classy blue pantsuit, Breanne always smelled like a queen.

"So how are your folks?" she asked. "I've been meaning to call them."

"Actually," Phillip replied. "they're in Europe - on another cruise or something."

"How nice for them. What about your software program? Is that coming along?"

"Slow and steady progress, but it's still going to take a while."

"Well, good luck with that. Tell me about Grandma. How's she doing?"

"Chipper as ever. Actually, she's part of why I'm here."

Breanne tilted her head slightly. "Oh? How so?"

"It's sorta complicated—"

"Then just gimme the bullet points."

"Okay. I met this woman—"

"Stop right there. Is my godson in love?"

Phillip grinned. "I admit it. I bought a large trike - you know, a motorcycle with three wheels. I also adopted a little dog as a companion and began a cross-country journey to see other places and people, and to think about some of my work."

"Sounds adventuresome."

"The idea was to sleep in cheap motels and campsites to save money. Then, in Utah, I met Miranda. She was scared and running from somebody. I could tell she needed me. So, we travelled together for a few weeks. She's kind and wise. I really like her."

Breanne bobbed her head. "Okay. So, what does this have to do with Grandma?"

"Well, I felt sorry for Miranda and wanted to impress her, so I bought her a few things and then more things. I kept thinking she would dump me and move on, but we just got tighter and tighter. Then I rented a crazy deluxe airbnb on the Mississippi River and that's where we fell in love."

"Grandma info, please."

"Well, JuJu gets copies of all my purchases and discovered that I'd spent a full six-month stipend from my trust in a few weeks."

"God love her. So, she called you home to take you out to the woodshed?"

"You got it. We're not crossways or anything like that, but she thinks Miranda is a bad influence and put me on a meager allowance to teach me a lesson."

Breanne grinned. "Don't tell me you want to sue her to get your allowance increased."

"No! It's nothing like that."

"I didn't think so, but you should cut her some slack. It's been a long time since she was in love. So, why are you here?"

"It's about Miranda and why she was hitchhiking."

"Oh?"

"Yes. She needs you. I need you. I just know she's innocent."

"Innocent? So, we're talking about a crime. You don't want me. I'm too expensive. I could find you somebody else who could help her for a lot less money—"

"No. No. No." Phillip said. "You don't understand. Miranda has to have the best attorney there is. That means you. I'll give you everything I own if you'll just talk to her. You'll see. She's a good person in a horrible situation. You can literally save her life."

"Save her life? Is it really that serious?"

"Yes, yes, yes. But we have to hurry. She's on the verge of doing something that could end everything."

"Alright then, my young godchild. If it's that important to you, I'll give her a call, just for you."

"Thank you. Thank you. I knew you would help me."

* * *

After Phillip left, I had a pretty rough time without him. Then in the late afternoon, after Killer and I went for a walk, he called me on the motel's line. He didn't say why he went back home but thankfully he'd booked a return flight and we'd have another run over to Cody's neighborhood where I might get a peek at my precious son.

The adult in me should have recognized that it wouldn't be the end of the earth if I had to wait one additional day to see Cody. But the anxious mom inside me had never really seen her son and could be taken back to prison at any hour of any day. I could never forgive myself if I made it this close and never got to see him.

As the hours slipped away, I paced and paced while fearing that my whole world could crumble at any minute.

Finally, I heard a car door. There was still a half-hour of light. I hoped Phillip would take me the 18 miles to Cody's home. I placed Killer in her carrier and stood ready at the door. Then, I heard his key in the lock. I felt like a whimpering dog who'd spent the whole day waiting for her human to return.

"Thank God, you're home," I said, wrapping my arms around him. "I know it's late, but if we hurry—"

"Can't," he said sternly. "We have to wait a few minutes. I'm expecting a call."

"But we're running out of time."

"I know that, Miranda, but this is important too. It concerns you."

I stopped, motionless. "Me? You told somebody about me? But I thought—"

Just then, his cell phone rang. "It's her," he said. "I'll put her on speaker. Hi Breanne. How'd it go?"

"Hi, Phillip. Quite frankly, it's rather interesting. Are you with Miranda now?"

"Yes, she's right here."

What the heck? I had no idea who that was nor what she was up to.

"Good, can both of you hear me?"

Phillip opened his laptop and turned to me. "Come sit next to me, Miranda. I've got somebody for you to meet."

Not sure what I should think, I shrugged and moved closer. "Hello," I said to the lady on the monitor.

94

"My name is Breanne Hize. I'm an attorney in California. I also happen to be Phillip's godmother. He came to see me regarding your case."

I glared at Phillip. "I wish you would have told me you were going to do this."

He shook his head. "Don't worry. You've got attorney-client privilege. Breanne can't say anything to anybody without your approval. Isn't that right, Brianne?"

"Close enough for now," she said, before speaking to me again. "If you're up to it, there seems to be a decent chance we can improve your situation."

"My situation?"

"Phillip tells me you were in prison for some serious crimes, broke out and now you're on the run. I did a little checking and discovered that you have confounded the police. They don't know where you are, but they sure want to find you."

Not knowing where this conversation was headed, I kept quiet and let Ms. Hize do the talking. "A colleague and I think we might be able to get you a new trial or get your sentence reduced. But we will have to do a lot of research beginning with this call. I need to ask you some questions to verify some things that Phillip told me. Is that okay with you?"

To say I was dumbfounded would be an understatement. "Well, I guess I don't have anything to lose."

"All right then. Near as I can tell, this all starts with your brother. What was his name?"

"Mickey. He was my twin brother and my buddy."

"All right. Mickey had a life-long mental disorder. Is that right?"

"Yes. He was institutionalized his whole life."

"If you don't mind my asking, what happened to him?"

"He got worse and needed expensive treatments but we didn't have any money. Eventually he died, earlier than he needed to."

"What happened before that? Was his behavior irregular?"

"Yes, he had to take medication to keep calm but occasionally he would go in trances and get wild."

"And what about you, Miranda? As I understand it, you also had these blackouts and trances. Is that right?"

Hmm. This woman was very captivating. "Yes, especially when I was stressed."

"When was the last time that happened to you?"

"About a year after I arrived in prison. The guards made me have sex with them and it stressed me out. I passed out in my cell—"

Stunned, Phillip turned his head my direction.

"Wait a minute," Breanne said. "Back up. Tell me that again."

Wow! This was the first time I felt like I could say anything about the laundry room days. "They called it sugar. Several of us had to take turns keeping the guards busy when the supply trucks were being unloaded."

"Why would you do that?"

"I didn't want to, but it was an arrangement between the inmates and the guards, so that contraband could be slipped to the other inmates. In exchange for doing that, the bad girls left me alone and made sure everybody else did too."

"But you're telling me you were forced to have intercourse with the guards? Do I have that correct?"

"Just two of them, separately, once a month, and it was more than just intercourse, if you know what I mean."

"Well, this is shocking news. I'll have to ask you more about it later, if that's okay with you."

"I guess so. It would be nice if they had to account for what they did."

"Damn right, but getting back to the more immediate question, were your blackouts similar as what happened to your brother?"

"Yes."

"And you both had brain tumors removed. Is that correct?

"Yeah, they examined his brain when he died."

"And you had a similar tumor. Is that correct?"

"Pretty much, a doctor removed it after I'd been in prison for a few years."

"Are you sure it was the same thing?"

"That's what the doctor thought. Mine didn't grow as fast as Mickey's did. I told people about it but nobody cared."

"Well, the truth doesn't mean anything until it bounces between the correct ears. That's why I'm here. Do you still have trances?"

"Not really. I have some strange dreams but that's about it."

"I want to go back to this Don fellow for just a bit. As I understand it, he was your boyfriend and basically dragged you into a plot to steal money from a trust? Don lost his temper and killed a woman. Were you involved in any of that?"

"I agreed to steal the money because the woman had insurance. But I didn't know that Don was going to hurt her and that's when I freaked out and went into one of my trances. Next thing I knew the police arrested me and said I was involved in that death plus two others, but I swear I didn't know what happened. I just pleaded guilty because I thought the police wouldn't lie. Dumb, huh?"

"Not if you were naïve and didn't know what was happening. After you got arrested, what was the interrogation room like? Did you have an attorney present?"

"Yes, but I was brain numb and didn't know what was going on."

Breanne shook her head. "What about your Miranda rights?"

"Yeah," Phillip, said from off to the side, "All Mirandas should get Miranda rights."

"Cute," Breanne said, returning her attention to me. "What about it? Did they read you your rights?"

"I don't honestly know. I was in a stupor. They said I did it so that was it."

"How about later? Did you have a court hearing?"

"Yes. I think so."

"Did you have an attorney?"

"Yes. A young girl stood with me at my table, but she didn't do very much."

"Did anybody ever propose that you see a neurologist?"

"No. They had me meet with a psychiatrist, but he couldn't prove whether I had blackouts or not."

"That's very interesting. Are you certain you didn't see a neurologist? You would have had an x-ray and gotten an MRI."

"No, I just saw the shrink."

"What about when you had that tumor removed? Do you know where I can reach that doctor?"

"That might be in my file. His name was Dr. Burns."

"What about witnesses? Is there anybody who can corroborate your story?"

"Not really. Do you think I have a case, because another attorney told me there was nothing they could do?"

"Well, we don't all operate in the same way. I can tell you it won't happen overnight. We have to do a lot of investigating and round up new experts and see what they think."

"Well, I'm just grateful somebody is finally listening to me."

"You can thank Phillip for that. He's your number-one cheerleader."

"Oh, I will," I said tapping at Phillip's nose. "You can be sure of that."

"Alright, we've covered a lot, but there's a couple additional things before I can help you."

"Like what?"

"This is going to be very, very difficult for you, Miranda, but you have to go to the police department immediately, and turn yourself in."

"What? I don't want to do that. What if I don't win the case? Then I'll be behind bars again. Can't you just do your work and then when we know more, we can decide what to do?"

"Sorry. I don't work like that. The DA will want to see a big positive good faith gesture on your part, and it impresses juries. Not to mention that the Fugitive Apprehension people might find you on their own. Then you wouldn't have any leverage."

"Yeah, but if I do that, am I guaranteed anything?"

"I wish that could be, but you'll just have to take your chances. If it makes you feel any better, I think you have a legit opportunity to get your sentence reduced. But bottom line, I can't help you and won't help you unless you turn yourself in. Not only that, they'll probably ask you who helped you escape and you'd best come clean. Whoever that is could get a few years, but you're looking at a heck of a lot more time in prison than they are."

"But this means I won't see my son?"

"Your choice. Now, is there anything else you think I ought to know?"

Phillip sat up. "I have a question. What about me? Am I in any trouble?"

"I'd say you're on the edge of a knife," Breanne said. "If I understand you, once you understood that Miranda was an escaped inmate you went right to a lawyer. I think we can establish that you did the right thing. Now, I want Miranda to tell me more about those guards who exploited you."

95

AFTER SPEAKING WITH PHILLIP'S GODMOTHER, I knew that the stakes couldn't have been any higher. If I turned myself in, I could end up right back where I came from with more years added to the thirty-one years that I'd not yet served.

Of course, the wind blows in many directions. For instance, there was a remote chance that I'd never get caught and I might devise a way to meet Cody. That would certainly be far better than decades of misery as inmate 1516103-A.

Combating that concept, Breanne was a very sharp woman and very convincing. If she could pull a rabbit out of the hat, I might have a real future. God knows I would love to go out in public without looking over my shoulder the whole time.

While I wrestled with my apprehensions, Phillip threw all his support behind his godmother. Since he had a much clearer mind than I did, I elected to follow his lead one more time.

I must have dropped a thousand tears on the ride to the sheriff's office. Phillip drove slower than he usually did just so I'd be free for a few more minutes. I could only imagine what they might do when a fugitive walked in the front door and surrendered.

Ultimately, we ran out of road. The sheriff's office was

right in front of us. I don't know how a body can produce so many tears but my torso and lap were noticeably wet.

We parked and dismounted. Phillip grabbed me. "You know that I love you, don't you?" I surely did, but I didn't have the strength to say so. "You don't know how much I admire you," he added, "but, while we're being honest, I have some news for you. When I took that flight back home, I was actually in some trouble of my own. A while back I got a stipend from my grandmother. That money was supposed to last me for months. But then Killer and I met you."

I remember that I actually smiled when he said that. "Don't tell me. You spent it all on me."

"Yeah. I wanted to impress you, and I'm glad I did; but now I'm broke. My fabulous grandmother put me on a modest allowance as if I'm a little kid. She just doesn't understand technology and that I'm writing a software program that will be worth millions. Anyway, since I was heading there already, I got a wild hair and called Breanne."

I kissed his cheek. "You are a very precious man."

"So, you don't mind what I did?"

"No, Phillip, I completely understand. We both withheld information for the benefit of the other person. I love you for that."

After a long and wonderful kiss, reality returned. So did the tears. I sniffled. "I hope you'll stay in touch."

"Of course, I will, Miranda. Breanne will know where they send you. I'll write and call and send text messages - whatever they'll allow."

"That's another thing," I said. "Breanne said I'll be in a county jail for months. They have fewer frills than the big house. It's going to be torture."

"Yeah, that's a bummer. Hopefully the time will fly by."

"I sure don't expect that. What are you going to do now?"

"I think I'll work my way back to the west coast and concentrate on my software program."

I wiped away more tears. "You take good care of our dog. I'm sure going to miss her."

Phillip gently tapped my lips. "She's going to miss you too, Miranda."

I glanced at the entry doors to the sheriff's office. "I guess the time has come."

"Do you want me to go in with you?"

"No. I might not be able to let go of you."

"Okay then, I guess this is it," he said before giving me a hug and kiss I'll never forget. We pulled apart. His ring finger was the very last friendly thing I touched.

I walked to the door, went through and turned around for a final goodbye, a final wave, and to mouth the words, "I love you." I could see the tears in his eyes, which brought forth even more of my own. I turned back toward the reception area, squared my shoulders, and stepped up to the desk. "My name's Miranda Munchak. I'm an escaped convict from California and I'm here to turn myself in."

96

It had been two months since I walked into a sheriff's office in Ohio and essentially traded my unstable freedom for a shot at genuine freedom. Before I knew it, a duo from the Fugitive Apprehension Team out of California swooped me into the back of a jet and dropped me in this ugly jail cell, inland from San Francisco.

There's no courtyard, no library, no carpeting, no cafeteria—just a few magazines, a worn-out mattress and a stool in the corner of my cell. Modesty be damned. Quite honestly, I think this borders on inhumane.

Regardless, I was told that my suite of cement and steel bars was better than the cells downstairs where they pack in drunk drivers and fighters and domestic abusers, especially on weekends. Maybe I was better off than them, but there were moments when I would have gladly traded my solitude for one of those loud people to talk with.

Breanne Hize drops by once every other week. The first of such visits brought bittersweet news. Part of our strategy was for me to rat out Roomie and Randal but come to find out they were already in custody because Randal beat the brains out of his wife's boyfriend. Apparently, there was a lot of back-stabbing and double-dealing going on and Randal wasn't even the man's real name.

Looking back, I had mixed feelings about the man who called himself Randal. I never would have tasted freedom or met Phillip were it not for him, but overall, he was a narcissistic, sex-crazed jerk.

My attorney said that those things weakened my case because we had planned to identify Randal and Roomie as accomplices in the escape and as the parties that stole the Utah car and the other things that they pawned.

On the plus side, Ms. Hize said she had managed to salvage some of my powder by agreeing that I'd be a corroborating witness in Roomie and Randal's trials, if needed.

Anyhow, after that early meeting with Ms. Hize, her information became a chain of tedious lawyer speak. At each meeting we scooted off to an interrogation room that was supposed to be private, but everybody knows that those rooms have two-way mirrors and cameras and microphones.

This morning Ms. Hize came by for another round of blah-blah-this and blah-blah-that.

"How you holding up?" she began. "Are you staying sane?"

"Barely. Sometimes I wish I hadn't turned myself in."

"Trust me. I get that, but they make this process drag out to keep insincere inmates from exploiting the system. What about my godson; does he come by?"

"Phillip is my rock. He writes me a letter just about every day and comes by for an hour on visiting day. I don't know how I'd get by without him."

"Well, good for him," she said, tapping at a file she'd brought with her. "Back to your case, we're making some progress. It's slow but promising."

"I just want to get out of here. At least the big girl's prison has things to do."

"I know, but it's going to take time. I've asked for your prison records, so they hired counsel, who told me to get a subpoena, which is a sign they're stalling. I have a hunch that they've got information that could be useful to you."

"Good."

"I've also had a chat with the doctor who did the autopsy on your brother. He said that your brother's tumor seemed similar to the one you had. He wouldn't go any further than that without seeing all your records, but it appears that both you and your brother had blackouts when stressed, which certainly supports your claims that you were 'not there' mentally when the crimes transpired."

"That sounds promising."

"I spoke with an excellent neurologist," she went on. "He said that it's genuinely possible that when you were under extreme stress, you fell into something akin to a hypnotic state in which you were oblivious to your surroundings."

"That's what I kept saying but nobody cared."

"I know, but you were just speaking to the wrong ears. As I was saying, Dr. Frampton is willing to state his opinion in court if requested. I'm going to get a second opinion just to be certain. Then I'll present all of that info, and more, to the DA and push for them to vacate the remainder of your sentence."

Surprised, I shifted in my chair.

"Will they do that?"

"Not likely, but we'll give it a try. Regardless, we have a better chance of getting you a new trial. If the doctor will say that there's a genuine possibility that you were nothing more than an unknowing bystander when those murders took place, then that will strengthen our claim for reasonable doubt."

A bit excited, I said, "That's fine with me, Breanne. Let's do that."

"We can try, but that approach has flaws, too. It could easily take six months to a year to get a trial."

The pit of my stomach tightened. "A year? Would I have to stay in this gawd-awful jail all that time?"

"Afraid so. But worse, you could lose the case and I don't know if you'd ever get another appeal hearing. That would be terminal. That's why I want to cut a deal with the DA. Unless something changes, their case isn't very strong, especially since there have never been any witnesses to your crimes. The DA made their case based on your confession and we both know that was a shallow confession."

"Yeah, they told me I committed those murders and I trusted them. I can't believe I was that stupid."

"The good news is, they don't like to lose, so they just might be willing to compromise."

"When can you do that?"

"Not for a while. I gotta wear them down first, and do it without implying that their department screwed up. I plan to admit that they had no way of knowing that you had that tumor - after all, you didn't even know you had it until your surgery. I'll concede that they worked with what they knew at the time. It wasn't malicious or even mistaken. It was simply a lack of evidence."

"I don't understand why it takes so long."

"There are theories about that, but for now, I see your case as similar to the DNA cases. When new information comes in, it can prove that the wrong person was imprisoned. That's why I'm hopeful they'll vacate the rest of your sentence or cut you a deal of some type. Otherwise, you should be granted a new trial. That's why I don't want you to give up."

I blew out a breath of frustration. "Now what?"

"Well, I'd like to find out why the staff or the doctors who removed your tumor never put two and two together. If somebody had realized that your problem mirrored that of your brother's you might have gotten a new attorney to look into the matter as I am doing."

"I agree. That would have been fair. What about St. Nick and that other guard? Do I get any brownie points for turning them in?"

"Yet to be determined. You've definitely raised some eyebrows, but it's not relevant to your case, so I want to stay focused on getting you out of here."

"Thank you, but be honest with me. How do you think this will all wash out?"

"Hard to tell. Could be anything from complete exoneration to return to prison and serve out your original sentence plus some additional time for your recent actions. I'm guessing you'll land somewhere in the middle."

"When will we know?"

"After I do all the homework and package it up, we could have a decision in four to six months or so."

Talk about stunned. "Four to six months? I don't know if I can live that long in here."

"I know, but the wheels of justice are slow and rusty and bogged down. They just don't move every time somebody squeaks."

"Too bad for me."

97

Throughout my years of confinement, I assumed that no facilities could be worse than the state penitentiary, but seven additional months in the county jail felt like seven years in solitary confinement. Everything including the prison clothes smelled like urine-soaked cement. Further, there were no frills and very few people to talk with. Sometimes I wondered if I'd already gone insane. I wondered about Helena and Killer and Roomie.

Thankfully, Phillip came by once a week for the measly two hours they set aside for visitors. In between visits, he sent me romantic letters like they did in the pre-internet days. I read them over and over again and still have all of them.

My attorney dropped by once in a while to give me updates, but it felt like we were merely going through the motions, with no real intentions to change anything. Nonetheless, Breanne persisted. After speaking with experts, she kept telling the DA that I was innocent because I didn't know anything about the murders that took place around me.

She also came up with a powerful argument involving the sexual assaults in the laundry room. She said if the juries were to hear what went on in there, I would likely garner a ton of sympathy, all of which could easily get in the news and that was the kind of publicity that the Department could do without.

Actually, I was fortunate that Breanne was so persistent because there were occasions when there was so little progress, I just wanted to surrender and get back into big-girls prison where there were people to talk with and a TV and a commissary.

Then another typical Breanne visit rolled around. A deputy led me into an interrogation room, where Breanne was waiting, stone-faced, with two Cokes and her laptop open.

Still skeptical, I may have been a little irritable.

"I don't mean to be rude," I said right out of the chute, "but we both know that these meetings are a waste of time. We talk about the same things, then go back to our routines and wait out another month."

Breanne actually grinned. "Not this time. The DA has finally made a proposal."

I almost spit out my Coke. "Really? What's the catch?"

"No catch, but it's a take-it-or-leave-it deal. You won't like some of it, but I think you should be open-minded."

Cynical but cautiously optimistic, I sat up.

"I'm listening."

"First, your brother, God rest his soul, has been your biggest ally. Without him, we never would have gotten this deal. The DA recognizes that you and he had the same kind of tumor and blackouts, which could have been a form of temporary incoherence. Therefore, it's possible that your story is true; you had no actual knowledge of those crimes until after they were over."

"That's what I've been saying all along."

"I know it, and people are not supposed to be convicted when there is reasonable doubt. On top of that, you've never had any additional spells after they removed your tumor so that too helped your case."

"God bless Mickey."

"Yeah, but the next thing works against you. They started with the fact that you conspired to steal a lot of money from a rich woman. When you decided that the victim would be made whole by the insurance company, it amounted to 'conspiracy to commit insurance fraud' and that's a big strike against you."

All I could do was nod and sigh.

"Aside from the murders, they can bring new crimes such as breaking out of prison and everything that happened in the Utah home."

"Hold it," I insisted. "First off, it was a hospital, not prison, and I didn't break out. I was recovering from surgery when my friends pulled off that kidnapping caper. I was drugged and couldn't even walk on my own."

Breanne nodded. "They know that too from the hospital surveillance cameras. You might have gotten some leniency if you had turned yourself in right after you knew what happened, but you stayed in the Utah home until you got better and then went straight for that truck stop in hopes you could get farther away."

"I had no reason to go back, Breanne. That would have been dumb."

"True, but that's a distinction without a difference."

"...and I did turn myself in after you told me too."

"True again, but when we balance things out," she said holding out her hands like plates on a scale, "they think they've got enough charges coming your way to keep you in prison for a long, long time."

"But that's not fair. I wouldn't have done any of those things if—"

"I know it feels that way, Miranda, but I told you to look at everything as a whole. In a minute they're going to give you something else that you'll like."

I shook my head. "I hope so because, so far this sounds one-sided."

"Just hear me out. As we established, they've got a whole lot of new charges they could bring. Among those is conspiracy to commit insurance fraud. They want you to plead guilty to that, and agree to serve five years for doing so."

"Oh, goody goody," I said with all the sarcasm I could muster. "What's next, a free ball and chain?"

Breanne gave a wry smile. "Anyway, here's the biggie for you. If you'll agree that you conspired to commit insurance fraud and a few more things, we can wipe away the remainder of your present sentence."

My jaw nearly dropped. "Really? All thirty-one years of it?"

"Yes, but like I said, you have to serve five years for the insurance fraud and accept a few other things."

"That figures. There's always a catch. What else?"

"This is where the escape charges come in. They think they've got enough to add ten more years to your new sentence."

"I knew it was too good to be true. So, I trade in thirty-one years for five years plus ten years and what else?"

"Not exactly. They're actually offering to apply time served to those charges."

"Time served? Exactly what do they mean by that?"

"Good question. They're talking about the ten years you've served in prison, plus the time in here. All of that pays your debt for the ten years they could add to your current sentence. That means you're back to five years for the conspiracy charges – and that's it."

"Really?" I said sitting back. "Why would they do that?"

"Quite frankly, I think that they came to the conclusion that they couldn't get twelve people who would find you guilty of those murders. After all, we've got experts who can lend credibility to your defense regarding your hazy phases. In addition, they're exposed to the publicity of the laundry room matters."

Suddenly I got the picture. "Is that it? Does this mean I get out in five years?"

"Sort of, but not quite. We still have to deal with the authorities in Utah. They want to sentence you to two more years for breaking and entering and stealing food, but there's a kicker to that too. Due to your leadership skills as indicated by your handling of the painting crews, you can shave off those two years if you agree to participate in a CAP program."

"What's that?"

"It stands for Community Awareness Program. They want you to join other inmates and talk with troubled school-age women about the consequences of misbehavior. We don't yet know whether the Utah folks will drop their charges because of your participation, or if our state will give you early parole to allow you to serve two years in Utah, but either way we're back to five years and nothing more."

"This is beyond wonderful. Is that it?"

"There are a few other minor wrinkles but that's the gist of it. You'll still have a criminal record but you won't be a murderer."

"I guess I can live with that. What else?"

"You have to agree not to bring any charges against them for what the guards did to you."

"Does that mean the guards get off?"

"No. it means they want to handle it internally so the press doesn't get a whiff of it."

"Alright, at least they'll get their comeuppance. Do I have to go back to the same prison?"

"Heavens, no. You're going to a nice minimum-security facility. It's almost like a college dorm."

"Can Phillip visit me?"

"And you can have private time. Oh, yeah, I almost forgot; if you don't get in any trouble, you can leave the new facility for a week each year on the honor system. You'll just have to wear an ankle bracelet."

My hands shot to my mouth. "I can't believe this. How soon do I get out of here?"

"Would forty-eight hours be too soon?"

"Oh, my God. Breanne. That's fantastic. I'm so sorry I doubted you."

"You're forgiven. So do we have a deal?"

"Yes, yes, and yes. I'll be pacing all night." I wrapped my arms around her. "I love you."

98

After nine full months in the county jail, I had a birth of my own. I was delivered to a minimum-security facility known as The Light House in Glendale, California. That was three months ago.

The new facilities are as advertised: well maintained and similar to a sorority house for recovering law breakers. The first day was almost like checking into a small motel for a long-term stay. Everybody was respectful and civilized.

There are still guards on duty, but they wear civilian clothes and refer to us as "residents" rather than inmates, and we're all on a first name basis to project a friendlier environment.

One of the guards, Diane, led me to a clean room, with a private bathroom, where I met my roommate, Georgella Spangler, a short and lovely African American who once had a lot of drug problems. We hit it off right away.

I'd only been here a month when I got word that St. Nick and Huff and Puff were both charged with multiple sex crimes. Apparently, Nick Stome couldn't take it. After he posted a large bond, he drove to the prison gate, stuck a gun in his mouth and had a bullet for lunch. I think he genuinely felt guilty for his past, but it's very difficult to forgive somebody like that.

Last month, I applied for a job as a dog-walker and poop

wrangler at a not-nearby doggie shelter. I haven't gotten an answer yet, but if I get the job, I'll enjoy the long bus ride just like Killer loved riding the trike.

Speaking of Phillip and Killer, when he got back to California, he sold his trike. He comes by twice a week, sans Killer, who is struggling with her health. I'm just thankful that Phillip rescued her. She deserved his kindness.

It's a long drive for Phillip to come visit me, but I try to make it worth his while when we have some genuine privacy. We may not have fourteen pillows to work with, but we get the job done in a twin bed. We try to keep the animal noises down, but I think most of the ladies shrug it off as I do when they have visitors.

At the moment, I'm thinking about this morning, when I was waiting for Phillip and his parents, whom I'd not yet met. I suspected it would be awkward for formal people, so I was on my best behavior. A large picture window enabled me to watch for a classy dark blue Mercedes. When they parked, Phillip and his father slid out of the front seat. His mother swung a back door open. And then the other back door opened. Somehow, Phillip had persuaded his upright grandmother to meet his jailbird lover.

"There she is," Phillip said, when they stepped to the outer desk to register. I waved. So did Phillip. So did his mother and father. His grandmother didn't play the game.

Diane was called upon to do the pat-downs just in case these grey-haired terrorists were trying to sneak in a case of grenades. When she felt up Phillip's grandmother, the elder woman puckered up like she'd just won first prize at a lemon-eating contest. I dutifully restrained myself.

After the pat-downs and introductions, hugs were allowed. I got a daddy hug, a mama hug and a "just right" hug from Phillip. Grandma must have thought I was the Big Bad Wolf because she held back.

I showed them my room, the dining area and the large back patio with a nice flower garden. Another resident went inside so we could have the patio to ourselves. Phillip and I held hands while everybody got to know me. It felt like a real family. Then, a short hour later, Grandma had had enough.

"I'm hungry," she said. "Why don't the three of us old people go get some lunch and leave the lovebirds alone?"

"Good idea," Phillip said. "I'd like some alone-time with Miranda."

They were barely out of sight, when he asked me if I'd ever considered changing my last name. I assumed that he thought a new name would make it more difficult for anybody to figure out who I really was.

"I did when I got married," I said, "and then changed it back when my ex was such a creep. Why would you ask that?"

All of a sudden, the kindest man I'd ever known dropped to a knee and opened a ring box. "Miranda Munchak, I've never known a more interesting woman than you," he began. "You even served time in prison because you were trying to help somebody else. I can't let you get away from me. Would you please, please marry me and become Miranda Pilday?"

Naturally, I'd imagined his proposing someday, but my heart thumped anyway. "Oh, my goodness Phillip, I'm truly honored, but a kind man like you can do much better than a stained person like me."

"I don't want anybody else. I want my Miranda. Besides, you didn't do anything wrong."

"Yes, I did, Phillip. I agreed to steal money that didn't belong to me."

"Maybe so, but that money was for Mickey's medical care, so it doesn't count."

"Yes, it does. I was also willing to commit insurance fraud and I shouldn't have done that."

"No way. They never actually issued a check, so it doesn't count either."

"But we also broke into a home in Utah and pawned some of their belongings. That's breaking and entering and theft."

"None of that counts either. You didn't know what you were doing when you first got to that house, and you believed that Randal knew the owner. Besides, Randal was the one who pawned things and when you left there you sent that woman a thousand dollars right after I met you. That's when I knew that you were so special."

"But I'll be 50 years old when I get out of here."

"And I'll be 40. So what? All that matters is I'll take good care of you. We'll have at least thirty years together."

"But a woman your age can give you a baby. I can't do that."

"Again. So what? If we want kids, there are ways to get them. I just want to be with you, and we both know that I'm good for you." That comment rang as true as anything I'd ever heard. He'd already proved it. Speechless and deeply touched, I didn't know what to say. Then my eyes figured it out. The happy tears gushed forth.

"Is that a sloppy yes?" he asked, bobbing his own head up and down.

I nodded. "I know how truly special you are, Phillip. I promise to be the best wife I can possibly be in every way."

We reached for each other and hugged like strong bears and kissed passionately. I smiled and admired my ring for a long moment. Suddenly he glanced at the clock.

"Oops, I almost forgot. I have a surprise for you. Happy-faced, he picked his laptop off the couch. "They should be waiting now."

Seconds later a middle-aged couple with comforting smiles shared the screen. "Miranda Munchak," Phillip said, "Meet Bertie and Chester Montgomery. They want to say something to you."

"We sure do," Chester said. "We're very pleased to meet the woman who saved our son's life. You don't know how grateful we are."

Tears flooded my eyes. "Oh my God, this is so wonderful."

Then Bertie tapped her eyes with a tissue. "I'm so glad to meet you, Miranda."

"Me too. This is the best phone call ever."

Chester smiled. "We heard about your case and are glad that things worked out."

Phillip couldn't help himself. "The charges are dubious, at best, but it would have been too risky to fight with all those lawyers."

"I'm sure," Chester added. "We want you to know that we'll look for a good opportunity to tell Trevor about you. Depending on how that goes, we might encourage him to speak with you sometime."

I grinned from ear to ear. "I'd love to tell him about his Uncle Mickey."

"Listen, Miranda," Bertie said. "Would you like some pictures? We have tons of them. I can email them to you or put them on a flash drive, if that's okay."

"Yes, yes, yes! That's definitely okay. Oh, my God!"

From there, we squeezed in a few more head-shaking minutes in which I learned of some of my son's quirks and family members. I loved it all. When we hung up, I'd lost enough tears to fill a sink. This time they were happy tears. I admired my ring and hugged my husband to be.

Then Phillip's family returned and endured another pat down. He hustled their way. "Guess what? Miranda has agreed to marry me."

His parents were thrilled, but grandma eeked and covered her ears.

Oh well, I'll have five years to win her over. Make that 1,728 days - but who's counting?

ABOUT THE AUTHOR

Like most Americans I liked my career of several decades but I have to admit that I didn't always approach the mornings with wild enthusiasm.

But then, I retired and discovered something I never would have guessed: When the day is mine, I love to get up even earlier. Now I'm the guy who wakes up the rooster. I still work as much as I ever did, only I now work on things that bring me a different form of compensation. Like writing books.

Some have asked me where I get my ideas, but it's no mystery. I had a storied youth with six sisters and a wild family. When I wasn't engulfed in that world, I spent a fair amount of my time wandering the alleys and streets of our neighborhood. A fellow learns a lot from all of those people even before he arrives for his first day of school. If he has the ability to recall the characters and the activities in which they engaged, and blend that with a dash of make-believe, there's a goldmine full of fodder from which to draw his inspiration.

AWARD WINNING BOOKS
BY THIS AUTHOR

NON-FICTION

Instant Experience for Real Estate Agents

Stop Flushing Your Money Down the Drain

FICTION

Three Deadly Twins

Monday's Revenge

Grandma's BFF Does Coke

Zero Degree Murder

All books available in paperback or ebooks

**Books may be ordered from
Amazon or other online bookstores**